Walkoff Wedding

Cover Design: Maren Moore
Couple Illustration: Chelsea Kemp
Editing: One Love Editing
Proofreading: Holly at Bird and Bear Editorial Services

For all the girls still waiting for their Prince Charming.
Love isn't always easy.

But with the right one… it will be.

To Monty Jay:

My soulmate. My twin flame.
No one will ever burn as bright as you.
I love you until the stars call us home.

louisiana dictionary

I realized when writing this that some of these terms/sayings/pronunciations may not be known so I wanted to include a cajun/creole guide!

** These are a mixture of my own definitions as well as a few pulled from various public websites.
Please do not consider this an official translation/dictionary in anyway.
*This is purely for **fun**!*

<u>**Cher-**</u> Cher (shaa) - Cajun and Creole slang, derived from the French. A term of affection meaning darling, dear, or sweetheart.

Bergeron- (baj-ron)

Arceneaux- (are-sun-oh)

Barrilleaux (bear-uh-low)

playlist

Accidentally in love- Counting Crows
Anywhere But Here- Hilary Duff
I'll Be- Edwin McCain
Best Day of my life- Jesse McCartney
Drops of Jupiter- Train
Paper Rings- Taylor Swift
Semi-Charmed Life- Third Eye Blind
Yellow- Coldplay
Linger- Royel Otis

To listen to the full playlist click here.

orleans university student information forum

We're two weeks out from Orleans U's annual spring art fundraiser! Please see the flyer below with all information and don't forget to share this with all of your friends on social media to get the word out. More shares = more money for OU Art!

User1: Yesssss! My favorite time of the year. I wonder if we'll get to paint that naked guy again.

User2: His... fruit was the best part of that fundraiser. IYKYK

User3: A true work of art.

User4: I say we petition the faculty to bring him back as part of our fundraising efforts.

> ArtGirl: I mean... he did raise a lot of money for the department... however unorthodox it may have been.

User5: Exactly.

OrleansU11: Speaking of guys and fundraisers... popping in to let everybody know the baseball team is doing a date with the player auction. All proceeds go directly to the Hellcats athletic department 😄

ArtGirl: Wow, you just slid right in there and went for it huh? This post is for the art department not for jocks raising money for what... heated bathroom floors? Vibrating shower heads and saunas not enough?

OrleansU11: Familiar with the inside of the guys locker room are you?

ArtGirl: Avoiding the real question, are you?

ArtGirl: God, you jocks are something.

OrleansU11: Is this your way of flirting, ArtGirl? If so, I'm kinda into it.

ArtGirl: In your dreams.

User2: Uh... maybe you two should like... get a room?

OrleansU11: Good idea.

private message request:

OrleansU11: Funny way to ask me out on a date, but I accept.

ArtGirl: Ah, egotistical and delusional. You've got the whole package going.

OrleansU11: Confident and hopeful* is what you really meant. I know.

ArtGirl: Do you always slide into girls' dms like this?

OrleansU11: Only the art activists.

bulletin

Here's your friendly reminder that with only one week left, the art department is still accepting donations for this year's spring fundraiser. Support your local artists!

OrleansU11: I donated to the art department's fundraiser today. You're welcome, ArtGirl.

ArtGirl: The art department thanks you.

OrleansU11: Nah, I did it for you. I'm a gentleman like that.

ArtGirl: 🙂

bulletin

A win for one hellcat is a win for all.
Just in: The art department scores a
sizable grant only two weeks after a
record breaking fundraiser!

OrleansU11: Heard about the grant that the art
department secured. Congrats, ArtGirl.

> ArtGirl: Thanks, Jockboy. I'm sure the auction
> next week will raise a ton of money for all you
> jocks.

OrleansU11: Yeah, mostly because I'm up for
grabs, but you know, money is money.

> ArtGirl: You're ridiculous.

OrleansU11: You like it.

> ArtGirl: Still delusional. 😌

STUDENT FORUM

bulletin

Hey Hellcats! Wanna win a date with Orleans' hottest baseball bachelors? You could be the lucky winner by attending tomorrow night's auction. The prize? Maybe the man of your dreams 🤍

OrleansU11: Last chance to bid on me, ArtGirl. You're going to miss your shot.

> ArtGirl: You don't think it's… weird that we're still talking? We don't even know each other's names. I mean I know that's what I asked for… but still.

OrleansU11: Nah. I like talking to you. Who else is going to bust my balls?

> ArtGirl: Someone's gotta humble you, Jockboy. I'm just the lucky girl with the job.

OrleansU11: A menace is what you are.

> ArtGirl:

> ArtGirl: Good luck tomorrow. Hopefully a sorority girl wins a date with you, and not a fifty year old cougar wanting to relive her glory days.

OrleansU11: Jesus ArtGirl, it's a date, not an escort service. Plus, women age like fine wine. I don't discriminate.

bulletin

STUDENT FORUM

The hellcat baseball team sure knows how to heat things up on campus y'all... last night's auction was a wild success bringing in lots of new backers and funding for our beloved players. Thanks for supporting your fellow students!

OrleansU11: Just wanted to let you know that a very sweet lady named Gertrude scooped me up for a date, and we spent the night talking about her late husband Harold.

ArtGirl: Glad your virtue is safe then.

OrleansU11: Probably wouldn't go that far...

ArtGirl: Of course not. Then you wouldn't fit in the stereotypical, playboy jock persona.

ArtGirl: Out of curiosity... if you weren't that guy. Who would you be?

OrleansU11: Who says I'm that guy? I don't like labels. I'm just... me.

ArtGirl: And who are you, Jockboy? Who are you really? Not the athlete label that everyone knows, but the real you under it all?

OrleansU11: Mmm that's deep ArtGirl, but I'll bite. I don't know. I'm the guy who loves classic rock, and his mom's cooking. I like poetry, even though I'm pretty sure if my teammates knew that they'd never let me live it down. I'm a hard worker, and I guess I'm the guy that my friends come to when they have a problem. It's kind of my nature to solve them. I've been told I give good advice.

ArtGirl: Wow. Yeah, I'd never take you as a poetry kind of guy. Who's your favorite poet?

OrleansU11: See... this is why you can't judge a book by its cover. As cliche as it probably sounds, Robert Frost. I like that he sees things for more than what they are. Beauty in the ordinary.

OrleansU11: What about you, ArtGirl? Who are you besides an activist for Orleans U's art department?

ArtGirl: Hm... let's see. Nothing as deeply moving as loving Robert Frost. I'm just a girl who loves to paint, and sketch. I like baking, and I'm kind of obsessed with astrology and the universe. Also, the kind of girl whose only friend miiiiiight be some strange guy she met on the internet.

OrleansU11: Nah, that can't be true.

ArtGirl: Pathetically, it is. I'm actually really shy and quiet in real life.

OrleansU11: Okay, now I know that can't be true. The girl who busted my balls from the very first conversation? Nah, no way, ArtGirl isn't shy.

ArtGirl: It's different when you're online, and not face to face. It's... easier through a screen.

OrleansU11: Yeah, I guess that's true.

OrleansU11: I'm glad that we have each other then. Bet you never thought we'd end up being friends from that first message, huh?

ArtGirl: Who said we're friends?

ArtGirl: Just kidding. Some would call that fate.

bulletin

STUDENT FORUM

You're invited! One last hoorah: a charity ball supporting Orleans U! This year's end of school ball theme is: masquerade! That's right, throw on the most gorgeous ball gown you own and join us for a sayonara to the school year all while raising money for yet another good cause. Masks: not optional.

OrleansU11: Very important question, ArtGirl.

ArtGirl: I'm listening...

OrleansU11: Pineapple on pizza. Yay or nay?

ArtGirl: Only psychopaths eat pineapple on pizza.

OrleansU11: Phew, I thought I was going to have to block you.

OrleansU11: How was your day?

ArtGirl: Sorry, I'm still stuck on the fact that you just considered that a "very important question."

OrleansU11: You can tell a lot about a person by the kind of pizza they eat and tonight @ Jack's my boys got a pineapple pizza and I thought I might vomit. Gross.

ArtGirl: I'm a veggie only kind of girl. I want alllllll the veggies. And my day was... stressful, honestly. But, at least I'm not eating pineapple pizza.

OrleansU11: Way to look at the positives. Wanna talk about it?

ArtGirl: Not really, but thank you.

OrleansU11: What can I do to make you smile, ArtGirl?

ArtGirl: You're already doing it.

ArtGirl: Why are you on here talking to me on a Friday night instead of out at a party or something? Stereotypical, playboy jocks are usually at a frat house on the weekend.

OrleansU11: Good thing I'm not one then, huh? Didn't feel like going out tonight. I felt like talking to my secret pen pal. Why are you not out at a party or protesting on campus somewhere like a good little activist?

ArtGirl: You know that I'm not a party girl. Clearly, I prefer to stay home and talk to strangers on the internet.

ArtGirl: And fortunately for you, there were no rallies tonight so I'm home, talking to you while I work on a sketch.

OrleansU11: Then I guess that settles that. We're both exactly where we wanted to be. Now, tell me something I don't know about you already, ArtGirl. Like your name? Please?

ArtGirl: For the thousandth time, no names. Remember? ArtGirl and Jockboy forever. I'm just... more comfortable this way. I like being anonymous.

OrleansU11: Alright, fine. It was worth a try. Tell me something else then? Something interesting that no one else knows.

OrleansU11: Something just for me.

> ArtGirl: Forewarning, I am the absolute furthest thing from interesting.

OrleansU11: Bullshit. I think you're probably the most interesting person I know.

> ArtGirl: Apparently, you don't know many people at all then, Jockboy. I'm boring, and... I'm okay with that. I like my quiet solitude where I can blend in, in peace.

OrleansU11: Trust me, I know plenty of people, and I've still never met anyone like you. This might be weird but sometimes I feel like a girl I've never met knows me better than most of the people I see every day.

> ArtGirl: Not weird. I feel like that too sometimes.

> ArtGirl: Okay, something "interesting" about me...

> ArtGirl: I've got an obese corgi named Augustus. Auggie for short. He's got the biggest personality of anyone you'll ever meet. He's got a little blue bow tie on his collar and it makes him look like a proper gentleman.

OrleansU11: That's fucking cute. I love corgis, they kind of waddle when they walk.

> ArtGirl: LOL yeah, he does. I might have to get him a doggy treadmill or something. Okay okay my turn. Favorite movie? Of all time.

OrleansU11: Ah... that's a hard one. Honestly? The Sandlot. Probably sounds cliche, I remember watching it as a kid and it being the first time I ever wanted to play baseball. It wasn't just the thrill of the sport for me, it was also the brotherhood. The found family that I loved. I was five or something. I've probably watched it a thousand times since then.

ArtGirl: I love that. So, you always knew you wanted to be a baseball player?

OrleansU11: Yeah. I mean, I didn't know I wanted to enter the draft to play professionally until like my freshman year of high school, but it's always been a dream to play.

ArtGirl: The draft... like the NBA?

OrleansU11: I know you did not just say the NBA, ArtGirl. Please tell me you're joking.

ArtGirl: Just kidding ;)

OrleansU11: Hell, don't make me panic like that. We're about to have an impromptu baseball lesson. Maybe you should watch the Sandlot now that I'm thinking about it.

ArtGirl: I might not be interesting or a social butterfly... but I am pretty smart, Jockboy.

OrleansU11: Well, at least one of us is.

OrleansU11: What's your favorite food?

ArtGirl: Gino's lasagne... or strawberries.

OrleansU11: I'm thinking of something dirty right now, but I'll refrain from saying it since I'm a gentleman, or at least I am on the internet. With you.

ArtGirl: Me liking strawberries is making you think of something dirty?

OrleansU11: Everything makes me think of something dirty. I'm a guy.

ArtGirl: Fair.

OrleansU11: It's kinda crazy that we've never even met but we talk every day now. Honestly, it would feel really weird if we didn't.

ArtGirl: Yeah. It is. I'm glad though? As crazy as it seems, I'm glad that our unlikely friendship happened. Even if you are the stereotypical playboy jock.

OrleansU11: And even if you are a shy, determined art activist with a very fat corgi.

OrleansU11: What sketch are you working on?

ArtGirl: Do you wanna see?

OrleansU11: Holy shit, you're going to show me your… art. That feels pretty intimate, ArtGirl. You ready for such a big step in our relationship?

ArtGirl: 😏 It's just a drawing. Not my face or something.

OrleansU11: Or something 😇

OrleansU11: And fuck yeah, I want to see.

ArtGirl: It's still a work in progress. But, okay.

ArtGirl: Photo Attachment

OrleansU11: You gotta be kiddin me

OrleansU11: You drew this?

ArtGirl: Yes. I mean like I said... it's a work in progress so I have to finish a lot on it. Shading and stuff.

OrleansU11: This is incredible. Literally, my jaw is on the floor right now.

OrleansU11: This should be in a gallery somewhere, ArtGirl. You've been holding out on me.

ArtGirl: Yeah, right. But... that is my dream. To see my stuff in a gallery one day.

OrleansU11: Well, I have absolutely no fucking doubt that I'll visit one one day and see you on display. You're beyond talented.

ArtGirl: Thank you. Seriously.

OrleansU11: ArtGirl, what if we... met?

ArtGirl: Met?

OrleansU11: Yeah, like what if we pick a place, and we say fuck the internet, fuck the forum and we hang out in real life.

ArtGirl: Then everything changes. We're not two strangers who met on the internet anymore. Don't you like the anonymity of this? Or the fact that there's zero pressure here. What if this only works here? I don't want anything to change.

OrleansU11: Nothing has to change, ArtGirl. I'm the same guy you've been talking to for months... we'd just be doing it face to face instead of through the screen.

ArtGirl: You know that can't possibly be true. I'm just not ready. But, what if we just... leave it to fate?

ArtGirl: The stars. Let the universe do what it's supposed to do. If we're meant to meet... we will. Without having to orchestrate it. I'm a very firm believer in the universe working in our favor.

OrleansU11: That's leaving a lot to chance, babe.

ArtGirl: Yeah, but if it's meant to be, it will.

ArtGirl: What's your birthday?

OrleansU11: September 27th

ArtGirl: Ah... this explains literally so much. A Libra.

ArtGirl: Balanced, yet arrogant about things that you know you're good at. A little overconfident at times, funny. Charming, clever, calm. I bet you're really... hot too.

OrleansU11: Funny how you already know that I'm hot and yet you've never met me.

OrleansU11: I am hot. Really fucking hot, and if you ever want to find out for yourself...

ArtGirl: Shit it's three am, I have to go to bed. I have a big day tomorrow. Night Jockboy. Xo

BASEBALL PLAYERS BUTTS... FOR CHARITY? COME OUT TODAY FOR THE HELLCATS ANNUAL CARWASH. ALL PROCEEDS WILL GO TO THE SANDLOT. A LOCAL CHILDREN'S LITTLE LEAGUE PROGRAM.

ArtGirl: Hopefully you had a better day than I did. God, today sucked 😔

OrleansU11: You okay?

ArtGirl: Yeah, it's just been a really terrible day, and I would like to crawl under the covers and pretend it's not happening. Avoidance at its finest.

OrleansU11: What can I do?

ArtGirl: Unless you're prince charming under all of that cocky, athletic swagger then nothing LOL

OrleansU11: I can definitely be your prince charming, ArtGirl. If you saw this chiseled jaw, you'd know. You could see for yourself... I'm just waiting for you to take me up on my offer.

ArtGirl: If only. I honestly could really use a hug right now.

OrleansU11: And I just so happen to give the best hugs. Now how can I, your prince charming in all of my shining armor glory, help?

ArtGirl: This is going to sound crazy. Fair warning...

OrleansU11: How crazy can it be?

ArtGirl: Pretty freakin crazy, trust me.

ArtGirl: My evil stepdad is... trying to force me into some archaic arranged marriage type of thing. Really really long story short.

OrleansU11: Whaaaat?

ArtGirl: Told you. It's insane. He's insane. So unless you're my prince charming ready to drop down to one knee and marry me, then unfortunately I'm stuck in this... nightmare. It sounds so crazy to even type it. Obviously, I'm joking about the dropping to one knee part.

OrleansU11: Why? I'll marry you.

ArtGirl: Wow, so you're insane too? You don't even know my name or what I look like.

OrleansU11: Semantics. We have undeniable chemistry, babe. That can't be faked.

OrleansU11: When and where do I show up?

OrleansU11: Should I get the rings, or will you? Is there going to be a quartet?

OrleansU11: Oooh, what are our colors going to be? I'm partial to classic black and white.

ArtGirl: Haha, you're ridiculous. Clearly still delusional like you were when we first started talking. But, I am smiling so thank you.

OrleansU11: Okay fine. But, promise me this. How about if fate ever does bring us together and you're still in need of a prince charming husband, then you'll take me up on my offer.

ArtGirl: Sure, if that day ever comes, I'll let you marry me.

OrleansU11: Damn, I'll be the luckiest guy in the universe if you ever LET me marry you.

OrleansU11: I'm gonna hold you to that, ArtGirl.

OrleansU11: But just know, if you need me, night or day, I'm there. No questions asked. Stalking this chat like a weirdo. Okay?

ArtGirl: Thank you. For being my friend and for making me smile.

OrleansU11: What are future husbands for?

bulletin

Last chance to sign up for Hellcat cheer squads Bingo & Bikinis event! The title is self explanatory on why you should attend.

OrleansU11: What's my horoscope look like today, ArtGirl?

ArtGirl: You know that you can just look it up yourself, right?

OrleansU11: Yeah, but I like it when you tell me instead. Just like you have for the last four days... I won my game that night which means we have to continue doing it.

ArtGirl: Jocks and your superstitions. Fiiiiine.

ArtGirl: Communication could take some extra effort today, Libra. Your romantic partner could seem like they're keeping things from you. You might get some uneasy vibes and wonder if there's trouble with your partnership. Don't be afraid to ask. They probably won't tell you what the problem is, but will reassure you that it has nothing to do with you. If so, it isn't your business. Let it go.

OrleansU11: Hm. You hiding something from me, ArtGirl?

ArtGirl: It says romantic partner, Jockboy.

OrleansU11: I mean we are getting married someday, which means you're my future fiance, so we probably shouldn't start this marriage off keeping secrets, ya know. I'm a married for life kind of guy.

ArtGirl: Delusional. That's what you are.

OrleansU11: Subjective. It's Friday... what're your plans for the weekend? Something exciting?

ArtGirl: If working is exciting, then sure. Haha.

OrleansU11: You could take the weekend off and meet up with your secret pen pal. That's always an option?

ArtGirl: Adding relentless to your roster, I see.

OrleansU11: I usually am in the pursuit of things that I want. Persistent and driven. Is that in my zodiac chart thing?

ArtGirl: Yep. See? The stars don't lie, Jockboy.

OrleansU11: You really believe all of this? Fate? The universe? The stars aligning? You don't think it's just something made up for us to have hope?

ArtGirl: Of course, I believe in it. Don't you?

OrleansU11: I believe... there's always something bigger than us. I'd like to think that there's a bigger plan that we're all a part of.

OrleansU11: I guess the universe brought us together then.

OrleansU11: I mean, I can confidently say that I've never met a girl on the internet and cared about her. Until you.

ArtGirl: Aww. I care about you too.

ArtGirl: And yeah, you can thank the universe for that. Imagine if we hadn't seen each other in the comments of that post?

OrleansU11: I would know absolutely nothing about my moons, or whatever the hell it's called.

ArtGirl: laughing face Exactly. See, what you'd be missing out on?

OrleansU11: Yeah, I see exactly what I'd be missing ArtGirl, but the question is... do you?

ArtGirl: Of course I do. Honestly, with how crappy things have been going for me lately, talking to you is the thing I look forward to most.

ArtGirl: That probably sounds pathetic, I know, but it doesn't make it any less true.

OrleansU11: It's not pathetic at all. I know you probably think I'm a walking, talking cliche, but ArtGirl, most of the time, I feel like I can only be the real me with you. I know you won't judge me for reading poetry, or make fun of me because I'm a mama's boy.

ArtGirl: Your friends would make fun of you for that?

OrleansU11: No, I mean, maybe? I don't know. We all give each other shit. It was just us growing up so we're really close.

OrleansU11: Are you close with your parents?

ArtGirl: Uh, well it's just my stepdad, and you already know about that situation. My mom passed away from cancer when I was young.

OrleansU11: Shit, I'm so sorry.

ArtGirl: No, it's okay. I'm... I'm really glad you have such a close relationship with your mom.

OrleansU11: Yeah, me too. Sorry for bringing all of this up.

ArtGirl: It's okay, really. I'm glad you know. It feels nice to trust someone enough to tell them things, you know?

OrleansU11: Completely.

bulletin

Tomorrow's the night! Enchanted Eclipse... the masquerade ball of the season. Anyone who's anyone at OU will be there... but will you?

ArtGirl: You still owe me a truth.

OrleansU11: You want a truth? Okay.

Orleans U11: I think I'm... falling for a girl I've never met.

ArtGirl: How's that possible?

OrleansU11: I'll let you know when I figure it out.

OrleansU11: Meet me at the ball tomorrow. Please. Let's take fate into our own hands.

OrleansU11: I need to see you, ArtGirl. We'll figure it out. All of it. I just need to fucking see you. I'm going crazy.

OrleansU11: I promise, nothing's going to change. We'll still be us. Just trust me. Please?

OrleansU11: Tomorrow. Midnight. In front of the gazebo.

ArtGirl: Goodnight, Jockboy.

bulletin

STUDENT FORUM

See you next year, same day, same time, dudes. OU Rumor mill... Out.

OrleansU11: Why didn't you show up tonight? I waited for you.

OrleansU11: ArtGirl?

OrleansU11: Hello?

OrleansU11: Don't do this...

OrleansU11: You asked me how it was possible to fall for a girl I've never met, and I told you I'd let you know when I figured it out. Because I never realized what my life was missing until you walked in, and now... the stars shine a little brighter.

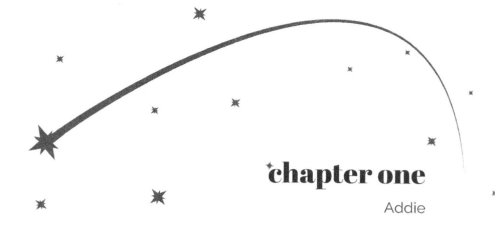

chapter one

Addie

ONCE UPON A TIME... *there was a girl who lived above the garage with absolutely no social life, like the most pathetic college senior in the history of the world, who was going to be forced into an arranged marriage by her evil stepfather.*

Delete.

Delete.

Delete.

My chipped blue nail jabs at the backspace key of my old laptop over and over until the glowing screen is blank again for the hundredth time... *tonight.*

I'm supposed to be working on my senior art thesis, a portfolio showcasing my artistic style in the form of a fictional fairy tale, but the only fairy tale I can write about my life is the one where Cinderella *doesn't* get her Prince Charming, and instead, she grows old with her fat, sassy corgi, locked in a proverbial tower, imprisoned by the man she's being forced to marry.

That's my fairy tale... more like a nightmare. It's as screwed up as it sounds.

Truthfully, it sounds *insane*, yet... it's my reality.

Groaning, I drop my forehead onto the keyboard, causing my

old, rickety desk to rattle noisily, and Augustus, the fat corgi in question, whines grumpily when he's awoken from his nap.

"Sorry, Auggie," I mutter dejectedly, still face-planted into the keyboard of my ancient MacBook.

There's no way I'm going to be able to create a fairy-tale depiction of my life. Because for girls like me, there is no happily ever after, and I'm very much aware of that fact. Which is making it nearly impossible to create a fictitious one in my head for said senior thesis.

It's not like me *graduating* college weighs on this or anything.

When I hear footsteps tromping up the stairway leading to my room, I begrudgingly lift my head from the keyboard and see Amos standing on the top step. He's the closest thing I've had to... family since my mom passed away.

He runs my family's bakery, conveniently located right next door to our house, which makes it easy for him to drop in to check on me. He's really the only person who cares enough to check on me.

His long, gray ponytail swishes as he makes his way over to me and reaches down, plucking something off my forehead, then holding it up for me to see.

The J key from my keyboard. Apparently in my melodramatic theatrics, it popped off and stuck to my forehead.

Unsurprisingly fitting for my mess of a life.

"Don't ask," I quip, swiping it from between his fingers and popping it back into place on the keyboard.

Amos's brow furrows deeper, a look of concern washing over his face. "Have you been here all day?"

I nod as I drag my gaze back to the blank screen and sigh. I've been at it for an embarrassing amount of time, and I've gotten exactly... nowhere.

"Well, it's a good thing you're done for tonight, then, huh?"

He reaches past me and pushes the computer screen shut. "You, my darling girl, are going to a party."

A laugh bubbles from my lips until I realize by his sudden serious expression that he's not joking.

"Uh, what?" I sputter. "I don't go to parties, Amos. So, that's obviously not happening. "

"Exactly. Cher," he says, using the term of endearment he's called me since I was a small child. "All you do is work, go to class, study, and stay cooped up in this room making art. So tonight, you're going to go out. With people. *Actual* people."

"I… hang out with people," I retort defensively.

His gaze narrows. "People *your* age, Addie. Earl and I do not count. We're your family. You need to be around people your own age, doing something besides work or school. Having fun. Which is why tonight you're going to go to the back-to-school bash on campus. Before you ask, you left the flyer on the counter in the bakery."

Crap. I meant to throw it away after finding it on the wind-shield of my car at school, but it clearly never made it to the trash can.

The thought of me going to a party, a *frat* party at that, is actually ludicrous.

Me.

At a party.

Yeah, right.

Standing from the computer chair, I walk over to my unmade bed, scooting a snoozing Auggie and all of his belly rolls over, and then crawl between the star-patterned blankets.

"In case you've forgotten, I'm betrothed to an evil toad and will be forced into an arranged marriage soon. These are my last weeks of… freedom." My tone is jokingly light, but the truth is

3

I've been looking for some way, *any way*, to stop this insanity from happening. We both have.

Except... time is running out, and therefore, so are my options.

When my stepfather, Brent, approached me with this plan over a year ago, I thought he had truly lost his mind. Need to be committed to a psych ward kind of crazy.

My mother's bakery, Ever After, was her pride and joy that she'd dedicated all of her love to before she got sick.

And he ran it into the ground.

Now, the bank is on the verge of taking it, and his solution is to marry me off to Dixon Barrilleaux, believing his family's money will save the hole that he's dug our family's business into. So, either the bank takes it, or he'll sell it to pay off the mortgage.

My choice is to lose Ever After or to agree to this archaic scheme and hold on to the only piece of my mother I have left.

It was never really a choice, and he knows that.

I couldn't lose Ever After, no matter what it cost me, which has led me here. The clock is ticking, and the figurative guillotine lowers closer to my neck by the second.

"Addie," Amos murmurs softly as he sits on the edge of my bed and pulls the covers down to peer at me. "I truly cannot imagine what you're feeling right now, my darling, and we *won't* stop trying. We won't stop looking for a way to prevent this from happening. But in the meantime, you can't stop living. This is the time of your life to be free and young and wild before the real world creeps in. Cher, you are the most responsible person I know. You've had to weather things most kids your age haven't. You're levelheaded, driven, and focused in a way that many adults never are, but I want you to experience all of these things before you start the rest of your life."

My laugh shakes Auggie from his nap again, earning me another grumpy growl. He opens his eyes just long enough to give me that notorious judgy corgi look. "Sometimes it just feels impossible to look ahead, Amos, past the impending *nuptials of doom*, you know? What's the point anyways? And besides, I'm perfectly content here, painting, reading, and pretending that I'm not a college student with no social life, about to be sold off in marriage."

I think putting myself out there and actually attempting to talk to people and make friends would be considerably worse than being here alone in the first place. While I'm comfortable around Amos, I'm painfully shy around basically anyone else.

The campus wallflower.

And most of the time, the people I go to school with don't even *see* me in the first place. I'm practically invisible. It reminds me of a scene in one of my favorite '90s rom-coms where the shy, quiet girl literally gets *sat* on by a jock in the courtyard.

That's my everyday life.

Except no one sat on me—they just walked right by without ever noticing my presence instead.

It seems pointless to form relationships anyways when, essentially, I have no control over my future.

"Oh, come on, cher. Go out and have a night of fun. One single night, just for a few hours. That's all I'm asking for. Try to let go of the things weighing on you for *one* night. Enjoy yourself. You deserve it," he pleads, his dark hazel eyes holding mine.

Sighing, I sit up, wrapping my arms around my legs and resting my head on my knees, "Is it really this important to you?"

"Yes. Because *you're* important to me, and I want to see you *live* a little. I'm putting my foot down. Up. Up. Let's go." Within

5

a split second, he's on his feet, shooing me out of the bed. "You can thank me tomorrow."

As much as I'm dreading it, I agree. Only because I don't want to disappoint Amos.

Much like Cinderella, I'm waiting for the clock to strike midnight. Because once it does, my promise to Amos will be fulfilled, and I can leave this stupid frat party that I never wanted to come to in the first place.

The deal was I'd stay until midnight.

But... I never promised that I'd actually stay *at* the party. Only that I would attend.

Clutching my sketchbook against my chest as if it'll protect me from unwanted attention, I make my way through the crowded, unfamiliar house in search of the nearest exit.

Relief floods my chest when I slide open the glass door at the back of the house and find the patio deck completely, *gloriously* empty.

Possibly the first and only thing that has gone in my favor tonight.

After stepping outside, I slide the door shut behind me, then walk to the edge of the wooden deck that overlooks the backyard and carefully sit along the edge. I set my sketchbook down next to me and peer out into the darkened wood line of looming cypress trees beneath a sea of bright stars.

It's kind of peaceful once you take away the loud, obnoxiously drunk frat guys and the absolutely horrid music they're blaring through the speakers. Yet another reminder that this whole party scene *is* not—and will not *ever* be—my thing... not that I needed one.

I pull my favorite drawing pencil from the pocket of my cardigan, open my sketchbook to my work in progress, and pick up where I left off. Like always, I quickly get lost in the details on the page, completely oblivious to the world around me.

Until I hear the back door sliding open and the sound of someone stepping out onto the deck, interrupting my quiet oasis.

My gaze slides to the intruder, a tall, dark blond guy who's stumbling toward the banister on the other side of the deck. He's either ignoring the fact that he's not alone... or he doesn't even realize that I'm here. Which makes sense because I'm generally invisible. I'm going to go with the latter because he begins fumbling with what I assume is the zipper of his pants, the dark gray T-shirt stretched across his shoulder rippling as he struggles.

"Goddamn zipper," he grunts. "Fuck. Fuck. Fuck."

"Um... Hi. Can you please *not*... um, pee with me right here?" I say loudly, alerting him of my presence. Normally I revel in my invisibility, but it feels like a violation of privacy to be out here without making him aware of it.

His head whips toward me, and a pair of piercing blue eyes meet mine in surprise for only a split second before he loses his balance and pitches forward over the banister railing, tumbling into the bushes below with a loud, pained grunt.

Holy crap.

Immediately, I jump to my feet, dropping my things and sprinting across the deck to the banister. My hands grip the railing as I peek forward over the side. The guy is half face down in a bush below with the other half of him sprawled on the ground, unmoving, and for a moment, I worry he might be dead.

Oh my god. Did I just accidentally… kill a guy?

Can tonight possibly get any worse? I'm going to faint from how fast my heart is racing.

"Please, *please* tell me you're not dead," I squeak loudly, leaning over further to inspect the mystery guy below. "Hello?"

When there's no answer from him, my stomach twists in a knot of anxiety.

"Please don't be dead," I mumble to myself. "Please don't be dead. Please don't be dead."

Finally, after the longest few seconds of my life, there's a deep, muffled rumble of a groan from below, and the guy lifts his hand slightly, alerting me that he is, in fact, alive.

I spring into action, taking the stairs leading down two at a time until I drop to my knees next to him. His head is still face down in the bush, so I truly have no idea if he's actually okay or not.

"Hi, are you hurt?" I breathe. "Should I… call an ambulance?"

It wasn't a very far fall, maybe a few feet at best, but he did just land face down on what looks to be a *very* prickly bush…

"Nope." More muffled words. "All good. Just need a second."

I find myself sighing in relief that he doesn't appear to need immediate medical attention. Nodding as if he can see me, I sit back on my feet and give him a moment. I feel so bad that I'm the reason he went sailing over this banister.

After a moment that seems to stretch, he pushes up off the bush, and I scramble forward, wrapping my fingers around his bicep to attempt to help him up.

I pause when I feel the hard muscle beneath the pads of my fingers.

Wow, his arms are extremely… *solid.*

I probably shouldn't be worried about how hard his muscles are right now, but it's also very difficult to ignore.

Once he rights himself, he flops down onto the grass, groaning as he leans back against the side of the house, and places his forearms on his bent knees in front of him. His dark blond hair is tousled from his fall, and there are a few leaves and what looks like a small piece of branch protruding from it. When our eyes meet, a sheepish grin flits to his lips, revealing a row of perfectly straight white teeth and a slight dimple on each side of his cheeks.

Wow. I mean... uh... Holy crap, this man is *hot*. Even with shrubbery sticking out of his hair, he is possibly the most attractive man I've ever seen.

So attractive that I forget how to speak for a second due to the fact that my heart is currently racing at breakneck speed in my chest, making my brain short-circuit.

"This might be the most painful way I've ever met a pretty girl, but I'll take it." His voice is deep and raspy in a way that makes the colony of butterflies in my stomach intensify with each syllable he utters. When I don't immediately respond, his grin widens into a blinding smile, and the dimples in his cheeks pop. He extends his hand toward me. "I'm Grant."

I glance down at his hand for a beat before slowly sliding my palm into his, shaking it. "Addie... And I'm so sorry that I almost killed you. Seriously, so sorry. Also, um, you have... something in your hair."

Reaching up, he drags a hand over his hair and plucks out the leaves before chuckling. "Thanks. I'll forgive you, Addie. On *one* condition."

"Okay, and what condition is that?" I say, arching my eyebrow in question. "I obviously can't leave here without your forgiveness. Almost killing someone is a *very* serious offense, so forgiveness is the very least I could hope for."

The deep blue of his eyes sparkles with amusement. "Agreed. So, yeah, I'm gonna need you to stay out here with me and save me from going back in there. If I have to go back into that party, I might really kick the bucket."

When my palm begins to feel clammy, I realize that it's still clasped in his. I tug it free and reach up to tuck my hair behind my ear. A nervous habit.

The pit of my stomach currently feels like there's a marching band inside of it, a steady flurry that makes my head feel light at the idea that this ridiculously hot guy wants *me* to stay here and keep him company.

This is turning out to be the most bizarre, possibly most interesting night of my life.

Even though I was looking for a way to escape, alone, I'm too curious to turn him down, so I drag my gaze to his with feigned confidence. "Okay. I accept your condition. And I'm sorry... again. I feel absolutely terrible. Are you sure you're okay?"

My eyes roam over his handsome face, pausing along his high, angular cheekbones down to the sharpest jawline, one that could rival that of a sculpture sitting in a museum somewhere, to his pillowy lips that make me wonder if they are as soft as they look.

A wave of embarrassment rushes through me when I realize that I've been openly staring, and I quickly avert my gaze to the grass beneath me.

If he realizes that I've been checking him out, he doesn't call attention to it.

"Yeah, I'm good. Don't feel bad. I should've paid attention to my surroundings instead of almost whipping my di—" He pauses, catching himself. "Sorry. I should've been paying attention, but really, I'm good. I do have one question though."

"Okay…" I trail off, waiting for him to ask the question as I move to sit crisscross on the grass next to him, smoothing my skirt over my knees and pulling my thick, yellow knitted cardigan tighter around me. Even though it's still August, there's an unusual chill in the air.

He plucks a blade of grass between his fingers as he speaks. "Why are you out here?"

The million-dollar question.

"That's… complicated."

It isn't really, but I also don't want to admit to him that I'm only here because I've got approximately zero friends and that Amos had to stage a mini intervention to get me out of my room. Or that part of the reason that I'm here in the first place is somewhat of a last hoorah before my life changes… *drastically.*

In a way that I have absolutely no control over unless, somehow, a miracle happens.

His brow arches. "Is it *really* though?"

Laughing, I shrug, my eyes sliding to his. "I made a promise that I'd attend tonight's party, but… not that I would participate in said party. It's just… I'm not really a party girl? Or a people person, really. And truthfully? There's an overpowering stench of sweaty socks and cheap liquor inside that I couldn't handle for a second longer."

"Yeah, that's fair." The deep rumble of his laugh settles around us. "How about another truth?"

Hiding my smile, I chew on the corner of my lip and nod. "Sure. But only if you give me one first. Why did *you* need saving?"

Grant lifts his hand and rakes his fingers through his hair, a sliver of hesitation ghosting over his face before his easygoing smirk replaces it. "I think I'm just... *tired*. I spend so much time feeling like I'm playing a part in someone else's life. You ever feel like you could just walk away from it all and not miss it even for a minute?"

"Yeah, I do." More than he probably could even imagine.

"Anyway, I just needed to get out of there. Get some air. You know... possibly be offed by a gorgeous girl wearing Mary Janes and a cardigan in the middle of August."

That has my gaze whipping to his and my cheeks catching fire.

He winks when he catches my furious blush under the pale moonlight. He's so effortlessly charming that it should be a crime. While my stomach is doing somersaults, he's the epitome of calm and collected. Which is slightly funny, seeing as how he just fell face-first into a bush.

"It's... unusually chilly tonight," I respond in defense.

"Oh? Should we go inside, then?"

I blanch, my nose wrinkling in distaste. "Absolutely not. You'll have to drag my cold, dead body back into that place."

His laugh echoes around us when he tosses his head back, exposing the strong column of his throat. "I like you, Addie with the Mary Janes. How come I've never seen you around before?"

Probably because guys like him don't notice girls like *me*. The pitiful, invisible wallflowers who are exceptional at blending in and never being seen or heard. I'm self-aware enough to know that.

Instead of the truth, I shrug. "Not a party girl, remember? Outside of class, I don't do much besides work. I'm the cliché quiet, studious loner girl. Maybe our paths have just never crossed."

A brief pause hangs in the air before he speaks.

"I would've remembered a girl like you. Something tells me

you're not very easy to forget," he murmurs, a reverent look shining in the depths of his blue eyes.

I can't explain the strange sensation of *familiarity* that tugs in my gut as our gazes lock, but it feels like even though we've just met tonight... that I know him somehow. That sounds crazy, even to me, but still, the feeling remains.

"You're ridiculously charming," I laugh as I shake my head. "Has anyone ever told you that?"

He nods, grinning proudly. "Maybe once or twice. Has anyone ever told *you* that you're incredibly beautiful?"

"Well, I me—" My words are cut off by my phone alarm sounding in the pocket of my cardigan.

Crap.

The clock has struck midnight, and my time is up.

I scramble off the ground as I fish the phone from my pocket, glancing down at the glowing screen showing the time.

Grant follows me to his feet, asking, "Where are you going?"

"Um, I have to go home. I'm so sorry. It was nice to meet you." I fumble to shove my phone back into my pocket as I quickly walk toward the stairs. He follows behind, calling out my name, but I don't slow my pace.

I spent the beginning of my night desperately wishing for midnight, and now, I find myself wishing for only a few more minutes with the stranger who made me smile. To hold on to this feeling for just a while longer. To pretend that this could be my life, even if only for a moment.

But I know that with midnight, reality comes rushing back. Girls like me don't get guys like Grant. The charming, confident, carefree guy with the playful smile and bedroom eyes.

There's no place for me in his world, and even if there was, my future is not my own. I don't think it ever was.

"Addie, *wait*..." he calls from behind me on the top step of

13

the deck. I glance over my shoulder at him when I make it to the back door, my fingers closing over the handle tightly. "I need to see you again. Give me your number, socials, anything. Please?"

I smile wistfully. "We're all playing parts in lives that aren't our own, Grant. Thank you… for tonight. Good night."

With that, I quickly slide the door open and hurry back inside.

The clock struck midnight, and my carriage has officially turned back into a pumpkin.

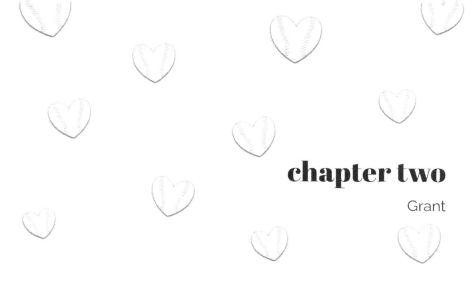

chapter two

Grant

IT'S a tale as old as time: *Drunk people do dumb shit.*

And drunk, horny college baseball players?

Yeah, well, we're a whole different ball game, and that's exactly why I'm currently back inside the party I never wanted to attend in the first place, trying to herd my teammates like a bunch of fucking cats.

It sounds *exactly* the way it's going.

"For fuck's sake, Guidry, will you stop trying to take your pants off," I grunt as my fingers curl around the fabric at the back of his neck, yanking him toward me. "I sure as hell don't want to see your pale ass, and I'm sure these ladies don't want to either."

Davis Guidry, our rookie pitcher, waggles his eyebrows suggestively to the group of girls who've gathered beside us and then blows them a kiss like they're his personal fan club.

Christ.

Not sure how looking after these idiots became my job, but if I don't keep an eye on them, we'll all end up running suicides until we puke.

And the very last thing I need? To end up on social media in yet another compromising position. Not after PANTYgate, which put me on very thin ice with my agent, who's probably going to drop me at any second because I'm not worth the headache.

His words, not mine.

It would probably be fine if it was *just* PANTYgate that was the problem. But... that was only one out of a slew of rookies-behaving-badly incidents that have put our asses in hot water with not just our coach but also the dean *and* the head of the athletic department. Once backers got wind of everything that had been happening, they threatened to pull their donations, and that was the final straw.

Needless to say, we fucked up. And I kept being in the wrong place at the wrong time, getting caught up in their shit. So, here I am, babysitting a bunch of college guys because I'm not letting them be the reason this sponsorship gets yanked away or that a scout decides not to come watch me play. My future's at stake here.

"Come on, Bergeron, stop being a party pooper," he mutters as he turns to face me, sweeping his dark, auburn hair out of his eyes and flipping his hat backward.

"Did you just call me a... *party pooper*? How old are we, five?"

"Yeah, well, you're being a numbnut and quite possibly the *worst* wingman in history. Did you see those girls? They were legit fucking me with their eyes. I probably could've fucked all three of them. *At once.* And you..." He pokes my chest drunkenly. "...keep ruining all the fun. You know, there's never any fun to be had with you around lately."

I roll my eyes as he pouts like a petulant toddler. "Do I need to remind you what happened two weeks ago? The last time you took your clothes off in public and ended up going viral? On more than one occasion? Actually, the better question is why do you keep trying to take your clothes off the second you start drinking?"

"No, I do *not* need you to remind me." He narrows his eyes with a scowl. "What I need is for you to reach back there and pull the stick out of your ass. C'mon, man, this is your last year of college. This is the time where you live it up. You get fucked-up and do stupid shit you'll tell your bros about when you're forty and reliving your glory days. Can't relive the glory days if there were none. Which is exactly why you have *me*."

"Pretty sure you're just filling in as the number one pain in my ass now that Reese is gone," I retort, referencing my best friend, who graduated in May and moved to Washington state, where he's catching for their minor league team.

A busty redhead dressed as a naughty teacher passes by with a tray of plastic shot glasses, and Davis swipes two, tossing her a wink before thrusting one toward me. "Call it what you want, but admit it, life would be pretty fucking boring if you didn't have me around. Dull and fun-less."

"That's not an actual word."

His shoulder dips. "Semantics." Lifting the shot glass, he knocks it against mine, and we toss them back together.

The cheap liquor burns as it slides down my throat, and I squeeze my eyes shut until I can suck in a gulp of air. "God-damn, I almost forgot how bad that shit is. It's like rubbing alcohol."

Davis chuckles. "Cheap, nasty as fuck, but highly effective. Shit… I gotta pee. Let's go out back. I don't feel like waiting for the bathroom again."

My thoughts immediately flit back to Addie.

Mystery girl in her Mary Janes and oversized cardigan.

Fuck, she was *beautiful*. The kind of beautiful that knocks you right on your ass.

In my case, off the side of a deck and face down into a bush, but still.

Bright blue eyes, pink pouty lips, dark lashes, heart-shaped face with long, curly blonde hair that nearly reached her waist.

She looked out of place at a party like this. Like she was too good, too innocent to be around this kind of scene. Who fled before I really got the chance to know her. To get her number. Ask her out.

I *really* fucking wish I would've gotten her number.

"What, you need me to hold your dick while you pee?" I ask. I didn't realize pee breaks were a team effort.

Everything seems to be with this dude, and for a guy who values his solitude lately, it's sometimes exhausting.

"If you want." Davis smirks playfully. "I'm just saying for someone who's so worried about babysitting me, letting me venture out there all alone is a bit of a gamble, don't you think?"

Fuck me.

"Whatever. Let's go. But after this, I'm out, which means you are too. My babysitting duties are done."

He lifts his hand in a dramatic salute and brushes past me toward the back porch, pushing his way through the crowded house. It's well after midnight, and the party's still going strong, unsurprisingly. OU has plenty of places to party, but most people end up at Kappa or at the Redlight, the college bar down the street, depending on what's going on. Tonight's party is back-to-school themed, which means there are plenty of girls walking around dressed as sexy teachers. Hence Davis's insistence that we come out tonight, even though I wasn't feeling it.

After pausing to talk to a few guys from the team, we walk out back, closing the door and drowning out the party behind us. This seems to be the only place that I can take a second to breathe.

I hang back while Davis walks away, looking for a place to pee, and fish my phone from the pocket of my jeans, opening the group chat with Reese and Lane, my other best friend who graduated last year.

Not to be in my feelings, but I miss them. Having my best friends around, being on the team together. Being a redshirt senior means I'm here for another year playing ball, praying that I get drafted before I graduate.

"Oh shit."

Glancing up, I see Davis peering down onto the deck. "What?"

"I almost just pissed on this thing." He leans down and scoops what looks like a notebook into his hands, flipping it over to look at the back.

I stride over, swiping it from him before he can open it. "Lemme see. Can you please go pee so we can get outta here?"

"Fine, but I want to know what it is. Ooooh, what if it's a diary? I'm so fucking reading it," he mutters, sauntering down the stairs toward the darkened tree line.

"It'd be the only book you've read this year."

He flips me off and keeps walking as I chuckle, turning the book over to the front. I don't know what's inside, but it's definitely some type of notebook.

It's light blue, leather-bound, with a well-worn crease on the spine from frequent use. I pause as I go to open the cover. Shit, what if Davis is right and it is someone's diary or something? It feels... I don't know, intrusive or something to look at someone's private thoughts.

I run my fingers over the worn spine, feeling the smooth leather beneath the rough pads.

It might not even be a diary, who knows, and surely whoever left it behind did so by accident and probably wants it back.

So, actually, opening it to see who the rightful owner is would be the right thing to do.

Yeah.

Carefully, I flip the cover open and see the front page littered with hundreds of hand-drawn stars, varying in size and complexity, etched onto the page in dramatic smudges of dark charcoal.

The spot where someone would put their information is blank, instead filled with more of those tiny stars. Okay, well, I guess that's not going to help.

I flip the pages slowly, scanning the sketches on the paper, completely in awe.

Holy shit.

This isn't just a sketchbook. It's more than just drawings. It feels like someone's soul poured onto the pages. It's filled with mesmerizing pieces of art, and it's... *incredible.* The details. The linework. The shading. Whoever this belongs to is extremely fucking talented.

I continue to flip, lost in the art, until the next page has my entire body going taut, my heart thrashing wildly in my chest as I peer down at the book in my hand.

It's not the portrait of the Milky Way that causes shock to course through my body. Nor the fact that it's one of the most beautiful pieces of art I've ever seen, nor even that it feels like I could step right into the pages because it's so realistic.

No, it's not that.

It's the *signature* at the bottom corner of the page, the one that's so small I almost missed it entirely.

The artist's figurative fingerprint.

It's the fact that I know who this book belongs to without a doubt, without another glance, that has me frozen in place.

A swirly *A* that's drawn with the side of a star connected through the middle.

This is *ArtGirl's* sketchbook. This is *her* art.

The girl I fell for through a screen without ever even seeing her face. The girl who ghosted me and broke my fucking heart. I never even realized it was hers until it was too late. Until the damage was already done.

The girl I've spent practically a year dreaming about. Wondering where she went, if she was okay. Wondering if the things I felt for her were all one-sided and that's why she ghosted me.

ArtGirl was here tonight, and I had no fucking clue.

She was fucking *here.*

"Dude, the fuck?" Davis grunts loudly from beside me, my gaze landing on him. I'm so shocked I can hardly even think right now. "I've been calling your name for like three minutes. What is it? Is it a diary? I want all the juicy details, man. Apparently, this is the only juicy shit that's happening to me tonight." When he leans over to peer inside the sketchbook, I snap it shut before reaching up and dragging my hand through my hair roughly.

How was she here and I had no clue?

All I can think about is now that I have this sketchbook and it's hers... how can I find her? How can I *finally* figure out who she is?

"Rude." He scoffs. "Why are you acting so weird right now?"

"I'm not acting weird."

"You're *definitely* being weird, dude."

I sigh raggedly, dragging my gaze back to him, contemplating keeping this to myself like I have since the first day I met her on the forum. No one knows what happened or anything about her at all. I kept it private because... it felt like she was only mine, and I didn't *want* to share her with anyone else. Not even my closest friends.

Shit, am I really thinking about telling the Rookie about her? About this entire thing? All of it?

I look down at the book in my hand, brushing my thumb over the cover, realizing that I'm holding the same book in my hands that she did. Sounds fucking weird, but it's the closest we've ever been.

Under the same sky but never together.

"Alright, start talking." He quickly snatches the sketchbook out of my hands before I can stop him and puts it behind his back. "Or I'm shoving it down my pants, and then you're diving in there to get it. Ass sweat and all."

My lips tighten into a scowl as my gaze narrows. "Don't fuck with me, Davis."

"See, you're being weird about some random notebook—that I found, might I add—on a fucking porch at a party. So, spill."

Fuck it. As aggravating as he can be... maybe he can help me figure out what I should do. Desperate times, right?

"I know who that notebook belongs to, and before I tell you this shit, if you say one negative thing, I'm going to punch you in the dick. And if you tell anyone, I'm going to..."

He cuts me off with an eye roll. "Punch me in the dick, I got it. Don't worry, I'm pretty fond of Gustavo, so no jeopardizing him."

Gustavo? The fuck... Did this dude... *name* his dick?

You know what, I don't even care.

"First of all, give it back, then I'll tell you."

Eyeing me warily, he pauses, then produces the sketchbook from behind his back and hands it to me.

"Fine. Start talking."

I take it from him, blowing out a resigned exhale. "Over a

year ago, I met someone… on the OU student forum. A girl. At first, we were just talking shit to each other on a post, but then we just kept talking. For a year, we DMed on the forum almost every day, about life, personal stuff, and I don't know… everything. I tried to meet her in person, but she was adamant that we keep things anonymous. We never exchanged names or numbers or anything too identifying. I hated it, but I didn't want to stop talking to her." I pause and drag my hand down my face. "I kinda… fell for her, and then she ghosted me. I asked her to meet me at the masquerade gala last year, and she didn't show. She stopped responding completely, and I haven't heard from her since."

Davis blows out an exasperated sigh. "Damn, dude, I'm fucking sorry."

I expected him to talk shit, make fun of me for having feelings for a girl I've never even met, but he seems oddly genuine. There's no hint of teasing in his voice.

"Thanks, man. It honestly kinda fucked with me. I mean, I just fucking want to know who she is? I had no way to figure it out when she ghosted. I tried to figure out who she was after that, but I never could. I never had enough to go on. But this?" I hold up the sketchbook, shrugging. "Maybe this is the answer. I have to return it to her somehow."

For a moment, he's quiet, possibly for the first time in his life, and then his eyes widen. "Oh shit. I've got it. You know, this is very Cinderella vibes."

"Shut up."

"No, I'm serious. Like… Girl loses her sketchbook, and you find it, and now you're searching for her?"

"Davis. Get to the point." I sigh.

He lifts his hands in surrender. "Okay, okay. All I'm saying is that if you wanna find your Cinderella, then put the flyers up, and you'll find her. And lucky for you, I've been casually hooking up with a girl in the library since I moved in this summer, and you know what that means? *Free* copies!"

"Wait, you want me to put *flyers* up around OU looking for ArtGirl?" I scoff.

"Yeah?" His T-shirt-clad shoulder dips. "Why not? I mean, look, you wanna find your girl, what better way to do it? She's a student. We'll put signs up everywhere, and there's no way she won't see it and contact you. Easy. We use the sketchbook, and we draw her out. It's like Cinderella bait."

This sounds like a terrible idea, listening to the Rookie, and I have a feeling I'm probably going to regret it, but what if it *does* lead to finding ArtGirl?

She was right underneath my nose all night, and I had no clue. We probably passed each other at the party like two strangers. What if... What if the girl that I talked to earlier was her?

"Well? You in?"

I look down at the sketchbook in my hand and sigh. I guess Rookie's plan is better than doing nothing. "Fuck it, yeah... I'm in. Let's do it."

I *have* to find ArtGirl.

There's no way I'm letting her ghost me twice.

chapter three

Addie

"*HELLOOOOO?*"

A faint voice echoes around my bedroom, pulling me from sleep, and I crack one eye open groggily, lifting my head from the fluffy pillow.

"I *know* you're in there, Addie. Do not ignore me!" The same annoying voice grunts through the Alexa on my nightstand so loudly that my ears ring.

Groaning, I pull my pillow over my face and flop back down onto the mattress.

Of *course* this is my Sunday morning wake-up call. A sobering reminder of reality after the party last night.

"Add—"

"I'm coming, Tad, jeez. I was *sleeping*," I mutter against the pillow before abandoning it to glance over at the alarm clock on my nightstand. "It's only 7:00 a.m. What could you possibly need from me at 7:00 a.m. on a Sunday?"

I can practically see his eyes rolling as he speaks. "We took a last-minute order at the bakery, and Dad needs you to come prep the dough."

"It's Sunday, Tad. My *only* day off. Can't you do it today?" I sigh frustratedly. Even though I already know the answer to that question. My stepbrother would never lift a finger to help the bakery, even though it's what's paid for his lacrosse career and the all-boys private Catholic school he attended before starting at Orleans U. He's spoiled and entitled and honestly... just a jerk.

I'm the one who has to wake up at three in the morning to help Amos do prep in the bakery, barely skating out of the store in enough time to make it to my first class on most days.

Something Tad, nor my stepfather, has ever had to do.

I don't mind working in the bakery or helping in any way that I can. It's just the fact that it's expected of me and that my time is never taken into consideration.

Why would it be when I'm not respected by either of them?

If I was, then Brent wouldn't be trying to marry me off to the highest bidder to fix problems that he created.

Tad laughs haughtily, and for a second, I think about unplugging the Alexa and tossing it into the trash where he belongs but decide not to because then I'd never hear the end of it.

It's bad enough that they both drop into the device unannounced with absolutely no respect for my privacy. I don't think I could handle them showing up in the flesh, invading my little sanctuary in my room above our garage. I try to limit one-on-one... *anything* with them whenever I can help it.

"Can't. Busy. You know me and the guys brunch on Sunday. Sorry, little sis. Maybe next time though?"

I scoff, my words coming out in a frustrated rush of syllables. "I really need to work on my art portfolio. Can you please cancel brunch for the day and fill in? Please just help me this once."

"Nope, no can do. Guess you'll just have to stay up late to work on it. Not my problem. See ya." The blue ring of light on Alexa glows, signaling Tad's gone, and I grab the pillow and pull it over my face once more, only this time, I scream into it as loudly as I can.

It's not at all surprising that Tad's asking me to use my *only* day off to work on a last-minute order that he took because let's just say that the apple… doesn't fall far from the tree.

Those two deserve each other, and like always, I tell myself to hold it together. Be the bigger person. Ignore their snide remarks and shitty jabs because their cruel words are only a reflection of who *they* are.

That's something my mom used to tell me when I was a little girl. That people's actions are a reflection of who they are and not at all of who I am.

But some days, it's easier said than done to heed her words, especially on days like today when I have to deal with Tad's dismissive demands before I've even had any coffee.

Begrudgingly, I toss the covers off and head to my bathroom to shower, almost tripping over the pile of laundry that's accumulated in the middle of the floor. Auggie opens one eye at the disturbance before he settles back to sleep in my bed.

Sundays are usually the days that I get everything done that I've had to neglect during the rest of the week, which is why I'm even more frustrated that I'm having to sacrifice my one and only day off. Between my classes and work, sometimes I feel like I never get a chance to breathe.

The stolen moments of quiet are few and far between. And I really love the quiet.

I pause in the middle of my room by the laundry, my eyes scanning the yellowed, cracked, and peeling paint of the walls to the worn and rickety furniture that is older than me.

My makeshift bedroom above the garage is… rustic at best. There are more things wrong with it than things not, but it's also… my piece of solace away from the main house.

It's home. It might not be much, but it's *mine*. I spent most of my teens making it feel that way. Picking up pieces at garage sales and for super cheap while thrifting. Some of my best finds have been buried beneath what others would consider trash on the shelves.

Hues of burgundy, black, and emerald... warm, earthy browns decorate the walls in paintings, and shelves display decorative vases and vintage knickknacks. Pieces that make me feel happy and comfortable. Dark green plants with long, loopy leaves drape over my bookshelves, and bronzed candlestick holders sit on my mess of a desk, lighting the way for more nights than I care to say as I've sketched until I've fallen asleep on my sketchbook, only to wake up with smudges of charcoal on my cheeks and staining my fingers.

A smile tugs at my lips when my thoughts drift back to last night... and meeting Grant. An unexpected meet-cute that's been lingering in my thoughts since I got home.

There's a small part of me that wishes I could've given him my number when he asked, like a normal college girl my age who flirted with a boy at a party would.

Okay, a big part of me wishes that.

But the realistic part of me also knows that there are too many things that stand in the way.

The number one thing being that in less than three weeks, I'm going to be married to someone else. A guy who I can't stand. A carbon copy of my entitled, snooty stepbrother, except that my "fiancé" looks at me with hungry, leering eyes like I'm a piece of meat at a market.

The weight on my shoulders feels heavier than ever as I turn the shower handle all the way to the left, as hot as it will go, and the old pipes groan and creak loudly at the sudden rush of pressure.

I've been meaning to ask Earl to take a look at it, but there's been a hundred other things to worry about. I make a mental note to ask him today as I step under the steaming spray and try to push last night and Grant from my mind.

After my shower, I throw on a pair of old jeans and a work shirt before heading downstairs and through the gate outside my stepfather's house to the side entrance of the bakery. I've always loved that this piece of my mom has been right next door and never out of reach.

Before I even open the door, I know that Amos is inside, creating magic from his fingertips. The scent of fresh bread and cinnamon wafts through the air, and my stomach rumbles in response as I push the door open and walk inside.

There aren't very many constants in my world, but Amos Herveaux is one of them. I can hardly remember a time in my life when he hasn't been here, and I can't imagine a time when he won't be. He's been working at the bakery since I was a little girl.

"Well, good mornin', cher. Sleep well?" His dark hazel eyes twinkle, and he smiles as he looks up at me from the pan in front of him. His long gray hair is pulled into his signature tight pony-tail at his nape, the strands of his hair decorated with beads and ribbon that match the bracelets on his wrist. He's the most eccentric, lively person I know, and sometimes I envy him for his ability to be who he is so effortlessly.

I always tease him for being the absolute opposite, in every way possible, of his husband, Earl.

Earl helps with maintenance around the house and bakery, and while Amos is a swirl of boisterous energy who never meets a stranger, Earl is quiet, stoic, and reserved.

Amos is a practicing Wiccan and never leaves home without his crystals or his tarot deck. And Earl? Raised a devout Catholic who still buys a newspaper on Sunday and believes that we never *actually* made it to the moon.

They're living proof that no matter how different you can be from someone, loving each other is all that really matters in the end.

"Good morning," I say, walking over to the counter and reaching for my favorite coffee mug on the shelf above it. The pot next to it is still steaming, and I could cry with how badly I need the caffeine after the late night and early morning. "You have no idea how bad I needed this."

He laughs and lifts a finger, telling me to pause before turning to the other side of the kitchen and returning with a strawberry cream cheese croissant, my absolute favorite thing he makes.

"The universe told me you needed one this morning, cher, so I woke up a little early and made you a fresh batch."

I snatch it from his hand eagerly, but not before quickly throwing my arms around his neck and kissing his cheek. "Thank you. Thank you. Thank you. I might cry over this fresh baked goodness, however sad that might be. Thank you for coming in to help me with this order too. I'm sorry Tad took it at the last minute. God, what would I do without you, Amos?"

Amos's deep chuckle vibrates against my chest as he holds me tightly to him in a hug. "I'm your fairy godmother, so you'll never have to find out. It's nothing, Addie. You know I'm always going to be here for you. Now, eat up because you know I wanna hear *all* about last night."

Pulling back, I take a giant bite of the fruity deliciousness in my hand and moan around the soft, flaky dough.

God, I would honestly do terrible things to have one of these… maybe two… every morning. It's truly heaven-sent.

"Nothing to tell," I hedge.

His thick, bushy brow arches, and the expression on his face tells me that I am not getting out of this kitchen without talking, so I hop onto the counter and sigh before taking another quick bite of the croissant.

"It was… fine. I can confidently say that I will never be a frat party kind of girl. It was a once-in-a-lifetime experience and not a great one. I'll never get the smell of stale beer out of my favorite cardigan." My nose wrinkles.

"Did you make any friends?"

My thoughts drift once more to Grant, and I shake my head.

"I did… not. Make any friends." The little white lie slips past my lips easily, and for a second, I feel slightly guilty for it. I guess, though, technically, it *isn't* a lie because we're not friends.

He's just a guy that I happened to meet last night and spent a few precious moments talking to about nothing at all. Just a guy that I… can't stop thinking about?

"I—" I'm cut off by the door of the kitchen flying open and my stepfather barreling through, a look of annoyance on his face. My heart lurches in my chest.

Crap.

I quickly hop off the counter and shove the rest of the croissant in my mouth.

"Addie, I thought Tad told you what I needed from you today?" His jaw steels while he glances between Amos and me with disdain.

I nod. "He did. I, uh… was just grabbing breakfast really quickly."

I want to tell him that I'm not going to do it, and if he has a problem with that, then he can shove it, but I don't, and I likely never would.

Because that's exactly who I am as a person, a passive doormat, and it's the one thing I hate about myself. My inability to stand up for myself despite the things I've dealt with my entire life from both Brent and Tad.

"Well, please, take all the time you need. It's not like we have a crisis on our hands," he says with venom-laced words.

"But there—"

He lifts his meaty hand, cutting me off abruptly. "The *last* thing we need is to not complete this order for the promised time, Addie. It's for a prominent New Orleans business, and I'd like to not tarnish our reputation because of your dawdling. Which means that I need you to take care of this as soon as possible, minus any excuses."

I nod hastily. "Got it."

"And as a reminder, we'll be celebrating your engagement next weekend with a party, so please be sure to be on time and wear something… *appropriate*. Need I remind you how important this is for our family and *the bakery*?" His jaw ticks.

Inside, my stomach is twisted into knots of hurt and frustration, but I press the feelings down, as always, keeping my mouth shut as I nod again.

I'm the dutiful stepdaughter because, at the end of the day, I know how important this bakery was to my mom. How much time, love, and dedication she put into every nook and cranny, and seeing it fail isn't an option. It's the reason that I've agreed to this stupid, archaic plan. Because if I don't… we could lose Ever After, and I truly can't live with that. I cannot fathom a world without it.

Without another word, he turns on his heel and stalks out of the kitchen, letting the door slam shut behind him, rattling the frame.

Only once he's gone does it feel like the air returns to the room, and I suck in a shaky breath.

"Cher, do not put a single ounce of stock into what that ass says. You know I could put him in his place anytime," Amos says, stirring the pot with more vigor. "A wedding? God, he has lost his mind."

"I know, but I need you around, so don't aggravate him into firing you. I've got it handled. I'll figure it out. Somehow. I'm going to get started on preparing the order, but I'll tell you more about last night later, 'kay?" I muster a small smile as I jump down from the counter and pat his arm. "Love you."

"Love you, my darlin'." His eyes are soft and his smile full of pity. Even though I appreciate the love and concern, I hate that I'm the recipient of his sympathy.

One day, I'll stand up to Brent. It just… won't be today.

As it turned out, I didn't get to catch Amos up on what happened last night because I worked the entire day prepping hundreds and hundreds of mini king cakes, and before I realized it, the sky was dark, and my stomach was growling fiercely. Unsurprisingly, it took the entire day to complete the last-minute order, and honestly, I have no energy left to even be mad about it any longer.

I'm exhausted, down to my bones, and as I plop down into the chair at my desk, my eyes are already bleary. I'm not sure how I'm going to make it through the next few hours of working on my project. But I don't want to fall behind on developing ideas for my thesis.

I reach for my sketchbook while staring at the computer screen but stop short when I realize it's not in the spot it usually is.

I spend the next hour tearing my room apart to the point that it looks like a hurricane has hit it and come up empty-handed.

My sketchbook is not here, and I groan when I realize where I might have left it.

chapter four

Grant

I REALIZED one of two things pretty fucking quickly with this elaborate plan of Davis's.

One was that I should *not* have let him be in charge of what actually went *on* the flyer since he idiotically put my cell phone number on the flyer that we're putting up around the entire campus.

And two... I will never under any circumstance let him talk me into anything *ever* again.

"Will you stop freaking out? Shit, man, you're making *me* nervous. And do you know how hard it is to make *me* nervous?" he says, taping another bright blue flyer to a light pole in the common area. "It's gonna work. *Chilllllll.*"

Is it though?

Because as of right now, I am not convinced that it will. What I *am* convinced of, though, is that this is the worst idea I've ever had. My phone chimes in my pocket for the hundredth time in the last hour, which cements that feeling.

I narrow my eyes at him, shaking my head. "I'm going to kill you. With my bare hands."

"Okay, fine, maybe we shouldn't have put your number on

the poster, but what else were we gonna do? We have to find your Cinderella, which means you're going to just have to deal with it. Now, quit complaining, take these, and go put them up on that bulletin board." He shoves a stack of papers at me, points to a board across the commons, then walks off in the opposite direction.

Great, now I'm taking directions from the Rookie.

This girl is probably going to think I've lost my mind, and you know what, maybe I have. That's probably why I agreed to this in the first place.

But fuck… I just want to find her, get her sketchbook back to her, and finally meet her after all this time.

I get three signs up before my phone rings in my pocket… *again.* I pull it out, ready to turn it off, when I see my best friend Reese's name on the screen.

I put it to my ear, answering with a cheery "Well, hello, stranger."

"Dude, we literally *just* FaceTimed yesterday. So, you wanna tell me why there's flyers posted all over OU social media and up all over campus with your phone number on it that say, *'Prince Charming searching for his ArtGirl.'* What the hell happened in the last twenty-four hours, man?"

How is he playing in the minors all the way in Washington yet still knows what's happening on OU's campus?

"Rosie heard about it and sent me pictures," he says, answering the question I didn't even need to ask out loud.

Of course she did. His younger sister, Rosie, goes to Juilliard in New York, but most of her high school friends go to OU, which means she's the plug for info.

I sigh, narrowing my gaze at Davis, who's now flirting with a perky cheerleader without a care in the world instead of hanging up the fliers. "It's a… long story."

"Yeah? Good thing I've got time," Reese retorts. "Wait till Lane hears about this, Prince Charming."

I can practically hear his shit-eating grin through the speaker, and I groan. "Fuck off. See, this is why I didn't tell you two."

"The disrespect! I'm your best fucking friend, dick, and just because I graduated and moved across the country does not mean that you don't have to fill me in on your life."

I know he's just giving me shit, but damn it, he's right. Walking over to a nearby bench, I drop down onto the seat. "I know. It's just a new… development. Super fucking new."

"I'm listening…" He trails off, waiting for me to continue.

I quickly fill him in on what happened last year: ArtGirl ghosting me, the crazy-as-fuck twist of fate of me finding her sketchbook, and now me following along with Davis's plan to find her with these stupid fucking flyers.

By the time I'm done, my chest feels slightly lighter. I probably should've told him a long time ago, but part of me was fucked-up about the fact that I had these feelings for her and she ghosted me. And a selfish part wanted to keep whatever it was between us to myself.

"You really wanna find her, huh?" he says when I'm done.

"Yeah, I really fucking do."

"I mean, the fact that you're going along with something Davis has come up with says it all, my man."

"Tell me about it," I laugh as I scan the courtyard looking for him. He's a royal pain in my ass, but I will say… when the kid gets something in his head, he goes all in, puts every fiber of who he is behind it. It's why he's such an asset to the team. I appreciate that, though I'll never tell him because his ego is already too fucking big. "I hope it works. I hope she doesn't see it and run in the opposite direction."

She was so insistent that we never meet before, and in the

end, she blew me off. Maybe she just really didn't want to be found. Maybe I came on too strong, or maybe she just wasn't interested in the same way that I was. I mean, all of this could totally blow up in my face. But… it was worth the risk. She told me to leave it to fate… and fate led that sketchbook right to me.

"Nah, dude, women love grand gestures, and this is an epic grand gesture. Probably shouldn't have put your number on there though." Reese laughs, and I nod in agreement.

"Fuck, don't I know it? I was about to turn my phone off until I saw it was you calling. My shit's been blowing up all day, which means determining who's *actually* ArtGirl and who's not is going to be a bit of a problem." I drop my head into my hands, tugging at the short strands of my hair. "Probably should've thought that part through."

Reese pauses, hesitation hanging in his tone. "I mean, if I've seen it, you know who else has seen it?"

"Hmm?"

"Jeremy."

I stiffen at the mention of my agent. Fuck, I didn't even think about him seeing this. Damnit, I should've at least given him a heads-up. We're so close to signing this sponsorship I hope I didn't inadvertently fuck things up more.

"Shit," I curse before glancing down at the flyers.

"I take it he's still riding your ass?"

I exhale, my fingers tightening around the flyers until they're nearly crumpled. "Yeah, something like that. There's just so much riding on this sponsorship, and I feel like every way I turn, I'm fucking things up. Jeremy thinks this is pivotal in making me more noticeable for the draft, but I'm scared I'm not going to land it, and it'll fuck up my chances."

"Nah, you'll get it because you're going to do whatever it takes. *Whatever.* You hear me? Look, before you know it, you're going to be headed to the minors. On your way to the majors. You've worked your whole life for this, and you're not going to let it, or this sponsorship, slip through your fingers. You've got this."

I appreciate the pep talk from my best friend more than he knows. Makes it a little easier knowing the phone call I have to make. "Thanks, man. Probably should call him before he has a coronary. Can I call you later?"

"Yep. Keep me posted on your search, *Prince Charming*."

I roll my eyes, my laugh gruff. "Yeah, yeah. Later."

I hang up and peer down at the screen before opening my messages. There's got to be at least a hundred texts in here, most of them claiming to be ArtGirl. There are pictures of random people, and hell, there are even a few nudes in here, which I know are not her.

She's not like that.

But the fucked-up part is, even if she *did* send a photo of herself... I wouldn't even know if it was her because we never exchanged photos. Or names.

I was willing to latch onto anything that I could find her with, and that's why I agreed to this shit in the first place. Because having this sketchbook means I can maybe draw her out but still let her be the one to make the move since the flyers put the ball in her court.

"Alright, I think it's time for a new batch," Davis says as he flops down next to me on the bench.

I turn my phone toward him to show him the screen. His dark eyes widen slightly when I scroll, showing him the number of messages.

"Damn."

"Yeah," I grumble. "How do you suppose we vet all of these girls claiming to be her?"

Silence meets my question until he says, "Easy. Ask her to message you on the forum. Only the real ArtGirl will know where to find you there, right?"

True. Yeah. Jesus, why didn't he think of that in the first place? Then my number wouldn't be floating around campus.

He plucks the phone from my hand. "You go hand the rest of these out, and I'll work my magic."

"Not sure if I trust your magic right now."

"You'll be thanking me later when my genius plan works and you find your girl. Mark my words, Bergeron."

I successfully avoided Jeremy until the following morning when he blew my phone up so many times that I knew if I didn't answer, he'd be showing up at the front door and ripping me a new asshole.

Leaning back against the couch, I sigh as I swipe my finger along the screen and answer.

"Jeremy, what's up?"

His scratchy, deep voice rings through the speaker. *"What's up? You know what's up? You continually making my job harder than it's supposed to be, Bergeron."*

Yeah, I knew this was coming, hence the fact that I avoided his phone call as long as possible. I knew he was going to be pissed.

He doesn't wait for me to respond before he goes in because his question was actually rhetorical.

"I'm fucking tired. You know what's at stake here. We've had this same conversation over and over. Not only do I see you

posted your damn phone number on a flyer all over the campus looking for a random girl, but there's photos from a frat party the other night with you and Davis Guidry where he appears to be taking his pants off in front of a group of girls."

Goddamnit. Fuck.

I drop my head back against the couch and bite back a groan. That dumbass. Of course photos of me would end up on socials, even though I was trying to keep the situation under control.

"Okay, in my defense, I was trying to keep his pants *on.*"

Jeremy sighs raggedly, and I can tell he's sick of my shit. Hell, I'm sick of my shit at this point. "You know how you stay out of situations like that? By not going to the damn party in the first place. Grant, this sponsorship could change your life. Not just put you on the map with other potential sponsors but financially too. I know how important it is to you to get drafted and set yourself and your mom up. These companies aren't investing big money into a kid who's partying hard and acting like a horny campus playboy, cycling through a new girl every week."

"I do not fuck around like that..." I trail off in frustration. Just because I go to parties and hang out with females doesn't mean I'm sticking my dick in all of them.

"Doesn't matter whether you do or not because that's how it's perceived. Image is everything, and right now, you need to clean it up, or they're going to pull from this deal."

Fuck no, I can't lose this deal. I've been working so hard to make it happen that I can't let it slip away, not when it's this close.

"Okay, I understand."

Dragging my hand down my face, I blow out an exasperated breath.

"Settle down, Grant. Stop going to parties, stop getting drunk with your guys. Get off social media if you have to. I don't care what you do. But we need your image to be squeaky-clean. So get it together, because if they pull it, there's not gonna be a second chance. I can only do so much."

"Got it."

"Talk soon."

The line disconnects, a short beep sounding in my ear when he's gone, and I drop the phone onto the couch cushion next to me.

I heard him, loud and fucking clear. Even if I'm not actually out there fucking off, social media makes everything look different than it really is. And the team can get a little rowdy.

Honestly… I'm over partying. Lately, it feels like a chore even going to the Kappa house, especially when I'm the sober one trying to keep the guys from doing some dumb shit.

I don't know. Maybe I'm just over college life. I've done it, and it doesn't appeal to me anymore.

What do I want?

I *want* to find ArtGirl. I want to spend my nights talking to her the way that we used to.

I swipe my phone from the couch and open the forum only to be disappointed yet again that there's no message from her.

Who knows… maybe she'll never see the posters. Or if she does, maybe she'll think it's ridiculous that I put flyers up looking for her and will never reach out.

Who knows… maybe it was all for nothing.

I just really fucking hope it isn't.

chapter five

Addie

I CAN DO THIS.

I can do this.

I can do this.

I recite the mantra for the hundredth time as I peer into the mirror in front of me at my reflection, exhaling shakily. I keep telling myself the same line over and over in hopes that I'll convince myself that it's true.

That I will somehow make it through this "engagement" party unscathed. I've thought of a hundred different excuses to try and get out of it, but I know that if I don't show up, the consequences will be far too great.

"Ready?" Amos says softly, stepping off the stairs into my room. The expression on his face is tight with apprehension and worry, the same feelings that are weighing heavily in the pit of my stomach, along with the looming sense of dread.

I drag my gaze from my reflection to him and sigh. "What am I doing, Amos? I *can't* go through with this. I can't believe he's even expecting me to go through with this. I barely know this guy, and what I do know isn't good… and I'm supposed to *marry* him?"

I walk over to my bed and flop onto the edge of the springy mattress, pulling Auggie's chunky body into my arms and squeezing him tightly against me. He cuddles into me, somehow always knowing when I need his comfort.

"You *don't* have to do anything, Addie. He can't force you into this," he says, joining me on the bed. "You can tell him no, and we'll figure something out. There has to be another way, and we'll find it."

A humorless laugh escapes my lips as I brush my fingers over Auggie's soft fur. "You know that's not true. If I don't do this, we lose Ever After. There's no other option. I've been searching for months for a way to save things, and I've found nothing. No last-minute Hail Mary. I'm just... going to have to do it. If it means saving the one place my mother loved more than anything, then I have to."

He reaches out, taking my hand in his and squeezing. It's a small gesture, but somehow, his quiet reassurance gives me strength. Strength to do this. To go to a party in a room full of people that I don't know and pretend to be celebrating an engagement to a man I don't want to be with.

I'll hate every part of what I'm being forced to do, but I'll do it for the bakery. To hold on to this piece of my mother, to not allow anyone to take it from me. The *last* piece I have of her. Her legacy.

"There's still time. Just make it through this party, keep your chin held high, and we'll figure it out. I promise, Addie. *We* will figure it out together."

I know he's talking about him and Earl, but it's not their responsibility. Or their debt. They're my family, but this is my problem.

Ever After is supposed to be mine, and I can't just give it

away without trying everything in my power to save it. I can't let it be taken away from me.

Putting on a fake, cheery smile, I suck in a deep breath, then put Auggie on the bed to return to his umpteenth nap of the day. I steel my spine and stand, smoothing my slightly rumpled dress down.

"It's now or never. I've got an engagement party to attend."

Downstairs, the dining room and foyer have been transformed into something out of a magazine. A very bougie magazine, and immediately, I wonder how in the world Brent paid for this. If the bakery is struggling as badly as he says, how did he afford an... ice sculpture? Waitstaff... *caviar*?

I've always known that appearances are everything to him, but this is completely over-the-top, even for him. And it makes me furious he wasted what little money we have left on this frivolous sham.

Rolling my eyes, I swipe a glass of champagne off a passing server's tray and take a large gulp. I'm not much of a drinker, or really a drinker at all, but I need all the courage I can muster to make it through tonight, even if it's in the liquid form. The bubbly, bitter liquid burns as it slides down my throat, and I wince, my nose wrinkling in response.

Jeez, that's terrible. My first, and probably last, drink. I set the still-full glass down on a table and make my way through the room, quickly realizing that I don't recognize... anyone. Not a single person in this room. I feel like a fish out of water as I pass men in freshly starched tuxedos and women in gowns wearing diamonds and expensive-looking furs.

The feeling only worsens as I pass the violinist playing an upbeat classical tune as I make my way deeper into the room.

"Ah, Addie, there you are," I hear from the left. When I glance over, I see Brent with a wide, albeit fake, smile on his face, standing with my faux fiancé and his family. "You remember Dixon's father, Judge Barrilleaux, and his mother, Elizabeth."

It takes everything inside of me not to turn in the other direction and flee, away from him and this ridiculous party.

Instead, I paste on a small smile and nod, offering them my hand. "Hi, yes. It's great to see you again."

Elizabeth shakes my hand, leaning forward to air-kiss each of my cheeks. "Hello. Addie, you look ravishing, darling." The haughty air of her words makes me cringe, but I keep the feeling to myself as I nod and then shake her husband's hand before turning and focusing my attention on Dixon.

We've met a handful of times, growing up in the same social circles, and since we were children, he's given me a feeling that makes my insides crawl.

I hate the way his gaze slides down my body, resting on my chest for far too long before coming back to my eyes. The slow perusal makes my stomach turn and I bite the inside of my cheek to keep from recoiling from his touch when he reaches for my hand.

"Hello, Addie," he murmurs, his voice low as he holds my hand hostage in his. His words slither down my spine in a way that makes me feel nauseous, but I make sure my smile never wanes, even as I forcibly tug my hand free.

I nod curtly. "Dixon."

"What a joyous occasion for us to celebrate!" Brent says, lifting his champagne glass high between us. Elizabeth, Judge Barrilleaux, and Dixon raise their glass in a toast, clinking against his.

We're celebrating an arranged marriage, I think to myself, bile rising in my throat. *A marriage that you've* coerced *me into, using the only thing I've ever truly loved as leverage to force my hand.*

There's nothing remotely joyous about this occasion.

"Addie, could I have a moment... alone with you?" Dixon says with an air of superiority, and everyone's gaze flicks to me.

I can't deny him in front of everyone, and he knows it.

"Of course." I give another forced smile as he sweeps his hand out toward the door that leads to the porch, gesturing me forward and away from our parents.

As I rigidly walk away with Dixon, my gaze finds Amos, who's standing in the corner, his jaw tight with worry. But he can't intervene.

Not with Brent here. The stakes are too high.

Subtly, I give a nod in reassurance and lift my chin, making my way through the crowd toward the exit. The sticky, humid night air hits my face the moment I step outside, draping around me heavily.

It's quieter out here, with only a few couples littered along the wraparound porch, providing Dixon the privacy he's requested.

The last thing I want to do is be alone with him, but I didn't see another option when he put me on the spot in front of his parents and my stepfather. I move toward the railing when he shuts the door and cross my arms over my chest to hide from his perpetually wandering gaze.

Clearly, it doesn't help when he slides his gaze down my body, making me feel like an object that he's attempting to possess. God, he's sleazy.

I clear my throat, and his eyes flick to mine.

"You wanted to talk?"

He nods before raising the champagne glass to his lips, downing the remaining liquid in a single gulp. From the outside, Dixon Barrilleaux looks like the epitome of his namesake. As the son of one of the most influential judges in New Orleans, he oozes privilege and entitlement from every pore of his body.

Custom-tailored suits, Italian leather loafers, a custom Rolex. Objectively, he'd be considered handsome, with perfectly styled hair, a chiseled, angular jaw, broad shoulders, and a too-perfect smile.

You wouldn't know the cold, calculated truth that lies beneath the polished facade. That the privilege of his upbringing has made him cruel, arrogant, and ruthless.

"Yeah, what's wrong with wanting to talk to my fiancée in private at our engagement party?" he rasps darkly, the irises of his eyes hollowing to almost black. When he steps closer, I retreat backward, hitting the railing behind me.

I glance around us before lowering my voice. "No need to pretend when we're alone, Dixon. You know this marriage is a farce just as much as I do."

A gruff laugh tumbles from his lips, devoid of any humor, the sound sending goose bumps along my flesh despite the late-August heat. "I know that you're my prize. The one I've always wanted yet never been able to have. You're finally going to be mine, Addie. *My wife.* In every sense of the word, whether you want to be or not. This marriage is happening, and if I were you, I'd be on my very best behavior... because I'm not the kind of man who tolerates disobedience."

That knot of dread twists deeper in my stomach as revulsion washes over me in pulsing waves. Surely... *No.* I've always known that he's wanted me, but not like this. Not when it's clear I'm not, and never have been, interested in him that way.

I suck in a sharp breath as I clutch the railing, digging my nails into the wood and trying to ground myself.

Reaching out, he drags the rough pad of his index finger across my shoulder and down the exposed skin of my arm, making me shudder. He smiles sinisterly as he whispers darkly, "Two weeks, and you'll be mine, sweet little Addie."

The words feel like a prison sentence, shackling me in place while my head swims.

As I open my mouth to speak, a voice interrupts.

"Addie, I need to speak with you." My gaze whips to Amos, who's standing by the door, his jaw clenched tightly as he shoots piercing daggers toward Dixon with his eyes. "Right away. It's important."

It's the only excuse I need to flee. Pushing Dixon off me, I brush past him without another word.

The moment Amos slides his hand in mine, tugging me back inside, relief floods my chest so powerfully that I feel like I could cry. A swell of emotions that have finally crested hits me at once.

Attempting to tamp down the emotions, I follow closely behind Amos as my heart pounds in my chest, still trying to make sense of the exchange that just transpired.

I'm disgusted… and for the first time, I feel truly hopeless. And *terrified*.

Amos pulls me inside Brent's study, where I find Earl already inside, then shuts the door quietly, flipping the lock and drowning out the party.

My brow furrows in confusion as I take it all in. "What's going on?"

Not that I'm not beyond thankful to have been rescued by him, to be far away from Dixon, but their expressions are terse, and tension sits heavily in the air.

Something's happened.

"This couldn't wait," Amos says. "Earl… tell her. Go on."

My gaze shifts to Earl's tall, hulking frame as he begins to pace the floor nervously. The feeling in my stomach tightens as I wait for him to speak. There aren't many times in my life that I've seen Earl nervous, and it does nothing but increase my anxiety.

"Honey, you're making her anxious," Amos says to him softly, and Earl nods, then pauses as he drags his meaty palm down his face.

"I... overheard something tonight," he whispers, his gaze fixed on me. "Something I know I wasn't supposed to overhear. But Addie..."

I swallow roughly, nodding. "Tell me."

"Someone broke a glass in the dining room, and I was walking past the kitchen to the supply closet, and I overheard... Brent talking to Judge Barrilleaux. I realize I probably shouldn't have been eavesdropping, but when I heard your name, I wanted to know what they were talking about." He pauses, looking at Amos for a moment. When Amos nods, Earl's gaze slides back to me, and he continues speaking. "I overheard them discussing your marriage to the judge's son. He said that Brent better make damn sure you never find out that you're to inherit Ever After when you get married. That it will screw everything up if you find out the bakery is yours if you marry *anyone*... not just his son."

My breath hitches, and my chest tightens at the revelation. What? I bring my hand to my mouth, covering it as I try to digest what he's saying.

"Addie... he *laughed* about lying to you about the will. Said your mama left *you* the bakery—it's yours the moment you turn twenty-five or if you marry."

I'm trying to process what he's saying, and I find myself swaying on my feet, "What? He's... he's lied to me? All this time? I... I— Why? Why would he do that to me? To take the bakery?"

Earl nods, and Amos steps next to him, smoothing his hand in a calming rhythm over his suit-clad arm.

There's no one in my life that I trust more than the people in this room, and if Earl says he heard it, then it's the truth.

"It seems like you inherit the bakery if either of those two things happen, whichever comes first, and I don't know why he's been keeping it from you, pushing you to marry this guy, but he's a snake, Addie. He's just as corrupt as the company that he keeps, and I know something isn't right. He's manipulating you with false information for some selfish purpose. I know it."

I nod. "I believe you, Earl. I know you'd never tell me anything that wasn't true. But... if this is true, then that means... he won't be able to sell the bakery. He won't be able to take it from me..." I pause, trying to process what I'm hearing. "If I get married *first*, then he'll no longer have a way to control me with it."

I'm shaking as I try to process all of this. As I try to wrap my head around everything that I've found out tonight.

If what he overheard is the truth, then I don't have to marry Dixon to save Ever After. To inherit what's always been mine.

I lift my gaze to the only real family I have standing before me, hot tears falling from my eyes and wetting my cheeks that I hadn't even realized had begun to well in my eyes until they spilled over.

"I don't have to marry Dixon. The bakery can be mine if I marry *anyone*."

Amos winces slightly, nodding. "Or... wait until you turn twenty-five."

Unease tugs at the base of my spine, unfurling through my limbs as I remember the other part of all of this. The most important part. "But that only solves one of our problems. If the bakery is going under, then we don't have until then. We have to do something now. Marrying him is still the only way to get the money we need to save it."

"But now we can form a plan. We can figure out how to avoid it now that we know the truth, Addie. Now, he can't threaten to take it from you if you don't cooperate," Amos adds with a soft, hopeful smile on his lips.

He's right.

This gives me hope. It gives me the Hail Mary I had been desperately wishing for.

Now, I just have to figure out what to do from here.

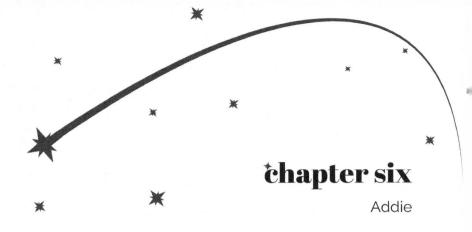

chapter six

Addie

THE MOMENT I get to campus, I realize something unusual is definitely happening, and as always, I am completely out of the loop.

My brow furrows as I pass another bright blue flyer taped to the wall of the art building, but since I'm already late after tearing my room apart again this morning on the off chance that I just somehow missed my sketchbook when I searched last night, I keep power walking toward my class.

Dr. Hart hates when we're late, and the last thing I want is to give him a reason to call me out when I'm already missing the most important thing I need for his class.

I'm screwed. Like royally, completely, totally screwed.

After everything that happened over the weekend with Brent, the party, and the revelations about his deceit, it feels like I haven't been able to catch my breath, and losing my sketchbook is truly just the icing on the cake.

The knot of anxiety in my stomach has unraveled slightly, knowing that I don't technically have to marry someone I'm disgusted by to keep the bakery. But there's still the heavy sense of unease remaining because I still have to figure out how I can save Ever After without marrying that jerk just to get us out of debt.

I slip into my seat just as the heavy door slams shut and breathe a sigh of relief. I made it.

Barely.

Pulling out a fresh notebook from my backpack, I flip to the first blank page and wince.

It's bare, and it shouldn't be.

It should be filled with my notes and sketches for my art portfolio.

I attempt to pay attention to his lecture, doodling in the margins of the blank pages until class is dismissed.

"Did you see this?" the tall, lanky brunette who I think is named Alison whispers to her friend next to me. "Apparently, *Prince Charming* has them all over campus. Literally, like everywhere. Seems like he's looking for an OU art student."

Prince Charming? My curiosity is piqued, so I glance over and see her holding the same blue flyer that I saw posted on every surface of the art building on my way to class.

"All I can say is whoever it is, she's a lucky girl. I mean, what a grand gesture, right? What guy do you know who would do something like this?" her friend replies, a dreamy expression on her face. "I can't wait to see if he finds his ArtGirl. So romantic."

ArtGirl?

My heart drops to my stomach when I hear that name. I… I mean, that's a fairly common name, right? It couldn't be…

"Um, hi, could I see that?" I mumble quietly, and the girl nods, thrusting the paper into my shaky hand. I barely notice them leaving as my eyes scan the flyer.

Prince Charming Searching For His Artgirl

*If you're her, then I found something special that belongs to you
and only fate can get it back to you.* -Jockboy

Oh. My. God.

The floor feels like it might have fallen out beneath me as I collapse into the lecture theater chair, holding on to the paper for dear life. I stare down at the flyer in my hand with wide eyes, exhaling shakily before reading it again.

And again.

And then... again.

This has to be just a crazy... coincidence, right?

I think back to the conversations I had on the OU forum with... Jockboy.

The boy who stumbled into my life by happenstance, who became more to me than I ever imagined he could. I flash back to all the nights spent talking to him until the early hours of the morning, only signing off when I could hardly keep my eyes open for a second longer. How I would anxiously await the next message from him the next day, like a lovesick fool. How I couldn't wait to tell him about my day or how I was feeling because somehow, it felt like he was the only person in the world I felt like I could just be *me* with.

It seems like a lifetime ago, even though it's been only nine months.

Not that I was keeping track or anything.

Bold serif numbers stare back at me from the bottom of the paper, and I find myself hesitating, even as I pull my phone out of the pocket of my cardigan.

There's no way... that Jockboy found my sketchbook. No, there's just no way.

How did he get it? Was he at that party?

That would be a serendipitous twist of fate, one that I'm not sure if even I believe is possible.

My fingers hover over the screen, talking myself out of messaging it because I know logically, there is just no way.

But...

Could it be?

I quickly type in his number with a simple, to-the-point message.

> I want my sketchbook back.

Then, because it sounded just a tad bit rude, I add:

> Please.

Standing from my chair, I shove the flyer into the side pocket of my backpack and lock my phone before putting it back into my pocket.

I'm sure that whoever this is, this must simply be a... coincidence... about the names. Well, besides that my sketchbook is, in fact, missing. But the paper doesn't specify what it is he's found anyway.

It could be anything. A sweater, a backpack, jewelry.

I make it halfway down the hallway before my phone vibrates in my pocket with a notification, and I hastily pull it out.

> How do I know it's really you?

My brow pulls tight as I quickly respond,

> So, you do have my sketchbook?

> I cannot confirm nor deny the object I have in my possession. If it's really you, then you know where to find me.

He's talking about the forum. He has to be—nothing else would make sense.

Holy crap. It *really* is him. Jockboy has my sketchbook.

I spend the rest of the day attempting to focus on my classes so I don't fall behind and desperately trying not to think about the fact that he's in possession of the most personal item that I own. My sketchbook is… a piece of me. Literally and figuratively. Like a diary of sorts. A place where I've bled my deepest, darkest secrets onto the pages through my art.

I can't just *not* attempt to get it back.

Later that night, as I sit in front of the glowing computer screen at my desk, chewing my lip anxiously, I glance over at Auggie, who's perched on his bed next to me, staring back with those judgy eyes.

"Don't look at me like that," I say.

His ears perk up as if he understands what I'm saying, popping into sharp little points that are entirely too cute.

"Would it really be so bad if I didn't get it back? I could just start fresh…" I mutter.

Of course, he doesn't answer back, instead cocking his head as if to say, "Just do it, you big weenie."

Sighing, I drag my gaze back to the screen, which is open to OU's student forum. Auggie's right. I need to stop being a baby and just do it. I'll meet up with him, and I'll get my sketchbook back. Even if that means facing Jockboy.

The nagging voice in the back of my head quips, "Yeah, the guy that you fell for and then ghosted. Easy."

Groaning, I drop my head onto my keyboard. It's not my proudest moment, disappearing on him. But... It had to be done.

It was the right thing to do, even if it didn't *feel* right at the time. A huge part of me regrets it, and another part of me has always wondered what would've happened if I'd actually met him at the gala that night.

I open the private message window and use my mouse to select the username I never imagined I would click again.

ORLEANSU11

ArtGirl: Can I have my sketchbook back now?

My stomach somersaults as I wait for a response. It's late, so there's a good chance that he won't even see my message until tomorrow. I should just shut my computer down and try to get a good night's sleep.

One where I don't think about... Jockboy or about what a cluster my life is turning into.

Just as I'm about to minimize the screen, a message comes through.

OrleansU11: Tomorrow. 9 PM. Dyer Park.

chapter seven

Addie

MY CLAMMY HANDS are shaking by my sides as I walk along the sidewalk toward the park. Almost as badly as the nerves churning in the pit of my stomach or the wildly unpredictable rhythm of my heart, which is racing in my chest.

I can't even believe I'm doing this right now.

Stopping abruptly with the thought of fleeing, I bring my paint-chipped nail to my mouth and chew anxiously on the tip.

Not only can I not believe I'm about to do this, but I can't believe that the person who somehow ended up with my missing sketchbook and who put flyers up around the entire campus searching for me is... *Jockboy.*

I ask the same question I've asked no less than a hundred times since our last message.

How?

How did he end up with my sketchbook? And out of all people, *him*?

I have so many unanswered questions, and it's not as if I can just get my sketchbook back and walk away and pretend it wasn't him.

No, this is... complicated.

Beyond complicated.

He's not a stranger, but yet, in many ways... he *is*.

What if he hates me for ghosting him? I wouldn't blame him, regardless of my reasoning.

What if I don't measure up to the girl he's imagined all of this time in his head? Or worst of all, what if he's indifferent to me? That he's not interested in finding *me* to reconnect... he just felt an obligation to find the owner of the art.

I know it shouldn't matter; it's not like he's meeting me because he's interested in me. It's just him returning something that belongs to me, but still, the nagging thought in my head won't retreat.

It's all I've thought of since last night.

I glance down at my rumpled linen skirt, smoothing my hands over the wrinkles in the fabric, second-guessing myself once more. I changed at least four times and finally settled on my favorite maxi skirt, pale pink with an array of red strawberries on it, and a white eyelet shirt paired with my favorite loafers and a deep brown cardigan. My stomach tightens with nerves, and I swallow roughly, trying to summon the courage to keep walking from somewhere inside of me, *anywhere.*

Except I come up empty, with only apprehension in the place of the courage I desperately need.

I can't do this.

He can keep my sketchbook, and I'll replace it. *Easy.*

But it's not easy. Just the thought of losing all the work inside my sketchbook for my thesis makes me feel ill. The foundations to my project are all inside it. What's worse... losing all of my art or the fear of finally meeting Jockboy face-to-face?

I turn on my heel and start back in the other direction. Nope, I can't do this.

"ArtGirl?" A deep voice from behind me stops me in my

tracks. The heel of my worn loafer skids along the sidewalk, keeping me in place.

No, no no no.

God, what am I supposed to do now? He's already seen me, so I can't just take off in a sprint and literally run the other way, although a very large part of me wishes that I could.

Doing that would be *far* more embarrassing. God, this was a terrible idea, and my heart thrashes in my chest as my feet stay glued in place while I try to determine a new plan of action.

The previous plan was to take off in the other direction. However cowardly that may be.

No. *No.*

I'm *not* running. *Get it together, Addie.*

I've waited this long to... see who he is. Not only that, but I really want my sketchbook back.

Slowly, I turn, my eyes squeezed tightly shut as my hands fold over my stomach, and I exhale the jittering nerves, squaring my shoulders and lifting my chin in an act of confidence that I don't truly possess right now.

"*Addie?*"

My eyes snap to his, and my mouth falls open, shock rippling through me in waves.

"*Grant?*"

He actually looks as surprised as I do, his deep blue eyes widened in shock, the sharp contour of his jaw hanging open, mirroring my own. His dark blond hair is tousled and mussed from running his fingers through it, and for a moment, I find myself wondering if it's as soft as it looks.

The black hoodie he's wearing is fitted to him, Hellcats Baseball Department stretched across his broad chest. Even the light-wash jeans he's wearing are molded to his thick thighs, fitting him perfectly.

Somehow, he's even more handsome than the first time we met. The first time we met...

"You're... *ArtGirl*?"

"You're... *Jockboy*?"

Our words run together in a tangle of consonants, and he chuckles, deep and low, a sound that tugs at the invisible clasp in the pit of my stomach, freeing a flurry of butterflies.

"Wow. Talk about fucking fate," he says quietly, stepping closer, so close that I can smell the fresh, crisp cedar scent of his bodywash. "I mean... I considered for a brief second that the girl I met at the party could potentially be the owner of the mystery sketchbook... but honestly, that seemed too... kismet to be true."

Jockboy is... *Grant.*

"I... You..." I trail off, my brain still trying to make sense of what's happening, but it seems to be short-circuiting because I can't find the words. The right ones, anyhow.

He chuckles. "Yeah. I can't believe that I'm finally meeting you. I can't believe that you're *you*..."

Immediately, I feel the heat rush to my cheeks as I drop my gaze from his. Is he disappointed by that? I can't tell, and suddenly, I feel stupid for even showing up to do this.

"Um... thanks?"

"Fuck, I said that wrong. No..." he says in a rush. "What I meant to say is that I can't believe that you're *ArtGirl*. That we actually hung out the other night, and I had no idea it was you. I would've never let you leave, Addie. Not without finding a way to contact you. Shit, I have so many questions."

I nod—if I had to guess, some of the same ones that I do. "This is unbelievable. I... You finding my sketchbook, the fact that we were around each other and had no idea who the other was. *All* of it..."

"Yeah, it is. But honestly, I'm really fucking glad. Are you...?"

Shyly, I chew the corner of my lip and nod. "Yeah."

Without a doubt, yes. Even if I'm having the hardest time rationalizing the insane twist that's been thrown our way.

"Some might call this fate, ya know?" The corner of his lip tugs up into a teasing grin, and I can't help but smile as he references one of our many conversations from the past. One I could never forget. Just the way I could never forget him, even though I tried.

"I mean, to be fair, you *did* put up flyers around the entire school, including the art department, so there was a pretty large probability that I was going to see it."

I watch as the dimple in his cheek pops when he laughs and shakes his head, his golden hair falling across his forehead. Honestly, I'm not sure what I thought meeting him would be like. I'd imagined a hundred different scenarios, but... it kind of feels like I'm meeting an old friend. While my stomach is still twisted in knots of nerves, a larger part of me feels comfortable around him in a way I didn't expect to. A sense of ease washes over me.

My throat bobs roughly as I drag the worn toe of my loafer along the concrete, my gaze lowered to the scuffed leather.

"Wanna sit with me?" He gestures to the wrought iron bench near us, and I nod.

I try to ignore the way my shoulder brushes against the hard muscles of his bicep as we walk to the bench, and I sit down beside him.

Instead, I focus on the way that my heart is still thrashing in my chest. I can't believe that I'm sitting here with... *Grant. My Jockboy.*

The faint rumble of thunder echoes in the distance, and a flash of lightning deep within the clouds catches my gaze. I've been so nervous about this meeting that I haven't paid attention to much else. Now, I can feel the light spray of rain in the air as it caresses my cheeks.

"I love thunderstorms," Grant says, his eyes trained on the dark clouds. "When I was little, my mom would always get on to me for going outside to the porch and watching it piss rain. She was convinced that I'd get swept away by a tornado or something. Didn't stop me though. I just kept going back."

"I remember you telling me about your mom. It's just you and her, right?"

He nods, his throat bobbing as he swallows, then drags his piercing gaze to me. "Yeah, my dad split when I was a toddler. It was always just the two of us. I gave that woman ten kinds of hell growing up."

"Something tells me you probably did." Teasingly, I bump my shoulder against his, and the corner of his lip lifts in a grin.

"Can I say something? Honestly?"

"Of course," I murmur.

"I've fucking missed you, Addie. I never stopped thinking about you," he rasps, the deep timbre of his voice settling around my heart with each syllable. "Even when I probably should've... I couldn't."

Hearing him say it out loud makes my chest feel warm, my limbs feel heavy with relief, knowing that the way I felt about our friendship wasn't just one-sided.

"I know. Me too," I say earnestly. "I'm sorry I pulled away. It's just... things are *complicated*, Grant. In my life. More complicated than you can imagine. I know that might sound like an excuse, but it's the truth."

The words feel heavy on my tongue as I speak. I hated that I pulled away from him when things became too much, but I did it with the best intention, even if the impact wasn't received that way.

His gaze lingers on mine, a beat of silence passing between us, and I can't read his expression. I'm scared that it'll be the reason he decides to leave, and I meant it when I said that I wouldn't blame him.

I can't imagine how it would've felt had he done the same thing to me.

Finally, he speaks, low and husky. "It's okay. I'm sorry things are complicated, but I can be there for you, the way I was before. I miss those days, fuck, I do. If you want to tell me about it or even if you don't, just... please don't disappear on me again, Addie. Okay?"

I can't get over how... handsome he is. Just like the night that I met him at the Kappa house, I was taken aback by it. I'm pretty sure I've never seen anyone as attractive as Grant, and internally, my stomach is flipping and my mind spinning at the thought of him being Jockboy.

This is the boy that I spent my nights talking to. The boy that I felt more seen by than anyone in my life.

And I'm sitting next to him on this park bench, so close that I can feel the heat of his body on mine.

It's a surreal feeling.

"Okay," I whisper shyly, tucking my hair behind my ear. Thankfully, it's dark enough that he probably can't see the way that my cheeks heat furiously under his lingering gaze.

Apparently, I'm not the only one who can't stop staring. He hasn't taken his eyes off me since he arrived.

"Can I hug you?" he says as he pushes to his feet. "I feel like I've waited so fucking long to hug you, ArtGirl. Would that be okay?"

"Yes."

He offers me his hand, and I hesitantly slide my hand in his. When his fingers close around mine, my heart begins to race erratically as he pulls me up from the bench.

And then, he's gently tugging me into his arms.

They wrap tightly around my body, strong and secure, as my cheek rests on the hard plane of his chest.

For a second, I just... *breathe*, melting into his arms, listening to the steady rhythm of his heart beating beneath his rib cage. I memorize the feeling since it'll probably be the only time that I get to experience it.

I imagined this moment in a thousand different ways. What it would feel like to touch him, to feel safe in his arms.

Yet, nothing could come close to the sense of comfort I feel sinking into his embrace.

Suddenly, thunder cracks in the sky, and I feel the first raindrop hitting my hair, the only warning we get before the sky opens up. Fat, heavy drops of rain begin to fall, and in a matter of seconds, I feel it soaking through my shirt and into my skin.

"Oh shit," Grant mutters, dropping his arms only to hold out his hand for me. I quickly take it, and then he's pulling me toward the covered awning on the other side of the park.

Before we even make it there, we're both completely drenched and laughing so hard that I can't tell if it's the rain or him that's making it hard to see.

"God, I feel like that came out of nowhere," I say once we're safely under the pavilion.

He laughs as he shakes his head side to side playfully, sending a spray of water my way. "Seems like a lot of things have come out of nowhere for us lately, huh?"

"That's the thing about fate. You never see it coming," I say, averting my gaze when his burns through me. It feels like he's not just staring at me but into me.

"Who's that?"

Glancing up, I see a hooded figure aggressively walking

through the onslaught of rain toward the covered awning where we're standing. At first, I have no clue who it is. It's raining too hard, and it's too dark to see almost anything.

But once they get closer, I realize exactly who it is, squashing the flurry of butterflies that were fluttering inside my chest and replacing them with unease. "Oh god," I whisper with wide eyes. "This cannot be happening."

Grant's brow furrows in confusion. "What? What's happening?"

I don't answer immediately, mostly because I'm trying to figure out how Dixon even knew where I was, so Grant reaches out and grasps the tips of my fingers gently. "Addie?"

My eyes dart to his, and I sigh, knowing that as much as I don't want to say goodbye, I have to. "Just... I have to go, okay? Thank you for meeting me tonight. I appreciate it, and Grant, I'm really, really glad that it happened this way."

I hate that he looks... disappointed, the crease between his brow deepening as his jaw works. I'm already messing this up again, but Dixon showing up here tonight proves what I knew nine months ago, that it has to be this way. I don't want Grant to see this turbulent part of my life, so there is no other way that this can go.

Softly, I pull my hand free and start to walk away, one step back at a time, until I hear Dixon growl my name.

The sound sends chills down my spine, and I wince, tearing my gaze from Grant's to face my disgruntled, forced fiancé.

"What are you doing here, Dixon?"

When he steps under the awning, he throws his hood off his head and sneers at me. "That's a question I should be asking you, isn't it, Addie?" He says my name with such force that I jolt back slightly.

Dixon sways on his feet before reaching out to steady himself against the metal beam of the awning.

Even from a foot away, I can smell the overwhelming stench of alcohol permeating off him. It's enough to make me gag.

He's drunk. Not only is he drunk, but I'm guessing he drove here like this in a thunderstorm, putting everyone's life at risk.

Out of the corner of my eye, I can see Grant stepping closer to me, his shoulders tense as he glares at Dixon, his eyes hard.

"How did you even know I was here, Dixon? Do you realize how creepy this is?" I say quietly.

When he laughs, it's devoid of humor, a mocking sound that does nothing for the trepidation building inside of me. In the dim street light, I can see how bloodshot his eyes are.

"Not important. What is important, though, is the fact that you're at a park in the middle of the night with another guy."

My hands are tightened into fists at my side as a wave of anger coils through my body.

How dare he show up like this? Drunk and acting unhinged and possessive.

"You're drunk, and you need to leave." My voice wavers as I speak, nerves shooting through me and stealing any conviction I had. "You never should have come here."

"Addie, who is this guy?" Grant asks. When I glance over at him, I see all of the questions in his eyes, and I wish that this wasn't happening right now. I'm completely mortified by Dixon's behavior, and all I want is for him to leave.

Lifting my chin, I say, "No one. He's leaving."

Dixon chuckles darkly, "And you're coming with me, Addie."

"No, I'm not."

"You either leave with me, or I'll put you in the fucking car myself." He stalks forward, wrapping his fingers around my bicep and squeezing hard.

"Ow, Dixon, you're hurting me. Let me go!"

Tears prickle my eyes at the force of his grip, and I suck in a sharp hiss. When I try to wrench my arm free, he only tightens his hold, but before the cry even leaves my lips, he's on the ground in front of me.

"Keep your fucking hands off of her," Grant spits, his chest heaving beneath his hoodie. Anger radiates off him in thick, pulsing waves. "I don't know who you are or what's going on, but I do know that you will not put your hands on her again. Do you fucking hear me?"

Grant gently pulls me into him, rubbing the palm of his hand gently over the sore spot on my arm. He's so tender and attentive that it causes my chest to ache.

"Are you okay?" he asks quietly, worry flickering in his eyes.

I nod, biting my lip to hold back the tears that threaten to spill from my watery eyes. "I'm fine. Thank you." I look down at Dixon and shore up what little courage I can. "Dixon, leave now, or... I... I'm going to call the police, and even your daddy won't be able to get you out of this one."

My words sound more assertive than I feel. I'm shaken up and scared. But I'm completely done with this.

With him.

"This isn't over, Addie." Dixon seethes as he rises to his feet and flips Grant off. "We'll see each other soon." His threatening tone makes me wrap my arms around myself protectively.

With one final glance, he pulls the hood back up and disappears into the stormy darkness.

"What a fucking prick. Who is that guy?" Grant asks once he's gone.

I don't know how to answer that question, so instead, I suck in a deep, shaky breath and put distance between us.

My emotions are in overdrive, and I can feel my anxiety snaking up my spine. Dixon showing up tonight after meeting Grant for the first time burst the little happy bubble that I tried to surround myself with, and now, reality has rushed back in with force like never before.

I can't do this. Not then, and not now.

"He's... no one. I need to go, Grant. I'm sorry." I turn and run out from under the awning into the rain. It pelts my skin rhythmically as I make my way to my car. The sidewalk is slick and wet under my feet, and I pick up my pace, nearly to my car when a hand wraps around my wrist, gently stopping me.

Turning, I see Grant standing there, his golden hair wet and dripping and sticking to his forehead. Rain droplets cascade down his face and cling to his dark lashes.

"Why do you keep running away from me, Ar—Addie? Are you running away for that asshole?" he asks over the thundering sound of the storm.

I reach up, pushing my drenched hair out of my face as our eyes stay locked, and I suck in a deep breath.

This is all such a colossal mess.

"I don't have a choice, Grant. I'm supposed to *marry* him in less than two weeks."

His lips part in shock as the crease in his brow returns. Fat droplets of rain trickle down his face as he shakes his head. "Married? You're engaged... to *him*? Is that why you ghosted me? You were engaged the whole time?" He pauses, collecting himself, and rubs his hand over his jaw. "Addie, you can't marry that piece of shit... I mean, look what he just said to you. What he *did* to you," Grant says gently.

"I don't have a choice! You think I *want* this?" I cry. I look down at the ground, laughing humorlessly. "Of course I don't *want* to marry him. I don't even want to be around him, let alone married to him."

This time, it's me who pauses as I try to regain a semblance of control, sucking in ragged breath after ragged breath as the rain punctuates every word. "Do you remember when I told you last year... about my stepdad trying to force me into a marriage? Well, that hasn't changed."

Silence hangs between us. The only sound is that of the wind whipping through the air as rain falls, the trees swishing in the night. And then I unload it all on him.

"Do you remember me telling you about my mom's bakery? Well, my stepfather has been threatening to take it away from me if I don't marry Dixon. The bank is on the verge of taking our business because of my stepfather's financial troubles, and this is his solution. Dixon's family is beyond wealthy. If I don't agree, he's going to sell it to punish me."

Tears well in my eyes as it all comes tumbling out. I dare a glance at Grant, searching for any sign of judgment on his face, but there's none, so I continue, even though it's hard to lay it all out like this. All I see is warmth and empathy.

"But a few nights ago, my friend overheard my stepfather admitting that he lied to me about my mother's will. Turns out the bakery can be mine now, *when* I get married or turn twenty-five. But that doesn't really solve the problem. My stepfather is going to sell if I'm not married to Dixon in two weeks. So, he's still my only option. If I don't, then I'm going to lose my mom's bakery, Grant. I'm going to lose the *only* piece I have left of her. He'll take away all I have left of my mother. I have no choice."

My chest is heaving with adrenaline when I stop speaking, my entire body beginning to shake from the wet, cold rain pelting my body and soaking me to the bone.

Grant steps forward, taking my hand in his. His palm is warm and comforting, and for a second, I close my eyes, squeezing them shut, willing my lungs to suck in a breath. But I know what's about to happen.

This is where he walks away from me, just like I always thought that he would.

Because my life is an unappealing mess.

But when he opens his mouth, he shocks me to my core.

"You always have a choice, Addie," he rasps. My eyes snap open as I peer up into the deep blue pools of his.

"Not anymore I don't," I reply defeatedly.

Silence hangs heavily in the air, our gazes locked so intensely that it feels as if he's staring straight into me. And then he says the words that change everything.

"You do. Because you can marry *me* instead."

chapter eight

Grant

"WHAT? Y-YOU... CAN'T MEAN THAT," Addie says with wide eyes.

We're standing in a fucking thunderstorm, soaked to the bone, and yet I can't stop staring at the girl in front of me. I can't stop thinking about how fucking cute she is wearing these little lace socks that ruffle around her ankles or how her lips are the same color as the strawberries on her skirt. She's *ArtGirl*. And it's surreal that she's here... after all this time, and more beautiful than I could have ever imagined.

A fucking vision, and as wild as it seems, I'm one hundred percent serious about my proposal.

"I don't say anything that I don't mean, Addie. Over my dead fucking body would I let you marry that asshole." My voice shakes slightly, my anger returning at the thought of him ever putting his hands on her again.

Her cute-as-fuck button nose wrinkles along with her brow as she soaks in what I'm saying.

"The will says you have to be married, not that you have to marry *him*, right?" When she nods, I nod along with her. "Then marry me."

"You're *crazy*," she breathes quietly. "Completely out of your mind."

"Yeah, probably so. But I'm serious. Marry *me*, Addie."

I don't think my heart has ever beat so fast in my damn life. She's right—I'm probably out of my mind, asking her to marry me. A girl I only know online, yet... I feel like I know her better than anyone. I knew her heart before I knew her face.

And there's no goddamn way I'm letting her tie herself to that piece of shit. No way.

Seeing him threaten her and put his hands on her made me see a violent shade of red-hot anger like I've never experienced in my life. I wanted to put my fist through his face, and I probably would have had I not heard her whimper from behind me. I didn't want to traumatize her further.

"But Grant... we haven't even *spoken* in almost a year," she starts, but I shake my head, stopping her.

"So? That asshole's any better? At least we *know* each other, Addie. Really know each other. I think you knew me better than anyone in my life. You knew the real me when it felt like no one else did. Not a single person. Do you realize what that meant to me?"

She shakes her head, pulling away again as she pushes her hair out of her eyes. The rain seems to be falling harder, and we probably look like two idiots standing in the middle of a storm having this conversation, but ask me if I give a single shit. "Do you even understand what you're offering to do? Why would you want to do that... for *anyone*, let alone me? You saw how Dixon was... my stepfather is even worse. I don't want you getting into this mess. I can't do that to you. I won't. We're talking actual *marriage*, Grant."

"We were there for each other last year... let me help you and be there for you now too. I wouldn't offer if I wasn't willing to do it." I duck my head to look her straight in the eyes so she sees I'm serious. Rain begins to fall harder around us, and as I reach for her hand to keep her close, I feel her trembling beneath my touch. I can already tell she's getting ready to deny my offer again, so I add, "Besides, it could be beneficial for us both."

"What do you mean?" she asks with a serious expression.

"You need someone to marry to save the bakery who isn't that prick… and I need help cleaning up my image a bit. I'm on the cusp of signing a huge sponsorship with a national athletic wear company. They're nervous that I'm viewed by the public as a careless playboy, and settling down could clear up that problem. Show them I'm not a risk to their brand. That I'm not this party guy that I've been perceived to be, and even if I was, those days are over. We could do this, Addie. Do it for *both* of us."

For a moment, she stares up at me silently, chewing on her lip. I can practically see the wheels turning in her head.

"This is…" She blinks, a look of hesitation and confusion evident on her face.

"Genius, maybe. The answer to both of our problems." I pause, taking her in for a moment. Water sticks to her thick, dark eyelashes, her blonde hair drenched and sticking to her face. She's shivering, either from the rain or the shock about everything that happened tonight. Either way, I don't think this is the place for this conversation.

"Look, we're kinda standing in the middle of a hurricane right now. If you're comfortable with it, let's go back to my apartment and talk about it further? Get out of the rain?"

Her eyes are as stormy as the one we're standing in, questions flickering within the depths. "Okay. Yeah," she whispers finally, and I nod, taking her hand in mine and leading her toward my truck and out of the rain.

Thank fuck I was so nervous about meeting her tonight that I anxious-cleaned the shit out of my apartment just to keep my mind busy. It was a wreck, and though I truly had no intention of bringing her back here tonight, I'm thankful for the first time in my life that I clean when I'm stressed.

She's hesitantly standing by the front door, shivering with her arms wrapped around her torso, when I walk back into the living room with a fresh towel and some clothes in my hands.

"I brought you an old hoodie and a pair of sweats for you to put on too. I'm sure they'll be way too big, but at least you can get out of your wet clothes."

"Ye-s-s, please. I'm f-freezing," she says between chattering teeth as she takes the clothes and then wraps the towel around herself like a blanket.

Pointing toward the door at the end of the hallway, I say, "Bathroom's right there. I'm gonna change too, but if you need anything, let me know, okay?"

She nods. "Thank you."

When she disappears into the bathroom, I head to my bedroom and grab a towel to dry off before I throw on a pair of clean gym shorts and a hoodie. When I walk back out into the living room, I find her sitting on the couch with her legs pulled up to her chest.

Of course, my clothes swallow her tiny frame, but something strangely primal flares in my chest at the sight of her wearing them.

Fuck, I can't even believe ArtGirl... *Addie* is in my apartment right now.

I feel like I've been trying to convince myself that she's actually real all night and that I'm not caught in a fever dream.

"Better?" I ask as I sink down on the cushion next to her.

"Yes. Much." She nods her head, giving me a small but genuine smile before her dainty features turn more serious again. "Grant... I'm so, so sorry about tonight. About Dixon showing up. That you had to even be involved in that. Honestly, I'm just completely mortified, and I can't stop thinking about it," she says quietly, her eyes holding mine intently. I can see the shame in her expression, and I hate that she's feeling embarrassed over that fuckwad's behavior. I rein in the sudden urge I have to pull her into my arms to comfort her.

"Hey, don't apologize for him. You have nothing to be sorry for, Addie. He's the one who acted like a dick, not you. You have absolutely *nothing* to feel embarrassed about," I reply lightly.

The crease in her brow deepens as her eyes flicker with emotion. "I know. It just... that was so crazy, and he's never done anything like that before. I mean, we've never really been alone, though, without our parents. I knew he was kind of a jerk, but nothing like *this*. Not until tonight... I guess I saw what's been hiding in plain view all this time."

As she speaks, my gaze travels along the delicate slope of her nose, which is scattered with faint freckles, then to her cheeks, which seem to finally have some color back in them now that she's warm. Thick, dark lashes frame her pale blue eyes, and her pouty pink lips are pulled downward into a frown. A frown that for some reason I would give anything to erase.

I probably shouldn't be staring at her, drinking every inch of her in, but I can't stop myself. I've waited so long for this moment, to see her face-to-face, and now that she's here... I'm memorizing everything about her, committing it directly to memory. That way, I'll never forget.

"You should never be alone with him. *Never.* No man who puts his hands on a woman is worth a fuck. He's dangerous, Addie. He could really hurt you."

She sighs raggedly, her entire body deflating. "I know. I don't want to. Trust me, I wish that I wasn't in this... mess with him to begin with. He gives me the creeps."

Reaching out, I grasp her chin between my fingers gently, turning her gaze to me. Her eyes widen, and I watch as her throat bobs. "You don't have to be around him ever again if you don't want to, Addie. I meant what I said—"

"About marrying me," she interrupts, and I nod.

"Yeah, about us getting married. I meant what I said, and I know it probably seems rash. Which is why I think we should both sleep on it. Talk about it more tomorrow when we've had a chance to think about things with a clear head?"

"Yeah, it was just a lot at once. I should probably go." Pushing off the cushions, she stands like she's going to leave, and before I can stop myself, I reach out and gently grasp her hand.

"Wait. Addie, I didn't mean you had to leave. Will you stay for a bit? So we can just... talk? Not about anything that happened tonight but just like we used to? It'll give you a chance to warm up."

I'm hoping like hell she says yes because I'm selfish, and I want just a little longer with her. As long as she'll give me. But I also understand that tonight had to have been hard on her.

A beat passes, and she finally nods, sinking down onto the couch and leaning back against the arm before pulling her knees up to her chest. The black hoodie she's wearing is so big that it covers her entire body, and I can't help but grin.

"What's funny?" she asks.

My shoulder dips slightly. "Just never thought I'd see you in a baseball hoodie. You know, since you're so *anti-sports*."

"That is *not* true." She blanches. "At all."

"Bullshit."

When her jaw falls open, I smirk. "I distinctly remember your hatred for all things sports related. Don't you remember how we met?"

"Of course I do, but that was simply because I felt passionately that the athletic department gets favoritism over the arts, and I was just saying that we should all be equals. That's all." The determined expression on her face is fucking adorable.

"Mhmm," I hum cheekily. "Always the activist. I see some things never change."

Like me teasing her every chance I get. Except now… it's face-to-face, and I can enjoy the adorable flush of her cheeks that she's trying to hide. The tilt of her lips as she tries to restrain her smile, but the twinkle of her eyes gives her away.

I could never see that through a screen. And fuck, I love it.

Those pale blue eyes roll as she pulls her bottom lip between her teeth before releasing it. "Does that mean you're still delusional?"

My head drops back as the laugh bubbles from my throat. "Yeah, ArtGirl. I guess so. Tell me what I've been missing for the last nine months."

And just like that… we fall right back into the way things used to be, as if we never missed a beat. We both realized that the whole point of us meeting up was to return her sketchbook, yet I left the damn thing in the truck because I was so nervous to see her for the first time. She tells me about the bakery, about her art classes, and how her corgi, who is currently staying with a friend, is still as chubby and grumbly as ever. About how she's working on her art thesis portfolio so she can graduate come May. I tell her about my last baseball season and my current training. About how Reese and Lane have graduated and moved away and how they both are basically married at this point. And of course, I tell her how Davis is a literal pain in my ass.

She's shy at first, and I can tell that I make her nervous, but the conversation continues to flow for so long that I lose track of time.

"Yeah, so basically, I've become the team's fucking dad. I feel like I have a bunch of toddlers running around, even though they're grown-ass men. Especially Davis. He's the ringleader, and I swear the universe sent him to destroy me because I finally got a reprieve from Reese. I love them—they're my teammates, and we're family—but I also need them to stop getting me into shit that jeopardizes my future. That's why I'm keeping us on the straight and narrow, whatever it takes," I mutter after giving her the rundown of how things have been on the team.

Addie laughs quietly, then reaches up and covers her mouth as she yawns.

Shit, it's got to be after midnight at this point. I reach for my phone and check the time, seeing that it's actually almost 1:00 a.m.

"Shit, I didn't realize how late it had gotten. Do you want me to take you home?" I ask, turning my phone to show her the screen.

Pulling her bottom lip between her teeth, she hesitates. "Oh. Um... yeah, sure." She wraps her arms around herself protectively, suddenly seeming uneasy at the thought of going home.

"Or... you can also stay here instead," I say lightly, "If you wanted? And tomorrow... we can talk more about things?"

An instant look of relief flickers in her eyes. "Honestly? I really don't want to go home tonight. I don't want to chance facing my stepdad."

"Stay here. You can have my bed, and I'll take the couch."

"Really?" she says quietly, tucking her damp hair behind her ear.

I nod. "Yeah, of course. I'd honestly feel better about you being here instead of there anyway after everything that's happened."

"Okay. Yeah, I'll stay… if you're sure."

There are a lot of things I'm not sure of right now, but the one thing I *am* sure of?

I don't want to let her go again.

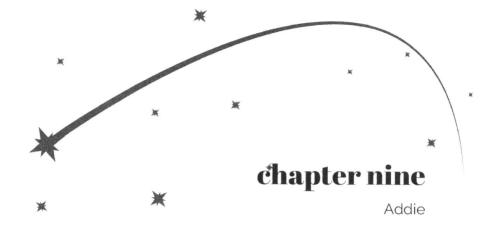

chapter nine

Addie

WHEN I WAKE up the following morning, I *almost* forget where I am, whose room I'm in… whose *bed* I'm in, if it wasn't for the fact that I'm nestled between blankets that smell *exactly* the way Grant does.

Clean and crisp, with a masculine hint of cedar.

I'm surrounded by it, and I burrow further beneath the blanket, sighing sleepily.

My eyes slowly open to an assault of warm morning rays, bathing the bed and room in bright sunlight. Last night, I was so emotionally and physically exhausted that I crawled beneath the covers and immediately passed out.

Which I was thankful for because I was worried that my brain would never shut off. I was internally freaking about everything that had happened and even more so about the fact that I was with *Grant*.

I didn't really have a moment to look at his room until now in the daylight. The walls are painted a bright white, plain with no decorations or mementos. But tucked into the corner, there's a tall wooden bookshelf that's stuffed full of paperbacks. Most of the spines are worn and cracked from being read, and I can't help the smile that pulls at my lips.

I bet a large portion of them are poetry books.

It's something I've always loved about him, the fact that he's a paradox. The fact that he's this dedicated athlete, but he's also... reserved, smart, and reads *poetry*.

And he's also devastatingly handsome. Even more than I thought he would be.

My gaze shifts to his desk and the textbooks stacked haphazardly on top of it, along with a pile of hardbacks and opened notebooks.

Turning to lie flat on the mattress, I stare up at the stark white ceiling.

Did last night actually even happen?

I mean, if it wasn't for the fact that I'm currently in his bed, then I would think it was only a dream.

That him offering to marry me was simply a figment of my imagination. But I know that it's not because I haven't been able to stop replaying last night in my head, over and over.

Could I really... marry *Grant*?

I tug my lip between my teeth and then flip to my side, placing my palms beneath my cheek as I think about that question. About the reality and the weight of what it really means.

If I think about it in black and white, it *seems* simple.

I was going to marry Dixon to save the bakery, even though it was the absolute last thing in the world I wanted to do. A guy who I hardly know, and the things I do know, aren't great. *Especially* after last night.

Then there's Grant, who once teased me about being my Prince Charming, my knight in shining armor who would swoop in and save the day... turns out he really is.

He's offering something that seems impossible and that… just might be crazy enough to work.

And my other option? Marrying Dixon… It's not really an option.

I know now that it never really was.

It seems so simple, the easiest solution in the world, to marry Grant, but a part of me knows that nothing in the world is ever really quite that simple, and that's what scares me.

Pulling myself from my thoughts, I send a quick text to Amos to check on Auggie and let him know I'll be by to pick him up soon. I texted him last night when I first got to Grant's, asking him to check on him since I was "studying with a friend," and he'd offered to take him home with him for a sleepover because Earl was dying for his "little" guy to come over. I sit up and push the covers off, then stand, making my way to the bedroom door, my thoughts currently moving at a breakneck speed I'm not equipped for this early in the morning.

Quietly, I open the door and pad down the hallway toward the kitchen. I'm surprised when I turn the corner and see Grant standing in front of the stove, the tan muscles of his back on display as he pushes a wooden spatula around a pan. His gray sweatpants are hung low on his hips, revealing dimples along his lower back.

My heart begins to pound wildly, and I realize how much I am not prepared for this moment. Just exactly how out of my element I am.

"Good morning," I say shyly.

That was stupid. I should've said something other than good morning, like, you know… hi again, thanks for offering to marry me to save my family's bakery, almost beating up my crazy "fiancé," and letting me spend the night in your bed while you slept on your couch.

That might have covered it, but *good morning*?

For goodness' sake, Addie. Could you have thought of anything more lame to lead with?

I wince, pushing my hair behind my ear in an attempt to calm the nerves swirling in my stomach. At this rate, I'm going to have to braid my hair just so I'll stop nervously fidgeting with it.

He turns toward me, a lazy grin on his face. His eyes are still heavy-lidded from sleep, giving him what I'm convinced is the best *I woke up like this* face. "Good morning. I hope you like eggs because I cooked way too fucking many. And I also cooked, um... bacon, toast, hash browns, and... waffles?" He gestures to the kitchen table, which is covered in enough food to feed a family of seven.

My eyes widen, and I bring my hand to my mouth to cover the giggle that's about to burst past my lips.

"Yeaaaaah, *I might* have overdone it a bit, but I didn't know what you liked, and I figured you'd be starving after last night."

It's actually really... sweet of him to do that, and I reply, "Thank you. Anything is fine with me. I love all of it."

His grin widens into a smile as he nods and turns back to the stove.

I walk over to the kitchen table and pull out a chair while he finishes cooking the eggs. As much as I try not to, I can't help but stare at him as he cooks.

My cheeks are probably as red as the jar of strawberry jelly sitting in front of me, but I'm praying that he'll be too focused on eating to notice.

This is the first time I've ever slept over with a guy before. Even if we did sleep in separate rooms.

That fact is just now hitting me, and combined with the fact that he's shirtless and has more abs than I think I've ever seen in my life, I'm a bit… flustered.

"Addie?"

My gaze whips to him, and I mumble, "Sorry, did you, uh, say something?"

"I was asking if you wanted orange juice?" He laughs, the sound still raspy with sleep.

I realize then that he's holding a container of pulp-free orange juice. The bottle actually looks small compared to the size of his hand, which makes me…

"Yes. Yes, please," I say in a rush before ducking my head and hiding the fire on my cheeks.

I do this thing when I blush—my entire body turns red with it, and it's *almost* as embarrassing as the last twenty-four hours of my life have been.

Truthfully, I'm not sure why this morning I'm ten times more nervous than I was last night, but it's probably because my brain is less occupied by what happened with Dixon and instead focused on the way-too-attractive man in front of me who *literally* proposed I marry him.

That's definitely it.

Avoiding his eyes, I put a little of everything on my plate and only glance up when he pours the orange juice into my glass and sits down beside me.

His hair is sticking in a hundred different directions from sleep, and I focus my eyes there instead of the sculpted muscles on his chest.

"How'd you sleep?" Grant asks casually, spreading butter on his toast.

God, I'm literally watching Jockboy spread *butter on his toast*, and I feel like I'm living on another planet. Maybe an alternate universe.

"Uh, I slept fine," I say, clearing my throat. "How did you… sleep?"

"Well, my couch is not meant for tall people because my knees hung off all night, so I think I might need to see the chiropractor." He winces when he twists in his chair. "Good thing I know a few."

When he winks, my stomach does a somersault.

"God, I'm sorry, I should have taken the couch. I didn't even think about the fact that you're a giant."

He laughs before shoving his toast into his mouth and shakes his head vehemently. "Nah, I'm a gentleman, ArtGirl. Like I'd ever let you sleep on the couch. Plus, it was worth it. I'm really glad that we got to talk last night."

I push the eggs around my plate with my fork and whisper, "Me too. It just feels… surreal though, right? Maybe it's just me, but I can hardly believe that we're even sitting here right now. *Together.*"

I hope that didn't sound as stupid as I think it did. It sounded much better in my head.

"No, it's totally fucking surreal, Addie," he agrees, rubbing his hand over the fresh scruff on his jaw. "Honestly? I thought I'd wake up this morning and you'd be gone."

"I'm sorr—"

"Don't apologize. I just… I feel like if I fucking *blink*, you'll slip through my fingers, and I want you to be a part of my life, however that may be. In whatever way that I can have you. I just don't want to let you go again."

My pulse races at his admission, and I find myself nodding. "I… I'm not going anywhere, Grant."

I'm not sure I can even truly make that promise, but I do anyway because the emotion flickering in his gaze grabs hold of me, twisting its way around my heart and taking root.

"We should probably talk about last night. About…" He trails off.

"About your proposal."

Grant nods as he sets his fork down and leans onto his elbows on the kitchen table, holding my gaze intently while he speaks. "I meant it. Every word of what I said. I get that it probably sounds crazy, but… it can't be any crazier than you tying yourself to that guy for life. Yeah, it would be an arrangement between us, something that we could both stand to benefit from, but Addie, I would never disrespect you. I would never treat you the way that he did. I would never touch you in anger or speak to you with anything but kindness. That's not the man that I am, and I think you know that by now. Wouldn't you rather marry a *friend* than that dick?"

I let what he's saying sink in, and I realize that… he's not wrong. Marrying him isn't really any crazier than marrying someone I feel completely unsafe with and honestly afraid of. What *would* really be insane is marrying Dixon. Especially after last night.

"I know. I do, I know, but I…" I trail off and blow out a breath. "I just… Grant, do you realize that you're offering to tie your life to me? Someone *you* barely know? Someone whose life is kind of a mess. It's *marriage*, not something we can walk away from when it suddenly feels like too much because we're legally bound together. If we're going to talk about this, or even seriously consider it, I think that we both have to be aware of what the cost of agreeing to this will do to our lives."

"It's not a cost to me. I'm not *sacrificing* anything to marry you, Addie. I mean, yeah, I'd be doing this for you. Because I feel slightly fucking murderous when I think of you ever being alone with that guy again and because I care about you. I genuinely want to help you because I care about you. But I wasn't lying when I said it can help me too. My agent is trying to close this sponsorship deal for me, and the company is worried about my reputation. Even though it's mostly just bullshit... it doesn't matter because it's how things have been perceived. I have to turn that around if I want to sign this deal because it's not just going to help my career. It's going to give me momentum going into the draft. That's what I want after college, to play professionally, and marrying you can actually help me work towards that too."

Okay, that makes sense and honestly makes me feel inherently better that I'm not the only one who's going to benefit from us being married. I feel guilty even considering involving him in the mess of my life, but when he puts it that way, it feels like less of a burden. I mean, marriage *is* only a piece of paper, right?

It's also not going to fix everything. Marrying Grant won't fix the fact that the bank is threatening foreclosure. But... at least it would prevent Brent from selling it out from under me and give me time to figure out the financials.

And it gets me away from Dixon.

I'm lost in my head again when he reaches out and grasps my fingers, dragging my attention back to him.

"Tell me what you're thinking. What's going on in your head right now?"

My lips part, and I laugh half-heartedly. "Everything? I'm thinking about all the things I don't know when it comes to what this marriage would have to look like in order to legally secure the bakery. Like if we do this, what's the end date? When do we decide that our arrangement has been fulfilled? This doesn't fix all of the bakery's problems... so what if the financial issues with the bakery affect you too? And afterwards, do we get an annulment or divorce, then walk away? What if you want to... be with someone else while we're married? Would I have to move into your apartment? Do we have to have a wedding? I have so many questions, and I know it's probably all just really stupid things, but..."

Grant squeezes my hand gently in his, his pillowy lips twitching in amusement at the word vomit that I just spewed.

Truly, I was unable to stop it. Which is generally not the case with me. I'm more of a not seen nor heard kind of girl, but this is... a lot.

"It's not stupid. Those are all legit questions and pretty big ones too. And I agree, if we do this, then we lay it all out. We need to know exactly what the plan is and what it would take to get the bakery. Then we can focus on the financial stuff—one problem at a time."

Suddenly, my mind spinning sends me to an answer that I probably should've landed on prior to now. I just hadn't assumed there would be another marriage option. Until now.

"I think we should talk to a lawyer. I mean, I think the first place to start is at the source. Have him confirm what Earl over-heard about my mom's will and that I do *actually* inherit Ever After if I'm married. I only recently found out about the will, and I planned on consulting a lawyer. I just hadn't had a chance before... all of this. Maybe they could help us answer some of these questions?"

Nodding, he offers, "Yeah, I think that's a solid first step. We can ask what would legally meet the inheritance criteria as far as the marriage goes and make sure there's not anything additional that you have to do. We can start there and then figure out what comes next? One step at a time."

"Yeah, I think that's perfect," I murmur with a small, hopeful smile.

"Then let's do this, ArtGirl." He smirks playfully before grabbing his fork and digging into his uneaten breakfast like we didn't just possibly decide to get *married.*

He's nothing like I expected him to be, but I think *exactly...* what I needed.

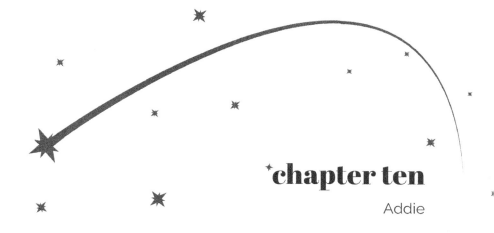

chapter ten

Addie

AS IF HE can feel my nerves from his chair beside me, Grant reaches out and squeezes my hand reassuringly, offering me a smile.

I'm not nervous to be meeting with my new attorney, but I am nervous about how this entire thing will go.

What if there was more to the conversation than what Earl overheard?

What if Ever After actually won't be mine? What if the whole idea with Grant won't work and all of this was for nothing?

What if… Dixon *is* the only option.

The thought alone sends chills shooting down my spine and anxiousness unfurling inside the pit of my stomach.

I don't think I'm prepared to hear any of those things, but I'm conditioned to expect the worst, so it wouldn't surprise me.

The door creaks open behind us, and then a man in his late fifties with midnight-black hair, a tight sports coat stretched over his protruding belly, and a kind smile appears. He rounds the desk, file in hand, and takes a seat in the chair opposite Grant and me.

"Good afternoon, Miss Arceneaux. Mr. Bergeron." He reaches

out and offers his hand for me to shake before turning to Grant and doing the same. "I'm William Morrison. Again, thank you for choosing my firm to assist with your inheritance and will matters. After our conversation on the phone this morning, I was able to pull the filed copy of your mother's will."

He glances down, opening the file folder in front of him, and pulls out one of the documents inside. "I know you were concerned with the will being valid, if I'm understanding correctly?"

I nod, swallowing roughly. "I am. I think... my stepfather has somehow obtained an altered copy. Or he is possibly, um... manipulating the truth? My mother passed away when I was a kid, so I've never seen the original."

Mr. Morrison's expression morphs in surprise. "Interesting. Well, I've got the original filing here. If there are any discrepancies from what you've seen or been told, then we can absolutely address those."

"I... I think that I'm supposed to inherit my mother's bakery, Ever After, upon turning twenty-five or when I get married. Is that information correct?"

I hold my breath until my lungs burn as I wait for his response. Grant must feel me tense because he gives another reassuring squeeze of my hand, and only then do I realize that he's been holding it the entire time, offering a sense of silent strength with just his touch.

A few painful seconds tick by as Mr. Morrison scans the document in his hand, then lifts his gaze to meet mine.

He nods at me. "That seems to be correct."

My lungs deflate, a hundred different emotions cascading through my body at once. Relief, shock... *betrayal*. While part of me wanted to hope, another part of me thought that somehow what Earl overheard wouldn't be true and all of this would have been for nothing.

That I would still be trapped in a situation that I couldn't control.

"It appears that you inherit the property, as well as the building and assets, upon turning twenty-five or upon marrying. Whichever is first. As of now, the property remains with the executor… which I'm assuming is your stepfather. Brent Arceneaux?"

"Yes. That's my stepfather. Until now, I was led to believe the bakery was left to him."

He stares pensively at me for a moment before speaking. "Do you anticipate him contesting the will during probate?"

When my brow furrows in confusion, he adds, "Probate is the legal process of actually obtaining the asset. In your case, the bakery."

"I'm not sure, honestly. I don't think so, but it's a possibility."

Mr. Morrison nods. "We'll be prepared to defend the will if need be. There are plenty of things in place for that situation."

My mind is moving in a thousand different directions, an influx of questions that I'm trying to sort through, when Grant speaks up. "Just to clarify… There are no other requirements for Addie if she gets married before twenty-five? She'll simply inherit the property then?"

"That's correct. Pending there's no contest, then the process would be fairly simple."

So…

"If he *were* to try and contest it or to make false claims, what would happen?" I ask quietly.

After all of the lies and deceit from Brent, nothing would surprise me at this point, and given how I was left in the dark about this until recently, I just need to know every scenario. Good or bad. Anything that could go wrong. It feels too… *easy.*

I marry Grant, then I get the bakery. Just like that. I don't think that Brent's just going to… roll over and take this. If he was willing to go to the extremes to manipulate and hide so much from me, he's clearly up to something not good.

"And what do you mean by false claims?" Mr. Morrison asks as he leans forward in his chair, resting his forearms on the desk in front of him.

"My stepdad is probably not going to be entirely… happy about my marriage. And I wonder if he were to cause any issues to try to prevent it, maybe say that my marriage isn't valid, what would happen?

Mr. Morrison leans back, a serious expression on his face. "Ah. Well, just speaking hypothetically, your marriage would have to be legitimate and valid to satisfy the inheritance clause stated in the will. If it were proven to be… duplicitous, then he would have grounds to contest the will on the basis of fraud… but as long as the marriage is real, there shouldn't be an issue."

Turning, I drag my attention to Grant, who's nodding, before shifting it back to Mr. Morrison.

"Okay, I understand. All of this has been very helpful. Especially confirming what the will actually says. Once we're married, I just need to provide you with… what?"

"Your marriage license," he begins, pausing to scan the document once more, then looking over at us. "After your license is obtained and signed, we can begin filing a probate and moving the property over to you. I'll try and make that process as easy as I can."

My head is spinning, and my heart is thrashing in my chest as all of this truly begins to sink in.

Ever After will be mine if I marry Grant. Brent will no longer be able to manipulate and control me. All we have to do is believably get married, and he can't sell it because it'll be *mine*. Well… if the bank doesn't take it first.

That's an entirely different problem to tackle.

"Uh, Mr. Morrison, one more question." I pause as he nods. "Do you have access to any of the financials? Do you know how far behind the mortgage is? I just want to figure out a plan of action for when it does transfer to me, given all the monetary challenges facing the bakery."

Reaching back into the file, he begins searching through the documents inside and finally stops, then picks a paper up and scans it.

"I requested the most up-to-date bank records in preparation for a potential probate process. It appears that Ever After is in good financial standing. There's nothing showing that the mortgage payments are behind or in the red. During probate, the business will go through a more thorough investigation period, but generally, there is nothing to indicate any financial distress."

What?

My jaw falls open in shock. Grant's hand tightens, and when I glance over at him, I can see the fury written on every inch of his expression. His jaw works as he shakes his head.

He's angry *for* me. Brent hasn't just lied about the will; he's lied about *everything*. How could I have not seen this coming?

The minute I learned I'd been misled about the will, I should have questioned *everything*. Of course, the financials were what was forcing my hand into his marriage scheme.

Somehow, I find the words even as emotion tightens in my throat, making it hard to talk. "Thank you, Mr. Morrison. I th-think… that's all I have for now."

My voice cracks when I speak, but even as angry as I am at being lied to for so long, an even bigger part of me feels nothing

95

but relief flooding my chest. This eliminates one huge barrier… once I get the bakery, I'm in the clear.

We say goodbye, and Grant leads me out to his vehicle, my hand still clasped tightly in his until he opens the passenger door and helps me inside.

I have so many things I want to say as he slides into the driver's seat, then pulls out onto the highway in the direction of his apartment. But… I'm still trying to process everything, to wrap my head fully around what I've learned, so instead, I gaze out the window at the vibrant city, sitting in silence with my thoughts.

Attempting to untangle the web of deceit that Brent has woven.

The ride is short and silent as Grant seems to perceive my need for quiet. By the time we get to his apartment and walk through the front door, I'm oddly… *calm.*

I walk over to the couch and sink down onto the cushions, thankful for the space he gave me to deal with everything in my head.

"Are you okay, Addie?" Grant asks as he sits on the coffee table in front of me, his eyes shining with concern.

"Surprisingly?" I start. "Yes." A laugh tumbles past my lips, and I realize it probably sounds a tad wild, but… I'm so relieved. "I expected to hear the worst. That… Ever After belongs to Brent, and there was no way it would ever be mine. Am I really angry that he's manipulated me for so long? Of course… but I honestly kind of feel relieved? The truth is even better than I expected. I don't have to consider marrying Dixon for money to save the bakery 'cause the money isn't actually a problem."

Grant nods. "You don't." He tugs at the collar of his button-up and begins to undo the buttons one by one until the taut, contoured muscles of his chest are on display. "Sorry, this shirt feels like it's fucking choking me."

"No, it's o-okay," I stutter nervously.

God, I have to get it together. It's just a chest.

And he's... *just* Grant.

"So, what do we do from here?" he asks as he flicks open the last button of his shirt. I purposefully avoid glancing down at his abs because I need my brain to work right now, and it absolutely misfires when he's involved.

For a second, I'm quiet again, chewing my lip in thought and looking anywhere but at him. Finally, I shift my eyes back to his, holding his gaze as I say, "I think... we get married?"

His eyes widen in surprise. "Yeah? You want to do this?"

Nodding, I reach up and tuck a loose strand of hair behind my ear. "I think it's the best plan. We get married and convince everyone that it's real. I get the bakery, and you sign your deal. And once the paperwork has been signed and the probate is complete... we can get it annulled."

Suddenly, this all has begun to feel more real.

I'm going to *marry* Grant. I'm going to own Ever After. I'm going to finally be free of Brent's hold.

It feels too good to be true.

"Okay. So that answers that. I'm in. But what about everything else? Are you going to move here? I mean... I can't imagine you want to continue to live with Brent, right? And our marriage needs to appear legit until it's done, right?"

Immediately, I shake my head. "No. Absolutely not. He's going to be angry, and so will Dixon. I can't stay there. I can move here with you if that's okay with you, but... there's one thing."

He looks confused, so I quickly add, "Auggie. My corgi."

Realization flickers in his eyes as his lips tug into a grin. "The

Maren Moore

two of you are a package, Addie. I wouldn't expect you to leave him with that asshole. Plus, I love animals."

"Okay. Good." Another question lingers in my mind, and I spit it out before I lose the courage. "Also… what if you want to be with someone else? While we're… married. I know it's not traditional, and, um… guys have needs."

That was mortifying.

Jeez, Addie. You're going to *marry* this guy—you have to be able to at least discuss things like this.

Grant laughs, the sound settling around the nervous flutter in my stomach as amusement dances over his features.

"That's not going to be an issue. Even if this isn't real, I'm a one-woman kind of guy, and… I have ways of taking care of my own needs."

Suddenly, it's hot in here. My palms begin to perspire as a furious blush works its way from my cheeks down my body.

Grant… Taking… Ca—

Clearing my throat, I nod and duck my head to avoid his gaze. A second later, I feel his finger tip my chin up, dragging my gaze back to his as he studies me with a serious expression.

"There's not going to be anyone else, Addie. Period. I'm committed to this, and I promise you that."

Exhaling shakily, I nod as his gaze remains holding mine. "Okay. And, um, not that you'd need to worry about this, but… me too. No one else… So, I guess, then… it's official. We're getting married."

"Guess that means I should *officially* propose, then?" he asks with a cheeky smirk.

My eyes widen, almost comically so.

What does he mean… officially?

Before I can even ask, he stands abruptly from the coffee table and disappears into the kitchen, returning with a napkin in his hand. He tears a piece of it off and fashions what looks to be a... ring.

Dropping to one knee, he reaches for my hand with the newly fashioned paper ring and peers up at me. "Will you fake marry me, ArtGirl? And make me the happiest *Jock* in all the land?"

It's absolutely cheesy and completely ridiculous, but even so, a flurry of butterflies takes flight in my stomach as I nod.

Because I know at this moment, Grant Bergeron is the only boy I'd ever trust enough to fake marry.

He grins harder, sliding the too-big paper ring onto my finger and swiping the pad of his thumb along the top of my knuckles softly.

"It's not much, but it's all I've got right now," he says with a wink.

I shake my head. "No. It's perfect. It's more than enough."

"When should we do it?" he says, still down on one knee with my hand clasped in his. "The sooner, the better, right? How about... right now?"

"*Right now*?"

He shrugs, the dimple in his cheek popping as he chuckles. "Why not? There's a twenty-four-hour wedding chapel down in the French Quarter. A buddy of mine got drunk married a few months ago, and the place was legit. We could go there. They do same-day licenses like Vegas does. We've got the details figured out, so now we just... do it."

Holy cannoli.

I'm about to get *married*. The thought is both terrifying and exciting all at the same time. Even if technically the marriage isn't real.

"But... I don't even have a dress," I say. "Or any of my stuff, for that matter."

Grant pushes to his feet and drops my hand as he stands. "Okay, pivoting. How about we stop somewhere in the Quarter and you pick out a dress?"

I chew my lip as I mull over the thought. One of my favorite thrift stores is in the Quarter, and I probably could find something that would be worthy enough to get fake married in. "Okay."

"Fuck. I just thought about something," he mutters, tugging at the short strands of his hair.

"What?"

"We gotta have witnesses for the license. I'm pretty sure that's how this goes? I can... probably call Davis and see if he'll do it, pending he's not hungover and still in bed. Do you have anyone who can be a witness for you?"

There are only two people who I would ever consider asking to witness a marriage, and I'm pretty sure if I didn't ask both of them to be there, they'd disown me.

"Uh... Do you think I could maybe have two?" I ask, wrinkling my nose. "I don't think I can do this without them."

"Whoever you want to be there is perfectly fine with me. How about I go take a quick shower, call Davis, and throw on something to wear? Shit, what do I wear to my own wedding?" he asks, a sudden look of panic on his face.

I glance down at his very naked chest and squeak, "Clothes. *Definitely* clothes."

The French Quarter is one of the most magical places in the *world*. Not that I've seen much of the world outside of New

Orleans, but it's something I just *know* in my soul. There is no other place like it.

It's a menagerie of charming cobblestone streets and wrought iron balconies that are adorned with flowers, beads, and century-old traditions. It's the heart of the city, full of rich culture that screams to be heard. And no one screams louder than the French Quarter.

While a twenty-four-hour wedding chapel was never a place I imagined myself getting married, I'm glad that it's here in the Quarter, in a place that will always feel like home to me.

And I realize that I probably shouldn't be nervous because our marriage is simply nothing more than an arrangement, but I can't help the swirl of butterflies in my stomach as we stand inside the small chapel.

It's quaint and undeniably charming. The inside resembles an old church, with vintage wooden pews that have small floral arrangements fashioned along the ends that face the aisle. Arched, stained glass windows line the walls, each pane a prism of light that paints the pews, walls, and small podium in the front in a kaleidoscope of vibrant colors.

I would imagine that there are *far* worse places to be married.

"Are you… sure this is what you want to do, cher? Absolutely sure?" Amos lowers his voice, whispering quietly.

Without hesitation, I nod. "Yes. I promise, I'm okay with this. This is what I want to do," I tell him as I reach out and lace my fingers in his, squeezing gently. "Thank you for being here. Both of you. I couldn't imagine doing this without you."

I look between Amos and Earl, and an overwhelming sense of peace hits me directly in the chest because I truly don't know where I would be without them. They're the only family I've ever known after I lost my mom. The only ones who have loved me unconditionally, through every season of my life.

"We just want you to be happy. Whatever that means, Addie," Earl retorts gruffly. This big, burly man who's never been one for emotion suddenly has unshed tears in his eyes, mirroring the fresh ones shining in mine.

"You know we'll always be here to stand by your side, cher. *Always*. To support any decision you make," Amos says.

He steps forward and wraps his arms around me, pulling me toward him in a fierce hug.

When I pull back, I suck in a shaky breath and smile. "This is just an arrangement between Grant and I, but I'm okay, and I'm ready to do this. I'll be able to save Ever After, and honestly? He's my friend. One of the only people outside of you that I trust. He's a really good guy."

I can still see the look of concern on their faces and the hesitation in their eyes, but I'm making the right decision. I can feel it in my gut.

Grant's the right choice.

I'm getting married today, and it *doesn't* at all feel like the death sentence it would have been had this happened differently. I'm not afraid, or disgusted, or despondent at the prospect of marrying Grant. Not the way I was when I thought I would be in this exact scenario with Dixon.

"Cher, you look like the most beautiful thing I've ever seen," Amos says, reaching out and brushing his fingers along my sleeves. He's wearing his best suit, with the most gorgeous array of colorful jewelry, and as always, I love his style.

I thought of him when I picked out this dress.

The vintage, cream-colored A-line dress I found in the thrift store is simple yet timelessly elegant. I knew it was the one the moment that I laid eyes on it. It's not a wedding dress, but it's perfect for... this. It has a square neckline with puff sleeves and falls below my knees in a soft linen material.

It's me, and it's perfect.

"Your husband-to-be is *very* handsome, you know. I'm not sure if you've stopped to notice that fact yet," Amos muses, his eyes twinkling with amusement. "Just sayin'."

My brow arches as I peer past him at Grant, who's standing in the front of the chapel, talking with the officiant and his friend Davis.

I'm very much aware of his handsome face, and it's concerning. For more reasons than I am ready to dive into moments before I'm supposed to marry him.

He's wearing a pair of black slacks, with a starched white button-down that he's rolled at the sleeves, showing off veiny, corded forearms that would make nearly any woman drool.

Which is why I am not, in fact, checking him out from across the chapel.

"Nope, I hadn't noticed at all, actually," I say, dragging my gaze back to the both of them and shaking my head.

I don't make it a habit of lying, but they don't need to know it's the only thing I've been able to think about since he walked out of his bedroom, wearing a smile that made my heart beat twice as fast.

Nope. No one needs to know that, which is why I'm keeping it to myself.

"You ready, Addie?" Grant calls from the front of the chapel, and I nod, offering him a small smile.

I'm ready to become… *Mrs. Grant Bergeron.*

chapter eleven

Grant

TRUTHFULLY, I never gave a lot of thought about what my wedding would one day look like. But I can guarantee my wildest imagination wouldn't dream up a twenty-four-hour chapel in the middle of the French Quarter with a girl I didn't think I'd ever meet in person.

Or that my marriage would be a fake one, at least not on paper.

But here I am, standing in front of an officiant with absolutely not one fucking regret.

Except that my ma might kill me, but we'll deal with that later because right now, all I can focus on is the breathtaking girl standing in front of me and the fact that she's about to become my wife.

Holy fucking shit.

My wife.

She's magnificent, an actual fucking vision in a dress that could only be described as made for her. Her long, blonde curls cascade down her shoulders, framing her heart-shaped face like a halo. The white fabric clings to her curves, making it hard for me to pick where to look. But when I drift up to the delicate freckles on her face and our eyes catch, my throat tightens.

"Do you, Addie Olivia Arceneaux, take Grant Alexander Bergeron to be your lawfully wedded husband? From this day forward, for better, for worse, for richer, for poorer, in sickness and in health, to love and to cherish, until death do you part."

I can feel the tremble in her hands, and I squeeze gently, reassuring her with touch. Arranged or not, marrying someone is a huge fucking deal, and I know exactly the thoughts that are running through her head because they're probably the same as mine.

A soft smile plays on her lips as she nods shyly. "I do."

The officiant turns to me before reading from the script in his book. "And do you, Grant Alexander Bergeron, take Addie Olivia Arceneaux to be your lawfully wedded wife? From this day forward, for better, for worse, for richer, for poorer, in sickness and in health, to love and to cherish, until death do you part."

"I do," I say without hesitation.

We're in this, for better or worse, for fake or for serious. There's no backing out now.

I shoot her a wink, and she giggles softly before rolling her lips together, stifling the sound.

Our officiant nods, glancing back down at his script, then asking, "Do you have rings?"

"We do," I say, dropping Addie's hand only to turn to Davis and grab the rings I picked up while she was shopping for a dress.

There wasn't much of a selection at the store she was shopping at, and I'm pretty sure it might turn our fingers green because they're only costume jewelry, but my options were limited with the time given.

I hand her the thin golden band I grabbed for me and wait for him to proceed.

"Whenever you look at these rings, may they remind you of this moment and the love you have promised to one another. Grant, please place the ring on Addie's finger and repeat after me."

I never take my gaze off her as I place the star-shaped ring at the tip of her finger. Her eyes are slightly wide as she glances up, her breath hitching.

It may have only cost ten bucks and be slightly bent, but I took it as a sign from the universe.

"With this ring, I thee wed."

I repeat the line, sliding the ring up her finger slowly, and then she does the same. The band is a tight fit for me, but since we decided to get married in less than three hours, it works just fine.

"By the authority vested in me by the State of Louisiana, I now pronounce you husband and wife. Grant, you may kiss your bride."

Unhurriedly, I lift my hand and reach for her, sliding my palm along her jaw before cradling it in my palm. The rough pad of my thumb sweeps along her smooth skin in a motion that shouldn't feel so intimate, yet somehow, it *does*.

When I lean in and pull her toward me, there's only the briefest moment of what looks like nervousness flickering in her gaze before her eyes flutter closed, and her lips part as she sucks in a sharp intake of breath. The moment that my lips press gently against hers, her fingers tighten in mine. The kiss is chaste and too fucking quick, but every nerve ending in my body comes alive at the feel of her soft, sweet lips.

I shouldn't, but I want to do it again, and again and again. I want to know the way she tastes more than I want to fucking *breathe*.

She pulls back slightly, her eyes still shut and her dark lashes fanned out along her cheeks as she breathes shakily. Still so close, I can feel her warm breath against my lips.

Maybe I'll regret it later, maybe I won't, but when she finally opens her eyes and stares back at me with those deep, dark azure eyes filled with trust, I decide to give a shit about the consequences later.

My arm slides around her waist, pulling her flush against me, closing the distance between us.

I kiss her the way I *should've* the first time.

The way I should *always* kiss my fucking wife.

Gone is the soft, tentative brush of our lips and the hesitation of experiencing a kiss together for the first time.

My lips move against hers, deepening with every second that ticks past until I feel her hands fisting in the front of my shirt. As if she's pulling me closer and holding on all at once.

It's the kind of kiss that should be written about in books. Played in movies. Plastered on billboards. The kind of kiss that would be used as a measure of time.

The time before kissing Addie, and the time after.

When a throat clears beside us, I pull back, slightly breathless, staring down at Addie in my arms with the same expression mirrored in her own eyes.

We're standing in front of a handful of people, but it felt like it was just the two of us, lost in a moment that only belongs to us.

"Congratulations!" the officiant says cheerily, glancing between the two of us. "I wish you a lifetime of happiness."

Addie offers him a small smile and turns her gaze back to

me. I realize I'm still holding her, so I drop my hands and step back.

Just like that... we're *married*, and for the first time since meeting her, I realize how much trouble I might actually be in. Because I liked kissing her far too much for an arrangement that is supposed to be fake.

We sign the marriage license shortly after, then say goodbye to Addie's family and Davis before heading out of the chapel to the parking lot.

I feel like I should apologize for that kiss, but shit, I'm not fucking sorry. I don't regret it for a second; I just don't want *her* to.

She's agonizingly quiet as she slips into the passenger seat of my truck, and I shut the door behind her. When I climb into the driver's seat, I turn toward her.

"I think I shoul—"

"Should we—"

Apparently, we're both still thinking about said kiss because our awkward words run together as we speak at the same exact time.

Her cheeks heat, and she ducks her head, tucking a stray piece of hair behind her ear. "Sorry, you go first."

I hate that she's too shy to look me in the eye, so I reach over the console between us and grasp her chin gently between my fingers, turning her to me.

Her gaze snaps to mine, and I watch her throat working as she swallows visibly.

"I should apologize for kissing you," I start, my voice low. "But I'm not sorry, Addie. I'm just sorry that I didn't run it by you first."

The dark blue of her pupils dilates, darkening, and she

shakes her head. "It's okay. This is what married couples do. They... kiss."

I nod. "Yeah, they do. They kiss. A lot."

She's my wife now. And I want to kiss her again.

A lot. Until she's breathless and clutching onto me the way she did in that chapel.

Her nod mirrors mine as the air between us crackles and hums with an electrified charge. A brief moment that feels as if we can reach out and grasp it between our fingers as our eyes stay locked. I try to decipher the flickering of something in them. Time ticks by, but it seems to stand still all at once.

A shrill ring reverberates through the cab of my truck, and then the spell is broken. Addie jumps, fumbling for her cell phone.

When she finally picks it up with a shaky hand, she answers and puts it to her ear.

"H-i-i, Amos."

I bite back a grin, bringing my hand to rub along my jaw to cover the twitch of my lips. She's just as affected by this as I am. I shouldn't like that as much as I do.

She doesn't say much on the phone but nods along with whatever Amos is saying. Then, she says, "Sounds good. Thanks."

Once she hangs up, she lifts her gaze to me. "Um... Amos says he's going to drop Auggie off later. They're apparently going for a walk and a pup cup. Like he needs more whipped cream. I'm going to have to get him a doggie treadmill soon or something."

Chuckling, I shrug. "I could take him with me on my morning runs, if you're cool with it? It can be a guys-only thing."

Addie's laugh singsongs through the truck, and she nods,

rolling her plump lips together. "He would probably hate it, but I think he could absolutely benefit from exercise."

"Cool. We'll make it a thing, then. Do you wanna go pick up your stuff? Not that I mind you wearing my clothes or anything, but you probably need supplies for class?"

"Yes. And I need to get Auggie's things. I don't have much, so it probably won't take me long to throw the important things in a bag."

"There's no rush. You can put me to work." I wink, relishing the shy smile she offers.

After she buckles in, I turn my truck on and put the address she gives me into the GPS before pulling out onto the highway.

It's only a few minutes from the Quarter, so it doesn't take us long to pull into a short driveway right off the road.

"This it?" I ask her as I pull to a stop at the end of the driveway.

"Yep. I... live over the garage though," she says as we pull up in front of a two-story Victorian with peeling shutters and massive white pillars. There's a small oval-shaped window above the garage, and that's where she points. Then, she turns to the building next door and points at the quaint little building beside the house. "And that's the bakery."

I park in front of the garage, and we walk to the side. She pushes the side door to the garage open after unlocking it, and I follow closely behind her into the stairwell.

"It's kind of a mess, but..." She trails off once we make it to the top of the stairs and into the open studio floor plan that's her room. She's not wrong—the walls are painted with what I think used to be a bright yellow paint but is now dull, and peeling, and the beam that's hanging in the center of the room looks unstable at best, but... it's apparent she's spent a lot of time making the space hers.

Her art is everywhere—on the walls, on the massive easel near the window, in frames along the shelves, and I can't stop the smile that tugs at my lips.

"That's beautiful," I say simply, eying the half-finished canvas that sits on the easel before looking back at her.

That delicious pink flush is back, and now it's traveled down to her neck at my compliment.

"Thank you," she whispers, holding my gaze for a beat longer before turning and walking toward her makeshift closet.

Seeing everything she's done to her room, making it an extension of herself, makes me wonder what she'll do to make my apartment hers too.

Even though our arrangement is temporary… we didn't set a time limit, but it will at least be as long as it takes to get through probate. In the meantime, I want her to feel comfortable there too. It's just as much hers as it is mine now.

"You should paint something to hang above the couch," I say as I sit at the edge of her bed, watching her packing things into a suitcase.

"You want me to paint something for your apartment?" I can hear the disbelief in her voice, like me asking her that is so hard to believe.

"*Our* apartment," I say playfully.

She looks up, laughing softly, "Okay, *our* apartment," before going back to her packing. She's moved on from clothes to smaller belongings, shoving them into the zipper pockets. Pencils, notebooks… underwear.

I try not to think about what they look like on her and drag my gaze to the canvases on her wall.

"Fuck yeah, I want you to paint something. Whatever you want."

There's a stretch of silence, and then she says, "Okay. Maybe."

And that's better than no.

True to what she said in the truck earlier, she doesn't have much. Most of what she's packed fits into one large suitcase, her backpack, and an oversized duffle bag.

I know there's probably no love lost moving out of here, but I still give her a moment alone in her space and carry everything down to my truck. It fits easily into the bed.

I turn toward the staircase just as Addie appears, no longer in the dress she wore to our wedding but in a pair of jeans with a cropped top covered in daisies. Of course, she's in her Mary Janes. She looks cute as fuck.

"Hi," she whispers, staring up at me.

"Ooooh. She's back with the Mary Janes," I tease with a wink.

Suddenly, I hear the front door violently slam shut, and when I look over, I see a man barreling toward us. His posture is tight and his expression furious, which has me stepping in front of Addie, pushing her behind me protectively.

It dawns on me that this must be her asshole stepfather.

He's tall, but not quite as tall as me, with salt-and-peppered, graying hair that matches his beard. I know from the second I lay eyes on him that he's every bit of the piece of shit that I figured he would be.

Addie's body goes taut behind me, and she reaches out to grasp onto the back of my forearm. Her nails dig into my skin, and I realize that she's fucking scared.

She's *scared* of him, and it makes me see red. The fact that she's cowering away from him makes me want to protect her from him.

"Where the hell have you been?" he spits when he makes it

to us, his seedy gaze moving between me and Addie, who's standing still slightly behind me.

I hope he knows that he's not going to disrespect her with me here, and if he doesn't... well, he's going to learn really fucking quick.

"I... I just needed to grab my things, Brent. I'm moving out," she whispers timidly. So quietly that I wonder if he's missed it until I see the muscle in his jaw tick as he grinds his teeth together.

He steps toward her, and I move directly in front of him, blocking him from getting any closer. "That's far enough. You can talk to her from here."

"Yeah?" He laughs humorlessly before dragging his attention to Addie and then back to me. "And who the fuck are you?"

"Her *husband*," I retort with finality.

He freezes for a moment before it registers, taken completely off guard by that revelation. But his anger is palpable as he directs his scorned gaze back to Addie.

"Bullshit. You're marrying Dixon Barrilleaux in less than two weeks, and you know that."

Addie stands straighter, lifting her chin slightly as she takes a long, deep breath and says, "No. I'm not." When she pauses, she reaches for me, sliding her trembling hand in mine as if she needs the strength. I squeeze her hand reassuringly, and she continues. "I've been seeing Grant... in secret, for months now. W-We got married, and there's nothing you can do about it, Brent. And I also know you lied, about everything. About the reasons you were forcing me into this marriage with Dixon, my mother's will. All of it. I've already spoken to a lawyer, and I know the bakery is mine."

Pride swells in my chest at how strong she sounds, even though I know she probably doesn't feel it right now. I'm so fucking proud of her for standing up to him. For letting this asshole know he's not going to control her for a second longer.

Brent's entire face turns a crimson shade of red, and I'm waiting for him to fly off the handle when he truly lets what he's heard sink in.

"You're a stupid, spoiled little bitch, and over my dead body will you take that bakery from me." Spittle flies from his mouth as he spews, the vein on his forehead bulging with each word.

That's when the small semblance of control I have frays, turning the edges of my vision hazy with rage.

I step forward, our chests meeting as I shake my head and seethe. "Don't fucking talk to my wife like that."

"Your wife?" His laugh is quiet and menacing as he shakes his head over and over. "I hope you understand how badly you've fucked up, Addie. Secretly dating, my ass. You think I don't know that this is a ruse? A way for you to cheat me out of what I'm owed and attempt to cheat the will. This is a sham. And I'll fucking prove it before I ever let you have what's rightfully mine."

"The bakery has *never* been yours, Brent," she whispers fiercely. "It was always my mother's."

"And who the fuck do you think has been taking care of it since she died, leaving me with the mess, huh? Who took care of you when *you* had no one? I did. This is the payment I fucking deserve. Payment that I fucking earned for dealing with this shit for years."

Fucking prick. Fuck this, and fuck him.

"Addie, get in the truck. You're not listening to this bullshit," I tell her, keeping my gaze fixed on him in case he does something stupid and reacts.

She hesitates for only a split second, then walks to the truck and flings the door open but halts when he calls her name.

"You think you're so smart. You've got it all figured out, huh? Except you didn't account for the fact that I'm not walking away, and I'm going to prove that this marriage is bullshit and contest the will. I'll have eyes everywhere, Addie. It won't be hard to catch you in your lies. You're not getting away with this. I'm warning you not to fuck with me."

When his threat comes, I'm beyond fucking done with this asshole. Addie shouldn't have to be subjected to this shit.

The hypocrisy of this man. He's the one who's been lying and manipulating her for who knows how long. Trying to force her into an equally fake marriage but for *his* benefit. She's endured enough at his hands.

"Fuck you," I spit. "I'm warning *you*. Stay the fuck away from *my wife*."

chapter twelve

Grant

"THIS IS A DISASTER. A LITERAL DISASTER" are the first words out of Addie's mouth the moment we walk through the front door of the apartment.

I watch as she paces the living room, chewing nervously on her nails, stopping every minute or so to suck in a shaky, uneven breath and run her fingers through her already mussed hair.

Part of me wants to go to her and attempt to calm her down, but the other part thinks that I should give her a second to work through whatever's going through her head. If I didn't already know that her stepdad is a piece of shit, I sure as fuck know now.

He fucked her over in every way that he could, and the hateful shit he just spewed was unacceptable. It's clear from the conversation tonight that Addie's best interest was never a concern to him; all he wanted was to be sure that he secured his future by manipulating and using her.

I'm still shaking with rage. My need to comfort her soon wins out. Closing the distance between us, I reach for her, halting the hole she's currently pacing into the hardwood. Gently, my fingers circle her small wrist to still her, and she gazes up at me.

There's hurt and outrage in her eyes. It's written all over her face, and it makes me want to punch that fucker right in his smug, entitled face.

"Hey," I whisper, lifting my fingers to her chin and grasping it between them. "Fuck him, Addie. He'll *never* speak to you again if I have anything to do with it. He's a narcissistic asshole who's trying to scare you into submission. And we're not going to let him."

I'm not going to stand back and allow that to happen. I'm not going to let her do this alone. I'm going to support her every step of the way while we figure it out because I know how much Ever After means to her and how important it is for her mom's legacy to live on.

Maybe our marriage isn't real, but how much I care about her *is*, and I meant what I said when I told her we were in this together.

For better or worse.

"This is such a mess," she whispers defeatedly. "I'm so sorry for dragging you into this. This is exactly what I was worried about, the mess of my life bleeding out onto you."

"Don't apologize. I'm the one who's sorry that you had to deal with that. I should've just broken his nose," I mutter.

"You can't do that. You could break your hand, and those hands are going to be worth lots of money one day."

The corner of my lip tugs into a grin, and I nod. "That's true, but I'm pretty sure it would've been worth it."

"I… I just—god, he's such a jerk," she blurts out angrily. "I'm just so mad and so hurt that he's done all of this… simply for money? So he can sell the bakery and make a buck off of everything my mom worked for? Grant, he manipulated and exploited me my entire life. I'm not sure anything he's *ever* said to me was the truth. I've spent years suffering by his hand of calculated cruelty. I've had to deal with his lazy, entitled son while I carried the weight of everything around me, and they never cared. They never cared about me; they never loved me like a parent should. I did all of this for my mom because I can't imagine a world where I don't have a piece of her with me. I... Thi—I'm more angry than I've ever been in my entire life."

Her words fly out in a rush of frustration, and I just nod, giving her the space to unload and get it off her chest. This is the closest I've ever seen Addie to pissed, and I'm not going to lie, I'm happy as fuck she's letting all of it out.

I can't imagine what she's really feeling right now, and I want her to direct that anger toward the asshole who deserves it.

"He can't do this. I... I *won't* let him do this."

"No you won't, ArtGirl," I respond.

"I *won't*."

I love the conviction in her tone. I'm proud as fuck hearing it and seeing her lift her chin higher, squaring her shoulders as if the more she says it, the harder she feels it, the more she'll convince herself.

My lip twitches. "Nope."

"I know I keep saying it, but I'm *so* sorry, Grant. About all of this. This isn't what you... agreed to. And now we're married, and all of this drama with Brent, it makes it all even worse." She pauses before pulling her lip between her teeth anxiously. "The only way to secure the bakery is to prove that our marriage is legitimate, or this will have all been for nothing. He's going to do whatever he can to try and disprove our marriage. He *threatened* us, Grant."

I nod. "I know. Take a breath for me. It's going to be okay. I'm here."

She follows my directions and inhales shakily while nodding and continuing the motion, in and out.

"I can't believe… that I'm even going to ask you to do this for me after you've already done so much. Would you be willing to pretend that we're really married? Because that's the only solution, right? To convince everyone, publicly, that our marriage is legitimate and give Brent no ammunition or cause to contest the will? I know that's not what you signed up for, and I'm so sorry."

My shoulder dips slightly. "Okay, so we're going to have to show everyone that it's real. So what? We can handle that. We just need a plan."

Addie doesn't look any less worried, her blue eyes flicking back and forth between my eyes nervously, so I keep going, trying to reassure her that it's going to be okay. I mean, fuck, we just got *married*—if the only thing we have to do is pretend that it's real in public in order to prevent Brent from taking the bakery, then we do it.

"He's not ever going to prove that our marriage isn't real, ArtGirl. Because we're going to show him that it is. If he's looking for a way to prevent you from getting your inheritance, then we're going to have to convince *everyone* that this is legit for it to work. We don't give him a single opportunity to disprove anything. What better way to convince everyone than to be the sappiest, head over heels, crazy about each other couple they've ever seen?"

I can't imagine I'm going to have to try very hard to act like Addie's my wife. To pretend that we're a real couple.

When she nods hesitantly, I step closer and lift my hand to cradle her jaw, leaning in until my lips are a centimeter from hers. So close I can feel the warm fan of her breath as it hitches, ghosting along my mouth. Her eyes widen, and my lip tilts in a smirk.

"But… I think in order to do that, we're going to have to

practice being a couple in private first so you're comfortable in public. There can be no room for doubt, so we practice until you're comfortable with PDA. With me touching you. Holding your hand, putting my arm around your shoulders when we're around other people." My fingers trace her jaw lightly as I continue. "Your cheeks turn this fucking adorable shade of pink when I give you a compliment. And as cute as it is, it's clear you're nervous anytime I touch you. The only way we're going to pull this off is if we practice until we seem natural as a real couple."

Her throat works as she swallows and peers up at me with those wide, endless blue eyes that flicker with curiosity. "Are you... Are you going to be okay with that? Doing that in public? With me?"

I chuckle when she scrunches her nose and pulls back slightly. "Yeah, it's not a problem for me. Are *you* going to be okay with this?"

"Um... yes? I mean, I think that I probably won't be very good at it," she murmurs timidly as she drops her gaze to the floor and fingers the ends of her hair. "It's not like I have very much, um, to go on."

My brow pinches. "Holding hands? Kissing?"

I've picked up on the fact that she's nervous around me and really shy, but this is not a conversation we've had. Her experience with things.

"Today was my... first kiss."

Holy fuck. My heart drops to my ass, and my throat runs dry.

I was her first kiss?

I shouldn't like that so fucking much, but I do.

"Ever?"

"Ever," she whispers before swallowing roughly. "I mean,

unless you count in the second grade when Grady Owens kissed me against the monkey bars, but I am not sure that it does. Count, I mean."

A laugh slips from the back of my throat, and I shake my head. "No, I don't think it does, ArtGirl. So, we... start at the basics? Work our way up until you're the one initiating the PDA."

Her expression sobers, and she blows out a shaky breath. "Could you... teach me? What to do? So we can convince everyone?"

A heavy pause passes between us, and I lick my lips. I'm finding it hard to even process thoughts right now, knowing I'm the only one who's ever kissed... my wife. And that now the dynamic is changing, and I don't hate the way it's going.

"Well, married people kiss. A lot," I say gruffly, suddenly aware of how close her lips are to mine and how fucking much I wish I could taste them again. Her warm breath cascades along my lips, something I know I could find myself becoming addicted to if I'm not careful.

"So, we should... practice that?"

Smirking, I nod, my gaze lingering on hers. "Definitely. We should probably practice *a lot.* You know, just to make sure we get it right. So much practicing. Actually, all the practicing."

The rational part of me says how bad of an idea this is, barreling past lines that will too easily become blurred, but I'm not paying attention.

I'm too caught up in Addie. Later, I'll deal with my rational side, but for now, I'm going to be delusional and pretend that we're not getting ourselves into something we might not be able to come back from.

"That's the plan. We aren't letting this fucker win. We'll be the most convincing couple anyone's ever seen. They'll be sick of us by the time we're done showing them how real we are." My fingers gently trace her jaw, and I smirk. "Let's do this, *wifey*."

chapter thirteen

Addie

AFTER SPENDING the majority of my life on a bakery schedule, 3:00 a.m. wake-up calls usually aren't so bad. You kind of just get used to waking up when it's still dark outside when you've done it for so long.

Except this morning, I've already snoozed my alarm three times because I can't seem to drag myself out of Grant's ridiculously comfortable bed. Seriously, it feels like I'm enveloped in the warmest, fluffiest cloud imaginable, and the last thing I want to do is leave it. Not only is it the most comfortable bed I've ever slept in, but the sheets smell just like my new husband, and the scent is intoxicatingly *maddening*.

When my alarm goes off for the fourth time, and I glance over at my phone, seeing the time is now three thirty, making me late… I groan quietly before tossing the covers off.

I can count on one hand how many times I haven't shown up to work at Ever After since I started working there when I was barely a teenager. And most of those were days that I was so sick that I could hardly get out of bed.

So, missing a morning because I'm too *tired*, even after all the drama of yesterday, isn't happening. It's my responsibility, and that means I have to show up, even when it's hard. I got married yesterday, and I'm still going to work.

Since it's technically still the middle of the night, I quietly tiptoe around the bedroom, shedding off my T-shirt and sleep shorts, careful not to be too loud. The couch is right down the hallway, and I don't want to wake Grant up this early.

Which is a lot easier said than done because it's pitch-black in here, and I have no clue where half of my stuff is. After searching mostly blindly for a few minutes, I find the bag I shoved my uniform in and get it on before heading to the bathroom to brush my teeth and put my hair up.

Once I'm finished, I turn the light off and wrench the bathroom door open, running smack into a warm, hard chest that groans groggily at the collision.

"Shit, Addie?" Grant's raspy, sleep-filled voice fills my ears, and I realize that my hands are splayed on his hard, sculpted chest. Not that I can see a single thing because it's so freakin' dark.

"Yes. Sorry," I squeak, immediately dropping my hands and stumbling backward, inadvertently bumping my hip painfully into the door handle in the process. "Ouch."

Seconds later, the hall light flicks on, and Grant peers down at me, his hair mussed from sleep with only one eye cracked open.

Suddenly, it's harder to breathe, not just because of the pain radiating up my hip from the stupid doorknob but because he's standing in front of me wearing nothing but a tight pair of black boxer briefs that leave absolutely *nothing* to the imagination.

My mouth runs dry. I'm actually in danger of swallowing my tongue.

His briefs hang dangerously low, revealing the two sharp

dips of his hips and a dark trail of hair that disappears beneath the waistband. I try to count the number of abs on his stomach but then realize how inappropriate it is to be checking out… my husband.

I'm pretty sure I'll *never* get used to that sentiment, whether it's fake or not.

My cheeks flame as I tear my gaze from his stomach and drag it up to meet his eyes, where he's grinning arrogantly.

"Morning?"

"Morning," I mumble in response as I rub my hip, which is throbbing painfully.

He leans one muscled arm against the doorframe and scrubs his hand down his face with the other before bringing it to thread through his already sleep-disheveled hair.

It dawns on me that he has no clue why I'm awake in the middle of the night, and I'm simply staring at him like I've lost my mind.

I *clearly* have.

"God, I'm so sorry for waking you up," I say finally when I snap to my senses and stop standing there like I'm mute. "I was trying to be quiet and clearly did a terrible job at it. Sorry."

Grant's laugh is raspy and deep, still heavy from sleep, "Stop apologizing, Addie, but why *are* you up at 4:00 a.m.?"

"Oh, um, well, because I have to go to the bakery for my shift."

His eyes widen slightly in surprise. "At four in the morning?"

I nod. "Yeah, I'm sorry I didn't mention it last night—it kind of just slipped my mind with everything happening. We have to start baking so we can have everything out for the morning shift. We open at five thirty."

And speaking of… I'm *really* freakin' late now.

"Technically I was supposed to be there at 3:15, so I really have to go because I'm late, and I'm actually never late, so... um, see you later? I'm sorry again for waking you up. Again," I say in a nervous babble as I duck beneath his arm, attempting to flee before I say anything else to embarrass myself this early in the morning.

I make it to the end of the hallway before he calls my name, and I turn back to face him.

"Since I'm up, what if I came with you?"

"To... Ever After?" My brow furrows in confusion.

He shrugs while nodding. "Yeah. You know, it's been a dream of mine for a long time to... make baked goods."

It's so ridiculous that my laugh flies out before I can even attempt to stop it. I'm pretty sure this man hasn't thought about a baked good in any form except when eating it, but who am I to call him on it?

"Okay, sure, if you want to. But, fair warning, Amos will absolutely put you to work. We have a lot to do before opening," I say, crossing my arms over my chest.

"Cool. I'm good with that." He smirks. "But can I be compensated in beignets?"

Giggling, I roll my eyes. "Sure. *After* all the work is done."

"Yes, ma'am."

After Grant quickly gets ready, he drives us the ten minutes from his apartment near campus to Ever After and parks behind the building in the employee spot, looking entirely too excited to be *working* at four thirty in the morning.

I'm not surprised that he takes this unexpected early morning wake-up call in stride because it seems to be who he is... taking anything that's thrown his way with a smile and no complaint.

"This place is cute," he says as I open the back door with my key and walk into the small office in the back.

The building itself is way older than I am, but it's charming and has been in my mom's family for nearly a hundred years. There are so many pieces of her scattered within the walls that when I'm here, I truly feel like she's still here with me.

"I'm really proud of it. My mom made sure that every inch of this place had her touch. From the front case to the napkins. And we've kept it all because it was her legacy. Plus, these recipes have been my family's secret recipe since the beginning," I tell him, grabbing us both an apron from the rack and handing one to him.

Brent tried his hardest to take control and change everything, *modernize* it. Take away the small-town charm, the little touches that my mom worked so hard for, but the changes he made weren't... well received by our customers, so he ended up leaving things the way they should be.

Thank god for small miracles.

Grant lifts the dark green apron over his head, then secures it behind his waist. "You should be proud, Addie. It's your mom's legacy, and from the looks of it... you've done an incredible job of keeping it that way. Now, put me to work. These hands were made for more than just baseball. They were made for *dough*."

He shoots me a wink and lifts his massive hands, which I am sure were made for many things that I refuse to let myself think about.

It's been less than twenty-four hours since we got married. Since the kiss... and the plan, and I haven't stopped thinking about it.

How much I loved it and how I really, really shouldn't be thinking about that. It makes this arrangement between us that much more dangerous.

"Okay, let's go." I lead him into the kitchen, and of course, the moment we walk in, Amos looks up from the rack of apple fritters he's standing over, a look of amusement on his face.

I already know that I'll *never* hear the end of it. Of course, one of the only days I have ever shown up late, I show up with my… with *Grant* in tow. Not to mention, I haven't exactly had the chance to drop the bomb on them that our fake marriage is not going to seem very fake. Most of the time.

"Well, good mornin', cher. And… her new beau," he says, eyeing Grant.

I narrow my gaze at Amos, telling him to cut it out until Grant turns, and then I quickly put on a wide smile to cover the fact that I'm silently yelling at Amos with my eyes.

"Good morning. Grant… asked to come to work with me today because apparently, he has a hidden love for baking, so here we are."

Grant smirks. "It's true. I'm a man of many talents that are just waiting to be mastered. I've always wanted to learn to bake."

"Oh, well, you've come to the right place, then," Amos says, gesturing toward me with a flourish of his hand. "Addie's the real talent in here, and don't let her tell you anything different. You'll be learning from the best."

He's the best baker here, but I know there's no use arguing with him.

While Grant's with Amos, talking to him about prep, I walk over to the massive refrigerator and lift out a pan of chilled dough that's going to be cut into our signature beignets and carry it back to the prep table.

It never fails—no matter how many we make for the breakfast crowd, they *always* sell out. So, I try to get as much done as I can before the doors open at five thirty.

"That's a massive piece of dough." Grant's deep baritone comes from behind me, a soft caress to the shell of my ear, causing me to jump in surprise. I was so lost in thought and my routine that I didn't even hear him walk up.

I can feel the warm rumble of his chuckle against my skin, and I do everything in my power not to shiver, to show him that I'm affected by something so simple.

Maybe it's just cold in here.

Clearing my throat, I nod, turning to face him. "Uh, yeah, we make literally hundreds of these every morning, so it takes a lot of dough."

"What can I do?" I notice that he's rubbing his hand along the back of his neck, like there's an ache there, and my brow furrows.

"What's wrong?"

"Nothing. I think I might have a crick in my neck from sleeping on it wrong or something." He rolls his neck on his shoulders before shrugging. "I'll be fine. Put me to work, woman. I need to learn the ropes."

Guilt tugs at my stomach. I feel terrible that he's sacrificing comfort just so I can have his bed, and even worse that I woke him up in the middle of the night just to put him to work at the bakery.

"Grant, you should totally go home and get some sleep. I feel horrible for waking you up when you're already sleeping uncomfortably on the couch because of me." I chew my lip. "I'll get Amos to drop me off at class later."

He shakes his head adamantly. "Hell no. If I didn't want to be here, I wouldn't be, ArtGirl. I *want* to be here. I wanna help you make the best damn beignets in the city, so… tell me where to start?"

I try not to smile at what he's saying, but it feels impossible.

Finally, I nod and gesture to the dough in front of us, then start to explain the simple but time-consuming process of rolling it out to the perfect thickness and cutting the dough into beignets that we then drop into the fryer.

Grant listens intently and follows along as I show him each of the steps, a look of sheer determination written on his face.

I set the large roller down in front of him and sprinkle some flour along the prep counter. "Now, you try."

Before I can move out of the way, he steps behind me, bracing his hands along the counter on each side of me. I can feel the heat of his hard body behind me surrounding every inch of me as his massive hands cover the handles of the roller, and carefully, slowly, he begins to roll the dough out. His movement is slow and precise as he attempts the measured thickness, like he's nervous he's going to break the dough.

"Like this?" he asks from behind me, his breath warm along the sensitive spot near my ear.

Nodding, I place my trembling hand over his, showing him the amount of pressure, and help him with it. The hardest part about rolling out dough is finding the perfect amount of pressure to get the dough just right.

My heart begins to race at the contact, but I swallow down my nerves and repeat the motion with him. I have to keep reminding myself that the only way to seem convincing is to stop being so nervous around him. I have to stop freaking out when we touch. It won't seem real to those watching if I keep making it painfully obvious that I'm so nervous.

It's just easier said than done.

"You're a natural," I admit, lifting my gaze. "It's almost like muscle memory once you get it down. I think I could probably do it in my sleep at this point."

I've been officially working at Ever After since I was thirteen.

But even before then, I'd spent countless hours here as a child watching everyone bake. At first, it was simply so I could spend more time with Amos and Earl when he was around. And because I desperately wanted to be anywhere but with Brent and Tad. And oddly enough, even though Brent seems desperate to own the bakery, he rarely spends any time here.

But once I started working here, I realized how much I liked to be a part of things, contributing to my family's business. And I loved creating something that made people happy, even if it wasn't my art.

As I get busy with my own prep, I feel Grant's gaze lingering on me, even though he never stops rolling his dough, and my stomach flips from his attention.

I realize in this moment how much I like the way that he looks at me. All my life, I've felt invisible, but with Grant... I don't feel that way. I feel like he sees me. All of me.

"I think you might be the most creative person I've ever met, Addie. This might not be oil painting or charcoal, but it's still an art form that you're incredible at," he rasps, causing my pulse to race wildly.

It seems to be something that happens pretty regularly when I'm around him. It's both unnerving and exciting in a way that I've never experienced. Is this normal?

My throat works as my shoulder dips slightly, and I plaster on a small smile. "It's just something I've always done. Art's just the way I express myself. I wouldn't really say that making beignets is an expression of myself. But I do like making something others enjoy."

The air around us seems to grow thicker as something I can't place hangs between us. Whatever it is causes my stomach to flutter as our gazes linger.

Finally, he speaks, his tone soft yet firm all at once. "Still seems like an expression of you to me. I have a feeling every-thing you touch turns to art, Addie."

"Addie, how is the first round looking?" Amos interrupts from behind us, causing us both to jump, the moment between us broken.

I suck in a shaky breath and whip to face him. "Uh, we're about to drop them now."

His brow shoots up as a knowing expression passes over his face, causing his lips to curl up into a grin. "Just wanted to check. We're opening in thirty minutes."

Crap. I've been so caught up in Grant that time has gotten away from me. Seems to be an ongoing occurrence this morning.

"Those are looking good, Grant. You might be a natural baker like our Addie," he adds with a smirk before turning and leaving us alone in the kitchen.

"Sorry, I didn't mean to distract you," Grant says seriously once Amos is out of earshot. "I think I can handle this if you want to work on something else. We can knock it all out."

I nod, stepping back and putting distance between us in hopes that it will calm the fluttering in my stomach.

"Yeah, I'll work on frying these once you finish cutting them all out."

With a lazy grin and a wink, he focuses on his task as I busy myself with getting everything else prepped and ready to go in the case and then start frying up the beignets.

Before I know it, we've got several pans of puffed beignets ready to be powdered and then put out for the morning rush.

"My favorite part," I say with a wicked grin as I pull out the large bag of powdered sugar. "I've got a bit of a sweet tooth. I guess that's expected when you work in a bakery?" I add when his brows tug together in confusion.

Handing him the sifter, I open the bag and pour a little into it, then close my hand over his and guide it over the beignets, showing him how to shake the sifter to spread the sugar evenly over our creations.

Once we've done a few together, I grab my own sifter and begin working on another pan. Together, we knock them out in only a few minutes. While I have been admittedly distracted with him here, we still work together well, and he's actually been a lot of help today.

"Wow. Baking is absolutely fascinating," Grant exclaims genuinely once we're done.

I giggle. "Is it though?"

He nods with a lazy grin. "Definitely, even though it seems like a lot of work. There's so much to learn. I think I might have to come back a few more times, maybe more—you know, to soak in all of it."

I bite back a grin. "Mhmm. Yeah, definitely not something you can learn in a single day. Takes a lot of practice. Consistency."

His laugh settles around me, warming my insides, and when he pushes himself off the counter, leaning forward close to me, my breath hitches slightly.

"You've got…" He trails off, reaching up with his thumb and swiping the pad of it tenderly along my cheek. "Something here."

When he pulls his thumb back and I see the smudge of powdered sugar on the tip, my cheeks flush.

Of course I'd end up with powdered sugar all over my face.

Blinking slowly, I shake my head in humiliation, hoping he doesn't see my blush. "Thanks. I… That is embarrassing."

"Nah," he replies, his eyes never leaving mine as he brings

his thumb to his lips and sucks the sugar off the tip in a way that is entirely too hot. "Guess you're not the only one with a *sweet tooth*, ArtGirl."

chapter fourteen

Grant

THE SACCHARINE TASTE of powdered sugar lingered on my tongue for the remainder of the day, long after we left the bakery.

I told myself it was because I fucking love sweets, but that's a lie. It's because I wanted to taste Addie instead.

We both had class early this morning, so after work at the bakery, we headed to campus, and I haven't seen her since.

I had classes, weight training, and then a meeting with Jeremy that went surprisingly better than I anticipated.

He's not *entirely* happy that I got married without any warning when he had no idea I was even *in* a relationship, but he *is* happy that this could help turn my image around with potential sponsors and help close the deal we've been working on. He agreed that, at minimum, me being in a seemingly long-term relationship couldn't hurt.

Works for me.

"Addie?" I call out as I walk into the apartment, shutting the front door with my foot while attempting to balance a stack of pizza boxes in my hands.

"In here," I hear quietly from the living room. When I walk through the door, I see her cuddled up in the armchair in the corner of the room. She's wrapped up in a thick, oversized, dark pink cardigan with her sketchbook open on her lap. Auggie is snoring steadily in the plush dog bed next to the chair.

Her gaze lifts to mine, and those blue eyes widen as they drop to the pizza boxes in my hands. "Hi. Um... Are you having people over?"

Laughing, I shake my head as I set the boxes down on the coffee table. "Nope. I just wanted to bring home dinner because I figured you'd be hungry, and I remembered you liked veggie, but didn't know if that included supreme, and other kinds? So, I just got... a lot of them."

"You could have just texted me." She laughs. "Instead of... bringing home five pizzas?"

Admittedly, that would've been the smarter thing to do, but I didn't know if she was studying or sketching, and I didn't want to bother her after she's had such a long day.

Plus, Jack's Pizza never lasts long around here. It'll get eaten, eventually.

I shrug, a grin tilting on my lips. Leaving her with the pizza, I walk into the kitchen and grab two plates, bottles of water, and a few napkins, carrying them back to the living room.

"Thank you," she says, closing her sketchbook and putting it on the small end table. "For being thoughtful and bringing dinner. I was starving but was also too tired to cook or go anywhere, so I was honestly just planning on skipping dinner tonight." She wrinkles her nose in that adorable way that makes me want to kiss it.

"Sorry, ArtGirl, no skipping dinners in the Bergeron household. I'm a growing boy. And since you are a Bergeron now, that includes *you*."

Her cheeks flame, but that sweet smile appears on her lush lips, causing my own grin to widen. "Okay. Got it. No skipping meals for Bergerons."

After she chooses her pizza, the veggie one, I load four slices of pepperoni onto my plate and flop down onto the couch.

"I'm surprised you didn't get pineapple," she muses. I glance over at her, my brow raised in surprise, and see the grin she's trying to hide behind her hand.

She remembered how much I fucking hate pineapple pizza, and she's teasing me.

I don't know why the fact that she remembered surprises me, in a good way, because it's not like *I've* forgotten a single conversation we shared back then. I can't help but like that she remembers these details about me. Like the conversations were as important to her as they were to me.

"No blasphemy in this house, please," I groan gruffly before taking a bite of my pizza to hide my grin. "But ordering dinner made me think. If we're going to be living together, ArtGirl, we've gotta learn the basics. You know? Things that make coexisting easier, things a husband would know about his wife… Like your favorite kind of pizza so I don't get five next time."

"Veggie, always." She giggles and shrugs. "But honestly, I'll eat most types of pizza. Besides pineapple, that is."

My lips curve into a grin when I hear the light, teasing tone in her velvety voice. After another bite, I mumble, "Good to know."

For a moment, comfortable silence settles around us as we eat, but I soon break it with a question that I've been wondering ever since I walked in tonight.

I nod toward her sketchbook on the end table beside us and ask, "What were you working on? When I got here."

"Oh, uh… just something for my art thesis project. It's nothing, really." She ducks her head, lowering her gaze to the pizza in her lap.

"Can I see?"

Her head whips up, and her gaze meets mine, her brow arching in surprise, "You want to see my art?"

"Yeah. I mean, if you'd be okay showing it to me?" I say hopefully.

I've only seen a few pieces of hers so far, including the canvas from her room the other night, but I want to see more. I feel like her art is part of the Addie puzzle, of knowing her better. And I *want* to know her. I want to learn everything about her, especially the parts of her she keeps hidden. I want her to trust me enough to share those pieces.

"It's probably... stupid and not very good," she mutters sheepishly.

My brow furrows, and I sit up, setting the plate down on the coffee table in front of me to give her all of my attention. "Addie, do you really not know how talented you are?"

Even in the dim light of the lamp, I can see the telltale pink flush of her cheeks traveling down to her neck, despite the fact that she's desperately trying to hide it by wrapping her sweater more securely around her.

"Show me. Please?"

For a moment, she stays put, her wild blue eyes holding mine while she chews her lip, silently debating something, but then finally, she nods and reaches for the sketchbook, flipping it open to the most recent page.

There's a tremble in her hand when she turns it to face me, and I hate that she's so nervous to share her talent, that she's not more confident in herself. She should be, and I want to tell her over and over until she believes me.

The page is still mostly blank, aside from a half-drawn portrait of a woman that resembles her. The girl has the same elegant slope of her nose, the same pouty lips, the same delicate features. The drawing is amazing, but even as talented as Addie is, she doesn't quite capture on paper how beautiful she is.

Or maybe she just doesn't see herself the way that the world does. The way I do.

"You think this is *stupid*?" Disbelief laces my words as my gaze shifts to her.

It's anything but stupid. It's fucking extraordinary.

"It's just… It's a rough sketch. A *verrrry* rough sketch. I want to finish it in painting once I get the full idea down. Right now, I feel like I'm just feeling my way around in the dark and throwing stuff against the wall and praying that something sticks."

"If this is your definition of a rough sketch, I can't imagine what it will look like when it's finished, Addie. *Holy shit*," I mutter, dragging my attention from the drawing back to her.

Her throat swallows roughly before she slams the sketchbook closed and tucks it against her lap hastily, like the positive attention is too much for her. She tucks a loose strand of her blonde hair behind her ear. "Thank you. I'll have to show you when it's finally done. Whenever that may be."

My mind is still blown that this girl truly believes that her art isn't incredible, and I vow here and now to make it my life fucking goal to convince her otherwise. Has no one ever told her how incredible she is?

"Can I help?"

She shakes her head. "No, I don't think so, but if I need help, I'll let you know." Pausing, she picks up her phone on the arm of the chair and glances at the time before shifting her gaze back to me. "Ugh. Three a.m. is going to come entirely too early. I guess I should head to bed."

Auggie lifts his head from where he settled on the couch next to me, his ears perking up at the mention of bed. I swear, he naps more than a toddler but is also the chillest dog I've ever met.

"Auggie and I are going on our first jog tomorrow, so he's gonna need to be *very* well rested. Big guy's got a lot of calories to burn," I tease, pausing to shift my gaze to Addie. "And… I was thinking, we're going to need to go out soon. So we can be seen together. But we probably should practice? You know, before we really take things public. Make sure you're comfortable."

"Okay. Uh… I think that's great. I'm ready when you are."

I've been ready.

I nearly choke on my own spit when I walk through the front door the following morning and find Addie folded over like a pretzel in the middle of the living room.

She's got her hands flat on the mat in front of her, with her ass perched high in the air as she listens along to some guided meditation thing on the TV.

And I'm pretty sure I've forgotten how to breathe, or think, or no… fucking *both*.

The tight purple leggings she's wearing are molded to the curves of her hips and ass. Somehow, I summon willpower that I never knew I possessed and drag my gaze from her and shift it to Auggie, who's still panting from our run at my feet.

Think about fat corgis. Think about Auggie, Grant.

About how you had to carry his cute but heavy ass for the whole last mile because he'd decided he had enough of your shit and promptly plopped down like a sack of potatoes in the middle of the street, refusing to move another inch. It was the laziest tantrum ever.

Don't think about your new wife in those tight pants, or how flexible she is, or how you would sacrifice just about anything to see what other ways she can ben—

"Grant?"

My head snaps up, eyes landing on her pink parted lips as she calls my name. My gaze follows a rivulet of sweat that languidly drops from her neck to the center of her chest, trailing lower and lower before disappearing between her sports bra–covered cleavage.

I bite back a groan. I'm getting hard just watching her fucking sweat. I've got to get my damn shit together.

"What's up?" I reply casually, lifting my shirt to wipe sweat from my brow. "Didn't know you did yoga."

When I drop my T-shirt, I see her wide eyes, and a shit-eating grin lifts my lips. I love that I affect her as much as she clearly affects me.

"Careful, ArtGirl. People might think you're checking out your husband."

I'm teasing her simply to see her flush my favorite shade of pink, which she does immediately, averting her gaze and turning toward her mat. She begins rolling it up. "Yes, I love yoga. I try to do it at least three times a week. Usually if I have time before class after leaving the bakery. I find it centers me. Have you ever done it before?"

I shake my head. "Nah, but… maybe I should. Actually, it looks very *bendy*."

If it means I get to watch *her* bending like that again, consider me the next yoga master.

"You should try it. I've heard of a lot of athletes using it to strengthen their core and to improve flexibility. It's supposed to help prevent injuries."

Before I can respond, there's a hard knock at the front door, dragging both of our attention toward it.

Auggie's pointy white ears perk up for a millisecond before he decides that it's not worth leaving his spot to investigate, instead laying his head back down on the floor, eying us warily.

"I'll get it," I say, walking over to the door and wrenching it open.

When I see Davis on the other side, my eyes narrow. "Are we just showing up uninvited now? That what we're doing?"

He reaches up and pushes the dark hoodie off his head, then shrugs, his signature shit-eating grin present per usual. "I was in the neighborhood, figured I'd stop by. See what was up since you haven't responded to my texts. All ten of them."

True, I didn't text back. But also, I'm calling bullshit. He lives in the dorms, and let's be real, he's only here because, if I had to guess, knowing him the way that I do, he couldn't last another second without coming over to find out whatever he could about Addie. Obviously, the thirty minutes he was around her at our wedding wasn't enough to get his fill.

I'm not saying he's the equivalent of a hormonal teenage girl, but I'm also not... not saying that.

Sighing, I lift my arm and open the door wider so he can step through. Even though I'd much rather shut it on his face and let him sit out there, I know I'm not getting rid of him that easily.

He's persistent if nothing else.

He ducks beneath my arm and brushes past me into the

apartment, and I slam it closed behind him with a little more force than intended.

"Hey, Addie. We didn't have a chance to really talk the other day, but I'm Davis, Grant's *bestie*," he says as he crosses the living room to Addie. "Welcome to the family."

I can't hear what her response is because he reaches out and drags her against his chest in a hug so tight that it makes me want to rip his arms off and beat him with them.

Yeah, he can't ever touch her again.

And trust me, I realize that's a little fucking much, but I… just *don't* like him touching her. Or talking to her. Or even looking at her, for that matter. Considering he's one of my closest friends these days, I probably shouldn't be so irrationally jealous. But here we are anyway.

A problem for later since he's still hugging her, and that's long enough.

"Hands off, Davis," I growl in annoyance.

I'm truly having a Jekyll and Hyde moment, and I'm not sure how the fuck I'm supposed to feel about it.

His gaze whips to mine, and he smirks knowingly before shrugging and stepping back from her.

"Nice to see you again," Addie says with a small smile.

"Not sure you'll be saying that after you get to know him," I mumble.

Chuckling, Davis walks over to the couch and flops down on the cushions, spreading his arms along the back. "So, how's married life treating you lovebirds?"

Yeah… I kind of didn't tell him anything about our arrangement.

As in that it's fake. I wasn't sure what Addie would be comfortable with, and I don't really trust him not to keep secrets. So, I told him that when we reconnected that day in the park, we realized that we're madly in love and didn't want to wait another second to get married.

He believed me, so clearly, it was convincing enough. Plus, dude was practically giddy that he had a role in helping us reconnect that he probably would have believed anything. Now, we just have to convince everyone else that it was love at first sight that led us to acting impulsively.

"It's... great," Addie says shyly. "Even better than I imagined it could be."

Thatta girl.

"Grant's the best guy I know, and I'm happy for you two. I'm assuming this means that you'll be in the stands this season, cheering our guy on?" he asks.

She nods. "Um... Yes? I've actually never been... to a baseball game. Or *any* kind of game, for that matter."

Holy shit. ArtGirl really is anti-sports.

Kind of ironic that now she's married to a baseball player who's entered the draft.

"Damn, girl. Well, perfect timing. Your husband's gonna have all eyes on him this season. Scouts from all over the country now that they know he's entering the draft in June."

Mention of the upcoming draft has a feeling of unease churning in the pit of my stomach. I'm nervous as fuck that even after all of the work I've put in, I still won't make it. I haven't really told anyone about my fears, but it's been weighing more heavily on me with every passing day.

There's a chance I *won't* get drafted. A big possibility, and if so, I'm not sure what the future holds for me. Baseball is the only thing I've had my sights on since I was a freshman in high school, and until recently, I never really let myself imagine a world where it *didn't* happen.

I've spent the last fifteen years with tunnel vision, and now that it's closing in, I'm facing the sobering reality that it might not happen for me.

Unlike some of my teammates, baseball hasn't always come easily. I'm not as naturally talented as Reese and Lane are, and I'm self-aware enough to know that. I always had to work harder at it than most guys, had to practice more than others to reach the level I'm at now. I've known that since I started at OU as a redshirt freshman, and I've had to put in twice the work to prove myself just to show my coach I deserve to be on the starting lineup.

I'm not saying I'm talentless. I wouldn't be playing for a D1 college if I wasn't skilled. I just know that the vast majority of college players never make the big leagues, and if I want to be drafted come June, I've got to bust my ass and be at the very top of my game.

Addie's sweet voice breaks through my thoughts, saving me from going too far in my head. "That's amazing, Grant. Congratulations. I bet you're going to get drafted to the best team."

Laughing, I walk over and slide my arm around her shoulder, tugging her gently to my side. A primal side of me wants to erase Davis's touch from her. She tenses for only a moment before relaxing against me. Her wide, blue eyes dance as she stares up at me. "Thank you, ArtGirl. We'll see what happens. But... until then, I've gotta bust my ass and put in the work. I've got a long way to go."

"Yeah, we're going to be unstoppable this year. Watch," Davis proclaims. The side of his lip curls into a grin when Auggie saunters over to the couch and hops into his lap. "Yo, this dog is actually so fucking cute." He pats Auggie's head and offers him a scratch behind his ear.

"That is Augustus. But he prefers to go by Auggie," I tell him.

"Him's so cute. Who's the goodest boy? You are. Yes you are, aren't you?" Davis coos saccharinely, causing Addie to bury her face into my shirt and giggle.

He continues to prove my point of how ridiculous he is. At all times.

"As much as I don't want to leave this little guy, I gotta split. I've got a..." He trails off, glancing at Addie before clearing his throat. "*Date* tonight. I'll come back and visit Auggie soon, but I was thinking we all go out soon? Celebrate? Maybe the Redlight? We haven't been there in a while."

I mean... It's not a terrible idea. We actually have to be around other people in order to convince them that this marriage is real. Maybe after tonight, she'll be more comfortable acting married.

"Yeah, maybe. We'll talk about it, and I'll let you know for sure later," I say as he pushes to his feet, much to Auggie's dismay.

He nods. "Sounds good. See you tomorrow at the gym. Later, *lovebirds*."

Once he's gone, my attention shifts to Addie, who's chewing the corner of her lip, lost in thought. I drop my arm from her shoulder and walk over to the coffee table in front of her and sit.

"I know you're probably not interested in going to a party... or a bar, and honestly, neither am I. I haven't been in a party mood in a while."

She nods. "It's not my thing, but if it's something you really wanted to do, then I'd be okay with it?"

"Nah. But maybe this is the perfect time to... practice? Not something like a stupid party with Davis, but maybe we could just spend some time together and practice before we do something more public? Not a party."

Her lip curves upward as she smirks. "Yeah, I'd like that."

"Yeah?"

She nods with a hint of shyness shining in her bright blue eyes.

Now, I just have to plan the perfect fake date for my fake wife.

chapter fifteen

Addie

I WONDER if tonight is *actually* a date.

There's no official guidebook on how to fake marry someone, so it's unclear how all of this should go, but I can't stop myself from wondering if *Grant* considers this a date.

Or is this simply just... practice?

Peering into the mirror in his bathroom, I scan my reflection, sighing as I run my hands down the front of the beige dress I'm wearing, wondering if this is what I should wear if it is considered a date.

Or... even if it's not.

It's times like this that I wish I had girlfriends. Someone my own age to talk to about clothes and my lack of knowledge about makeup and boys. But I've just never been great at making friends. I've always been painfully shy, much better at blending into the background. It's why I've mostly stuck to my art, working at the bakery, and Auggie. Most of the time, I'm content with that, but sometimes, I wish that I had someone to confide in.

Instead, I've got Auggie, who's currently staring at me with his judgy eyes and making me second-guess my outfit choice for tonight.

But before I can change for the third time, there's a light rap at the bedroom door, and then Grant's voice drifts through. "Almost ready?"

"Um, yes. Give me just one more second!" My stomach twists in a flurry of nerves as I blow out a shaky exhale and take one final look in the mirror.

This dress is fine for *whatever* tonight ends up being. It's basic but still flatters the small amount of curves that I have. And the dainty strawberry earrings I grabbed at the last minute are the perfect accessory for the soft waves I did my hair in.

It's *fine.*

At least that's what I keep telling myself as I grab a thin pink cardigan off the bed, then give Auggie a quick head scratch before walking over to the bedroom door and opening it.

Grant's standing in the doorway, leaning against the wooden frame on one veiny, muscled forearm.

His lips slightly part, and his eyes trail down my body in a slow, unhurried perusal. I can nearly *feel* his gaze as it travels over me, a shiver racing down my spine in response and sending my already frayed nerves into overdrive.

"Is this okay? I can go cha—"

"No. No," he stops me, his blue eyes finally lifting to mine. "You look *stunning*, Addie."

Heat flushes my cheeks at the compliment. His gaze feels more intense than ever, or maybe I just haven't noticed how much until now.

"Thank you," I murmur shyly.

Tonight, he's wearing a simple black cotton T-shirt with a faded pair of blue jeans and a well-worn pair of Converse. He's styled his hair and shaved, which somehow makes his sculpted jawline appear even more prominent.

I never knew that was a feature that I would be so... attracted to until Grant. Not that I've had a lot of experiences to go on.

He's standing so close, only a few inches away, that I can smell the clean scent of his bodywash, and I want to inhale, breathing the cedarwood scent in.

Jeez, Addie, no. *No.*

That sounds creepy even in your head. Imagine if he knew you wanted to *smell* him.

My nerves are clearly clouding my thoughts and making me think like a lunatic.

After saying a quick goodbye to Auggie, we walk out of the apartment, and I feel Grant's palm brushing along the small of my back as he guides me toward the truck.

It's the most innocent of touches, but it sets my skin on fire.

When I reach for the door handle, he stops me by placing his hand over mine and shaking his head. "Let me."

He pulls on the handle, opening the door with a smile.

I'm confused for most of the drive and when we pull into the parking lot of the school's baseball stadium my brows furrow together.

I glance over at him with wide eyes as he parks in the front row but he just chuckles, reaching over and gently smoothing the furrow between my brows with the pad of his thumb.

"Don't worry, ArtGirl. We're not here to *play*. I know how *anti-sports* you are." His tone is light as he teases me with a playful grin that makes him that much more handsome.

My heart races inside my chest at his touch, something that seems to always happen.

"I wasn't... worried."

His smirk is the only response I get to my denial.

We get out of the truck, and he leads me to a side entrance that reads *FACULTY ONLY* across the door in big, bold letters. He pulls a small white key card from his pocket and presses it against the entrance scanner.

When it beeps, unlocking quietly, he pulls the door open and waves me inside. "*Wifeys* first," he says playfully.

Stepping inside, I clutch my cardigan tightly to me and wait for him to follow me into the building. I can't stop wondering *why* we're here, of all places, and what he has planned.

Whenever I asked him what his plans were, he insisted that it remain a surprise.

"This place is kinda creepy when it's empty," Grant mumbles quietly as we walk down the long stretch of dimly lit hallway.

I nod, scanning the frames of memorabilia along the maroon walls. "Yeah. It is really eerie."

I follow behind him to the end of the hallway, and he points to the right, where another long hallway leads. "I would give you a tour, but it's not all that exciting if you're not a fan."

"I am *not* anti-sports, Grant," I exclaim, even though we both know that it is… slightly true. "Even if I *was*, it wouldn't matter now that I'm… married to a baseball player, would it?"

His lips twitch as he nods. "Touché, ArtGirl. Touché. But, nonetheless, I'll save the tour for another time because we've got somewhere important to be."

A combination of anticipation and nerves blooms in my chest as I follow closely behind him out of the double doors at the very end of the corridor. We're back outside, but now, it's within the fenced stadium. The chill I felt while inside disappears when the muggy night air settles around us.

Obviously, I've never been inside any kind of stadium before, but it's even larger than what I expected. The tall lights above the field are off, making it hard to see as we make our way forward, but Grant knows this place like the back of his hand.

He takes us directly to a side entrance and unlatches the gate, pushing it open. I step through and realize... we're actually going onto the field.

The narrow walkway leads to the dugout, and we walk through, my eyes scanning the championship years painted along the wall above the bench to the waist-high fence that over-looks the diamond-shaped field.

"And this is where the magic happens." He grins, sweeping his hands toward the darkened field.

It seems so much larger than it does on a TV. Even in the dark.

"Wow," I breathe. "It's... *big*."

Grant laughs, the sound tugging at something deep in my belly, before he nods and steps out of the dugout onto the grass. "Yeah, it can be a little overwhelming sometimes. Especially when the stands are filled with ten thousand screaming people."

"Holy moly," I mumble, dragging my gaze to the rows and rows of empty seats. I would probably have a heart attack if I had to do something, *anything*, in front of that many people. It's way more attention than I care to ever have.

"Yep. Talk about performing under pressure, huh?"

When I nod, he gestures for me to follow him along the grass toward the corner of the field. Only then do I halt when I see what's in front of us.

The *reason* he's brought us here tonight. Apparently, my surprise must be written all over my face because he chuckles deeply, stepping so closely beside me that I can feel the heat radiating off his body.

"I figured that our first date should be a combination of things we both love?" he whispers near my ear. The bare skin of my forearms erupts with goose bumps, and I wish that I could say it's from a chill in the air, but no. It's entirely Grant.

I clutch my cardigan tighter, the fabric bunching between my fingers as I attempt to pull in a shaky breath.

There's a large quilted blanket spread out in the middle of the field with dozens of battery-powered tea light candles emitting a soft, warm glow. A small lantern sits next to a picnic basket with a large bottle of pink lemonade. There are large fluffy yellow pillows along with a bag of my favorite candy.

Every detail of it is beyond sweet and carefully thought out, but it's not what has my heart thudding so hard in my chest that my head feels light and my vision swims.

It's the nearby *telescope* pointed toward the starry night sky that's making my throat feel tight with a hundred different emotions.

"D-date? This is a… *date*?" I fumble the syllables out when I'm finally able to speak, dragging my attention away from the setup to where he's standing beside me.

The space between his brows is creased. "You're my wife, Addie. You date even once you're married. We kinda did shit ass-backwards, so yeah… I think this is our first date."

Of course, he means that's how it should be perceived by everyone around us, I know. I *know.*

The only way that we're going to pull off this entire arrangement is to make our connection seem realistic. That we're just two out-of-our-mind-in-love college kids who got married on a whim because they were so in love that they couldn't imagine another second not being together.

But I think to make it seem believable, it has to *feel* believable.

And this? Feels… like a date with a man who could easily steal my heart.

"This is amazing, Grant. All of it, truly. Thank you," I say, rolling my lip between my teeth as I peer up at him. "It's so thoughtful and so sweet... and I'm just really glad that we're doing this. Um... I mean, that we're getting to know each other better."

His lips curve into a smile. "Me too, ArtGirl. Really fucking glad." After a brief pause, he continues. "Now, since our date has *officially* started, let me show you the best part."

The best part isn't the telescope that I'm currently drooling to get my hands on? I can't imagine him topping that on this fake date, but he's done an incredible job of surprising me so far.

Smirking, he turns toward the blanket, and I follow behind him until we're both seated beside each other on the soft blanket he's spread out. He reaches for the picnic basket, his large hand closing around the handle, and pulls it toward him. When he opens it and begins pulling out the contents from inside, my jaw drops.

I would recognize that packaging anywhere.

"Gino's? Oh my god, Grant, it's my *favorite.* How did you make this happen?" I ask in complete shock.

He remembered everything from that semester we spent getting to know each other through a computer screen.

Even after I... ghosted him and left with zero explanation, he never forgot a single conversation.

A single detail mentioned in passing.

My god.

I... I can't believe he did all of this. This clearly isn't something he threw together at the last minute. He put so much thought into arranging all the little details, kept it all a surprise.

My chest throbs at how achingly sweet he is.

His grin turns cocky, and his shoulder dips nonchalantly as if him pulling this off for a date is nothing. "Called in a favor. One of the team's backers is an investor. He hooked me up."

My eyes widen further as my mouth begins to water. I can't remember the last time I had Gino's famous lasagna. It's been my favorite restaurant since I was a kid and yet another detail that Grant remembered.

It feels like he's thought of it all.

"You know, I think any future date I have may forever pale in comparison to this fake one." I giggle softly.

For a beat, I swear that I almost see disappointment flash in his eyes… as if the idea of me going on a date with anyone else irritates him. But that couldn't possibly be true, so I chalk it up to a combination of my nerves and the flicker of the candles and reach for the container.

"Have you heard from Brent?" he asks, changing the subject.

I shake my head and grab the fork he's extended toward me before pulling the top off my takeout. "He sent me a text this morning, saying that he'll be by the bakery soon, but Amos told me to ignore it and that he would handle it if he shows up. Kind of easier said than done."

Grant's eyes darken, his expression hardening as his jaw clenches. "I fucking hate that guy. I've been thinking though… since Davis asked us to go out to the Redlight earlier, if Brent really is having us followed or whatever the hell he's threatening in order to disprove things, then we're going to have to make sure we're out *in* public. We'll use his own threat against him." He pauses, shoveling his food into his mouth and chewing. "We can't stay holed up in the apartment or the bakery."

"I know. I just… can't even believe he's doing this, Grant. I mean, I guess I can believe it, but part of me doesn't *want* to believe it," I whisper between small bites.

Part of me wants to hate him for the things he's done. For lying to me and trying to force me into a marriage built on deceit with someone cold and calculating and likely abusive. For trying to take the bakery away from me when it's rightfully mine. For being so hurtful and cruel toward me for my entire life, as if I had wronged him simply by *existing*.

Then there's another part of me that… can't fully hate him. Because despite the mistakes that he's made and the wrong that he's done, he did take care of me when I had no one else. He put a roof over my head, clothes on my back, and gave me food to eat. He did the bare minimum, but at least he let me stay in my home. That's the part of me that feels a little indebted to him. Besides, it's not in my character to hate anyone, so it all feels like so much at once.

And maybe both things can be true, but I'm still struggling, trying to reconcile these feelings.

"We're not going to let him win, Addie. He's an asshole, and he doesn't deserve a second of the worry you're giving him. I promise you I'm going to make sure that he never hurts you again. Okay? Trust me."

Sincerity shines in his eyes, and I allow myself to feel security in what he's saying, that no matter what, we'll figure it out. Even if it's not easy.

"Okay."

Thankfully, the conversation steers away from Brent and all of the heavy stuff and back into lighter territory when Grant completely misses his mouth and drops the very last bite of his lasagna onto the blanket. It sends me into a fit of giggles, causing my stomach to begin aching from how hard I'm laughing.

I try to stop. Really, I do. "I'm-m sorry. It's not f-funny," I wheeze, very ungracefully, but the crestfallen look on his face as he dropped it was possibly the funniest and most adorable thing I've ever seen.

Grant chuckles along with me while he cleans up the mess

and puts his now empty box back into the picnic basket before stretching his long denim-clad legs out on the blanket.

Unlike him, I'm much slower since I savored every single bite, and I find myself hoping that it won't be the last time we have my favorite dish together. Hoping that there's going to be another date like tonight because this might be the best meal I've ever shared with anyone.

And not only because of the food.

It's obvious that the reason Grant did all of this is not just because he's attentive and considerate but because he knew it would make me feel more at ease, less nervous. Even though we're still learning about each other, he somehow knows me in a way that no one else does.

Once I'm done and my empty container is put away, I move closer to his spot on the blanket.

"Wanna lay with me and look at the stars? They're really bright tonight without the city lights," he asks, lifting his gaze to the sky, then back to me.

"Yeah, I'd… love that."

Tugging my dress further down on my thighs, I carefully lie back on the blanket next to Grant, our shoulders nearly touching as we gaze up at the endless midnight sky littered with sparkling constellations.

Beneath the stars is my favorite place in the world to be. It's the one place I feel an overwhelming sense of… peace.

"Do you ever think about how *somehow…* we exist in a universe that's endless? Like there's this entire Milky Way full of planets and stars and cosmos and galaxies. It's vast beyond comprehension. And yet, somehow, *we* exist. We're created with hearts that beat in different rhythms and souls that are tethered to fate," I whisper quietly, turning my head to look over at Grant.

I expect him to be staring at the same stars that I was, but he's not looking at the sky at all. He's looking at *me*, and his dark, stormy eyes hold mine with an intensity that I can feel somewhere deep in my chest.

Seconds tick by as his eyes linger on mine, but time feels slower.

"It makes you feel kinda… small," he replies. "But still… significant. When you think about how we're floating on a rock in the middle of the galaxy, but we're all under the same sky, no matter where you are. I completely get it."

Nodding, I turn back to the sky, my eyes finding my favorite constellations by muscle memory. "When I was little, I would constantly search for the constellations at night. I'd lay on the hard concrete in the middle of the driveway and memorize their shapes after spending the day reading book after book until I could spot them without any help. I never got tired of searching for them. It was comforting that, no matter what, I knew the constellations would never disappear. That the stars would always shine. A constant that I desperately needed."

A hard knot of emotion forms at the base of my throat as I speak. This part of me, the part that's still a tangled mess, feels the thorns of vulnerability digging deep beneath my skin.

As hard as it is to be open… Grant makes me feel secure. Even if this marriage is fake and the feelings we're feigning aren't real, he still feels like a safe place to land.

Where our two hands rest closely together on the blanket, his pinky brushes gently against mine, and in another breath, he's hooking them together. The smallest touch, the barest brush of his skin, yet it feels incredibly powerful.

I'm attempting to control my breathing in order to not reveal the racing of my heart but failing miserably. I'm not sure if it's a good or bad thing that I have this response to him. It makes me feel so… out of control of my own emotions.

"I'm glad that as endless as the universe is… I exist in the same time and place that you do, Addie." When I glance over at him, his smile makes the flutters in my stomach intensify. An eruption of butterflies that make my head feel light and my limbs feel heavy.

And I don't bother hiding the smile that tilts my lips, much like his own. "Me too."

His pinky leaves mine, and his hand slides slowly, tenderly, along my palm until my fingers are intertwined tightly with his.

The gentle swipe of his thumb along my skin makes me realize for the first time… my heart's not racing because I'm nervous.

It's racing for *entirely* different reasons.

chapter sixteen

Grant

I KNOW this isn't supposed to be an actual date. This is supposed to be practice at being a real couple so that Addie feels more comfortable when I touch her in public.

But I'm having a hard time pretending that it's *not*.

Maybe we're just caught up in the moment... or maybe we're not. Who fucking knows, but what I do know is that I'm not in any rush for tonight to come to an end.

Rising from the blanket, I sit up and peer down at her. "How about we use the telescope? I have absolutely no idea what to do, but I figured that you probably would."

Excitement dances in her eyes at the mention of the telescope that Davis somehow borrowed from the astronomy club, and she nods eagerly, sitting up.

I was a little worried that she would think it was lame that I set all of this up or that it was too much, but seeing the expression on her face when she first saw it, I knew that I made the right decision.

Even more so now when she bounds over to the telescope and starts twisting the knobs without hesitation. Art and space are Addie's things. That much I know, even if I'm still finding out the rest.

"I'm not sure I even want to know how you just so happened to have a Bushnell handy for tonight." Her blonde brow arches as she glances from the telescope and then back to me. The expression on her face is a mixture of awe and something that I can't quite decipher.

My lip twitches, and I chuckle with a shrug. "Called in another favor. But I have been threatened with bodily harm if I don't return it in the exact condition that it was stolen in."

"Stolen?" Addie squeaks, her ocean eyes wide. "Grant…"

"Just kidding." Winking, I walk to where she's standing beside the large telescope. "You know how to work it?"

She nods as she tucks a wave of her hair behind her ear. "Of course. I mean… I've never owned one *this* nice, but I saved for two years when I was a freshman in high school so I could get one off of eBay. Mine was secondhand and primarily for hobbyists, but most, not all, work universally… no pun intended."

Even in only the pale moonlight and dim light of the candles, I can still see her cheeks flush red at the cheesy pun, and I laugh, the sound echoing around the empty field.

"Alright, ArtGirl, do your thing, then."

I watch as she nods and bites her bottom lip. She glances at the sky a few times, then turns toward the telescope and uses one eye to peer into the lens while adjusting several of the knobs on the side.

It's pretty fascinating watching her work, clearly full of knowledge that I'll never possess. She's brilliant.

"Okay, you should be able to see Telescopium," she mumbles, still peering into the eyepiece. "Just be careful not to jostle it."

When she steps back and to the side, I take her place, looking into the eyepiece, holding on to the sides of the telescope. I see… nothing but black.

"Do you see it?"

Shaking my head, I pull back slightly. "No, all I see is darkness?"

"It's just kind of hard at first because even the slightest movement will cause you to lose the target."

When she steps closer, I feel the warmth of her bare arm brushing against the front of my shirt, the strands of her soft curls drifting along my skin. So close that I lose my head, and now the problem is… I'm not thinking about the stars or the damn telescope any longer. I'm thinking about *her*.

About how sweet she smells and how warm her body is next to mine. How my hands itch to touch her. How all I want to do is pull her to me and kiss the fuck out of her.

Taking the smallest step back, I murmur, "Maybe you can show me what I'm doing wrong, then? Maybe I just need a… *lesson*?"

My words feel heavy with what they really mean, and I expect her to nod and scramble away, but instead, her rosy pink lips part, and her eyes flicker with… something new.

There's the same hesitancy, but not like before. There's heat in her gaze.

I'm not the only one that feels the chemistry between us. The invisible string of… *something*… constantly pulling taut when we're together.

Everything would be easier if I *didn't* have this attraction to Addie. This *want* that I can't seem to push away no matter how much I try. It complicates everything, makes this entire situation a tangled fucking mess. But a large part of me doesn't even care because I don't think I've ever been so attracted to *anyone* before.

"We should probably… practice?" she breathes, her eyes dropping to my lips as she speaks. "Right? That's why we're here?"

"We can do whatever you're comfortable with, Addie. It's your decision."

Her throat bobs as she swallows roughly, her gaze lingering on mine, and then she nods. "Yes. I-I think we should."

Thank fuck. I want to kiss her so badly that everything inside me *physically* aches, but if she wasn't comfortable with it, I would've waited forever. If that's what she needed.

"I have an idea. About…" I rasp as I gently reach for her fingers and intertwine them in mine. "*Practicing*."

She nods, biting that plump little rosy lip, gazing up at me with wide eyes.

Stepping back, I lead her back to the blanket and gently pull her down beside me.

"I think the only way to make you more comfortable… is for *you* to feel in control. Your consent is everything, Addie, even if this is just an arrangement. I will never touch you without your permission." Lifting her hand, I bring it to my face and place it along the curve of my jaw. "I want you to touch *me* first. Until you no longer feel nervous or anxious. Is that okay?"

"Yes," she whispers in a rush of breathless words, whether from nerves or anticipation, I can't tell, but I stay still, waiting for her to make the next move. "Yes. It's okay."

My gaze is steady on her as she lifts a shaky hand and tentatively sweeps the pad of her thumb along the edge of my jaw before trailing her fingers to my lips and ghosting them across. The barest of caresses, yet I still feel my spine stiffening and my breath catching in my chest.

Her fingers trace my bottom lip softly, and I watch as her

eyes shift down to where her fingers meet my mouth, and she swallows roughly.

I'm not sure if she's even noticed that she's leaned in, closer and closer with each brush of her fingers. Her hand moves lower until it's resting along my jaw, and then she slides it to my neck, to the back of my nape, gently tangling her fingers in the hair there.

A shiver races down my spine, and an audible hiss tears from my lips before I can stop it, causing her to pause and glance up at me.

"Is this okay?" she asks so softly that it's almost a whisper.

I nod, remaining silent because I don't trust myself to speak right now.

"Would you... kiss me?" she breathes so quietly that I almost miss it. "Like you did at the chapel?"

My eyes land on hers, her eyes sparkling with trust. "You want me to kiss you again, Addie?"

Rolling her lip between her teeth, she nods. "Yes."

Now it's me who swallows roughly, my throat working as I bring my hand to her face, cradling her jaw tenderly in my palm. When I lean in, our gazes locked, I feel her fingers tightening in the hair at my nape as if she's anticipating this almost as much as I am.

There's no way that she doesn't feel *whatever* this is between us.

It's like every cell in my body is screaming to kiss her, and I know at this exact moment that I'm hopeless in my pursuit to deny this pull.

Gently, I tug her closer until we're only centimeters apart, both of us breathing heavily until my lips *finally* touch hers... a crescendo of longing that finally peaks. I move my lips over hers gently at first, unhurriedly committing what she feels like to memory. Each movement is deliberate, a languid exploration that we weren't afforded the first time.

My tongue traces the seam of her lips, tasting her, savoring her until her lips part and her fingers tighten further in my hair. A quiet whimper escapes as I pull her even closer and slide my tongue into her mouth, kissing her the way I've been dreaming of since we stood at the altar.

Since I made her my wife.

Every sweep of my tongue along hers feels more intense, a buzzing beneath my skin that only she seems to ignite, and I'm completely drunk off the feeling.

Drunk off *her*.

She pulls back, panting as she gazes up at me with hazy, unfocused eyes. "Was it okay? Am I-I… doing it right?"

I almost fucking groan at her question, so sweet and innocent. Instead, I pull her back to me, both of my hands on her neck, thumbs caressing her cheeks, and murmur against her lips, "Mmm. Too soon to say. Gonna need to try it again. For educational purposes."

I feel her smiling, and then I'm capturing her lips again, slipping my tongue back inside her mouth and gently threading my fingers through her hair as I angle her head to kiss her deeper. It still isn't close enough.

I want to haul her into my lap and never stop kissing her.

Suddenly, the stadium lights flick on, one after another, illuminating the field and causing us to both stiffen, then jump apart.

Oh shit.

I pulled a few strings to come here tonight, but… that doesn't mean I'm technically *supposed* to be here. I've got a lot of perks being a player, but sneaking into the stadium when it's closed isn't one of them.

With the lights, I get my first true glimpse of Addie since we arrived. Her cheeks are flushed red, her lips swollen and puffy from kissing me while her eyes flare with a mixture of heat and trepidation.

I don't have time to drink in the sight of her as much as I really fucking want to, though, because we're about to get caught.

"Shit," I mutter. Lacing my fingers with hers, I tug her to her feet and pull her toward the dugout. "We gotta run. Like… actually run."

She squeaks, her eyes wide, but she keeps up as we sprint. With her small hand squeezed tightly in mine and her other hand clutching onto her cardigan like a vise, we somehow make it back inside before the security guard, booking it down the hallway.

We run all the way to the truck and tumble inside, both of us breathing hard as I turn on the engine.

After a second of anxious silence, she erupts into giggles, throwing her head back and sinking into the seat. It's the sweetest sound, her laughter, and I realize just how much I love it. How it might just be the best sound I've ever heard. Maybe my favorite. And then, we're both laughing until tears form in our eyes from the exertion.

"That was scary but also kind of exciting? I've never in my life done anything like that before," she mumbles once she can finally breathe. When she looks over at me, there's the cheekiest smile tilting her lips, and it takes everything inside of me not to haul her over the console and kiss her again.

"Sometimes doing something scary makes you feel alive. And we all need to feel alive."

Shyly, she tucks her hair behind her ear and nods. "Thank you for tonight, Grant. It was amazing... All of it."

I bite the inside of my cheek to stifle my grin and fail. I love teasing her almost as much as I love kissing her. "You trying to tell me you like kissing me, ArtGirl?"

Her cheeks bloom red as she ducks her head and covers her face with her hands. "God, I'm so inexperienced, and it was probably terrible for you. I'm so so—"

I reach out and gently close my fingers around her wrist, tugging her hand down until she looks up at me, stopping whatever nonsense was about to come out of her mouth.

"It was the best fucking kiss I've ever had, Addie. There's no question." And I mean it.

I say nothing else because I want to let what I'm saying fully sink into her. That this kiss has ruined me for all other ones, that I don't even want to think about kissing anyone who isn't her.

Not that I can tell her that, not yet, but it's true.

Finally, she nods, and I give her a smirk as I put the truck in reverse and pull out of the parking spot. We never stop talking the entire drive home.

It's never been like that with anyone in my life, even the guys, and it's a little staggering, if I'm being honest. When we get to the apartment and walk inside, I toe off my shoes and hang my keys on the rack by the door.

Addie hangs her cardigan up and then walks over and sits beside Auggie, who's looking as excited as I've ever seen him. *I get it, Augs. I miss her when she's not around too.* She scratches his ears lovingly, then rubs his chunky belly, wearing an adoring smile that she reserves just for him. His pudgy body vibrates with happiness.

It's easy to forget that besides Earl and Amos... Auggie is her closest friend, and they share a bond that a lot of people never have with their animals. And I'm really happy she has him.

I stretch my arms over my head, a yawn escaping in the process, and she glances up at me, her brow furrowed.

"Crap, I'm on your bed, I'm sorry." She pushes to her feet quickly, but I stop her before she can escape to the bedroom.

"It's okay. I'm just tired from my workout this morning. I've been training harder than I normally do to get ready for preseason. Trust me, I'm in no hurry to hang off that thing all night. Stay as long as you'd like." I wink before disappearing through the entryway to the kitchen for a bottle of water.

I grab us both one and walk back out into the living room, where I find her staring off into the distance, chewing on the tip of her nail, lost in thought.

"You can sleep with me," she blurts out suddenly, her eyes widening in alarm as she starts to backtrack. "No. I mean... literal sleeping. We can share your bed. I-I... I don't want you to have to keep sleeping on this couch. You're too big for it, and it's uncomfortable, and I feel terrible when I get in bed at night and I have to think about you out here on the sofa that makes your back hurt. Especially with your training." She's nervously rambling, and it might actually be the cutest thing I've ever fucking heard. "I mean, *not* that I lay in bed and think about you all night. I just mean when I'm thinking about you out here being uncomfortable. This is coming out all wrong." Finally, she pauses, blowing out an exasperated breath before restarting, this time less rambly. "What I'm *trying* to say is... we're both adults. We can share the same bed platonically. It's literally huge. That way, your back won't hurt anymore, and I won't have to feel guilty about stealing your bed. Easy-peasy."

My brow arches in amusement, and she winces. "Please put me out of my misery because I want to die currently."

I close the distance between us and set the bottles of water down on the table. "Please don't die. I'm way too young to be a widower." When she gives me a small smile, I shoot her a playful wink before my expression sobers slightly. "Addie, if you're comfortable with sharing a bed with me, then great, I'd take you up on it, but also, if you're not and just feeling obligated to offer… There's absolutely no pressure. I'm perfectly fine out here on the couch, or I wouldn't have offered. Besides, Auggie's been sneaking out to sleep with me, and he and I are becoming fast friends, thanks to the spooning."

She shakes her head rapidly. "No. I'm sure. Every night, I feel ridiculously guilty that I've inadvertently kicked you out of your own space, and it's fine… no big deal. We can totally do this."

"Are you really sure?"

"Yes," she says, her voice steady.

"Okay. You go get changed first, and I'll take Auggie out? Give you time to get settled?" I say, glancing over at Auggie, whose ears perk at the mention of his name.

Addie nods and reaches up to tuck her hair behind her ear. She opens her mouth as if she's going to say something but then abruptly closes it and disappears down the hallway into our bedroom.

Thankfully, Auggie's not interested in staying outside in the hot, humid heat, so he quickly takes care of business. I hang up his leash on the rack once we're back inside, watching as he pads back to his signature spot on the sofa and flops down like the outing took every ounce of his energy. When he cocks his head to the side and stares at me with a look that can only be construed as judgy, I shake my head.

"Don't look at me like that. I know exactly what you're thinking." My brow arches. "It'll be fine. I can handle platonically sharing a bed."

Somehow, he looks as if he doesn't believe me. Not sure how that's possible since he's a dog, but then again, here I am having a full conversation with him like he's going to participate.

The real problem though?

I'm not sure if I'm trying to convince *him* or myself.

chapter seventeen

Addie

I'M IN DEEP—*TREACHEROUSLY* deep—trouble.

I realize that fact as I'm standing in front of the counter at the bakery, running my fingers over my lips, absentmindedly thinking about *the kiss.* Which is what I've decided I'm referring to it as from this moment on.

But *the kiss* isn't the sole reason I've found myself in trouble.

No.

It's also the fact that I laid in bed last night beside Grant, close enough that I could feel the heat from his body and the steady rise and fall of his chest, with my heart racing all night until it was almost time for my alarm to go off this morning.

I'm running purely on adrenaline at this point. Yet here I am, still obsessing over kissing my husband.

It's all supposed to be for show, all that we did just for practice. But… if that's true, then why can't I stop thinking about the way his lips felt as they moved against mine? How safe I felt to be in his arms? Or how nice it was to give control over to someone else, even if only for the smallest moment of time?

None of last night felt fake. Not the date, or the kiss, or

falling asleep surrounded by his scent, listening to the rhythmic sound of his breathing beside me.

It was the kiss to end all kisses.

Technically, it was our second kiss. The first being the day we were married, but this kiss felt completely different. Different because it burned… *brighter*. More intensely. I felt the singe of his touch along my skin, the feeling traveling inside my veins until something deep and hot pulled inside my belly…and between my thighs.

A feeling I've never really felt before.

I'm not experienced when it comes to… most things, but I'm not a total prude. I've… touched myself before, explored parts of myself that no one else ever has.

But now, after *the kiss*, I can't help but wonder what it would feel like to be touched by *Grant*.

Hence, the *very* deep trouble that I'm in.

"Cher, you are distracted this morning. What's going on?"

Startling, I glance over to Amos, whose hands are resting on his apron-clad hips, his expression laced with worry.

"Just a little tired this morning, that's all," I reply with a small smile. "I didn't sleep well."

… or hardly at all.

Amos tuts, shaking his head so hard that the little beads in his gray ponytail clink together. "Go home. You deserve a break. I've got this. You need rest."

"But I—"

His brow arches. "No arguing with me, cher. Go. You can get a few hours of a nap if you go now. So go. Out. Out."

I blow out an exasperated sigh. I should stay and help. I've got a hundred different things that I can be doing, but instead, I reach behind my back and untie my apron. I know there's no use arguing with him, and as always, he knows me sometimes better than I know myself.

I really could use some sleep. Maybe then I can convince my brain to think about something else besides Grant.

"Thank you, Amos," I murmur as I hang my apron on the hook in the back. "I owe you one. A big one."

I slide my arm around the small of his back, my head dropping to his shoulder as I sink into a hug, reveling in the comfort of his embrace. He holds me close against him, brushing his hand lightly over my hair.

There have been so many changes in my life lately, even if they're not all bad changes, and I could still use the comfort from one of my constants. Lately, it feels like my entire world has been flipped upside down, and I'm left clinging to the small amount of familiarity that I have.

Amos and Earl are that for me.

"This is all I need right here, ma cher," he murmurs against my hair, tightening his hold. "I just want you to be okay. To be happy, to follow your heart no matter the path."

I nod against him. "I'm trying. I am... happier. Now that I no longer have to be around Brent. Although, I've seen him lurking outside when I've gotten here to open the bakery a few times, and it's just... weird. He even sent a text the other day saying that I should pay attention because anyone could be watching. He's acting insane. I'm just so hurt and angry about everything he's done and is *still* doing. I hate even giving him that. He doesn't deserve another thought from me."

"Promise me that if you feel unsafe, you'll call the police. I don't trust him, cher. Not for a damn second. Maybe we should make sure I always get here first in the mornings from now on," he says.

"No, it'll be okay. He won't do anything... he just wants to intimidate me."

Amos looks skeptical but gives me a nod. "Okay, cher. But please be careful. And you're right, he doesn't deserve anything from you, but that doesn't mean that *you* don't deserve the space to work through those feelings, Addie. It's never easy when you've been betrayed by someone, and you have every right to feel it all. Give yourself time to feel. To purge them. Healing is not linear. Remember that, okay?"

When his arms tighten around me, I sigh and nod against his shoulder. He makes it seem so easy when it feels anything but. "You always give the best advice. You know that?"

His deep chuckle vibrates between us. "Comes with old age. When you've been around as long as I have, it comes naturally. Wait and see, cher. Now, go on and get some rest, and I'll see you in the morning."

With one last squeeze, I drop my arms and step back.

"Oh," Amos exclaims, lifting his finger to make me pause. He brushes past me and picks up a to-go box. The clear plastic on top is fogged over, which tells me that it's fresh. "Put some breakfast together for your new beau. He's got a sweet tooth like you, I noticed."

My cheeks burn as I take the box from him. "It'll make his day, I'm sure... Thank you."

Auggie greets me the second I step through the front door of the apartment. He's more energetic than normal, probably because he smells the box of goodies that are most definitely not for him, even though he tries to sweet-talk me with those cute little eyes.

"Good morning, Augustus," I murmur, squatting down and petting the soft fur on the top of his head. "These are not for you, but I promise to feed you in just a minute. Okay? Sorry, big guy."

Sometimes, I swear he's part human, almost as if he can understand what I'm saying, because in response, he grumbles unhappily and marches toward the couch, hops onto the cushions, and settles in for a nap. Apparently, Grant's couch is his new favorite napping spot.

"Grumpy old man," I mutter to myself as I turn and round the corner to the hallway. I'm halfway to the bedroom when the bathroom door opens and Grant steps out, steam billowing from behind him in a thick cloud.

He's. Completely. Naked.

I wish I could say that I didn't let my gaze linger, that I didn't drag my eyes slowly down his hard, glistening body, drinking in every rivulet of water as it slid down his skin.

But I did. Frozen at the sight of him.

My fingers tighten on the box in my hands as I struggle to breathe. He... I...

Holy. Cannoli.

Logically, I know Grant is an athlete, and it's not the first time I've seen him shirtless, but seeing him *completely* naked... I'm actually speechless.

Mostly because I'm in shock because he's naked. And because of how incredibly built he is.

And because of the dull throb that begins to form between my thighs once again, an unfamiliar ache that pulses through me.

My gaze follows the water that drips down the center of his

chest, along the space between the sculpted muscles of his abdomen, and further down the trail of hair that leads to…

Oh my god.

His dick… is hard and *so* big that my eyes almost pop completely out of my head. It's only then I realize that I've been ogling him for an embarrassing amount of time, so distracted that I almost crushed the box of beignets in my hands.

"I'm so sorry, oh my god," I cry, lifting the box to cover my eyes so I don't have to meet his because I am so mortified I might actually die. Right here with a handful of baked goods after an eyeful of my husband's monster penis.

Now would be a good time for the floor to open up and swallow me whole.

"I—" I'm panicking and searching for the right thing to say and coming up empty. "I'm home early. I mean, obviously, I'm here early. I, uh… here, I brought you these."

With my eyes squeezed shut, I thrust the box of beignets in his direction as a low, gravelly chuckle fills the air around us as he takes it from me.

"Addie… it's okay," he murmurs quietly, and I squeeze my eyes shut tighter in response. One, so I'm not at all tempted to open them and look again, and two, because… I'm seriously so embarrassed.

Shaking my head rapidly, I mumble, "I'm sorry, that was incredibly rude of me to… gawk like that. I'm so sor—"

I feel his finger against my lips, and my pulse skyrockets, sending my already racing heart thrashing within my chest. He's touching me… while he's naked…

"It's okay," he repeats, his voice coming from a respectable distance. "I thought you'd be working a full shift this morning, and I forgot my boxers. I'll make sure I'm better about grabbing them before I shower, just in case. But I'm your husband… seeing me naked is totally fine. Completely. No big deal."

Is he trying to convince me or himself?

I swallow roughly as I nod. "Yep. Totally."

My words come out as a squeak, and I hear him laugh again. "Let me get changed. I'll be right out."

A beat passes, and then I hear the bedroom door shut. My lungs finally deflate, and I fall back against the wall, finally opening my eyes again and dropping my head back against it.

I cannot believe that just happened.

I can't believe I just… saw Grant naked.

Or that he's working with an actual monster in his pants.

And that I'm currently pressing my thighs together at the mental picture that's never ever leaving my brain.

This is bad. So. So. Bad.

I am so in over my head, and now I'm lusting after my husband, which is a problem that I did not prepare for.

Abandoning my spot along the hallway, I walk into the kitchen, grab a drinking glass from the cabinet, and turn on the faucet with a slightly shaky hand, filling it to the brim.

Then, I chug all of it.

As if staying hydrated is going to help the monumental mess that I've found myself in.

"You good?"

Grant's deep, gravelly baritone comes from the entryway of the kitchen, and I set my empty glass in the sink before turning to face him.

Thankfully, I can breathe more normally since he's now dressed in a pair of dark gray sweatpants and a loose T-shirt bearing the Hellcats Baseball logo. His hair is still damp from his shower, and he's got it pushed messily off his face as he grins playfully down at me. "Stop freaking out. It's okay. I promise."

I groan, dropping my head in my hands. "It doesn't feel okay. I'm mortified, Grant. I invaded your privacy, and I feel like I can't look you in the eye ever again."

Grant closes the distance between us and gently wraps his arms around me, pulling me into his warmth. My hands connect with his strong chest as I keep my face buried behind my palms.

Great… and now I'm imagining him naked again. Did I ever really stop?

"Would it make you feel any better if I saw you naked?" he counters with a smirk.

"Oh my god. No!" I blanch, freezing in his hold. "No, it wouldn't. In fact, I think it would be inherently worse."

His chest vibrates with laughter as he pulls me tighter to him. Even though I'm on the cusp of a shame spiral, I can still admit how nice it feels to be in his arms. I feel safe.

The truth is that I'm only *slightly* embarrassed over seeing him naked. It was an accident, I know. It's the thoughts that I'm still having, the ones that I can't admit to him, that are making this such a big deal.

The fact that I'm… *turned on*, and it's not like I can just blurt that out as if it's nothing.

"Well, we have to live together and continue being married, so *eventually*, you're going to have to look at me again," he teases. Finally, I glance up at him and realize that he's just entirely too attractive to look at when I'm feeling so… *flustered*, so I duck my head and bury my face into the front of his shirt again.

"Debatable," I mutter against the fabric.

His chest shakes with another laugh, and he pulls back, then tips my chin up, dragging my gaze to his. The deep blue of his irises seems to blaze as he says, "Trust me, ArtGirl, I'd be having very different thoughts if the roles were reversed. Don't worry about it."

My heart is pounding so hard that I can hear my pulse thrumming in my ears.

And by that, he means…

When his brow arches and his eyes darken, I put it together quickly, but before I can say anything, he speaks again.

"I was thinking we could go to Jack's for dinner? My teammates are harassing me to meet you, and it's the best place on campus." He pauses, reading my confused expression. "If we wanted to be seen acting married in public. Which we do. What do you think?"

"Yes. Sounds good. I, uh… I'll be out of class by four. Should I meet you there?"

Grant nods as he begins to slightly loosen his arms from around me, "Yep. If you get there before us, save us a table and order whatever you like. I've gotta head out for an early workout and then practice after class, but I'll see you later?"

Nodding, I step back and clutch the counter behind me as I watch him grab a bottle of an electrolyte drink from the fridge and a packet of preworkout out of the container by the table.

When he walks across the room and grabs his bat bag that's leaning against the wall, he looks back over his shoulder with a grin. "Oh, and ArtGirl? Try not to spend the rest of the day thinking about your *husband* naked, 'kay?"

Then, with his trademark wink, he walks out of the kitchen like he didn't just cause the fire in my cheeks or the uncontrollable flutter of butterflies in my stomach.

I'm a complete nervous wreck as I walk into Jack's Pizza for dinner later that evening. Mostly because I've had the entire day to replay this morning's disaster and to psych myself out about tonight.

I realize that it's not that huge of a deal, meeting Grant's friends for the first time. But this is *also* the first time we've been out in public together, trying to convince everyone that we're a real married couple, and I'm just worried that I'm going to do something to mess it up. That I'm going to be the reason that this entire plan comes crashing down.

But I square my shoulders and attempt to push away my nerves as I pause near the hostess stand.

The restaurant is completely packed. All of the fifties-style booths and tables are full of people, loud and animated as they share huge pizzas and Jack's signature sundaes. As I scan the restaurant, I notice a few familiar faces from class and find myself hoping that no one recognizes me.

I'd be more surprised if they *did* though.

Pretty much all of my teen and college years have been spent perfecting the art of blending in, doing whatever I could to not draw attention to myself, and that's the way I've always wanted things.

But suddenly, it feels like an impossible feat. Now that I'm married to Grant, someone everyone notices—even from the other side of the room, I spot him and his friends at the back corner booth. Not because they're the loudest group in here, which they are, but because everyone's attention seems to gravitate toward them. Girls walk over, twirling their hair and batting their eyelashes as they flirt, and the thought of one of them flirting with him causes something unfamiliar to stir in my gut.

Is that jealousy?

The feeling takes me by surprise because it's one that I've never experienced before when it comes to a guy, but I guess it's another first I've experienced since meeting Grant.

Even so, it's still a feeling that settles heavily in the pit of my stomach. One that I don't like.

Crossing the busy restaurant, I make my way toward the table in the back, and when I stop in front of it, Grant's piercing blue eyes flit to mine. The smile that spreads on his face makes it impossible not to mirror with my own. I couldn't stop my smile even if I tried. He looks happy to see me, and that does something funny to my chest.

My earlier nerves seem to wilt away, just like that, and all I can focus on is the man in front of me.

"Hey, baby," he rasps, sliding out of the booth and sidestepping the girl who was desperately trying to get his attention. The smallest sliver of satisfaction runs through me as he does.

Baby.

That's new. I think maybe I like hearing it even more than ArtGirl.

"Hi," I reply quietly, reaching up to finger the end of the braided pieces of my hair as he peers down at me with his lopsided grin.

His large palms settle on my hips and then slide along my lower back, gently tugging me to him at the same time his lips slant over mine for a kiss. He kisses me like he's... marking his territory in some way. And I think that I *like* it.

Letting him... claim me like this.

It's the hottest thing I've ever experienced.

His fingers press into my skin as he groans against my mouth hungrily, tilting his head slightly to deepen the kiss. When I feel the trace of his tongue along the seam of my lips, asking me to open to him, my knees feel like they might actually give out.

How is it even possible that he *kisses* this good?

Not that I have anything else to compare it to, but still, I know it can't get better than this. It's all-consuming, and every inch of my body feels like it's on fire. It makes me wonder, if he's this good at kissing, what other things he must be good at. My cheeks burn yet again at the thought.

When his friends begin whistling and catcalling from the table, he groans against my mouth and then tears his lips away, leaving me breathlessly staring up at him.

His gaze lingers on my eyes for a moment before he drops down to my lips for one more quick peck and then leans in and brushes his lips along the shell of my ear, inciting a shiver down my spine. "I wish you could see what I do right now. You, thoroughly kissed by your husband. Those pouty, pretty little lips, swollen and red. Your cheeks flushed my favorite shade of pink. You look like a piece of *art*, Addie."

If I wasn't already about to melt into a puddle of mush at his feet, I am now. I bite back a smile as I glance up at him through my lashes.

I keep telling myself that this is supposed to be fake, but it's the moments like this when everything feels too real. It's both confusing and exciting, a hundred different emotions running through my head.

None of them are close to the feeling that pulls in my belly. A fire that he's somehow started with nothing more than a brush of his lips. It's dangerous because I know that if I'm not careful... I'm going to get burned.

"Guys, this is my wife, Addie," Grant says to the table of

guys in front of us, lacing his fingers in mine and squeezing reassuringly. "Be respectful, or I'm beating your asses."

My smile is shy as I lift a hand and wave. I feel like I'm a new student standing in front of the classroom and having to introduce myself. "Hi. Nice to meet you all."

There's a chorus of hellos as everyone begins to greet me and offer their name, but honestly, I don't remember a single one… except Davis, since we'd already met. He gives me a flirty wink when it's his turn to introduce himself and says, "If you ever get sick of this guy and want a man to treat you right, you know where to find me."

Grant tenses beside me, and the only way to describe the look on his face is murderous, so I tighten my fingers in his. When he looks down at me, I surprise even myself when I rise on my tiptoes and press a sweet, quick kiss to the corner of his mouth. Apparently, I'm not the only one who's been feeling jealous.

Rightfully or not.

After the introductions, I move to slide into the crowded booth next to Grant, but he wraps his arms around my waist and settles me into his lap instead, tossing me a playful grin. "You've got the best seat in the house, baby."

For the second time tonight, the term of endearment has my pulse racing. I keep reminding myself that this is all for show, that we're just playing the part that we said we would, but this man is the best actor I've ever seen. He plays his role effortlessly, without a single ounce of hesitation, so well that even *I* start to believe it.

"You like that?" he whispers into my ear when the guys get into a heated debate about whether cheerleading is considered a sport or not. Spoiler alert: it is.

I'm quiet for a second as I consider the answer.

"Yes," I admit. "I do. It's… sweet." When I shift slightly in his lap, he sucks in a sharp breath, tightening his arms around me, causing me to freeze. "What? What's wrong?"

"If you keep wiggling in my lap, every guy at this table is going to see how hard I get for my wife," he whispers against my ear, the deep, gravelly baritone sending another involuntary shiver down my spine.

Oh my god.

Before I can respond, one of his teammates interrupts. "Grant, you want us to leave so you can have a date with your girl? 'Cause it feels like we're intruding."

The other guys snicker, each of them giving Grant a hard time until he shakes his head. "You mean *my wife*? She's not just some girl, Heath."

"Ohhhh, you heard the man. That's his wife. Put some respect on it." The dark-headed guy beside Heath elbows him in the side, resulting in a smack on the back of the head from Heath in return.

The entire exchange has me grinning, and when Davis notices, he tosses me another wink before adding, "Stop giving my man shit, y'all. Clearly, he's in love and happy. Let him be."

It seems that way—with how well Grant handles all of this, he makes it so easy to believe that he's in love, that this marriage isn't just a means to an end.

Shortly after, pizza is delivered to the table, thankfully none with pineapple, and we all dig in.

"Mmm, lemme taste yours?" Grant asks after devouring his slice in 2.5 seconds flat. The one thing that never ceases to amaze me is the man's ability to eat. He's like a bottomless pit, and I truly do not understand where it all goes. He's the most fit guy I've ever seen, and apparently, everything he eats goes straight to his muscles.

My brow arches. "You want *mine*? You've got an entire pizza right there."

His shoulder dips as he nods. "Yeah. But I'm fucking starving, and yours looks way better. What is it?"

"It's veggie."

I hold it out to him, and he takes a giant bite, licking away the excess sauce that clings to his lips while he chews. When he's finished, a playful smirk curves his lips. "I guess it tastes better because it's yours, baby."

The way he holds my gaze, his eyes darkening, it feels like we're not even talking about *pizza* any longer.

Once we've finished eating, Grant excuses us, and I say goodbye to all of his teammates, feeling much better. Tonight went way better than expected, and I'm feeling less nervous about the situation as a whole.

Only now… I'm feeling on edge. Tense. Completely wound and pulled taut.

After spending the night seated in Grant's lap, his fingers brushing delicately along my skin, his breath fanning hotly along my neck, a hundred little touches that have somehow surmounted into something much bigger, I'm nearly squirming in my seat as we pull up to the apartment.

He shuts off the engine, then opens his door and rounds the truck to open mine, offering his hand. Always the gentleman. When my palm slides against his, it feels like a current of pent-up electricity hums between us, and I wonder if he's as affected by tonight as I am.

It seems impossible that he couldn't be when the tension in the air feels so… *tangible*.

"Hey, Auggie man," Grant coos when we walk through the front door of the apartment, and I use the moment to escape into the kitchen for a bottle of water that I'm hoping will help the erratic pounding of my heart.

Twisting the top from the bottle, I bring it to my lips and take a gulp, hurriedly sucking the water down when I feel heat behind me, followed by the sound of Grant's low, gravelly voice invading my ear.

"You okay?"

A shiver catches my spine at his close proximity, a strange heat flooding my lower belly. His hands bracket the fridge in front of me, caging me in, and if he stepped any closer, he'd be pressed against me.

"Yes." My voice comes out steadier than what I feel, and it surprises even me. As I shift from one foot to the other, my thighs rub together, the friction catching me so off guard that my breath hitches audibly.

I feel Grant's breath on my neck, gliding along my skin like a caress. "You sure? You seem a little... jumpy."

Ducking beneath his arm, putting much-needed distance between us, I turn toward him and plaster on a smile. "Y-yep. Uh... I'm just going to go shower. Right now."

He laughs low and slow, and I'm nearly panting. "Cool. I'm going to hang out with Auggie for a bit, catch up on some game highlights. I'll be in later."

I muster a nod and then all but sprint from the kitchen to the bedroom. I desperately need a moment to collect myself.

Although I have a feeling that there's nothing that could help except the one thing I can't have.

My husband.

chapter eighteen

Grant

THINGS I SHOULD CURRENTLY *NOT* BE DOING:

1. Thinking about my wife in the shower, naked and soapy.
2. Number one *again*.

Groaning, I drop my head back against the couch cushion and adjust my rising cock in my gym shorts.

Again.

I'm fucked, and I'm only now beginning to realize just how badly.

I told Addie I'd come to bed later because I wanted to watch game highlights, but the truth is, I'm trying to get my shit together. Ever since that damn kiss, then spending the entire night with her in my lap, I've been attempting to direct my thoughts back to safe territory.

Usually, I'm the kinda guy with an abundance of control, but when it comes to her... I feel that control fraying until there's virtually nothing left.

Which is why when she went to shower and go to bed, I

opted to stay on the couch with Auggie, blankly staring at the TV in hopes that I could focus on something other than the thought of her sweet little ass squirming on my lap. And the taste of her pouty lips.

Clearly, that plan is fucked because it's the *only* thing I've been able to think about.

I reach for my phone and open the text thread with Reese and Lane. They've unsurprisingly been texting nonstop since I called them both out of the blue to drop the bomb that I got married… to a girl they've never met.

> Reese: I'm gone for like a second, and Grant gets fucking married. Without us. And invited fucking Davis to be his best man? I don't think I'll ever recover from this type of betrayal.

> Lane: I'm just annoyed that I wasn't the first one to get married.

> Reese: Even Boo is offended that she wasn't invited to her uncle's wedding. We could have dressed her up to be the flower girl.

> Reese: SMH

I ignore the messages and quickly type out what's been on my mind for the night.

> Grant: I think I might be fucked.

> Reese: And you think that…why? I was just kidding dude. I'll forgive your shotgun wedding. You know you'll always be my bestie.

> Lane: *eye roll* What happened?

> My fingers hover over the screen for only a second.

Grant: I want to fuck my wife.

Grant: Clearly, this was not part of the plan.

Reese: Not really seeing a problem here?

Lane: For fuck's sake Reese. The problem is that this is supposed to be a mutually beneficial arrangement between the two of them. Which means he's supposed to be keeping his hands to himself.

Grant: Exactly, and since that seems to be becoming a problem, I'm realizing that I might be really fucking fucked.

Reese: Why can't you just... Idk, have a "friends with benefits" kind of thing?

Lane: Because that shit always complicates things.

Reese: Yeah, well what's wrong with a little complication? That worked out for you and Hallie. And, look how great Viv and I turned out.

Grant: Subjective.

Reese: Shut up. All I'm saying is if you want her, then go for it.

Lane: Possibly the worst advice in history. But, then again, Grant's usually the one giving the advice so...

Before I can respond to their messages, there's a loud thud against the bedroom wall that causes me to freeze. My brows pinch as I glance up at the door, wondering what happened.

Shit, what if Addie slipped in the shower? Immediately, I'm on edge, listening for any sign of distress. And then... a few seconds later, it happens again. And then... again.

I toss my phone down onto the cushion and jog over to the

closed bedroom door, pressing my ear against it and listening intently. I feel like a creep, but I just want to make sure she's okay and doesn't need me.

It's not like we aren't technically sharing the bedroom now anyway.

But when I hear Addie's strangled voice crying out *my* name for help, I don't hesitate for even a moment.

I wrench the door open and burst inside, skidding to a complete halt when I see her sprawled out on the bed, her soft blonde hair spread around her like a halo, wearing nothing but an oversized T-shirt that falls around her hips. Hips that are writhing on the pillow stuffed between her legs. She lets out a frustrated sigh and groans, still not realizing I'm even here.

Motherfucking god.

Is…

Suddenly, Addie stills, her eyes popping open, revealing pools of inky blue as they notice me in the dim light of the lamp.

"*G-Grant*? Oh my g—" Her voice is low and hoarse, barely recognizable as she yelps, then scrambles to jerk the blanket over her. "I… I…"

Sweet, innocent Addie was… getting herself off. In *my* bed.

And she said *my* fucking name as she did it.

I'm frozen in place, my feet glued to the floor as if they've become a permanent fixture on the hardwood. I should look away, or… I don't know, leave, but I can't seem to bring myself to do it. Not when I know that it was *my* name she was saying as she was trying to make herself come.

"Addie…" I murmur hoarsely. "I thought something was wrong. I'm sorry, I shouldn't have…"

I trail off when she disappears beneath the covers, pulling the comforter up so high it covers the top of her head. Walking around the foot of the bed, I sit at the edge of the mattress, gently pulling down the covers to reveal her pretty face. Her cheeks are bright red as she squeezes her eyes shut tightly, avoiding looking at me at all.

"I shouldn't have busted in without knocking. I'm sorry, I just... I was worried and thought you needed me."

She groans, bringing her hands to her face, hiding from me further behind her slender fingers. Something I know she does when she's really embarrassed, but she shouldn't be. If only she knew how fucking hard it makes me to think about her touching herself... thinking of *me*. I wish she knew how beautiful she looks right now, with her cheeks flushed and her chest still heaving from exertion. So beautiful it makes me physically ache with the need to touch her.

Maybe then she wouldn't question herself for a second longer.

Which is why I decide to not hold back. I say exactly what I'm thinking, consequences be damned.

"What do you need, Addie?" My voice is so husky it surprises even me.

Her body tenses as she drops her hands from her face, peering up at me with hesitant eyes. "W-what do you mean?"

"What were you doing when I walked in?"

I watch as her throat works and her nostrils flare as she sucks in a shaky breath, holding my gaze on her steadily. I already know what she was doing, but I want to hear it from *her* mouth. I want her to tell me that she was trying to make herself come with my name on her lips.

I *need* to hear her say it.

"You don't have to be embarrassed or ashamed of anything with me, Addie. Ever." My voice comes out rougher than I intended as my hands ball into fists to stop myself from reaching for her.

After what feels like the longest stretch of time, she finally nods. She pulls her lip between her teeth before blurting out, "I… was… touching myself."

Fuck. Fuck. Fuck.

I can feel my dick throbbing to the same beat as my heart. She's not even touched me, but the mental image of her fingers exploring her body with thoughts of me is enough to have my dick straining painfully against the fabric of my gym shorts.

The blush on her cheeks spreads lower until her pinkened skin disappears beneath the collar of the T-shirt, and she ducks her head. "I'm *so* embarrassed."

"You have nothing to be embarrassed about." I reach out, dragging my fingers along her cheeks and brushing her hair back from her face as her gaze snaps to mine. "Not a fucking thing, Addie. I heard you… call out my name."

She gazes up at me with doe-like eyes, "Y-you did?"

"Yeah, baby, I did," I rasp darkly. "Do you have any idea how fucking crazy it made me hearing that?"

Her face softens with a shy smile when I call her baby, and I realize how much she likes the endearment, and I make a mental note to call her that again. As we stare at each other, her pupils expand, turning hazy and unfocused, darkening, her chest rising and falling in rapid succession. It's the only confirmation I need to continue.

I know this is probably crossing a hundred different lines that we created, but right now, I don't have it in me to give a single fuck about it.

"That sweet, frustrated little sigh you made was almost enough to bring me to my knees. Tell me why you were so frustrated?"

Silence meets my question, but her gaze holds mine. I can see the moment she lifts her chin and decides to put it out there. All of it.

"I can't... By myself. I..." She swallows, pulling in a ragged breath. "I can't make myself..."

"Come?" I supply for her.

She bites her lip and nods. "It's... Sorry, it's so humiliating to say that out loud. I can't even make myself... finish."

Unable to stop myself, I reach out and run my fingers softly along her jaw before cradling it in my palm. "That's why you had the pillow?"

Never in my life have I wanted to be a fucking pillow. Until now.

"I thought it might work this time since I've been..." She trails off, tearing her gaze away and dropping it to the chipped yellow paint on her nails.

I tip her chin up, dragging her attention back to me. "Been *what*, Addie?"

"Turned on," she stutters quietly as her gaze lingers on mine. "All... day."

I spent the entire night trying to think about anything other than the feel of her in my lap, the taste of her on my lips, and she was feeling the same thing, fighting the same battle and failing.

I know I shouldn't... but I can't stop myself from dipping my head down to her mouth. I brush my lips gently along hers, pausing when I feel her breath hitch. "Tell me what it feels like." Pulling back, I stare down at her, drinking in her blown pupils, wide eyes, and those pretty pink, parted lips.

She swallows visibly, lifting her hand to trace the curve of my jaw. Her fingers tremble as they ghost along my skin, and a shiver runs down my spine.

"It... *aches*. Like something is pulled tight inside of me that I can't unravel." She murmurs so quietly that I almost miss it, even being only a breath away from her lips. I can feel her panting, her breath fanning along my mouth as her chest moves in rapid succession.

I have to bite the inside of my cheek to hold back the ragged, feral fucking groan that threatens to erupt from somewhere deep inside my chest.

My wife is *aching*.

"It's my *job* to take care of *my wife*," I rasp, brushing my lips against hers. The barest touch that has us both breathing heavily and her fingers digging into the bare skin of my arms. "I took vows. And... I take my vows *very* seriously," I continue, never taking my eyes off her.

Another nod, and then she breathes, "V-very. Grant, would... you... touch me?"

This time, I can't stop the groan, the noise low and deep vibrating from the back of my throat, as I drop my forehead against hers and squeeze my eyes tightly shut. "I want to so fucking bad, baby. You have no goddamn idea how badly I want to touch you... I just... I don't want you to feel like I'm taking advantage of the situation."

I feel her shaking her head, and when I pull back, the serious expression on her face has me momentarily sobering. "You're not. I want you to, Grant. Nothing in my life has *ever* just been mine. I want this moment... to be *mine*. I want to be the one in control. I want to be the one to decide."

Fuck. My throat is tight with need as a mixture of emotion and desire flickers in her eyes.

Who am I to deny my wife? Especially when I want her more than I need to fucking breathe.

"Are you sure?" I ask.

A beat passes, and she nods. "Yes. I just... Could we go slow? With, you know...?"

Even as she tells me she's sure, I hear the vulnerability in her words, the tremble in her voice from nerves. I know she's never done this with a guy before, so I know this is a huge fucking deal to her, and the fact that I'm the one she feels comfortable enough to experience it with has my chest swelling, my heart beating faster than it ever has in my life.

"I know this is fake and we're only pretending…" she adds before I can respond to her question, and I stop her.

"It's not all fake. We're attracted to each other, Addie. We've got chemistry off the fucking charts. I think that much is clear. If we're going to be married, sleeping in the same bed, living our lives together… why can't we explore something physical between us? If that's what you wanted and were comfortable with, then I want that with you too."

"I do," she murmurs breathlessly. "Want this."

"Then let me take care of you." My knee hits the edge of the bed as I slide in beside her, turning to my side. Her back to my front, we're so close I can feel the heat from her body. The oversized T-shirt she's wearing has ridden up, exposing her thighs and the curve of her hip. "I need you to do something for me, baby," I breathe quietly near her ear before slowly dragging my nose down her neck. "Don't think. Close your eyes and trust your *husband*. Can you do that?"

I hook my arm around her waist when she nods, her eyes fluttering closed as I tug her back until she's fitted against my front.

Of course she fits perfectly, as if there was ever the chance that she wouldn't. She fits me like she was *made* for me, and I have to swallow down the tight knot of raw need settling in the base of my throat that's making it hard to breathe.

I remind myself that we're going slow and moving at Addie's

pace. That this is not only her learning her own body but getting comfortable with someone else touching her.

I'd wait forever if she needed me to. Because she's worth it.

I never imagined I'd have the privilege of touching her, no expectations that we'd ever do anything like this.

But somehow, I'm the luckiest fucking guy in the world given permission to do so.

I press my lips along the sensitive spot beneath her ear, a searing kiss along the juncture of her neck and shoulder, one along her nape. She shivers, a needy whimper falling from her lips as she arches, pushing back against me.

"Tell me if you want to stop. At any time," I murmur against her skin.

Her head shakes. "Don't s-stop. Please."

I slide my palm beneath the worn fabric of her T-shirt, trailing the calloused pads of my fingers up the soft skin of her stomach until they ghost along her rib cage. I want to spend the rest of the night learning every inch of her, memorizing every curve of her body, every dip of her creamy skin. Learning what she tastes like, what she feels like as I move inside of her, the sounds she makes when she's on the edge of an orgasm.

But this isn't about my pleasure. It's about hers.

Sliding my hand over the top of hers, I slowly drag them lower until we reach the elastic band of her pale pink panties. They're simple, cotton, and not meant to be sexy. Yet, on her, they are, somehow innocent and erotic at the same time.

When I dip her fingers beneath the waistband, I pause before continuing. "Keep going?"

She nods breathlessly. "Please."

I drag her hand lower, torturously slow, until she sucks in a shaky breath. Her entire body goes taut as her fingers brush along her clit. Even with her hand beneath mine, I can feel the heat from her pussy on my fingers, and I bite back a groan when I feel how wet she already is.

Fuck me.

She's completely drenched, and I want to crawl between her thighs and suck on her clit until her cum's dripping down my chin. As badly as I want to taste her, I want even more for her to know that *she's* the one in control and that she *can* bring herself to orgasm.

I press the pad of her middle finger gently against her clit, inciting a surprised whimper that has arousal jolting through me.

It's the sweetest fucking sound I've ever heard, and I want to be the reason she does it over and over again.

Together, we circle her clit slowly, my movements controlled and purposeful as her head falls back against my shoulder and her lips part on a sigh.

"Just like that," I praise. "There's no rush, baby. Take your time, let it build."

I continue to move her fingers in slow, languid circles, even when her hips begin to writhe, trying to speed things up. Instead, I drag my tongue along the flutter of her pulse and gently nip at her skin while keeping a steady pace, drawing out her pleasure.

Her breathing turns choppy, a sharper intake with each strum of her fingers, her body telling me everything I need to know.

"I…" She pants, squeezing her eyes shut. "Grant…"

Our fingers are coated in her arousal as she begins to pant, the neediest little breaths that have me gritting my teeth in restraint.

Goddamnit, she's a dream. An actual fucking dream, and she feels like mine.

Her hips rock against our fingers, chasing the feeling that has her muscles coiling and her body pulling taut.

I press my lips against her neck, my other hand curling into her hair as a strangled breath rolls off her lips.

"I… I can't-t."

I move her fingers faster, adding more pressure to her clit. "How does it feel, baby? Making yourself come while your husband watches, like a good little wife?"

I don't know if it's that she finally allows herself to let go, if she's finally shut her brain off long enough for her pleasure to take over, or if it's the words I whispered in her ear that do it, but her thighs slam together, her back arches, and she cries out loudly as she comes.

"Grant."

My name is whispered like a prayer from lips that are worthy of divine worship. I'd fall to my knees for her. She draws out my name as her orgasm powers through her, hips writhing with the slowing motion of our fingers along her sensitive clit. Her thighs tremble, and my gaze never leaves her, never falters.

I'm cataloging every breath, every whimper, every moan. Memorizing the feeling of being curved around her, the scent of vanilla and cinnamon surrounding us and making me dizzy.

Gently, I pull my fingers back, resting them along the flat expanse of her lower stomach. I don't want to move a fucking muscle. I want to savor every second of what she just trusted me with.

"Um…" She finally finds her voice, raspy and hoarse from her climax.

"Are you okay?" I murmur.

She nods languidly against my shoulder, sinking further against me. "Yes. I… was I okay? Was I—"

I use my flattened palm to pull her closer to me, burying my face in the spot between her shoulder and neck, planting my lips softly along her heated skin.

"You're perfect. Every single thing about you."

Gently, she turns toward me, peering over her shoulder. "But what about... you?"

My dick has possibly never been so hard in my life. If she moves and brushes her ass against me again, I may actually come in my pants... but this isn't about me.

It never was. It was always about her.

"I'm good, baby. This was about you and only you," I reply simply.

Her gaze lingers on mine for a beat before she nods, then gently turns in my arms until her head is pressed against my chest.

"Thank you. Not just for... that, but for helping me feel comfortable and safe. I-I wouldn't have ever wanted that moment with anyone else."

The sincere tone of her voice washes over me, and I tighten my arms around her, pressing my lips to her hair. "Always."

It doesn't take long for her breathing to slow and her body to go slack as she drifts off to sleep against my chest. I should probably get up, move to my side of the bed. Do anything but hold my sleeping wife in my arms, thinking of how good it feels to do something that blurs the lines between us. That complicates everything.

But I don't. Because nothing has ever felt right the way that Addie does.

chapter nineteen

Addie

STOP THINKING ABOUT IT, *Addie. Just. Stop.*

I tell myself for the hundredth time as I walk through the front door of our apartment after working on my art thesis for most of the afternoon.

Except that's the problem. I *can't* stop thinking about it, and believe me, I've tried.

Can you blame me? My… husband not only looks like some mythological Greek god walking among mortals and is talented at basically everything he does, but he also does this thing with his fingers that should quite literally be *illegal.*

And of course, being the perpetual overthinker that I am, I've been replaying last night over and over in my head and thinking about how there's literally no way that we'll ever be able to go back to the way things were… before. And then there's also the tiny little detail that we didn't actually decide what happens from here, which has my thoughts going in a hundred different directions and making it impossible to focus on anything… other than my husband.

Groaning, I drop my backpack onto the foyer table and bury my face in my hands.

God, what was I thinking?

Oh, that's right… I wasn't. Well, now I'm thinking yet again about Grant's long, ridiculously talented fin—

"Addie?"

My head whips up, my hands dropping to my sides as Grant walks out of the kitchen wearing a cocky smirk and a backward baseball hat that makes my insides turn molten.

Why is that the most attractive thing I've ever seen? A dull throb begins to form between my thighs, and I have to press them together to stifle it.

What is happening to me?

"H-hi," I stutter, then clear my throat and try repeating the greeting. "Hi."

Grant strides toward me, closing the distance between us, and dips down, pressing the softest kiss to the corner of my mouth. I'm so surprised that I don't even have a thoughtful response, and instead, I'm stuck with my jaw hanging slightly open and my cheeks burning yet again.

I wasn't expecting him to be here this evening. I figured he would be working out with the team or out with Davis and the guys. Or… something.

And now, I'm feeling nervous and shy all over again, even though he's… you know… done that thing with his fingers.

"I can practically see what you're thinking from here, ArtGirl." He chuckles, brushing the pad of his thumb along my heated cheeks. "C'mon, let's go eat, and we can… *talk*."

Talking is good.

Great.

Wonderful even.

He turns, disappearing into the kitchen, and I take a single moment to attempt to breathe normally and collect myself before joining him. This is weird, but also *good* weird? I don't know what I'm feeling. Besides… horny, that is.

I feel like I don't even know who I am right now. My body is betraying me in ways I've never experienced, and I'm not sure what to make of *any* of this.

Auggie whines from the floor by my feet, so I crouch down and give him a few scratches before leaving him belly up on the floor.

"Wow. You cook?" I ask as I walk into the kitchen, taking in the fully set table and steaming food already on plates. Apparently, he's full of surprises.

He pours water into our glasses with a satisfied smile, his shoulder dipping nonchalantly. "Sometimes. Growing up, since it was just my mom and I… there were a lot of nights I had to cook when she worked overnights at the ER. I got tired of mac 'n' cheese and ramen pretty quickly, so I watched some YouTube videos and learned the basics. Helps now that I'm on my own. Well, I *was* on my own."

I walk over and sit in the chair beside his, scooting forward as he joins me. I've noticed that when Grant talks about his mom, he gets this look in his eyes, a softness that is reserved just for her. It's clear how important she is to him… and I love that he's not afraid to show his emotions. A lot of people, including myself, have a hard time showing vulnerability, and I just love that about him. And I love that I'm beginning to know these things about him.

"Well, I'm really impressed, and I bet she's really proud of you," I say, picking up my glass and taking a small sip of water before setting it back down on the table. "Not only because you learned to cook. But because you're selfless, kind, and compassionate, Grant."

Usually I'm the one with the incessant blush constantly

staining my cheeks, but this time, a hint of pink colors his, and he grins in response. "Thank you. I just figured that you're probably tired of living off Jack's and microwavable stuff."

"Maybe a littttttle?" I tease, squinching my nose.

His laugh is gravelly as it carries around the kitchen, making my own lips curve into a wide smile.

"That's fair. And plus… I can't keep up these abs if I keep eating pizza every day. It's a tough job. Sacrifices must be made." He brings his hand to his stomach and pats, tossing me a wink.

I try not to let my eyes travel to his T-shirt-covered abdomen, but apparently, when it comes to him, my self-control is nonexistent.

Entirely his fault.

Now that I've seen what's beneath that shirt, I can't help the image that comes flooding back from the day in the hallway where I counted each of those muscles in slow perusal, and suddenly, *I'm* the one blushing.

"We should… *talk*," I blurt out, unable to hold the thoughts in my head inside any longer. "About last night."

God, I probably sound so stupid, but he just nods, leaning in toward me. "We should."

"About what happened."

Grant nods again, his eyes lingering intently on mine.

"W-what did last night… mean for us? Where do we go from here? I feel silly asking that, but my brain hasn't shut off since, and honestly, it's exhausting, and I'm probably doing everything wrong, and I'm second-guessing everything. I know I have no clue what I'm do—"

Grant reaches for me over the table, sliding his big hand along my nape, and pulls me toward him, sealing his lips over mine and swallowing all of my rambling words. They die on my tongue as my eyes flutter shut, and I whimper against his mouth.

Far too quickly, he tears his lips away and peers down at me, heat flaring in his gaze. "Does that answer your question? I want *you*, Addie. Not only because you're my wife but because I can't stop fucking thinking about you. I can't stop replaying how you felt last night or how perfect it was to hear you come apart, for *me*. Baby, I barely touched you. I barely even saw you, and yet it was the hottest thing I've ever experienced."

Me? The girl with absolutely no experience in... any of this? He wants *me?*

His fingers brush tenderly along my nape as he continues, thankfully, because I think I'm too stunned to speak. "If you want to stop, we stop. If you want to keep going, then we'll keep going, but it's your decision. You tell me. But Addie, I do know that I want you—there's no question about it. Not for me. And if you want me too, I don't see why our arrangement, our marriage, can't be mutually beneficial in other ways too..."

A beat of silence hangs in the air between us, but I already know the answer to what he's asking. To what he's *proposing*.

Because I *want* my husband.

Even though I'm nervous and terrified that I won't measure up to what he's used to because of my inexperience. But after last night... I can't deny what I feel with him. I would not only be lying to him but to myself.

"I... want this. *You*, I mean." My voice is a whisper, barely recognizable even to me, and when I lift my gaze back to his, his dark eyes flicker with heat.

"Good," he murmurs. "Then we're on the same page, and thank fuck for that because I've been dying to touch you again."

My heart races in my chest as a shiver passes through me.

"You know what I love?" he rasps, leaning forward and dragging the rough pad of his thumb along my bottom lip with a look that has warmth radiating through my body, heating my insides with nothing more than his molten stare.

"W-what?"

My throat works as he repeats the motion, hunger flaring in his eyes once more.

"That I can tell *exactly* what you're thinking, and you don't have to say a word." He reaches beneath the table and grasps the edge of my chair, hauling it toward him so quickly that I yelp.

I blink, trying to calm my erratic breathing and pounding heart, but the smile he gives me does nothing to help.

"When you're nervous or... turned on, *this* goes wild." His fingers brush along the curve of my jaw, sliding lower until his thumb ghosts over my wildly fluttering pulse. Then, he trails his fingers back to my cheeks as he leans in, pressing soft, featherlight kisses along them before dipping his head to my ear and whispering, "And you turn the prettiest shade of pink, almost as pretty as your perfect little pu—"

My hand flies out, covering his mouth before he can finish his sentence. I feel him smirking against my palm as his brow arches, the corners of his eyes crinkling in amusement.

Oh. My. God.

I fear I might melt into a puddle of nothing in this chair hearing him say something so... filthy.

The only sound in the room is the crackle of the tall candles on the table that are surrounded by our cooling dinner and the harsh sounds of our labored breathing.

His fingers circle my wrist, and he gently pulls my hand away from his mouth, only to press his lips to the racing pulse along the inside of my wrist. The kiss is tender and reverent yet still intensifies my already erratic breathing.

Arousal slides down my spine when his eyes lift to mine, and I can see the want flickering within the depths.

"Does that make your heart race? Hearing me talk about how fucking beautiful you are?" As he speaks, his thumb brushes back and forth along my pulse, and after a moment of trying to gather myself, I nod.

"I… I'm just not used to hearing things like that. I've never been the girl who gets told she's beautiful by a hot…" I catch myself and pause, clearing my throat. "By a guy."

Grant's pillowy lip curls up into a small smirk. "Will you come with me? I want to show you something."

Nodding, I stand, and he reaches out to hold my hand and gently pulls me toward the bedroom.

One second, we were at the dinner table, about to have a meal, and now we're here next to our shared bed, and I'm trying to digest everything that's happening. I'm confused about what we're doing, even more so when he walks us over to the full-length mirror tucked into the corner of the room and stands behind me. I stare into the mirror, my gaze flitting to his, and my brows pinch together.

"What do you see?" he murmurs near my ear, the proximity causing me to shiver involuntarily as I scan my reflection.

I see… a painfully dull girl who's done nothing but excel at being a wallflower for her entire life. It's not that I think that I'm unattractive. I'm just *ordinary*. There's nothing exceptional about me, and that realization is not something I care to admit out loud to him. So I don't answer, instead dropping my gaze to the hard-wood floor beneath my bare feet.

Grant reaches for my chin and tilts my face back up to the mirror, his stormy gaze locking mine in place. "Do you want to know what *I* see, Addie?"

Biting the inside of my lip, I nod silently.

I can feel the warm fan of his breath against the shell of my ear as he speaks, his fingers tenderly tracing my jaw. "I see the most beautiful girl I've ever laid eyes on, and I'm not going to stop proving it to you until you see the same thing that I do."

He slides his hands beneath the hem of my shirt, and I tremble beneath his touch. Not only because of the expected nerves but… with *anticipation*. His stormy blue eyes meet mine through the mirror, and his brow raises in question, asking if he should continue, and I nod.

Inch by inch, he slides my shirt higher with his large hands splayed along my hypersensitive skin, exposing my rib cage, then the cups of my cream-colored bra. There's nothing sexy about the old jersey fabric, but the way that his eyes flare when the swell of my breasts comes into view makes me feel that way.

With only a look, he makes me feel desired in a way I've never felt before.

"I see the most perfect body, one that nearly brings me to my knees," he murmurs, never letting his gaze leave mine. "I see these…" Trailing off, he slides his hands higher, cupping my breasts through my bra, causing my breath to hitch as I halt breathing altogether. "The *perfect* size to fit in my hands. Almost as if my wife was made *just* for me."

My lungs burn with the need to expand, but I'm afraid if I suck in a breath, my legs will give out from trembling.

The throb between my thighs pulses harder when he pulls the cups down, exposing my breasts fully. My nipples pebble from the sudden rush of cool air, and he palms them in his large hands, his thumbs sensually caressing my nipples.

Oh…

My head begins to feel dizzy as he touches my bare skin, more sensitive than ever before, and a hoarse whimper tumbles from my lips before I can stop it.

"I see delicate little nipples that I want to wrap my lips around and suck until they're an even rosier pink. I want to bite and flick them with my tongue just to see if I can make you come that way."

No one has ever spoken to me like this before, and realization rushes through me at how maddening it is. I'm nearly panting as I anticipate what he'll say next. What part of me he'll run his rough hands over. How my body will respond to his touch.

His hands drop before I can protest, and he reaches behind my back and unclasps my bra, letting my breasts spill free. But before he drags the straps down my arms, his gaze meets mine in the mirror, the silent question in his eyes once again.

"Please." My voice wavers. I'm practically begging, and I don't even recognize my own voice as I speak, low and hoarse... full of desperation.

I lift my arms, and Grant pulls my shirt up and over my head, tossing it to the ground by our feet. Then, slipping his fingers beneath the loose straps of my bra, he carefully pulls them down, leaving me in nothing from the waist up.

My heart thrashes inside my chest as he scans my reflection, a look of hunger lingering in his gaze.

I've never felt so exposed, so vulnerable in my life. Completely on display for someone with the power to break me if he chooses.

Yet, I still feel safe. I feel... beautiful and wanted.

He slowly slides his hands up my stomach, creating a trail of fire over every inch of skin that he touches, until he cups my breasts in his palms once more.

My skin feels like it's on fire as he brushes the pad of his thumb over my nipple, whispering roughly, "I never want you to question whether I want you, Addie. I never want it to cross your mind. Just feel what you do to me simply by touching you."

His hips press forward, his erection hard and thick against my back. My lips part on an audible gasp, and my throat works as I attempt to breathe.

It *feels* as big as it looks, and the dull ache between my thighs turns into an incessant pulse of pleasure that throbs in sync with my racing heart. Every breath tightens the pull in my belly, and I'm nearly delirious with the need for him to touch me again... there.

But I'm too... timid to ask. The thought of having to say it out loud is too daunting.

"Feel what my wife does to me." His breath tickles the shell of my ear, and I tremble. "I've never wanted anything as badly as I want you, Addie."

My voice shakes, matching the tremble of my body as I whisper, "Then... have me."

His groan vibrates against my skin, rumbling from his chest. "Baby, you wanted slow. And I'm trying to respect that."

I did say that, but when I said slow... I didn't mean the torturous kind. Now that I know what it feels like to be touched by him, I'm craving... more.

"Maybe not this slow?"

Grant's brows inch together as he holds my gaze through the mirror. "Are you asking for more?"

Shyly, I nod. My teeth graze my bottom lip when he sweeps his thumb across my nipple in an unhurried stroke.

"I'll never deny my wife. If you want more, then that's what you'll get, baby."

The husky, deep baritone of his voice has my thighs clenching, something he immediately notices through the mirror.

Suddenly, his hands fall from my breasts, and he takes a step back, his chest heaving like I've never seen.

"On the bed."

My eyes bounce from him to the unmade bed, and with only a second of a pause, I hurry over and sit on the edge of the mattress.

He walks over to where I'm sitting, his eyes never leaving mine as he reaches behind his neck and pulls his shirt over his head, tossing it aside.

My nipples are tight and aching as I watch him quickly strip down until he's in nothing but a pair of dark gray briefs that leave nothing to the imagination. I swallow roughly at the sight of his erection, hard and straining, pressing against the fabric.

I slide my gaze higher, roving over the rows of sculpted abs, to his broad chest, and finally to his face. His eyes are nearly black as he sits on the bed, leaning back against the headboard.

"Come here, baby."

I'm nearly shaking as I crawl over to him, the soft mattress sinking below my hands. Even though there's no one I'd rather give all of my firsts to, it's still as nerve-racking as it is exciting exploring these things.

When I stop in front of him, he reaches for me, curving a large palm over my hips as he hauls me onto his lap. My thighs fall to each side of his legs, straddling him. Feeling every inch of him pressed against my core, I bite back a traitorous whimper.

"Do you remember how I made you come last night?" he rasps. The pad of his thumb sweeps back and forth along the curve of my hip slowly, and I can't help but shudder as I peer down at him with unfocused eyes.

When I nod, he says, "I want you to make yourself come on my cock."

Oh god.

I glance down at my skirt, which is bunched around my hips now, exposing the pale yellow satin of my panties. Grant's hands move to my thighs, and he slowly inches the fabric up, higher and higher, until the only barrier between us is my underwear and his boxers.

"I… I don't know how." My voice is barely a whisper, and heat rushes to my cheeks at having to admit that.

He slides his palms to my hips and rocks me slowly over him until I'm gasping at the sensation. "Just like this."

"Oh," I choke out when my clit drags over his erection through our clothes. The feeling is… like nothing I've ever experienced. It's nothing like touching myself or using the pillow. It doesn't come close to how good it feels with his hands gripping my hips, rocking me over him.

I'm embarrassingly wet, and when I glance down, I see the damp spot I'm leaving on his briefs. My nails dig into his chest as he guides my hips slowly back and forth in a steady, languid rhythm that nearly drives me to insanity.

My eyes flutter closed, and I lose myself in the sensation until I feel his thumb dip beneath the fabric of my panties as he pulls them to the side, forcing my eyes to snap open. When they land on him, his pillowy lips are parted, and his hungry gaze is fixed on my core, watching me, devouring me with his eyes.

"You have no idea how fucking pretty you are. Fuck, I can't wait to eat you. I want you to sit on my face until I can't fucking breathe, baby."

His filthy words wash over me, stroking something inside of me that I never knew existed, and I buck my hips harder over his length. This time, the head of him rubs against my clit roughly, and a whimper rakes out of me.

"Mmm, does my wife like when I talk dirty to her?"

I can only manage a moan of approval as I rotate my hips with the guidance of his hands.

"I can tell you do by the way you're soaking my cock. Look at the mess you've made." I follow his gaze down to where we're fitted together and see now that the front of his boxers is completely soaked with the combination of us.

I bite back a moan and exhale shakily. His dirty mouth, the feel of him pressing against my clit, his hands at my hips, it's all too much. I'm already... close.

My muscles coil and tighten as I roll my hips, chasing the feeling.

Grant sits up and flexes his dick against me at the same time his mouth closes gently around my nipple, sucking it into his mouth. A ragged, hoarse whimper breaks free as I slide my arms around his neck and tangle my fingers into the short hair at his nape, holding him to me.

He rolls my nipple between his teeth, a new, foreign sensation of pain and pleasure that my body can hardly process.

"Grant. Oh... God. That. Th—"

The room echoes with a pop of his mouth pulling free, and he stares at me heavy-lidded, his chest heaving at nearly the same pace as my heart, a frantic beat that has my head swimming.

Light dances along the corner of my vision as he slides his arms around my back and holds me to him, flexing his hips as I search for my release.

"I'm..." I barely get the words out of my mouth as I detonate, my eyes slamming shut, my head falling back as my entire body seizes with climax. My legs tremble at the blinding intensity, wave after wave rocking my entire body until it feels as if every ounce of pleasure has been wrung from me.

Grant groans jaggedly against my chest, and I pry my eyes

open, watching as the muscles of his abdomen contract, his hips jutting against me as he comes.

It is absolutely the most intimate thing I've ever experienced in my life… and by far the hottest.

He continues to slowly rock his hips against me, drawing out the last of his orgasm. We're a mess, covered in a combination of the both of us, a sight that I never imagined could be this… sexy.

The only sound in the room is our labored breathing, a mixture of heavy pants and our attempts to control them.

Grant's mouth hovers over my sweat-slicked skin, pressing a path of kisses upward until he reaches my lips. His tongue sweeps inside my mouth, tangling with mine, until I have to tear myself away to suck in a ragged breath.

His lip twitches. "Sorry, I couldn't wait another fucking second to kiss you."

"Then by all means… Maybe you should do it again?" I respond in a low, sultry murmur.

And so he does.

chapter twenty

Grant

I CAN COUNT on one hand the number of times I've been inside the campus library, and today is one of them.

Not that I'm here to study. I'm only gracing the OU library with my presence to see Addie.

When she texted me this morning that she was going straight to the library after working her shift at the bakery, I wanted to make sure she ate something.

At least that's what I'm going to tell her. Because I can't admit that I just wanted to see *her*. I was so exhausted that when she crawled out of bed this morning at her normal 3:00 a.m. time, I didn't even stir.

I can't tell her how much I've gotten used to waking up beside her for the last couple of weeks or how much I look forward to spending our mornings together while she does yoga or we cook breakfast.

I can't admit any of that... not when this is supposed to be fake. The problem is that every day that passes, it begins to feel less and less like an arrangement and more like something different entirely.

Strolling past the circulation desk, I grin at the librarian and raise my hand in a quick wave as I make my way toward the back of the building. This place is way bigger than I remember, but then again, it's not somewhere I've frequented in the four years I've been at OU.

My phone vibrates in my pocket, and when I pull it out, there's a message from Addie.

Wifey: In study room 12.

My lips curve into a grin as I pocket it and continue walking to the back, where the signs direct me to the secluded row of individually numbered rooms. They're not huge, but big enough for a desk, a few chairs, and a large whiteboard. The top part of the walls is glass and the bottom a blackened-out partition that matches the door.

I had no clue these existed, yet another testament to the fact that I haven't spent any time here, but I'm not in the least bit surprised that my wife knows about them since she's the kind of student that every college dreams of.

I find her in the very last room in the corner, her head bent over her textbooks, chewing on the end of her pencil as she bobs her head to whatever's playing through her headphones.

She hasn't noticed me yet, so I take a second to admire her. Her hair is down and curly today, with a few tiny little blue flowers threaded within the strands. They match the flowers on her denim dress, and of course, she's got on her favorite Mary Janes. When she smiles down at whatever she's working on, something fiercely possessive blooms within my chest.

I wish she knew just how beautiful she is.

How every time I see her, I'm struck by it, like I'm seeing her for the very first time all over again. No one even compares to her. I just can't fucking believe that we somehow spent the last four years at the same university and never crossed paths.

Quietly, I slip inside and shut the door behind me before

walking over to her. I dip my head down to press a kiss to her head and set the coffee and muffin on the table in front of her.

She glances up from her textbooks, a bashful smile tugging at her lips, and pulls the headphones out of her ears. "Hi."

"Hi, baby." I pull out the chair next to her and sink down into it. "Brought you coffee and breakfast. Figured you probably didn't stop to eat this morning."

Heat blooms on her cheeks, and she nods, tucking her hair behind her ear. "You would be correct. I... forgot. My head's kind of been all over the place today. Thank you very much."

My brows pinch together at her comment. "What's going on?"

For a second, she's quiet, her gaze flicking between me and the books in front of her, and I realize that something's off.

"Addie, what happened? Talk to me." My voice is laced with concern.

"It's... it's probably nothing. I just, I could've *sworn* that I saw Dixon in the courtyard this morning. But that would be crazy, right?" She pauses, dropping her pencil onto the table and turning toward me before reaching up to rub at her bottom lip absentmindedly. "Since I was fairly certain that I was losing it, I kept walking, especially when I glanced back and saw the person was gone. It just... it left me feeling really weird and paranoid, and I haven't been able to shake it. It's all just too much. Brent has been hanging around a few times when I've gone to open up the bakery, which is insane because it's literally 3:00 a.m.... just watching creepily from his house. And there's those texts that he sent, which he makes seem harmless but feel so... *threatening*."

Before she's even done talking, I reach for her and pull her against my chest, wrapping my arms around her tightly. It better not have been Dixon. I was worried he'd be a problem, but after

Addie texted and told him to never contact her again, he's been a ghost.

"Why didn't you call me? I would've been there in a heart-beat. Addie, you have to tell me this stuff. You can't keep it all in, and I can't protect you if I don't know."

She leans back slightly, peering up at me, "It might not have even been Dixon today. I'm tired and stressed-out about this test, so it could've just been my mind playing tricks on me. I didn't want to make something out of nothing and totally disrupt your day. And with Brent, I mean he's technically not doing anything wrong since he lives next door, it's just unnerving. Even though I knew he'd be watching, hoping to catch us in a mistake."

"Hey, you not feeling safe *is* something. If you think you see either of them again or even feel like something's not right, call me. Or call the campus police and report it. Who knows what they're capable of now that they didn't get their way. Both of them. I'm not taking a chance when it comes to your safety, baby. Promise me you'll call me if you see either one of them. I won't let anything happen to you. Okay?" I assure her, reaching up to brush my thumb along her jaw.

The thought of him potentially being here, watching her, coming within a hundred fucking feet of her, sends a jolt of fury crashing down my spine. I grit my teeth together, my jaw working painfully at the idea.

I'll do whatever it takes to keep this promise to her, even if that means going to that fucker's house and handling this shit myself. Especially after that asshole put his hands on her. He'll never get close enough to make that mistake again.

If he did that with me there, I can only imagine what he'd do if she were alone.

No one touches my wife.

"Okay. I will," she mumbles quietly into my chest. "I promise."

I hold her for a few more minutes, finding comfort in the steady sound of her breathing until she pulls back, finally reaching for the strawberry muffin. "I honestly just want to forget about it. Thank you again for bringing me breakfast. I was planning on starving until lunch so I could get a few extra hours of studying done, so this is very appreciated."

My arms drop, and I sit back in my chair as she starts to pick at the top of her muffin.

"Seriously, text me next time. I can always bring you food or, you know... keep you company while you study." I give her a playful grin, and she smiles.

She gives me her first *real* smile for today, and it causes my heart to skip in my chest like a lovesick teenager.

"You're spoiling me, you realize that?" She giggles sweetly.

I fucking love her smile, but I love her laugh even more.

I stroke my jaw, shrugging as if it didn't make me want to pull her to me and kiss the fuck out of her. "It's my job to spoil you. Let me do it, woman."

Addie rolls her plump, rosy lips together to hide her grin as she drops her gaze down to her lap and fingers the embroidered flowers of her dress.

My favorite thing in the world is when she gets flustered from my attention.

"How's studying going anyway?"

She glances up at the spread of textbooks in front of her and groans before dropping her face into her hands. "It's not? I think my brain is just numb at this point. I've been staring at it for too long."

"Maybe you just need... a *distraction*." I reach for her and slide my palm along her nape, pulling her closer. My lips hover

over hers, close enough that I can almost taste her. "And I just so happen to be excellent at distracting my wife."

Her lips part when I sweep my thumb along her pouty bottom lip, gently tugging it down.

Fuck, she's so pretty.

I love how responsive she is whenever I touch her, how comfortable she's getting with me. Her entire body relaxes, sinking into my touch.

It's the ultimate sign of trust, and I'm so damn thankful that she's giving it to me.

"Should I distract you, baby?" I murmur against her lips, my mouth hovering over hers.

Addie exhales as her eyes bounce down to my lips, then back to my eyes as she swallows. The delicate column of her throat bobbing with the motion. "H-how are you going to do that?"

"Well, I'm going to start by doing this." I close the distance between us, my mouth meeting hers in a kiss that starts gentle but quickly transforms into a frantic clash of our lips. My tongue sweeps into her mouth, and I swallow down the sweetest little whimper that has my cock twitching in my pants.

She reaches up, sliding her arms around my neck, raking her nails along my nape as she kisses me. Our tongues tangle together desperately, growing needier with each passing breath. I nip at her bottom lip, pulling it between my teeth and nibbling until she's writhing in her chair.

That's my cue to touch her.

Tearing my lips from hers, I curve my palms over her thighs, my large hands covering them almost completely. Her soft skin glides along my hands as I move them higher, gently spreading her legs open.

My gaze lifts to her face, and it almost steals my breath.

She's fucking *magnificent*.

Disheveled hair, parted lips red and swollen from my kisses, cheeks flushed pink, piercing blue eyes that are heavy-lidded and dazed as she stares back at me.

She's never looked more beautiful.

And she's never looked more... mine.

The realization rocks through my entire body, making me dizzy with possessiveness. I drag my hands up her thighs until they disappear beneath the hem of her dress, and when they reach the top of her legs, her breath hitches.

"Can I distract you..." I brush the pad of my thumb along the front of her panties, nearly groaning when I feel them already damp. "*Here?*"

Her eyelashes flutter shut as she nods rapidly, her hands flying to the seat of her chair and curling around the edge.

"I need to hear you say it, baby."

"Yes. Distract me." The pleading, needy tone of her voice, along with her consent, is all I need.

Slowly, I pull her panties to the side and dip my fingers beneath the fabric, dragging them along her pussy. It's the first time I've touched her without any barrier between us, and she's already so wet that it slicks my fingers, coating them with her arousal.

"Fuck, baby," I murmur gruffly. "You're already a mess for me."

Her eyes fly open, holding mine as she drags her bottom lip between her teeth to hold back a moan. Finally touching her, feeling her wet heat soaking my fingers, seeing the evidence of her desire on every inch of her face is the hottest thing I've ever experienced.

I'm enthralled by her.

Enthralled by *my wife*.

I sweep my thumb over her swollen little clit once, watching as her knuckles turn white with her tight grip on the chair. She tosses her head back, and the softest, neediest fucking moan tumbles from her parted lips.

A sound I'll never forget as long as I fucking live.

"Does that feel good, baby?"

She nods rapidly, her throat working as she whispers raggedly, "Yes-s."

Chuckling, I rub tight circles on her clit, a slow, languid rhythm. I'm in no hurry—I could stay here all fucking day, watching her like this. I could spend all day making her wet for me.

I'm desperate for a taste of her, so I pull my fingers from her clit and bring them to my mouth. As she lifts her head, her gaze snapping to mine, I close my lips around my fingers, sucking the taste of her off them.

Goddamnit, she tastes just the way I imagined she would. Musky and sweet like strawberries. Like the best thing I've ever tasted.

Her bright blue eyes are wide with surprise as she watches me. I bring my fingers back to her pussy, only this time, I circle her entrance, discovering that she's even more fucking soaked.

"Does it turn you on knowing that I'm fucking obsessed with the way you taste? Because you're so wet for me, baby. Does it turn you on to know that if we weren't in this library where anyone could walk in, I'd lay you out on this table and eat your pussy until you were dripping down my chin and then lick up every drop?"

My favorite pink stains her cheeks, trailing down her neck, and she nods.

"Good, because once you let me taste you there with my tongue, I'm going to do it every fucking chance I get."

I get another little whimper in response, so I slowly push one finger inside, her pussy clamping down around it. Holy fucking shit, she's so goddamn tight. I can barely get my finger in despite how wet she is.

"Oh god." She moans hoarsely. "Grant. That... I—"

"Do you want me to stop?"

Her gaze snaps to mine, and she shakes her head emphatically, "No. No... please don't."

I swallow roughly, praying I don't come in my pants like a fucking teenager from touching her for the first time. I slide my finger deeper, gently hooking it up and easily finding her G-spot.

She grips the chair even tighter and inhales sharply, the tip of her tongue dragging along her bottom lip as I start to stroke her there.

"Have you ever come like this?" I ask, my brows furrowing. When she looks up at me with confusion, I skim my finger along her G-spot again. "Come with something inside you. With your fingers or a toy?"

"N-no. I... I've never been able to make myself... finish that way either."

Fuck. I'm going to be the first time she's ever come from penetration.

Using my free hand, I grasp her by the nape, pulling her to me, my finger still buried deep in her needy pussy, and close my mouth over hers, kissing her like a man possessed.

Maybe I am.

Knowing I'm the only one to ever touch her this way has an epic surge of possessiveness overtaking me until I can't even fucking think straight. All I can focus on is her tight little pussy clenching around my finger, sucking me in deeper, and the taste of her still lingering on my tongue as I kiss her.

I withdraw my finger and slide it back in, once, then twice, her pussy weeping for me each time, soaking my hand more with each thrust.

She's moaning against my mouth louder now, her hips writhing as she reaches for me, her fingers digging into my abs.

I pull back, peering down at her. "I need you to be quiet for me, baby. I know it's hard, but I don't want anyone to see what's mine. No one gets to see my wife soaking my fingers. No one else sees this sweet little pussy."

I swear to fucking god, she gets even wetter at the filthy words I whisper in her ear. Nodding, she buries her face into my neck and fists her small hands in my shirt, and I use my free hand to hold her tightly against me. Drawing out the movements, I take my time, adding my thumb to circle her clit as I fuck her with my fingers.

Her breathless little pants are hot against my neck as she lifts her hips ever so slightly to try to meet my fingers, rocking like she needs more.

I pull out of her completely before adding a second finger, slowly sinking them back inside of her. She's so goddamn tight that I move torturously slowly so she's able to adjust.

"Grant-t," she moans against my neck, the words vibrating me to my fucking core as her nails rake down my stomach.

"What, baby?"

"More. P-please."

She's trembling in my arms as her greedy little pussy swallows my fingers, taking everything that I give her. So, I give her exactly what she asks for.

More.

My movements change from slow and gentle to something different. I thrust my fingers harder, slamming them into her and curling them to massage her G-spot with every stroke. Her thighs shake as they fall open wider, and her dress rises higher, allowing me the briefest glimpse of her perfect pussy.

Pink and glistening, it's the prettiest thing I've ever seen. I lean back just slightly so I can watch her needy pussy swallow my fingers. I'm mesmerized as I admire my fingers sliding in and out of her, covered in her arousal and stretching her open wide. My cock is so hard it's aching as it strains against my pants. One touch and I'll probably come.

But I'm more worried about her coming.

"Come for me, baby," I murmur.

The wet, erotic sound of me slamming inside her pussy fills the room, and it's so goddamn hot.

I wish that I could see her face right now, how stunning she is in her bliss, but she's buried into my neck, attempting to keep quiet since we're in this fucking library.

The second I can, I'm going to spread her out on our bed and eat her pussy until she's limp. I'm going to edge her over and over until she can't take another fucking second. And then I'll eat her again.

"I… I think…" Her voice shakes, trailing off when I sweep my thumb along her clit more quickly and bury my fingers deeper.

Her orgasm builds, higher and higher with each thrust, and I can feel her tightening around me.

"Be a good little wife and come for me. I'm going to suck every drop off my fingers."

The seconds that follow are palpable. Her entire body goes taut, her fingers digging into my stomach, her teeth sinking into my neck as the orgasm rolls through her, and she lets go.

Wetness floods my hand as she comes, her body trembling with the intensity.

Her delicate, throaty little cries wash over me, sending a jolt of arousal pulsing through my body, so powerful that a low groan rumbles out of my chest.

"Good girl. You did so good, baby," I praise, moving my fingers slowly, drawing out every ounce of her orgasm until she's limp and sated in my arms.

Slipping my fingers out of her gently, I tug her panties back into place, my other hand reaching up to stroke her hair. When she sits up, peering up at me through a heavy-lidded stare, I do just as I promised and lick every fucking drop of her from my cum-soaked fingers.

And nothing has *ever* tasted so sweet.

I couldn't focus on anything besides my wife for the rest of the day. How could I after the unexpectedly fucking hot moment in the library this morning?

She's making it impossible to concentrate on anything other than her.

I worked out for over an hour today after class, stretching and weight training, but even then, it didn't take off the edge. The need to go home and repeat what we did this morning, only with my tongue as well as my fingers, is invading my every thought. I'm going to have to take the longest shower of my life tonight, undoubtedly.

As I turn the doorknob to the front door and push it open, the first thing I notice is it smells amazing. I can't figure out what it is, but something delicious. Which means that Addie must have cooked dinner.

Before I even shut the front door all the way, Auggie waddles over and jumps against my legs, his way of begging for a head and belly scratch, his usual way of greeting anyone who steps through the door. My guy is a slut for attention, and he always gets it.

"What's up, buddy?" I say as I bend down and scratch his furry head. I rub his favorite spot behind his ear, and his leg thumps against the hardwood. "Yeah, I know that's your favorite. Where's your mama? Let's find her, and then I'll give you a treat, okay?"

Also a slut for treats.

You and me both, big guy. As long as they come in the form of my wife.

"Addie? You here?" I call out, making my way out of the foyer and down the hall toward the kitchen. But when I poke my head inside, she's nowhere to be seen.

"In here!" Her voice comes from the bedroom, so I head there. I find her sitting in front of the window, the warm rays of the sun setting along her skin as she sits in front of her easel. She's wearing a big T-shirt that I think used to be white but is now stained with a hundred different shades of paint. Her hair is piled messily on the top of her head, and her lips are set in a firm line as she drags the brush along the canvas.

There's a spot of paint on the tip of her nose, and her fingers are stained with color.

Like every time I see her, my heart thumps erratically in my chest. I'll never get over how beautiful she is. No matter how long this arrangement lasts, I'll still want more time.

The thought of having to walk away from her makes an ache form in my erratic, thrashing heart. But that's not something I even want to think about right now, regardless of if it's inevitable for our future.

I've been so focused on her that I didn't even see what it is she's painting. My eyes scan the large canvas and the art that's taking shape.

"Hi, beautiful," I murmur as I walk over and press a quick kiss to her head before flopping onto the edge of the mattress. "How long have you been working on this?"

"For a while," she admits, giving me a radiant smile that lights up her heart-shaped face. "I couldn't focus any longer, so I came home after class and started on it. You told me you wanted something for the apartment, so I took a break from my thesis project to work on it."

"I love it already. Whatever it is."

There's not enough on the canvas to really make it out, but I have no doubt that if Addie's creating it, it'll be a damn masterpiece. She's naturally talented, and everything she creates blows my mind.

She nods, dragging her attention back to the canvas. We sit that way for a while, me watching her make small, calculated strokes of her brush, her working in silence. Every few minutes, she cocks her head, those blue eyes scanning the canvas as if she's searching for the perfect place for the next stroke.

My phone rings in my pocket, and when I pull it out, I see my agent's name on the screen.

I answer it with a quick swipe of my finger. "Hello?"

"Hey. I just heard from Aaron, and you've got the sponsorship."

What? *Holy fuck.*

I fly off the bed, turning to pace the bedroom.

"I got it? For sure?" I ask.

Jeremy chuckles. "Yep. I just got the call. They said they'll be sending over an email soon with additional information as far as getting you out there for an onboarding meeting, as well as some shoot dates. They did mention they'd love to include your new wife if that's something you'd be comfortable with. Turns out they really liked the happily married thing even more than I thought they would."

My eyes flick to Addie, who's abandoned the paintbrush and is staring at me with wide eyes.

"I can talk to her and let you know."

She stands from the stool and walks over, stopping in front of me. I reach out and loop my arm over her shoulders, hauling her against me.

Fuck, I can't believe it actually worked. I got the fucking sponsorship. This kinda money, attention... It's going to change our lives. Not just mine.

Ours.

"Yep, that sounds good," Jeremy replies. "They also mentioned a gala in New Orleans coming up and asked if you could attend. Smile for a few cameras, meet some of their board members. I think it's a good opportunity for you to rub elbows with a bunch of influential people. Couldn't hurt."

Thank fuck it's the offseason, or there'd be no way I'd have time for all this.

Nodding, I say, "Yeah. I think I can do that. I'm going to run things by my wife, and I'll give you a call first thing in the morning."

"Cool. Shoot me a message if you need anything in the meantime. Congratulations, Grant. You turned it around and made this happen. Go celebrate with your wife, but don't get in trouble."

I laugh. "You got it. Later."

After pressing the button to end the call, I toss my phone onto the bed and glance down at Addie in my arms.

"I got the sponsorship. It's done. I fucking did it, ArtGirl. *We* did it."

Her entire face lights up, excitement dancing in her eyes as she launches herself up completely in my arms. Her legs fit around my waist, her arms on my shoulders, and I slide my arms around her back, holding her against me as I bury my face in her neck.

"I'm so proud of you, Grant. So, so proud. I knew that you'd make it happen. They will be lucky to have you."

Pulling back, I reach up with one hand and cradle her face, sweeping my thumb tenderly along her jaw. "I couldn't have done it without you, Addie. Not just with the shit with my reputation. Just having you here means more to me than you know. Thank you."

Her head shakes adamantly. "You don't need to thank me. We're in this together, remember?"

I know she means together as in our arrangement, but I'm beginning to want more than the arrangement could ever offer.

chapter twenty-one

Addie

"YOU KNOW you don't *actually* have to walk me to class, right?"

Grant shrugs, offering me a boyish grin. "Can't I do something nice for my wife?"

"You already do *more* than enough nice things for me. You spoil me, remember?" I reply, brushing past him into the art building as he's holding the door open for me like the gentleman that he is.

"Mmm… you mean like last night when I—" I come to an abrupt halt in the middle of the hallway, slamming my hand over his mouth as I glance around to the throngs of people rushing past us.

He's impossible and absolutely determined to make me blush in the worst places possible with his mouth and… his hands. What I'm not going to do is think about how *nice* he was last night and then be unable to think of anything but him during class.

Which I'm beginning to think has been his goal all along.

"You. Are. Ridiculous. You know that?" I mumble while my

eyes dart around the hallway, hoping not to draw extra attention to us.

I realize that the goal of this arrangement is to convince people that our marriage is real, but I'm still trying to get used to the idea of being on anyone's radar after spending so long doing anything I could to blend in.

He places a hand on my hip, then slides his palm to the small of my back and hauls me to him until I'm pressed tightly against every hard inch of his front. Of course, he's wearing a pair of gray sweatpants to class today, even though they should be illegal for men, *especially* married men, to wear in public. Something I never really gave much thought to until recently.

My fingers grasp at the fabric of his T-shirt as I exhale shakily. It seems entirely unfair that he has this effect on me without even trying.

He takes two steps back until he's leaning against the wall in a more secluded part of the hallway, dragging me with him. While the building is still littered with people making their way to class, it almost feels like we're alone, the rest of the world fading away.

"What if we skipped class today? Went back home… spent the day doing other things," he whispers roughly as his gaze drops to my lips. It's already been established that I'm the equivalent of a girl in crisis when it comes to him, and today it's even worse because not only is he wearing the stupid gray sweatpants but a backward hat too.

I've never skipped a class in my life, but the heated look in his eyes has me considering it.

Just as I'm about to give in and tell him yes, I remember why I can't.

Crap.

Not today, of all days.

I shake my head. "I can't. We're painting a live model today in class, and Dr. Gatti says the project is worth twenty percent of our final grade. He has a no-makeup policy, which means that I have to be there."

Grant sighs. "Yeah, you definitely can't miss that. C'mon, let's get you to class so you can keep your perfect attendance, ArtGirl."

He tosses me a playful wink, reaching for my hand, and for the first time ever... I find myself wanting to *break* the rules instead of following them.

All for him.

Somehow, I still make it to class on time despite the fact that Grant used the few spare minutes I had to pull me into an empty classroom and kiss me until I was breathless and shaking.

He insisted on walking me all the way to class, even though I assured him I could make it the rest of the way without his help.

Once we're outside the door to my art class, I turn to him, my brow arched. "I have to go. Unless you plan on becoming an art student this late in your college career?"

His smirk spreads into a broad smile. "I mean, I have many talents. But... that is not one of them. See you later?"

I nod. But as I turn to walk away, he catches my hand, halting me. He pulls me to him and kisses me so fiercely that it has my body trembling. His soft yet firm lips capture mine, his tongue sweeping inside my mouth and dancing with mine in a way that I'm not sure is entirely decent for an audience.

A few catcalls and whistles later, he releases me with a grin, his dark ocean eyes hazy and unfocused. "Now, that's the kind of goodbye a husband needs from his wife, ArtGirl."

There's still this part of me that can't believe that somehow we've ended up in this marriage together, regardless of the events that led us here. The lines feel like they're blurring more and more each day, but I'm too afraid to say anything or mention how I feel because I'm worried that while it seems like he's interested in… the physical, I'm not sure that he would be interested in more, and the thought of things ending and him no longer being in my life scares me.

For the most brief moment, when he got the call from his agent, I was terrified that it would be over. Even though technically only one side of the arrangement would have been fulfilled, there was still this intrusive thought that he would leave.

That I'd go back to being alone.

I never knew how truly lonely I was until I met Grant. Sure, I have Earl and Amos and Auggie. And I love them dearly. It's just… it's not the same as what Grant gives me.

With him, I feel more like myself than I've ever been. I'm happier… lighter. The world doesn't feel like it's weighing down on my shoulders as heavily when we're together.

And as much as I love that feeling, it also *terrifies* me. I'm scared of what it's going to be like when it's over. How will I ever be able to go back to the way it was before I met him?

"Ms. Arceneaux. Good morning!" Dr. Gatti says suddenly from beside me, causing me to jump in surprise. I was too lost in Grant and my thoughts to notice his approach. Not sure how I missed him with his bright teal brocade blazer and matching pants, but clearly, I wasn't paying attention.

He's got on a matching shiny, iridescent silver headband and chandelier earrings that are made of a string of crystals in various shades of blue.

"Bergeron," Grant interjects suddenly.

My art professor turns to face him with a look of confusion written on his face. His thick, bushy brows pinched together. "Pardon me?"

"Her last name. It's Bergeron. She got married." His mouth

tilts up into a smug grin, seemingly proud of himself for the way he just publicly claimed me as his.

Dr. Gatti's face lights up, a smile overtaking his face at the news. "Well, then, congratulations are in order. I wish you both many years of happiness. I adore young love. It's so inspiring. So full of wonder and possibility. Finding your muse in a spouse for life… hang on to that, my dears. It is truly something special."

Dr. Gatti has *always* been my favorite professor, not only because he's incredibly talented and an incredible teacher but because he reminds me of Amos with his eccentric, larger-than-life personality.

"Thank you," I whisper, cutting my eyes to Grant, who's grinning cheekily. "I appreciate that."

"We have a little bit of a snafu on our hands today, unfortunately, so this was *just* what I needed to brighten my day," he adds, reaching up to rub his temples, exhaling loudly. "Our model for today canceled at the last minute. Food poisoning from bad sushi, unfortunately. I've been planning this for months, and it's going to mess up the entire syllabus."

Darn. Even though I was considering skipping today with Grant, I was actually looking forward to painting a live subject. It's not something I usually do.

"I could do it," Grant says nonchalantly.

Both of our gazes whip to him, my mouth parted in… shock?

"I mean… only if my wife was okay with it that is," he adds.

Pretty sure hearing him call me his wife will *never* get old, especially when it's around other people, which I guess is the point… but still. I kind of love the way he's making a statement about… us.

"I'm totally good. I mean, it's *your* junk that will be on display, big guy." I pat his chest teasingly, and he captures my hand with a laugh, hauling me to him.

My heart still races when he touches me, but it's different than it was in the beginning. Now it races because of how much I love it. I'm comfortable with Grant in a way I haven't been with another person, and it happened so gradually I can't actually pinpoint the moment that things began to change. Only that it feels inherently different.

"Hmmmm. You know this might actually be the perfect sprinkle of kismet," Dr. Gatti muses as he stares at my husband with a curious expression. He drags his gaze down his body in a slow perusal, then circles Grant, stroking his short goatee before moving back in front of him. "Would you mind… taking off your shirt?"

"Sure. I would be doing something great for the art department, and my wife is such an activist for the arts… seems like a no-brainer, right?"

Grant looks at me, and when I shrug, he slides his backpack off his shoulders, dropping it to the floor, then reaches behind his neck and pulls his T-shirt off.

Heat pools in my lower belly at the sight of his broad chest and rows of taut muscles, and I wonder if there will ever be a time where I don't feel so… affected by just *looking* at him.

Probably not.

My eyes follow the path of his chest, down the rows and rows of abs, along the trail of hair that disappears beneath his waistband, over the hollow dips of his hips that create the perfect V.

"This isn't a fully nude session, so he would still be in underwear. This project is all about capturing the essence of the human form, enhancing our students' ability to render all aspects of human anatomy in their own style." He gives Grant an approving look. "A lean body, sculpted muscles, a chiseled jawline. He checks all the boxes."

It doesn't bother me, if I'm being honest. He's the one that would have his body on display. I'd rather jump off a cliff than stand in front of a room full of people partially clothed.

Plus, this is how all classically trained artists practice. And my husband *does* have a body that's worthy of being painted and hung in the Louvre.

I look at Grant, and he catches my gaze for a moment before reaching out and grabbing my hand in his. "Can you give us a moment?"

"Certainly. I'll be inside if you decide to join us! Toodles!" Dr. Gatti says jovially before sauntering off.

Once he's gone, Grant looks at me with an earnest expression. "If you're not okay with this, then I'm good. I'm only offering because I know this class is important to you."

I nod. "Oh yeah. You'll be everyone's knight in shining armor with all of your muscles. How will the art department *ever* repay this favor?"

A beat passes, and the corner of his lip curves into a shit-eating grin. "Oh, *ArtGirl*, I can think of a few ways you ca—"

My hand flies to his mouth, covering it before he can say something else that causes me to actually catch fire in the middle of the hallway.

"Just go. God." I laugh, nodding my head toward the classroom. "Go. *Please*."

As expected, Dr. Gatti is beyond thrilled that Grant will be filling in for us today. As well as every woman and even a few guys, judging by the dreamy sighs and longing stares as he steps onto the raised platform in the center of the room in only a pair of tight, black boxer briefs.

Even *I'm* having a hard time focusing, and I see him every day.

Mostly with clothes though… but I am thinking that should change. Maybe. Not that I could say that to him.

"Okay, settle down, everyone. Settle down," Dr. Gatti says with a knowing smile, raising his hands above him to garner attention as he stands beside Grant, who's now perched on a velvet chaise in the middle of the platform. "As I'm sure you've probably come to realize, Ronaldo will not be joining us today. He's unfortunately come down with a case of food poisoning, but we were able to find a replacement last minute."

He sweeps a long arm toward Grant. "This young man has so graciously offered to join us for today's session. Everyone, please give him a warm welcome."

A chorus of hellos echo around the room, and he lifts his hand in a short wave, followed by a cocky smirk, not looking the least bit fazed to be sitting in front of a room full of people in nothing but his underwear.

I'm the one who's frazzled, and I'm not sure if it's because he's so ridiculously hot that I can't stop staring long enough to even get my charcoal out of my backpack and to secure my smock around my waist or the fact that every single eye in the room is on my husband.

He's comfortable with the horde of attention because he's used to experiencing it. The polar opposite of me.

I finally get my apron tied and my pencils out of the zipper pouch I keep them in and take a seat on my stool in front of the blank canvas.

Since meeting Grant for the first time, I've wanted to sketch him, but I've been too afraid to ask, so the fact that I get to do it for a grade is exciting.

My eyes flit back to the platform, where he's laid back on the crushed-velvet chaise. Dr. Gatti has posed him exactly the way he wants, with Grant's arm thrown over his head, strategically showing off all the sculpted muscles of his arms and abdomen but also in a way that looks as if he's ready to take a nap. And while I can appreciate his body, it's his eyes that make him truly magnificent. His dark, blue irises seem to smolder as they find me, holding mine for so long that my cheeks begin to burn. His lip twitches as he gives me a wink, and my throat runs dry.

How is he *this* hot?

It's ridiculous. For anyone to be so attractive, so effortlessly.

What's worse is I know all of the dirty, delicious things that he's capable of when it's just the two of us.

A dreamy sigh sounds beside me, and I glance over to see a girl staring at Grant with an awestruck look in her eyes. "God, he is the most beautiful man I've literally ever seen."

I do my best to focus on my sketch, but as loudly as she's talking to her friend, it's next to impossible to ignore the conversation happening. Every few minutes, she's got something new to say.

"And Jesus, do you see what he's packing? Those briefs are like god's gift to women. What?" She pauses when her friend giggles beside her. I see her elbow her through my periphery. "I'm only speaking the truth. You got eyes, girl."

I exhale, tightening my grip on the charcoal so tightly that I'm worried it'll snap. It's not like I'm blind—I clearly know exactly what she's talking about. I am *very* well aware that Grant is stupidly hot. I just didn't expect to feel so... possessive over him. So jealous that these girls are even having the chance to look at him.

That's ridiculous, I know, but I can't help it.

"I'm pretty sure I've heard about him, and apparently, the sex is amazing. Clearly not surprising because look at what he's working with." She giggles in a high-pitched voice that makes my ears ring.

My god. This is art, and this girl is behaving like a horny teenager instead of being respectful to the model, which is just… gross.

"Everyone," Dr. Gatti says loudly over the hushed whispers echoing through the room. "Let's take a break and reconvene in ten minutes." He hands Grant a robe that he shrugs into and secures around his waist.

I'm nearly fuming as Grant crosses the classroom toward me. I feel silly for feeling like this, but it was infuriating overhearing those girls objectify him like that.

He's more than just his looks and his… package. He's incredible, and they won't ever get the chance to find that out. Because he's *mine*.

"Hey, baby," he murmurs, his raspy voice velvet in my ears as he walks up and presses a lingering kiss to the corner of my lips. My gaze drifts to the girls beside me, and I almost laugh at the look of pure shock on their faces.

"Hi. You did amazing up there."

He grins, brushing his hair off his forehead with a shrug. "Not much to it, but I'm glad I could help out. And get to see you in your element. Makes me wish we had more classes together." His voice lowers as he leans in and whispers, "Maybe more study dates?"

My pulse comes alive, racing wildly at the memory.

"Grant," I warn.

His grin only widens into a smile that makes the dimple in his cheek pop. "Gotta go back up there, but I'll see you after."

When he kisses me this time, it's heated in a way that has me burning from the inside, wishing we weren't in this classroom. He pulls away, tossing me a quick wink before walking away.

"Uh… is that your boyfriend?" the girl beside me immediately asks.

"No. He's my *husband*," I respond smugly.

I pick up my charcoal and move back to my drawing, but before I can even press it to the paper, I pause, turning back to her, unable to stop myself.

"Oh, and just so you know, whatever you heard… it's *better*."

chapter twenty-two

Addie

THE MOMENT I step inside the bakery, I get an overwhelming sense of… unease. I can't even really explain it, but there's a sense of dread weighing heavily in the pit of my stomach, and the hair on the back of my neck stands up, sending goose bumps along my flesh.

My hand shakes as I feel for the light switch along the darkened wall and flip it on, illuminating the back room.

Nothing seems out of place at first glance, but still, the feeling of unease creeps higher along my spine, sending my senses into overdrive.

Maybe I'm just being paranoid, like the other day when I thought that I saw Dixon on campus. It's probably because I'm barely functioning on three hours of sleep and have been a little paranoid since the maybe-Dixon incident. I'm sure I'm just imagining things that aren't really there.

Amos should be here soon, and then I won't be so freaked-out.

At least that's what I keep repeating to myself as I turn back toward the door and lock the deadbolt.

I grab my apron off the hook, securing it around my waist

before walking through the kitchen, flipping the rest of the lights on. A flood of relief washes over me when everything seems to be in place. No serial killers hiding in the shadows.

You've worked yourself up over nothing, Addie. Just chill.

I exhale, blowing out a pent-up breath, and then make my way to the front of the bakery.

There, I find exactly where the feeling of unease and dread came from. The sight in front of me sends me into a state of panic and pure fear. My stomach plummets, and I begin to shake so badly that I'm worried my legs will give out.

Oh god.

I lift a trembling hand to cover my mouth as a pained, heart-broken cry tumbles from me, and hot, stinging tears well in my eyes.

Someone's… destroyed Ever After.

It's completely trashed. Pieces of wood and glass are strewn on nearly every inch of the floor from the shattered front windows, one of my mother's most favorite parts of the bakery, leaving nothing but a gaping hole.

The bistro tables in the front have been flipped, the wooden chairs lying in broken pieces next to them. The display cases are smashed, along with all of the plates that were on the counter.

With each new thing I discover, my stomach twists, and I feel like I'm going to be sick. Seeing my favorite place in the world this way does something irreparable to my heart.

I just… I just don't understand… Why would *anyone* do this? What could they possibly gain from destroying a bakery? Kids who thought vandalizing a business would be fun? But this just seems way more intense than a random case of vandalism. A hundred different scenarios play out in my head, and I just can't seem to make sense of the nightmare in front of me.

Everything's been thrown from the counters, bags and boxes

strewn across the floor behind the counter, yet… the only thing that seems to have not been touched is the cash register.

Why would someone break into the bakery and not take anything? This seems so hostile and targeted an—

Realization hits me with a force so powerful that I have to reach out and grip the wall to remain upright. *Dixon? Brent?*

Oh my god.

Did *they*… do this? Did my stepdad do this? Did Dixon?

Would they really stoop *this* low? To damage the bakery this way?

I honestly don't know anymore. I thought that I knew who Brent was, and then I found out that it was all a lie. That he spent the majority of my life lying to me and manipulating me. It doesn't seem too far-fetched to think that he could do something like this.

And that night at home… he threatened me.

The only difference between Brent and Dixon is that Dixon physically *hurt* me. He could have done this.

I'm spiraling, my thoughts moving in a hundred different directions, furthering the anxiety that's taken root inside of me. No matter who did it, there's nothing I can do right now besides call the police.

The damage is done.

My vision blurs as my tears fall in earnest, and a choked sob erupts from my chest. My heart hurts for my mother's beloved bakery. A beat passes before I'm able to suck in a shaky breath and wipe the salty wetness coating my cheeks.

It suddenly hits me that this is a *crime scene*, it's still dark outside, and I'm alone. I'm barely able to hold it together as I turn and flee to the safety of my locked car. I can hardly get my phone out of my purse because I'm shaking so badly, but I finally am able to pull it free. My fingers hover over the screen, and I can barely make out the numbers as tears cloud my vision.

Hold it together, Addie. You have to hold it together.

I know I need to call the police, but there's one person I need to call first. The only person that I want when the world is falling apart around me… the only person who makes me feel safe.

My husband.

I'm still shaking as I sit on the curb outside of the bakery, a blanket wrapped tightly around my shoulders courtesy of the police officer who responded to the 911 call. My teeth were chattering because I was shaking so badly, a combination of adrenaline and shock, as I attempted to give my statement about what I walked into.

My gaze lingers on Grant, who's standing near the bakery entrance, his arms crossed over his chest, talking with the officers. Every few seconds, he glances over at me as if he needs to reassure himself that I'm okay. His face is an uncontrolled mask of worry mixed with frustration as he speaks, his jaw clenching with each shake of his head.

I've never seen him look *scared* before. But he did when he pulled up, flinging his truck door open and leaving the truck still running while he ran to me, hauling my nearly lifeless body against him protectively. The moment his strong arms closed around me and I breathed him in, I just… broke. He let me sob into his chest, seemingly needing to hold me as much as I needed to be held.

Being in his arms was the safety I needed to let go, to purge all of the heartache and fear that had been building inside of me, not just this morning but over the last few months. He held on so tightly I thought I'd stop breathing, but I only pulled him closer.

Because Grant is my safe place to land, and I know without a doubt that I'm falling in love with him.

I'm scared to admit that, even to myself, but I think I've loved him since before I even saw him for the first time. I fell for the guy through a computer screen who saw me more clearly than the people I saw face-to-face every day.

The guy whose quiet, unwavering strength has gotten me through one of the hardest times of my life.

"Cher?" My gaze whips to Amos, who's standing on the sidewalk next to me. "Are you okay?"

Numbly, I nod, clutching the blanket tighter around me. "Yeah. I'm just sad. And angry. And scared that we'll never be able to fix everything that was broken tonight. This place is so important to me, Amos."

"I know, darlin'." He takes a seat on the curb next to me before curving his arm around my shoulders and tucking me tightly against his side. "I'm sorry that you had to go through that this morning. I'm sorry I wasn't here to protect you."

The sad, remorseful tone of his voice has fresh tears stinging in my eyes and a ball of emotion rising in my throat. I lay my head on his shoulder as a moment of quiet settles over us.

I guess the adrenaline is starting to wear off because I just feel exhausted. Overwhelmed with everything that's happened this morning.

I hate this. I hate that it's affected not only me but the people that I love. Amos, Earl… *Grant*.

"It's not your fault. Please don't apologize. I came in early because I was planning on making a special batch of cream cheese croissants for Grant." I laugh humorlessly, swiping at the tears on my cheeks. "I guess that plan isn't happening now."

Amos tightens his arm around me and lays his cheek on the top of my head. My eyes flit back to Grant, and I sigh defeatedly.

"It's going to be okay, cher. I know it might not feel like it right now, but it will. We've got insurance, and they'll cover the damages until the police arrest whoever's responsible for this."

I scoff. "You know who's responsible for it."

"I have an idea, but we don't know that for sure. That man's a *lot* of things, but I don't think he's that foolish. And I know this is devastating to us both, but I want you to remember something. Okay? I want you to remember that no matter how dark it gets, that sun is gonna shine again. And when you feel those warm rays on your face, all of the darkness that you suffered through will be a thing of yesterday."

I nod, sniffling. "I know."

"I think I've been telling you that since you were a little girl. Goodness, you would run around the bakery, hiding behind my legs from your mama when you played hide-and-seek. I still remember those days like they were yesterday."

I could never forget growing up in the bakery or the time I had with my mom before she passed. Most of my memories include Amos—he loved her as much as I did.

Grant strides over to our perch, dropping to his haunches in front of me. He reaches out, brushing my hair back from my face with a softness in his eyes that's so tender it makes my chest ache. "You doing okay, baby?"

"Yes. I-I think…" I whisper quietly. "I will be okay."

Amos presses his lips gently to the crown of my hair before sliding his arm off and pushing to his feet. "I'm going to go do some cleanup inside, make some calls to the insurance company, and see how quickly I can get someone out here to replace the front windows and repair the display case. Probably should get the locks changed just in case."

God, I hadn't even thought that far ahead. I hadn't really thought about anything other than making it through this morning. I was exhausted before I even got here, and now that the adrenaline has begun to wear off, my eyes are heavy, and my brain is not functioning properly.

"I'm coming too," I say as I pull the blanket off my shoulders and stand, swaying slightly from how quickly I got up from the curb.

Grant reaches for me, immediately wrapping his hand around my arm and steadying me. "Baby, you're dead on your feet. You need to rest."

I shake my head adamantly, bringing my fingers to my temples and attempting to rub away the ache. I can't just leave the bakery. Amos and Earl need me to help clean up the disaster that's inside.

"Grant, I can't just leave them with this mess. This is my responsibility."

"I understand," he starts, gently pulling me to him and wrapping me up in his arms, practically holding me up. "But you also need to take care of yourself, Addie. You went through something traumatic this morning. You need to take a moment, get some sleep. I called in some help… I figured we could use it."

My brows pinch in confusion. I try not to fixate on the fact that he referred to the situation at the bakery as *we* and how it made my heart flutter.

"What do you mean?"

"Davis and a few guys from the team. They're going to come by in a bit and get a tarp up over the front window to prevent anything getting in." He pauses to look over at Amos, who has the smallest hint of a smile that I can't quite read on his face.

"They're at your beck and call, Amos. Put them to work. Anything you need, they're here to help. I figured with their help, we can get the place cleaned up today, secure it as best we can until someone comes out to replace the windows and we can order new supplies."

God, my heart squeezes with each word that comes out of his mouth. I'm on the verge of tears again as I stare up at his ridiculously handsome face.

I think he might be perfect, and until now, I wasn't sure the perfect man existed.

But he does, and he's *my husband.*

"Grant," I whisper, and he glances back at me. His dark blue eyes are a hurricane of concern within the depths, and I can't take another second without touching him. I rise on the tips of my toes as I slide my arms around his neck, and then I lean in, sealing my lips to his.

It's the first time I've ever been the one to initiate a kiss. It's the first time that I've been so overcome by emotion that I physically restrain myself from pressing my lips to his. His arms tighten around my waist as he tilts his head, deepening the kiss, sweeping his tongue along the seam of my lips.

He pulls away with a small smile. "What was that for? Not that I'm complaining, but…"

"Thank you. Thank you for coming as soon as I called, for calling your teammates to come help clean up the bakery an—" I feel hot, fresh tears wetting my cheeks as my words tumble out in a frenzied rush, my exhaustion and emotion finally bubbling over.

"Hey. Hey," he whispers as he reaches for my face, smoothing his thumb tenderly over my cheeks and wiping the tears away. "You don't ever have to thank me, Addie. I will always come, no matter where you are. No matter what happens, I'll come, okay?"

I nod. His gaze lingers on mine, searching almost. I wish I could tell him what I'm feeling. That I could be brave enough to put it all out there, despite the fact that there's a huge chance he might not feel the way that I do. That this is just an arrangement to him with some attraction involved, and I'm just the foolish girl who fell in love.

"I promise you, Addie, I'm not going anywhere. And I know that promises are just words, but I'll prove it to you. I'll prove it with my actions."

Nodding, I sniffle, nearly swaying on my feet again. "O-okay."

"Now that we've got the bakery taken care of, at least for now… why don't you let me take you away for the weekend and get away from everything? I *know* that you're worried about everything going on here, but the guys have it under control. They'll get things cleaned up in no time. I can see how exhausted you are, and I know being here and stressing isn't what you need right now."

Even though there are a hundred reasons why I want to say yes, there are even more reasons why I can't.

I can't leave this mess for Earl and Amos. This is *my* bakery to look after.

"I—"

Amos interjects, cutting me off. "Don't say no, cher, because I already know you were about to. I think your beau is right. He's got a whole slew of strong, capable boys coming up here to get this place cleaned up, and you look far too exhausted to be help-ful. The police report is done, and once I make the call to the insurance company… there's not much more we can do until we get the windows and cases fixed. We'll have to be closed for a few days while we wait. There's no better time for you to get away. To take a break for the first time… maybe ever?"

I chew my lip nervously, trying to cipher through the thoughts in my head. All of that may be true, but it still doesn't mean that I can just up and leave the bakery.

"Amos, I just… I can't leave. There's so much that I need to be doing. I can't leave you with this mess. And then there's Auggie."

Amos places a hand on his hip and shakes his head, his long ponytail swaying. "All I hear is you making excuses. You know that nothing makes Earl happier than getting to spend time with Auggie." He pauses, arching a bushy brow. "There's nothing you can do right now, cher. As much as I know you'll worry, I think you should go and give yourself the weekend. Rest and recover."

My gaze flits between the two of them as I mull over what he's saying.

It seems so easy… to take off for the weekend and not worry about what I'm leaving behind, but it's not a luxury that I've ever had. I've fought so hard for Ever After, and I'm struggling with the thought of leaving it this way. It physically hurts.

But there is a huge, overwhelming part of me that wants to go with Grant. To have an entire weekend of uninterrupted time with him, away from all of *this*. Because I have a feeling whoever did this, Brent or otherwise, did this to hurt me.

I'm not just angry and hurt… I'm *scared*.

If he was willing to do something as underhanded as this, how much further would he go to hurt me?

The thought terrifies me, and a shiver racks my body as I start to tremble. Pure exhaustion settles over me in a wave so strong that if it wasn't for Grant's arms tight around my body,

I'd probably end up on the ground. As weary and afraid as I feel, I still feel safe and secure in his arms.

I guess… if there's nothing I can do while we're waiting on repairs, then I *could* go with him.

"Are you sure, Amos?"

Amos nods. "Absolutely. I've got everything under control. Go, enjoy a little quiet."

I drag my attention back to Grant, a beat passing between us before I speak. "Okay. I'll go away with you. But… where are we going?"

"Home."

chapter twenty-three

Grant

THE HOUSE I grew up in is only about thirty minutes outside of New Orleans, in a tiny town called Belle Chasse that sits right along the West Bank of the Mississippi River.

When I told Addie I was taking her home, she didn't realize that I meant the place where I grew up. And that she'd be meeting my mama for the first time. It's pretty ironic that my *wife* hasn't met my mom, but then again, we did everything ass-backwards, beginning with a marriage that started as fake but now feels more real than anything I've ever experienced.

After everything that happened this morning, I wanted to put a whole goddamn city between Addie and the asshole who I'm fairly sure I'll end up killing with my bare hands. I've never thought myself as a violent person, but when I think about Dixon and all of the fucked-up shit he's put her through, I see red.

The call that I got this morning... changed my fucking brain chemistry. Hearing her panicked voice sobbing through the phone so hard that she could hardly speak was something that I'll never forget. I'll hear it in my nightmares with the same feeling of fear that slithered down my spine and took me hostage.

I've never been so fucking scared in my entire life. I had no idea what I was walking into. I didn't know if she was hurt or if she had been threatened, and the entire ride was the worst form of torture.

The moment I saw her in a shaking, huddled heap outside the bakery, I nearly lost it, holding on to her so tightly that she probably couldn't breathe. It still wasn't enough to calm my pounding heart or lessen the feeling of dread weighing down my gut.

It was at that moment that I realized there's nothing on this planet I wouldn't do to protect Addie. No line I wouldn't cross, no fucking law I wouldn't break, no sacrifice I wouldn't make if that's what it took to keep her safe.

Because I *love* her.

And the thought of anything happening to her, or worse, *losing* her, is something I can't even fathom.

I won't.

From the very first conversation, I knew there was something about her that I would never be able to forget. She saw me more clearly than anyone in my life ever had, and I think I loved her even then. I'm pretty sure I never stopped.

I was a fool to think that I could pretend. It was never pretending for me, and today made that crystal fucking clear.

"Hey," her soft voice calls from the passenger seat, pulling me from my thoughts and out of my head.

My fingers tighten on the wheel until my knuckles are white, and I exhale the breath I had been holding for so long my lungs burn.

"Are you okay?"

I drag my gaze from the road for a second to look over at her. Her normally bright eyes are dull, and her face is etched with worry and exhaustion, and it does nothing for the storm brewing inside of me.

I fucking hate that she's hurt and that there's nothing I can do to take it away.

She should never have to bear the weight of something like this. She's too good. Too pure.

"I'm okay," I breathe, even though the last thing I feel right now is okay. I lie, for her. Because I'm not going to be another thing she has to worry about.

Which is why I'm going to keep that I realized I'm in love with her to myself for now. She has so much shit happening in her life, and I refuse to be another complication. I promised all this would go at her pace.

And there's always the chance that she doesn't feel the way that I do. I've never been in love before, so this is all new to me.

"Are you okay?"

I glance from the road to her and see her nod, sinking further into the seat.

"I'm okay. I'm just tired. Not just physically but emotionally. Mentally. I feel like I could sleep for a week." She laughs half-heartedly. "And also nervous because now I have to meet your mother, and I look like a zombie."

"You do not look like a zombie. You look beautiful, as always." When I quickly flick my gaze to her, her pouty lips curve into a shy smile. A smile that hits me directly in the chest, and for a second, I want to pull over and pull her into my lap and just fucking hold her. And not let her go. "Don't worry about meeting Mama. You'll love her. I'm actually worried she's going to love you more than me, and I'm a mama's boy. I need the love."

Her giggle floats airily around the cab of my truck, and I revel in it. After the morning we've had, I think hearing her laugh is exactly the medicine I need.

"I'm just worried because… well, you got married and…" She trails off.

"She knows everything, so you don't have to worry about anything. Trust me, she's the best person you'll ever meet. I promise it'll be great, and when we get there, you can go straight to bed if you want. It's been a long-as-fuck day. You need rest."

Addie hums in agreement but sits quietly, fidgeting with the string of the hoodie I gave her to wear. As much as I love seeing her in all of her cute, quirky outfits with her signature Mary Janes, I love seeing her in my clothes even more.

It makes the caveman part of me that I never knew existed until her rear its head.

Since I spent most of the ride to Belle Chasse lost in my thoughts, trying to work through everything, we're only a few minutes away. We ride in a comfortable silence until I pull into the driveway in front of a small, cream-colored Victorian that has been my childhood home since I was born. Despite the fact that it's been a while since I visited home and it's generally *my* job, Mama's got the flower beds looking great.

"Oh, Grant, this is the most precious house I've *ever* seen. The porch swing!" Addie murmurs excitedly as her eyes roam over the house. "Oh gosh, the windchimes. My mom loved them so much. It was her favorite thing to do. Sit on the back porch when a storm was coming, listening to her chimes going crazy."

My heart flips in my chest at the wistful, sad look in her eyes. Fuck. Reaching out, I take her hand in mine and lace our fingers together. "We should get some at the apartment porch. Next time it storms, we'll go out there and listen."

She looks like she may actually cry, and I open my mouth to

apologize when she suddenly untangles our fingers and then flings herself across the console into my lap, wrapping her arms around my neck and burying her face in it.

I slide my arms around her back and press my lips against the crown of her head. Neither of us speaks; we simply stay here, just like this, breathing together, holding on because it means more than words could.

After what happened this morning, I think we both needed this. I sure as fuck needed reassurance that she's okay. I needed to just hold her.

"You're the best husband in the entire world, Grant Berg-eron," she mumbles against my neck.

I took those vows with the intention of honoring them. For better or worse.

"Okay, so this one is from the time I entered him into a beauty pageant when he was... four? I think? And he won King. Look how adorable the little crown was with his little ringlets. He was so handsome in his little tuxedo. The best part was he didn't take it off for two weeks after it was over. I had to toss it in the trash when he fell asleep one night."

Addie's brows furrow, her lips turning into the cutest fucking smile I've ever seen as she peers over the baby book at me.

My wife and mother are currently bonding over the most embarrassing baby photos from my childhood... and they just keep getting worse.

Mama giggles, covering her mouth as they flip another page together.

Truthfully, I don't even care that she's seeing my naked baby ass in a galvanized bucket bathtub in the front yard. Because if it makes her smile like *this*, she can look at them forever if she wants.

I'd do just about anything to keep that smile on her face.

Fuck, she looks *happy*.

She and my mom hit it off from the second they met, not that I was expecting anything less, and after dinner, they immediately pulled out the baby books. I expected Addie to want to head straight to bed after our exhausting day, but she insisted on staying up to visit with Mama.

So… here we are.

"Gosh, he was the most precious boy. Gave me a run for my money sometimes, but he was always the sweetest, sensitive kid," she says, brushing her finger over the picture before lifting her gaze to me. "Anyway, just a mama getting all sappy over her baby boy who's all grown up. Even though he'll always be my baby, no matter how old *or* tall he gets."

I laugh. "Mama, I've been a foot taller than you since I was twelve."

"Twelve? That explains you being seven feet taller than me," Addie interjects, unable to hide the shock from her tone.

My shoulder dips as I lift the beer to my lips and take a pull. "Nah, you're just fun-sized, baby."

Addie's cheeks flame, and Mom's brows arch, a silent question of *what have I missed…* but I'll save that conversation for later. I could use her advice anyway… now that I know without a doubt that there's no turning back when it comes to Addie.

"It's pretty late. You wanna head to bed?" I ask my wife.

She nods, clearing her throat before turning to my mom. "Thank you for your hospitality, Mrs. Bergeron. For letting me stay at your lovely home this weekend and for being so kind."

"Oh, honey." Mama reaches out, placing her hand over Addie's. "You are always welcome. With or without my son. Actually, I'd love to get lunch one day soon, just us. If you'd be up for that?"

She blinks. "Yes, of course."

I drain the rest of my beer and try not to fixate on how much I love seeing Addie with the other most important person in my life. Bonding. How seeing her fit so comfortably in my life reinforces that I want *more*. For a second, it's easy to envision a future just like this.

I watch as the two of them say good night, exchanging a quick hug and whispered words before Addie turns to where I'm still sitting on the love seat.

"I'll be there in a bit if you wanna shower first?"

She nods, sparing me a small smile before heading down the hallway, leaving Mama and me alone. A few seconds later, the sound of the bedroom door shuts quietly.

"Grant Alexander Bergeron."

I exhale, shifting my gaze to Mama, who's leaning back against the couch, her arms crossed in front of her and shaking her head knowingly.

"You *love* that girl." Her voice is a mixture of certainty and awe.

My eyes shift to the hallway, then back to her, before I nod. There's no point in denying it. She'd see right through me if I did, anyway.

"Yeah. I do."

"I know you do. There's some things that a mother just knows, and your baby boy being in love is one of those things. Do you wanna talk about why you've got that worried look on your face?" Her eyes are as soft as her voice.

Sitting up, I place my forearms on my knees as I drag a hand down my face and up through my hair. "This morning was hard, and I just can't stop thinking about it. It made me realize that... I *can't* let her go, Mama. I don't want to. Regardless of how things started between us, I love her, and I don't ever want to be without her again."

It's the first time I've said it out loud, and I wish it was her that I was saying to. But I'm not sure she's ready to hear it yet.

"Does she know that?"

I shake my head as my fingers slide roughly through my hair, tugging at the root in frustration. "No."

Mom sighs, standing from the couch and coming to sit beside me on the love seat. She gently places her hand on my knee, dragging my attention to her. "Oh, baby, why?"

"I'm going to tell her. But Mama, look at what she's dealing with right now. Look at everything that's happening in her life. I don't want to add a complication. I think she might love me too, but I don't know for sure, and what if she doesn't? Our relationship is supposed to be just an arrangement, and maybe that's all she really wants it to be."

"Or... maybe she feels exactly the way that you do. And maybe *she* always has. You can't keep it from her because you're afraid of what her reaction might be, Grant. Trust her to take care of your heart just the way you will always take care of hers."

Sitting back against the couch, I exhale as I nod. She's right. I *am* going to tell her. I just... have to find the right time. And now doesn't feel like the right time.

"Thanks, Mama."

She squeezes my knee gently before putting her arm around my neck and pulling my hulking frame against her. "I told you that no matter what happens, you will always be my baby boy. I will always be here for you, Grant, no matter what season of life you're in. I know it can be scary to put your heart out there, but I see the way that she looks at you. It's the same way that you look at her. Trust her. Let her decide what she's ready for. Trust her to not only take care of your heart but also to make her own decisions."

That's the scariest part... *I already do.*

chapter twenty-four

Grant

"LISTEN, I've got news for you. You are *not* replacing me with that fucking Rookie. I will fight that motherfucker with my *bare* hands."

My jaw hits the floor when I open the front door and find Reese goddamn Landry outside, his lips twisted in a scowl, with Boo strapped to his chest in a bright purple cat carrier.

He frowns, shaking his head and narrowing his eyes at me. "Oh, you think you can just disappear from Swifties4Life and not text back for days on end and that we wouldn't show up?"

What in the fuck is happening?

Before I can even respond, Lane steps from behind Reese and folds his arms over his chest, mumbling, "Moneybags here rented a jet, and here we are."

"You weren't complaining earlier when you were joining the mile-high club, dickface," Reese retorts with a shit-eating grin.

A hand flies out of nowhere from behind him, smacking him directly in the back of the head.

Reese winces, his shoulders hunching. "Ouch, Viv. What the hell was that for?"

Suddenly, his five-foot-nothing, fiery girlfriend pushes

between the two of them with Hallie, Lane's girlfriend, in tow. I notice that Hallie's changed out her signature purple streaks in her hair to bright green ones, and my mouth curves up in a grin.

Holy shit… how are my best friends *here*? It's been so long since I've seen them. Too fucking long. And no matter how ridiculous Reese's reasons are for dragging them all here, I'm just ridiculously happy to see them.

I surge forward and drag both Viv and Hallie into my arms, hugging them so tightly they squeal in mock protest.

"Fuck, I can't believe you guys are here right now," I say.

After giving them both one last squeeze, I move on to my boys, giving Lane a lingering hug despite his grumbling, and the same with Reese, even though Boo's caught between us.

The dude takes "cat dad" to a whole new level.

"You gonna let us in, or are we gonna stand out here and braid each other's hair?" Lane says, brow arched in question.

Shit, I missed his grumpy ass. And Reese's over-the-top ass. I realize that while, yeah, he's been busy playing for a new team, and Lane's growing out his beard… we're the kind of friends who'll always pick back up where we left off, no matter how long we go without seeing each other.

We all head back inside the apartment, and the second that the girls see Auggie sitting by the coffee table, they lose their minds.

"You got a *dog*?" Hallie squeals excitedly, bouncing on the toes of her checkered Vans. She rushes over to him and squats to cover him in kisses as she rubs his ears.

To absolutely no surprise, he's eating the attention up, rolling over onto his back with his pudgy little legs and paws pointed toward the ceiling.

"God, he is so freaking cute," Viv murmurs as she joins Hallie on the floor to lavish Auggie with head scratches.

I'm pretty sure he's going to have a heart attack from the amount of attention he's getting.

Reese bends down, taking Boo out of the carrier and placing her gently onto the floor after giving her a few kisses on her head. Completely unfazed, Boo stretches before taking in her new surroundings. Clearly, she's gotten used to outings and other animals because she pads directly over to Auggie without hesitation.

She takes a furry black paw and pokes him with curiosity, but he just licks her face in response. Apparently, that's enough for her to consider him a friend because she lazily lies down next to him, cuddling up to Viv's side.

"So, you got fucking *married*, you got a *dog*, you signed a *six-figure* sponsorship. Anything else you care to tell us?" Reese says as he flops down onto the sofa, pulling his hat off and dropping it into his lap.

"Yeh, one more thing... I think I'm in love with my wife."

"Uh... duh?" Reese replies as if he's stating the obvious. "Are you just figuring that out or...?"

Lane chortles, covering his mouth. "Apparently so."

Part of me is glad Addie's not here for this conversation so I can get advice from my guys, but then an even bigger part of me can't wait for her to meet the most important people in my life, besides my mama and her.

She's with Amos working at the bakery, so she'll be home later this afternoon.

I walk over to the armchair and sink down into it, exhaling. "Yeah, well, it's complicated, remember?"

More complicated than I've even had a chance to tell them. So I quickly catch them up about all that has transpired in the past few days with the bakery, and our suspicions about who's behind it, and about the weekend spent with my mom. And the biggest update of all… that I have, in fact, realized I'm in love with Addie and have probably been in love with her longer than I even knew.

"Listen, I'm going to start making you schedule a weekly FaceTime call with us so you can keep us up to date on your life. And stop neglecting the group chat," Reese says exasperatedly. "I fucking hate that we're the last to know anything."

"For once, I agree," Lane adds with a solemn expression. "I mean, I get it. Life is busy, we're all on opposite sides of the country doing different shit, but we're your best friends, man."

I nod. It has been hard this year not seeing my two best friends every day. But as much as I hate that they're so fucking far away, I know they're all happy and thriving, and that's all that I want for them.

"Yeah, I'm pretty sure I caught Reese crying when he found out he missed your wedding," Viv says from the floor. Auggie's somehow halfway in her lap and halfway in Hallie's, taking what looks like the best nap of his life.

My lips twitch. Reese's brow furrows, and he acts completely shocked by her admission, quickly defending himself. "I was not… crying. I had something in my eye. Dust or something."

Viv rolls her eyes with a smirk. "Mhm. Dust. Whatever you need to tell yourself, baby. Just admit that you miss your friend."

"I do miss him, and I have no problem talking about my feelings. And even if I was crying, it's fine. Men have emotions and can express them too," Reese mutters matter-of-factly.

Shit, I didn't realize just how badly I missed this until now.

"Reese, focus. Can we go back to Grant's problem?" Hallie interjects. "So… you love Addie. Have you told her that yet?" she asks with a small smile.

I shake my head, and the room erupts in a chorus of groans.

"Dude, did you not learn anything from Lane?" Reese says, nodding toward him.

"I'm going to tell her. My mom gave me the same advice when we visited. I just... with everything going on, I don't want to complicate things further for her by moving too fast. It just feels selfish." I pause, flicking my gaze between all of them. "And I don't want my love for Addie to be selfish. She deserves everything. The whole world."

Viv's nose wrinkles. "That is the most romantic thing I've ever heard, Grant. This is why you *have* to tell her. She deserves to know how you feel about her."

"Yeah, what my girl said," Reese quips, staring at her adoringly in a way that used to make me want to hurl myself off a bridge. Not because I'm not happy for my friends—I am, and I always have been. It was just the fact that I was always the third wheel, and now... I get it. I so fucking get it.

I'm pretty sure I stare at Addie the exact same way. I guess it took falling in love to really understand.

"I know you're right, and I need to tell her. I just also... want the first time I tell her that I love her to be memorable. I want to do it the right way, to plan something that she'll never forget."

I expect the guys to give me at least a little bit of shit for wanting to do something sappy, but they genuinely just look like they're excited for me.

Reese hops up from the couch and claps his hands together enthusiastically, "So let's do this shit. We're going to help you plan the best fucking love profession to ever exist."

Lane chuckles. "Clearly, Reese has been waiting his entire life for this."

I'm vividly remembering times when I helped *both* of these idiots who were in love and didn't even realize it, and now I'm the *idiot* in love who needs help.

"Tell us about her. What does she like? What's she into? What's important to her?" Hallie asks as she tucks a black, springy curl behind her ear.

I drag my hand over my jaw pensively. "She's an artist and loves to sketch and paint. Baking. Her family owns Ever After, a bakery down by the Quarter, so she's amazing at it. She's also into space, constellations."

"Oh. What if you, like… named a star after her?" Reese says, and I can't hide the shock that morphs my face.

That's actually… a really good fucking idea. Brilliant, honestly.

"Babe, that's literally from *A Walk to Remember*. With Mandy Moore?" Viv points out with a soft expression.

"Shit. Is that the one you made me watch a few weeks ago?" he asks, scratching his head, suddenly looking a bit red.

Viv nods. "Yep. You got dust in your eye then too."

My lip tugs into a grin as I raise my fist to my mouth and attempt to hide it.

She is always outing that dude for his sensitive side. Of course Reese fucking Landry would cry watching *A Walk to Remember*.

"Uh… yeah, okay, well, it was just a suggestion," Reese replies as he walks over to Boo and picks her up, clutching her in his arms.

I stand from the chair and steal her right from his arms, cuddling her cute-as-shit, furry little body to me. I missed my Boo bear. I'm the worst uncle in the history of the world for not cuddling her the moment she got here, but in my defense, she was all too happy to be hanging out with Auggie.

"It was a great suggestion, man. I appreciate you all trying to help. But I… think I have an idea. Something that will be special to her," I say as I rub Boo's head affectionately.

"Whatever you decide, Grant, I know it'll be perfect," Hallie offers, and my gaze flits to her, a smile curving my mouth slightly.

"Thanks, Hal. Thank you all for hopping on a plane to come check on me. I'm really fucking glad that you did because I miss you guys."

"Thank rich guy over he—"

The sound of the front door opening cuts Lane off, and everyone's attention turns toward the entryway as Addie appears, her blonde hair piled high on her head and wearing my favorite dress. The one with little flowers all over it. The one I have very fucking fond memories of.

"Oh. Uh… hi," she mutters timidly as her gaze shifts to mine.

I didn't have a chance to text her and tell her that everyone was here since they surprised the shit out of me.

"Hey, ba—"

Hallie and Viv barely even give me a chance to open my mouth to explain and introduce everyone before they're both barreling toward her, pulling her into a hug as if they're not meeting her for the very first time. For a second, I see Addie's eyes widen, a flash of surprise flickering in them, but then she laughs nervously, reaching up to return their embrace.

"Hi, I'm Viv, and this is Hallie, and we've heard so much about you. I feel like I already know you? Which basically just means we're all best friends at this point," Viv rambles as she pulls back and smiles warmly at Addie.

Hallie laughs, stepping back. "God, Viv, give her a second to *breathe*."

"Hi. It's nice to meet you. I've heard so much about you guys too," Addie replies shyly, walking over to me. I've got a sleeping Boo against my chest, cradled in my arms, but I dip my head and give her a quick kiss.

"Sorry for just randomly showing up. My boyfriend has entirely too much money and a flair for the dramatic, and he missed his bestie," Viv tells her. "It was definitely a last-minute thing, and we wanted to surprise Grant. And meet you, of course."

Addie shakes her head vehemently. "No, I'm so happy you're here. I've been looking forward to meeting everyone, and honestly, this is a great surprise to come home to," she says genuinely.

After Reese and Lane introduce themselves and we all catch up for a bit, Hallie and Viv quickly steal her away for "girl talk," shooing us out to the patio. The three of them immediately hit it off in a way I truly didn't expect. Not because I thought that they wouldn't like each other, but because I know how shy Addie is and how sometimes meeting new people is hard for her. But clearly, that is not the case here. In part, because my friends are so welcoming to her, just like I knew they would be.

When she gives me a sweet smile, letting me know she's okay to be alone with the girls, I set a sleeping Boo next to Auggie on his bed, then join the guys outside.

"You're either blind or stupid because that girl loves you back, dude," Reese says when the patio door shuts behind me. "You both look at each other with fucking heart eyes. It's actually adorable."

Lane nods in agreement. "Can't believe I'm saying this again today... but he's right."

"Letting Reese be right? Damn, I know that wasn't easy for you to admit, man. Good for you," I reply, slapping Lane on the back with a grin.

Reese's dark brows furrow. "You know, assholes, I'm right more often than not. And I *know* I'm right about this. You gotta tell her, Grant. And so help me fucking god, if I'm not best man at your next *real* wedding, I am breaking up with you. Cold turkey, cutting your ass off. Nobody puts baby in the corner."

"You and Lane can rock paper scissors over it," I say jokingly, but knowing Reese, he's not going down without a fight.

But his joke also jolts me. I've been so caught up in thinking about just admitting my feelings to Addie that I didn't even consider what actually happens after I do. We're already married. We skipped a lot of fucking steps. If she feels the same way, do I just date my wife? What happens when the stuff with the bakery is over?

I don't want an annulment.

I sure as fuck don't want a divorce.

I want her to be mine, for real this time. I want to protect her, cherish her.

I want to be the man who puts *her* first, especially when no one in her life ever has.

I want all of it, and I want it with her. Even if we did it backward.

There's nothing I've been more sure of.

"You know, it's really nice being the one to dish out relationship advice for a change," Reese says with a smirk. "What would you two do without me?"

"Jesus Christ," Lane grunts.

"Need I remind you who got on their hands and fucking knees and crawled around a baseball field looking for tiny-ass little beads for you?" Reese sasses back.

I bite back a laugh because, you know… he's right.

Lane rolls his eyes as he drags a hand through his mop of dark blond waves.

"Tell me you love me, Lane. Go on," Reese mutters, crossing his arms over his chest and lifting a brow.

Lane shakes his head exasperatedly. "Fuck me. Why are you like this?"

Sometimes they drive me fucking nuts, and they bicker like an old married couple, but honestly... I'm just thankful because they're *here*.

These guys are my family, no matter how many miles separate us. No matter how much time passes. No matter what changes in our lives. Long past our time at Orleans U.

We'll always have each other. The kind of bond that can't be broken.

My brothers.

chapter twenty-five

Addie

I'M *SLIGHTLY* FREAKING OUT.

By slightly, I mean I'm currently on my… fourth batch of strawberry meringue cupcakes.

Clearly, there's a cupcake crisis happening. And it's *entirely* my husband's fault.

He's the reason there are forty-eight cupcakes cooling on racks on the marble countertop in our kitchen.

Because they're his favorite. And today's his twenty-third birthday. The first birthday we've shared together, and I just want today to be all about him. He does so much for me and is the most giving person I've ever met; he should have an entire day dedicated to *him*.

And even then, it doesn't feel like nearly enough.

Almost two weeks have passed since the break-in at the bakery, and now that the new glass on the front cases has been replaced, we should be able to reopen by the end of the week.

And Grant has been a pillar of unwavering strength through every step of the way.

He's kind and patient and reassuring when I'm feeling like there's no light at the end of the tunnel. He's attentive and protective of not just me but also the things that bring me joy. He respects Amos and Earl like they're my parents and understands that they are the most important people in my life.

He's become my *best friend*, and I'm so in love with him that it scares me.

That's part of the reason why I'm stress baking. Because I want tonight to go exactly as I planned.

After I set the last pan of cupcakes onto the counter to cool, I do a quick whirl around the kitchen and dining room, my eyes roving over all of the details I've been painstakingly working on since Grant left this morning for a meeting with the new brand he's working with.

Breathe, Addie. Everything's going to be great.

I keep telling myself the same thing, but it's done little to quell the wave of anxiety that sits in my belly.

Not only have I spent the majority of the day working on his favorite cupcakes, but I ordered Gino's for dinner and set the table with an array of candles. I'm wearing his favorite dress, the one with the tiny yellow daisies, and I picked out something... special for underneath it.

Hence the main reason my palms are clammy and my heart has been beating in an uneven rhythm the entire day.

I just don't want him to think all of this is... I don't know, silly.

It's the first time in my life I've ever attempted to do anything like this, which makes the sliver of self-doubt inside me bloom.

I want it to be perfect.

Grabbing a spatula from the utensil holder, I fill a pastry bag and start piping frosting on the cupcakes in an attempt to calm my heart and force my brain to shut off for longer than five seconds.

I'm in the middle of filling another bag to frost the second half when I hear the front door slam, nearly causing me to drop the spatula and the entire bowl of icing.

My god.

My hand shakes as I run it down the front of my denim dress, smoothing nonexistent wrinkles, and then brush the braided front pieces of my hair out of my face.

A second later, Grant walks into the kitchen wearing a broad, maddeningly handsome smile that almost causes me to melt into a puddle on the floor. His dark blond hair is combed back, and he's wearing a crisp white button-down tucked into a pair of fitted black slacks, the fabric hugging his muscular thighs.

His eyes find me the second he walks into the room, and it makes my pulse quicken, just as it always does. When he strides toward me, closing the distance between us, realization morphs his face, and he falters, his brows pulling together.

"Hi, beautiful. Uhhhhh… Why are there…" He trails off, his eyes flicking between the dozens of cupcakes on the counter. "So many cupcakes?"

I set the icing-covered spatula on the counter and launch myself at him before my nerves get the best of me, wrapping my arms around his neck. "Because it's your birthday and they're your favorite? Happy birthday, Grant."

I feel the rumble of his chest vibrating against me as he laughs and slides his arms around my waist, holding me tightly against him. "Thank you, baby. But you know you didn't have to make this many, right?"

He pulls back slightly, bringing his hand to my face and brushing his thumb lightly over the ball of my flushed cheek.

"Yes, well, once I started stress baking, I couldn't stop myself."

"Why are you stressed?"

I exhale shallowly. "Because I just want tonight to be perfect.

I've been working on it all week, and I want you to have the best birthday."

For a second, he's quiet, his dark blue eyes searching before he dips his head and presses his lips to mine in the sweetest kiss that has a riot of tingles coursing through me.

When he pulls back, lips hovering a breath away from mine, he whispers, "It's already the best birthday I've ever had."

"But you haven't even seen everything yet. There's more," I respond as my eyes lift to his in a daze. It's impossible to be kissed by Grant and not feel like the world has faded out around us.

"Doesn't matter. Because I've got the most beautiful wife in the world, and nothing could ever be better than that."

Okay, officially melting into nothing. I'm hopeless.

My arms tighten around his neck, and I lift on my tippy-toes, pressing another kiss to his mouth. His hands slide along my jaw into my hair, and he pulls me closer as his tongue sweeps along the seam of my lips, demanding access. In a matter of seconds, the kiss turns hungry and desperate, like neither of us can get enough. I'm all but climbing his chiseled body, as embarrassing as that sounds.

Grant tears his lips from mine, staring down at me with a look that I feel all the way to my core. "As much as I want to stay here for the rest of the night kissing you until you can't breathe, I'm fucking starving. Unless… you want to be my dinner?"

Oh my god. Heat rushes to my cheeks, and my eyes widen of their own accord, causing him to toss his head back and let out the raspiest, sexiest laugh I've possibly ever heard.

"W-well… I, uh, I ordered NOLA po' boys. B-But…" I stammer over my words and then just shut my mouth.

Because honestly, I'm squeezing my thighs together at the thought of Grant doing… that.

"I guess that's why my stomach is growling like there's something living in there," he says with a chuckle.

I slip my arms from around his neck and take a step back, turning toward the table. "I got your favorite shrimp po' boy and obviously cooked way too many cupcakes, but at least there's some for later?"

Grant walks to the table, pulling out the chair beside his and gesturing for me to sit. Once I do, he scoots it forward and sits down next to me. As we eat dinner, he tells me about how the meeting with the brand went and how things are going even better than he anticipated.

I love seeing the excitement on his face and how animatedly he talks about their values and how they align with his.

There's no one who deserves this more than him. It may be the off-season, and I haven't seen him play yet, but I *have* seen the way he trains relentlessly, putting in hours at the gym and training facilities to prepare. He's determined and driven, and I love being able to witness his hard work pay off.

I'm proud of him.

Once we're done eating, he helps me clear the table, even though it takes twice as long because he keeps stopping to kiss me until I can hardly remain upright.

Afterward, I tell him that he has to stay at least a foot away from me until Auggie and I are done singing him happy birthday because I can't even think properly when he's touching me, let alone kissing me.

"These are the best cupcakes of my fucking life, baby." He groans around a mouthful of icing as he leans against the kitchen counter.

"Thank you. I'm glad you like them. I… have something else for you." I walk over to the entry closet and grab the present that I wrapped earlier.

I'm second-guessing it, but it's too late to go back now.

He takes it from me with a boyish smile, one that lights up his entire face. "What did you say to me that one time about spoiling, ArtGirl?"

"It's your birthday. Everyone should be spoiled on their birthday."

I shift nervously on my feet as he slides a finger beneath the silver bow, deftly untying it, then tearing the paper off.

When he sees what's inside, his eyes snap to mine. "Baby..."

"I know it's probably silly, but I just..." I trail off, my gaze dropping down to where I'm fingering the hem of my dress nervously.

I feel him in front of me before I even see that he's moved, closing the distance between us so quickly that my breath hitches. The pad of his finger finds my chin, and he tilts it up, pulling my gaze to his.

"It's not silly. It's perfect, and I love it." He says it with such conviction that I believe him.

I swallow down the tight ball of emotion in my throat before I speak. "It's what I'm going to turn in for my art thesis portfolio. You... You were the only thing I could draw. I started over so many times because nothing ever felt right. I was so frustrated with myself, with my abilities, but then I met you, and... everything just kind of clicked into place. It was like drawing something I'd done a hundred times. It felt like I was drawing from my heart."

The words tumble out of me in a rush, and for the first time, I'm thankful for my nervous rambling because I'm not sure I would've ever had the courage to say any of that out loud otherwise.

Emotion, strong like a current, flows through the deep blue of his irises, and his throat bobs. "It's the best gift I've ever received, Addie." His words are laced with fierce sincerity, and it makes my chest ache.

The canvas he's holding is a sketch of him from the night that we sat under the stars and talked about how big the universe was. It wasn't that long ago, but so much has changed since then, and I was worried that drawing him as my subject would be… too much. But truthfully, Grant's the only thing that feels right anymore. A feeling that's both terrifying and comforting at the same time.

He sets the canvas on the counter and turns toward me, his hands finding my hips and tugging me to him before he wraps his arms tightly around my waist. He's holding me like I'm going to break apart in his hands, and it causes my chest to physically ache. The expression on his face is unreadable, his jaw set in a line as his eyes flick between mine, searching.

"I love you, Addie," he murmurs softly.

"Grant…" His name slips from my lips in a breathless whisper. My heart is thudding so hard in my chest that it feels hard to breathe. I desperately pull in a breath as he continues talking.

"I'm in love with you, and I've wanted to tell you that for weeks, but I wanted everything to be perfect. I wanted the timing to be right and the date I was planning to be something you'd never forget. Because you deserve that, and I want to be the guy that gives you everything. But, Addie, I couldn't wait another second to tell you that I'm in love with you. And that this marriage isn't fake for me. Not anymore. It's the most real thing I've ever felt."

My cheeks are wet with tears when he finishes, and I have a hundred different things that I want to say. But I physically can't stop myself as I throw my arms around his neck, a choked sob escaping against his mouth as I press my lips against his. After a beat of salty, tear-filled kisses, I tear my lips away and say, "I love you too. Just in case you didn't understand what that meant."

Grant chuckles, his breath fanning over my tearstained cheeks as he brings his hand to my face and cradles it in his palm, gently sweeping his thumb to dry them. "I was hoping that's what you meant, but I wasn't sure…"

His voice is light and teasing, and I laugh through a happy sob. "I was afraid to tell you how I felt because I was scared that you wouldn't feel the same way. Our marriage was supposed to be an arrangement, and I didn't want to make things weird between us if I was the only one who had these feelings. I thought maybe that you did, but this entire arrangement was built around pretending. I thought you were just playing the part," I whisper.

He shakes his head as he strokes my cheek, the expression on his face turning soft. "Baby, I'm fucking crazy about you. It hasn't been pretend for me in a long time—honestly, I'm not sure if it ever was. When I kissed you for the first time at that altar, I think a part of me knew, right then and there, that there was no turning back. That there would never be anyone besides you, Addie."

"It's real for me too. All of it, Grant," I murmur softly against his lips. "I… I want to be yours. Really yours."

God, I can't even believe this is happening right now and that I'm saying those words out loud.

"You've always been mine, Addie. Even before you realized it." His voice is low and full of conviction.

I think back to when we only knew each other through a computer screen, how I used to only allow myself a moment, brief and fleeting, to imagine what it would be like to be his. But I knew that my life was too much of a mess, and feared that if we ever really met, a guy like him wouldn't want a girl like *me*. I thought it would never be anything other than me wishing that my life was different.

Except, all this time later, Grant Bergeron *loves* me.

We said we would leave things to fate. And by whatever strings that control the universe, we somehow ended up together.

"I've wanted to be yours for longer than you even know, Jockboy," I say, my eyes dropping to his lips before I lift on the tips of my toes and brush my lips against his. I feel more brazen than I've ever felt, and I think it's because I'm comfortable with him like no one else. "Will you… take me to bed?"

chapter*twenty-six

Addie

GRANT LIFTS me off my feet at the same time that I wrap my legs around his waist, and he carries me toward the bedroom without ever breaking our kiss. It feels different somehow, charged in a way that it's never felt like before. and maybe that's because now we both know that this isn't fake. That the way we feel is real. And that changes *everything*.

It feels surreal, that as much of a mess my life has been, it led me here. To him.

He walks us into the bedroom, pushing the door shut with his foot, then tearing his lips away from my lips, trailing hot, open-mouthed kisses along my jaw, down to the sensitive column of my neck.

My head feels dizzy, and my pulse races. The feeling of his lips searing along my skin has my toes curling and my fingers sliding to tug at the short hair at his nape. Everything feels on fire, a tangible burn that continues to ignite with each press of his lips and drag of his tongue along my heated skin.

A whimper falls from my lips, and he lifts his head, his eyes connecting with mine. The hunger blazing inside of them gives me confidence I never thought I could possess. It gives me the boldness to show him just how much I love him and how safe I feel with him.

How much I *trust* him to take care of me. When there's never been anyone in my life that I could trust this way.

I unwrap my legs carefully from around his waist, sliding down every inch of his hard, unyielding body until my feet touch the hardwood. Pulling in a deep, shaky breath, I take two steps back and gaze up at him, holding his eyes as I reach for the hem of my dress and pull it over my head.

The matching bra and panties that I ordered probably aren't very sexy... it's not like I have a lot of experience in the matter, but I know that Grant loves it when I wear blue. The lace set hugs my curves and flatters my figure.

Clearly, my husband likes it because there's an audible hiss that fills the room when the dress hits the floor, and I drag my gaze back to his. I watch as his throat bobs, his expression a mixture of hunger and reverence.

Reaching behind me, I slowly unclasp my bra despite my trembling hands. I hold his eyes as I slowly drag the straps down my arms, letting the bra slide off to hit the hardwood.

Even though I'm nervous, I know with absolute certainty that this is what I want. That Grant is who I want.

My fingers hook into the waistband of my panties, and I languidly drag them down my hips until they're pooling at my feet, leaving me completely and utterly naked.

"Baby..." he murmurs darkly, his gaze dropping to my chest and lingering, making my core throb and my nipples tighten into taut, hard peaks. Heat pools in my belly as his eyes slide lower, doing an agonizingly slow perusal of my bare skin like he's memorizing every inch. I'm throbbing with every touch of his gaze.

There was a time where I felt self-conscious and so nervous

that I couldn't imagine ever being naked in front of my husband, but now... there's nothing I want as badly as the feel of his hands dragging languidly over my skin.

"I'm ready... I- I want you, Grant. I want to share this with *you*," I whisper, stepping closer until I stop right in front of him, the heat of his body radiating against my bare skin and sending a shiver down my spine.

A beat passes between us, the seconds tangible as his stormy eyes search mine before he lunges forward, his hands sliding along my jaw as his mouth crashes against mine. My hands fly to the top of his as he kisses me so frantically, so desperately, that I'm holding on simply so my legs won't give out beneath me. He teases at the seam of my lips, and the moment that I open for him, he delves in, his tongue dancing with mine, swallowing the needy, desperate whimper straight from me.

His hands slide down my body, palming my butt and lifting me off my feet, carrying me toward the bed. He gently sets me onto the mattress, hovering over me with impossibly dark and hungry eyes.

"Are you sure, Addie? I don't want you to feel pressured, because, baby, I'd wait for the rest of my life if I had to an—"

I stop him with a finger pressed to his lips and a shake of my head. "I've never been more sure of anything in my life. I love you, and I want this to be *ours*." My fingers brush along the dark blond hair brushing his forehead, pushing it back as I gaze up at him. "The only thing that has ever truly been my decision is this."

"And you have no fucking idea how much it means to me, Addie. How much *you* mean to me. I love you so much."

The words wash over me, causing my heart to thrash wildly, and I'm not sure if I'll ever get over hearing him say those words.

Grant rises, standing from the bed, and quickly makes work of his button-down and slacks. The sculpted muscles of his abdomen flex as he stands in front of me with nothing but those tight black boxer briefs that mold to every inch of his dick. It's hard and tenting the fabric, and I want to wrap my palm around him.

I want to feel him come apart the same way that I do when he touches me.

"Stop looking at me like that, baby," he murmurs hoarsely. My gaze lifts, and I see a tortured expression on his handsome face.

"Why?" I ask innocently.

I know exactly the way I'm looking at him, but I love when he says dirty things that make me throb.

"Because I want to last when I fuck my wife for the first time."

Oh. God.

My thighs press together, and my core clenches with each raspy syllable. I'm already so wet I can feel my arousal coating my inner thighs.

I'm almost ashamed of how turned on I am for him.

He strides forward, his large palms sliding up my thighs as the mattress dips and he hovers over me. He leans forward, capturing my hardened nipple in his mouth, sucking and biting until I'm nearly panting beneath him. Then, he moves on to the other, giving it an equal amount of tortured attention.

His teeth scrape along the peak, and my back arches as my fingers slide into his hair, anchoring him in place. Pulling back, he looks up at me with a slight curve of his lip. "I love how responsive you are."

Pressing a kiss to the center of my chest, he trails his lips lower, using his tongue to trace a heated path down my stomach until he grips my thighs, gently spreading them open.

He settles his broad shoulders between my parted legs and grabs my hips, pulling me to the edge of the bed. He presses sweet, searing kisses along the inside of my ankle, trailing his lips up over my calves until his lips meet my inner thighs.

I suck in a shallow gasp at the sensation. He's so close to my core that I can feel his hot, panting breath, and my heart thuds in my chest so hard that I feel like I may faint.

"Do you know how badly I've wanted to eat my wife's pussy? How badly I've wanted to fuck you with my tongue, to suck your sensitive little clit between my lips and see if your skin flushed the same pink as your cheeks?" he rasps.

I'm so flustered, so turned on, that I'm not sure I could speak right now even if I wanted to.

When he blows softly on my slick flesh, I whimper hoarsely, my fingers fisting into the soft sheets beneath me until they ache.

"It's all I've thought about. Tasting you, making you come on my face. Can I, baby? Can I taste how fucking sweet you are?"

Pulling my lip between my teeth, I nod. "Y-yes."

His palms slide up my inner thighs, and then I feel his fingers brushing against my fluttering center, causing me to suck in a stuttering breath.

Grant's barely touched me, and yet I feel like I could combust at any given moment already. It's dizzying. Using his fingers, he spreads me wide, the cool air hitting my exposed core, and groans raggedly.

"Fuck, you're so pretty. Already so wet and needy for me. Look at the mess you've made."

Rising on my elbows, I glance down to see him admiring me with such raw hunger and want in his eyes that I shiver, goose bumps erupting along my flesh.

Grant staring at me like I'm the most beautiful thing he's ever seen makes me feel desired and wanted in a way that I know only he will ever be able to make me feel.

He dips his head and drags his flattened tongue up my slit torturously slowly. The groan that spills from his mouth sends a vibration through me, and my thighs try to press together, desperate for any way of relieving the ache that's throbbing inside of me.

"Oh… god."

My husband between my thighs, eating me like a man possessed, is going to be seared into my memory forever. There's nothing sexier than seeing him be so turned on by bringing me pleasure.

My head falls back against my shoulders, my eyes squeezing shut as he begins to eat me, each swipe of his tongue sending me spiraling into a state of euphoria.

God, it feels… there are no words. My brain is hazy, my attention unfocused as I fall back against the mattress.

Over and over, he laps at me, circling my clit with this tongue, flicking my sensitive bud with the tip of his tongue until I'm writhing. And then he sucks my clit into his mouth roughly, working it between his lips, alternating the pressure, and my hips buck off the bed. Reaching up, he flattens his palm along my belly to hold me still while he licks my pussy as if he's starving.

"Grant…" Unable to stop, I cry out. My hands fly to his hair, grasping at the strands, tugging harder with each pull of my clit into his mouth.

He slides his thick finger inside of me, thrusting it in time with the flick of his tongue, and my back arches off the mattress, pushing my core against his mouth, chasing the blinding intensity building inside of me.

"Squeeze my finger, baby. Suck me into your greedy little pussy," he murmurs, curling his finger upward to rub the spot inside of me that has the corners of my vision darkening. "I can't wait to watch my cock sliding in your cunt, stretching around me, taking every inch of me." He adds another finger, and my back bows, my breath stuttering as the feeling of being full overtakes me.

The filthy words have me flooding his finger with arousal, and I realize just how much I love to hear him talk like this. I want to hear him whisper dirty words into my ear as he moves inside me, skin to skin.

I'm so close, my orgasm building higher and higher, pulsing as he thrusts his fingers, heat flooding my lower belly.

"Come for me, baby. Be a good little wife and soak your husband's tongue with your cum. "

It only takes one more pump of his fingers and lash of his tongue on my clit and I'm soaring, the most powerful orgasm I've ever experienced ripping through me like a torrential current.

I choke out a sated whimper, my voice no longer even my own. My fingers tighten in his hair as my climax pulses through me with such intensity that my legs tremble violently.

It's euphoria in its purest form, and I'm addicted.

I sag into the mattress as I pant, unable to hold my eyes open as he pulls every ounce of pleasure out of me until I'm a limp, sated mess.

"The most perfect little wife," he whispers against my heated skin, pressing a single kiss to my still-throbbing clit.

I'm quite actually speechless.

When he crawls up my body, hovering over me, only then do I pry my eyes open and stare up at him hazily.

"We can stop right here, baby, if you want and do nothing

else," he says with such fierce sincerity that my chest physically aches.

I can't believe that this is the man I get to love.

That he's *mine.*

"I want you. I want to feel you inside me," I say.

Reaching between us, I slide my shaking fingers beneath the waistband of his boxers and curve my palm around his erection. He's so big that my fingers don't meet, and for a split second, I consider changing my mind, only because... I'm concerned if he's going to fit. There's just no possible way, even with how wet I still am for him.

Apparently, my expression reflects the brief hesitation, and he chuckles lightly.

"Are you worried about something?"

Dragging my teeth along my bottom lip, I nod. "I... I'm not sure how *that* is going to fit in *there.*" My gaze shifts between us, and this time, he laughs, the deep timbre filling the room.

He reaches for my face, palming the curve of my jaw in his hand. "Trust me, wife, it'll fit."

Wife.

I'm truly convinced there is nothing better than hearing him whisper those words while my hand is wrapped around the evidence of how badly he wants me.

A deep, guttural noise rumbles from the back of his throat when I squeeze him in my hand and then gently pump him. "Fuuuck."

I repeat the motion, earning another sharp hiss as his head falls against my shoulder, and his eyes drop shut.

"Like this?" I ask.

His mouth parts, and he nods.

Only a second later, he's pulling my hand free with a tight

shake of his head. "I'm really fucking trying not to embarrass myself right now, but I'm about to come."

"I want you inside me. Please, Grant."

He whispers a curse, sitting up on his knees as he peers down at me and begins to work his boxers off. His dick bobs free, and my eyes widen at seeing the size up close for the first time.

God, it looks even bigger than it feels.

Long and thick. He's *impossibly* hard. There's a prominent vein running up the side and a thick, deep pink head that's glistening with a pearl of cum from the slit.

I swallow roughly at the same time I press my thighs together, the familiar dull ache returning as arousal spirals inside of me. My husband is that hard for *me*.

I want him. I want this with him, and I'm ready.

Reaching for the nightstand, he opens the drawer, and I hear the rustle of foil.

"I'll be as gentle as I can, baby, I promise," he whispers as he tears it open, sheathing himself in one swift motion before fitting his hips between my parted thighs. I can feel his dick, heavy and thick, pressing against me. Even though there is a part of me that's still nervous, there's an even bigger part of me that's beyond ready to share this with Grant.

He leans forward, pressing his lips gently against me, kissing me so tenderly that I feel hot tears well in my eyes. He's so attentive and gentle and always seems to know exactly what I need.

Like he sometimes knows me better than I even know myself.

His tongue tangles unhurriedly with mine as he reaches between us and gently hitches my leg up around his hip, then drags his erection through my pussy lips slowly, coating him with my arousal.

The head of his dick nudges against my clit, and I suck in a sharp breath against his mouth.

"If you want to stop, all you have to do is tell me, okay?" he says with sincerity, his hand gently rubbing my leg hitched around him.

I nod silently, sliding my hands around his hips to his back, pulling him to me.

His palm curves around my hips as he slowly pushes into me. The pain is sharp and searing at first, an unexpected gasp tumbling from my lips at the sensation.

Grant drops his forehead to mine as my eyes squeeze shut. "I'm so sorry, baby. I can st—"

"Don't you dare," I mutter, opening my eyes to peer up at him. "I want you to keep going. I'll be okay. I just need to get used to it."

Without another word, he nods and flexes his hips forward inch by inch, gently pushing into me.

I feel the moment where he breaks through the barrier inside of me that has fire coursing through me. It hurts, but it only lasts for a fleeting moment as he pushes to the hilt.

His arms shake in restraint as he holds himself above me, unmoving, giving my body a chance to acclimate to him.

Reaching between us, he skims his thumb along my clit, soft, steady circles that have me quickly forgetting about the pain altogether.

The combination of his rhythmic thrumming of my clit and the feel of him buried deep, stretching me, replaces the pain with an insatiable need for… more.

My fingers dig into his skin, signaling for more, and he lifts his eyes to mine.

"Are you okay?"

"Yes… You can move," I whisper.

His eyes darken, and he leans down, brushing his lips against mine, swallowing the whimper that escapes when he withdraws and slowly thrusts back in. Again and again, he moves slowly, winding up a string of something tight inside of me until I'm ready to beg for more.

Nothing has ever felt as good as feeling full of my husband. "More, please."

Grasping my hip, he thrusts harder, deeper, reaching a spot I've never felt, and my toes curl against his back as blinding pleasure courses through me.

"You feel so good, baby, so goddamn tight I'm losing my fucking mind," he rasps, surging forward and bottoming out inside of me. Every stroke of hips has his pelvis brushing against my clit, and the movement is sending my senses into overdrive. It's maddening, and I'm desperate to come. "I need you to come for me. I need to feel you coming on my cock for the first time."

Grant dips his head to my breast, sucking my nipple into his mouth as he rocks his hips, rolling the taut peak between his lips roughly, and pleasure rips through me, splitting me open wide.

The unexpected orgasm hits me with blinding intensity, my head falling back against the mattress as I clamp down, pulsing around my husband's dick.

"Grant, Grant, Grant," I chant.

His forehead falls to the center of my chest as he groans hoarsely and thrusts deep one last time. I feel the hot lash of his cum filling the condom, and it sends a wave of aftershocks through me, wringing every ounce of pleasure from my body.

My chest heaves as he sags against me, our sweat-slicked skin bleeding together until I don't know where he ends and I begin.

I've never felt so close to another person. Never felt so raw and vulnerable, and I know with all my heart that I'll always be safe with Grant. I'll always be cherished, and loved, and protected. He proves that every day, not just with his words but with his actions, and I've learned that is what really matters.

"I love you, Addie." His words are whispered against my skin, sinking into me. "I'm never going to stop loving you the way you deserve. You will always be the most important thing to me."

Tears well in my eyes as an overwhelming sense of emotions wash over me. I run my fingers through his damp hair, holding on to him so tightly that I never want to let go.

"I love you," I reply quietly.

We stay that way for so long that I nearly fall asleep, my limbs heavy with exhaustion but Grant finally lifts his head, pressing a sweet kiss to my lips before he lifts himself off me and gently withdraws from my body.

I wince at the movement, and his brow furrows, a look of worry sliding onto his face.

"Let me take care of you, baby," he whispers, pressing a soft kiss along my lower stomach. "Give me a second."

When I nod, he pushes himself off the plush mattress and strides to the bathroom, returning a minute or so later with a damp washcloth in his hand. I'm so exhausted that I can hardly keep my eyes open, but I attempt to as he climbs back onto the bed, and then I feel the warm cloth between my legs as he gently cleans my sensitive core with achingly tender movements. A comfortable silence hangs in the air, only the sound of our soft breathing as Grant does what he always does—takes care of me.

My fingers find the smooth strands of his hair, raking slowly through them. I'd never given a lot of thought to what losing my virginity would actually be like; I thought maybe awkward and only painful. But as Grant puts the washcloth away and crawls back into bed with me, I realize that I couldn't have imagined anything more perfect than this moment with the man I love.

"Are you feeling okay, baby?" His voice tickles my ear as he pulls me into his body, the scent of him surrounding me completely.

My head falls against his chest, hearing the steady, rhythmic beat that feels a lot like my own.

"I'm feeling like I love you, Grant Bergeron."

chapter twenty-seven

Grant

SUNLIGHT STREAMS THROUGH THE WINDOW, bathing the bedroom in a warm, golden glow. The sun is rising higher, so it must be almost seven.

I've been up for hours, since the sky was still dark and moonlight painted Addie's naked body as she slept, draped across my chest. My arm fell asleep a while ago, but I wasn't moving, not when I *finally* had her in my arms.

Not when I spent the entire night memorizing every inch of her body, committing every freckle, every curve, every whimper to memory. She was exhausted, and she needed to rest.

And I'd rather watch her sleep. It might just have become my new favorite way to pass the time. My eyes rove over her face, drinking in the thick, dark fan of her eyelashes that flutter as she dreams. Her rosy, pink lips are pursed, and I wonder if she's dreaming of me.

I feel like I've spent the last year dreaming of her, and I'm scared that if I blink, she'll slip through my fingers. That the past twenty-four hours have been one of those dreams, and once I wake up, it'll all be over.

If it wasn't for the fact that she's sleeping contentedly in my arms, then I would believe that it was all just a fever dream. It's the only thing that reassures me that she's *finally* fucking mine.

And not just because we signed papers to legally get married.

No, Addie is mine in every sense of the word, and I'm not letting her go. Not now, not when the probate process is finished, not when the bakery's finally transferred into her name. Not ever.

She's it for me, and after what she gave me last night... a piece of herself that she held so close, I know that there's no walking away.

Those warm rays of morning light move over her face, and she stirs slightly, the sweetest moan cascading from her lips at the intrusion.

I trail my fingers lightly down her spine and then back in a path that somehow feels as if I've done it a hundred times. As if *somehow* my soul knows hers, even in the dark, even when distance separated us.

"Mmmm," she hums sleepily, her eyes still closed as she burrows further into my chest. "Good morning."

"Good morning, beautiful."

Her pouty lips curve into a smile, and I brush my thumb along her bottom lip, suddenly thinking about how I spent the entire night kissing them until they were swollen and red.

And how I desperately need to kiss her again, or I might lose my mind.

I don't think there's anything that could surpass waking up with the girl I love in my arms and feeling her naked, sleepy body pressed into my side. I'd really fucking love to do it for the rest of my life.

"How are you feeling?" I ask. I'm worried that she'll be sore this morning, but I'm hoping that the pain relievers helped before she went to sleep last night.

She lifts her head from my chest, and a shy smile pulls at her lips as a slight flush works its way down her cheeks and to her neck. "I'm okay. A little… achy, but I feel fine."

I keep the steady swipe of my fingers along her skin as I wince. "I'm sorry, baby. I fucking hate that it hurt you. I wish that I could've taken it all away."

Her piercing blue eyes hold mine, and she shakes her head adamantly, "No, it was… It was *perfect*, Grant. It was everything I imagined it would be, and I don't regret anything. Do… Do you?"

Something in my chest constricts as her words wash over me, and I tighten my arms around her, wishing that I could somehow pull her even closer.

"Fuck no, never, Addie. The fact that you trusted me with something that special… It was *everything* to me. *You're* everything to me."

Rising on her elbows, she props her chin in her hands and smiles. The freckles that are scattered along her nose and cheeks are more prominent in the morning light, and I fucking love them.

Then, her sleepy smile shifts to a curious look. "So… what do we do now?"

My eyebrow arches as my lip twitches in amusement.

She quickly backtracks, her eyes widening. "I mean… now that, you know…"

I laugh. "Whatever you want, baby. I think you should let me run you a warm bath and make you breakfast, for starters."

At the mention of food, her eyes light up.

"You hungry?" I ask.

She nods. "Starving. My stomach is growling."

"I know," I tease. "I've been listening to it for the last hour while I watched you sleep."

Her lips part, and she stutters adorably, "Y-you were watching me sleep? Oh god, was I drooling?"

"No, buuuuut you do snore. Auggie poked his head in twice because I think he was worried the roof was about to come down on top of him while he napped."

Addie's face morphs into panic, and I chuckle, bringing my hand to her face to brush her messy blonde hair out of her eyes. "I'm just kidding. You're perfect, baby. Fuck, I had to recite the last twenty years of World Series winners just so I wouldn't get hard again from watching you."

She tosses her head back and laughs so loudly that Auggie pads back into the room, his head cocked to the side as if to ask what's so funny, and that only makes her laugh harder.

"Stop laughing at me, woman. I can't help it—you make me crazy. Now, let your husband take care of you. I know you're sore from last night, so I'll run you a bubble bath, and then I can make you… pancakes?"

"That sounds amazing." She smiles shyly as she starts to sit up, but before she can, I slide my fingers into the hair at her nape and tug her mouth to mine, capturing her lips.

She protests, pulling away before I can really kiss her. "I haven't brushed my teeth yet…"

I pull her back and chuckle against her mouth. "I don't care. I want to give you a good-morning kiss." I kiss her once, then again, before tasting her lips as I part them.

When I pull back, she's breathless and her pupils darkened.

"Come on before we never make it out of here," I say with a grin.

If it was up to me and I knew she wasn't sore, we'd never leave this bed. I'd lock us in here for a week and make up for all the time I wasted by not telling her how I felt.

But since I know that she needs sustenance for energy and

the warm water will soothe her, I get out of the bed and then bend and scoop her into my arms, lifting her from the mattress. She yelps, collapsing against my chest in a fit of giggles as I carry her to the bathroom and turn the faucet on.

I add in some of the girly, smelly shit that she loves, and after making sure that it's not too hot, I help her in.

The sound she makes as she slips beneath the bubbles makes my dick twitch, and that's my cue. It's impossible not to want to touch her, but I won't until I know that she's not feeling too sore from last night.

After I pull on a pair of briefs, I walk into the kitchen and make sure Auggie has food and fresh water, not that he would let anyone in this house go long without putting him first, and then I start on breakfast.

I grab some fresh strawberries from the fridge and then cut several to go with the pancakes because I know Addie loves them. Then, I get to work on heating the stove and preparing the pancakes.

Twenty minutes later, Addie walks into the kitchen with her hair still wet from her bath, wearing one of my baseball T-shirts that hangs down to the middle of her thighs.

Fuck, she looks so good in my shirt.

She looks like *mine.*

"Do me a favor and throw away every single dress you own. And the skirts. Everything. All of it. Gonna need you to wear nothing but my clothes from here on out, baby," I tell her, my voice hoarse and raspy, a mixture of sleep and desire. Her nipples are hard against the front of the shirt, and it nearly makes me groan.

I've always wanted Addie. Since the first day I met her, but now that I've had her... It feels like I'll never get enough. I've had a taste, and now I'm consumed by this overwhelming need for her. I only want her more.

"You're still delusional, I see," she says with a sassy smirk.

Laughing, I shake my head as I put two pancakes and two generous spoonfuls of strawberries onto her plate. "And this is still my favorite way of flirting with you, ArtGirl."

She grins widely before rolling her pouty lips together. I shoot her a wink and walk over to the kitchen table to set her plate down next to mine.

"Thank you for breakfast."

"I love making you breakfast. Not as much as I love you making me breakfast since you're inherently better at it than I am, but still, I like taking care of you."

Addie giggles as she drags the chair out beside me and sits before immediately diving into the strawberries. Of course, I was right. I knew she'd want them.

I've paid attention to everything about her, and I know exactly what she loves. Not just for breakfast but in general. In… everything. It's hard not to notice everything about your favorite person. To want to memorize every detail about them.

"You could always have some of the four dozen cupcakes that we still have left over from yesterday." She laughs.

"You know, that's an excellent idea."

My chair scrapes against the floor as I stand and walk over to the counter and grab the box full of the leftover cupcakes.

I still can't believe she spent all day on these or that she planned dinner and made that incredible painting for my birthday. No one has ever done anything like that for me before. God, I love her.

I walk back to my chair and sink into it. Fuck the pancakes—my wife made me cupcakes, so I'm going to have them for breakfast instead.

Her giggle floats through the air as I shove pretty much the entire cupcake into my mouth and chew it.

"Did you have a good birthday?" she finally asks, peering over at me with a curious expression.

I nod. "The best birthday I've ever had. It's going to be pretty impossible to top it. Thank you for everything you did yesterday."

Her icy-blue eyes sparkle. "I just… I really wanted you to have the best day, a day for *just* you. You do so much for me, Grant. You've been so selfless and generous with me. And I know that you always say it's nothing and that you want to do it, but I also want to do things for *you* too. I want to make you as happy as you make me."

Unable to stop myself, I reach for her, taking her hand in mine and lacing my fingers through hers. "You do, Addie. You have no fucking idea how happy you make me."

"Things have just been so much lately… with the marriage and the bakery and with all of this with Brent and Dixon. I hate that you have to deal with any of this," she continues, chewing the corner of her lip nervously. "And I don't know what will happen next… Does last night make us a *real* couple now? We're already married, and I just… I've never done this before, and I keep thinking that I'm going to mess everything up."

Fuck, I can't wait to get rid of those assholes once and for all. I don't care if I have to spend every goddamn cent of my brand money to hire the best attorney in the country. I'll do it.

Or I'll handle them myself if that's what it takes.

"I haven't done this either, Addie. You're the only person I have ever told 'I love you.' They aren't just words to me. They're a promise. A promise that I will never let you face anything alone again. That I will always take care of you and put you first. Protect you. Cherish you," I say with fierce sincerity. I need her to know that I'm not just saying this shit; I want to prove it to her with my actions. I'm going to prove it to her with every day that passes. "We started our marriage as an arrangement, but we've both said that it's no longer fake for us. I don't know what the future holds, but what I do know is that you're mine. No matter what happens, you're the one I want. I know that I *don't* want this marriage to be over, regardless of what it was in the beginning, because that's not the way I feel now. I want to be with you. I want this to be our life. I'd marry you again tomorrow if I could. Is that what you want?"

Her face crumples slightly, a look of worry flickering in her eyes as her fingers squeeze mine. "Yes. I-I don't want to be without you. I want you to be my future too, Grant. I'm just worried that… you're going to the MLB, and I'll be here an—"

"Baby," I stop her. "Nothing is going to change, even if I get drafted. Even if I have to go on the road for a bit, I'll fly you to wherever I am, or I'll come home every single weekend if that's what it takes. We'll make it work, no matter what life throws at us. We can figure it out as we go. As long as we're together, then that's all that matters. I just want to be with you, Addie. You."

I lift my thumb to her cheek and brush away the stray tear that's fallen. I fucking hate her tears.

I hate seeing her cry, regardless of the reason. It makes my chest feel tight.

"I want this life with you more than anything. You're the only place I feel *safe* anymore. Especially now… after the bakery," she whispers.

"Then, baby, that's all that matters. Me and you. And tomorrow, we're going to check in with the detective and see if they've made any progress on the break-in. I promise you that we're going to figure it out. All of it. So, you don't have to be worried or feel unsafe. I hate that these assholes make you feel that way," I tell her.

"Okay," she whispers. "I've just been thinking... Don't you think it's weird that we haven't heard anything else from Brent or Dixon lately? There's been nothing since the break-in, and I feel like I'm waiting on bated breath for the other shoe to drop. It feels entirely too quiet. It scares me."

Yeah, tell me about it, I think to myself but don't voice out loud. I don't want to make her feel any more anxious about the situation than she already is.

Either way, they're not coming near Addie ever again because I'll follow her around like a fucking shadow if that's what it takes to protect her.

That's my job as her husband.

"The police being involved probably scared them, as it fucking should. They fucked up, and now they'll pay for it." Reaching up, I slide my hands along her jaw, cradling her face as my eyes rove over the delicate slope of her nose and the constellation of freckles along her pale skin. I sweep my thumb along her jaw steadily.

"I promise you that I will never let anyone hurt you, Addie," I murmur.

And there's *nothing* in the world I wouldn't do to keep that promise.

chapter twenty-eight

Grant

I'M SITTING on the couch after a grueling session at the batting cages with Davis and an exhausting call with my agent about scheduling engagements for the brand deal when my phone vibrates for the fifth time in the last five minutes.

I swipe across the screen and bring up the group chat with Reese and Lane.

SWIFTIES4LIFE

> Reese: Have you told her yet? I'm starting to sweat, Grant. The miscommunication trope is not it. You're probably wondering why I even know what the fuck that is. It's because Viv keeps making me read these sexy books with her.

> Reese: I am quite enjoying them, but that's besides the point.

> Reese: Do not ignore me or I'm going to fly back down there and show up at your front door again. Only this time I'm not fucking leaving.

Lane: Reese, do you realize that you're a stage five clinger? Let the man breathe. He'll do it when the time is right. And then tell us, right Grant?

Reese: Now is the time Lane. Carpe fucking diem. It's time for him to go get his girl.

For fuck's sake. I groan, thumbing through message after message, a smile tilting my lips even though they're both ridiculous.

Grant: Stop panicking. I told her.

Reese: THANK FUCK. Now tell me everything. I've been waiting by my phone like an idiot. heart eyes X 9

Lane: You've been watching Paradise Island again haven't you?

Reese:... No. I have not.

Lane: Bullshit.

Reese: Fine. Yes, I watched a few episodes before I fell asleep with Viv. And no I do not know who Greer ends up with.

Reese: It wasn't Russ though, I'll tell you that much.

Lane: You're literally proving my point.

Reese: I saw it on insta.

Reese: Stop deflecting on behalf of Grant. Grant, spill the beans dude. For the love of God please give me the goods.

Grant: There's nothing to tell. I told her how I felt, and she feels the same, and everything's good.

Lane: Good. I'm happy for you, dude. You seem happy and that's all that matters to us.

Reese: Awwwwww, Lane. That was so sweet.

Reese: What he said though. I'm glad you got your girl, and that you're happy.

Reese: Plus Viv is obsessed with her and literally has not shut up about her since she met her. Which means it would be hella awkward if they had sleepovers and you two weren't a thing

Grant: Everything's good.

Reese: Maybe we should have a sleepover? That sounds fun

Lane: I'm blocking you

Reese: Yeah fucking right. Anyway, I gotta tell you about the playdate I took Boo to earlier.

Reese: It was the cutest fucking thing of my life, and now they're best friends.

Reese: picture of Boo with new bff

I'm about to respond to the cute-as-shit photo of Boo with a tabby kitten when I hear the sound of the front door opening and then shutting. Auggie springs from the couch with speed I did not know his chubby legs possessed, bounding toward the hallway.

A moment later, Addie walks into the living room with a smile when she spots me on the couch.

"Hi. How did batting practice go?" she asks as she sets her purse down next to the coffee table, along with a small takeout box from the bakery, and makes her way toward me. "And the meeting with your agent?"

Much to my dismay, she *didn't* get rid of everything she owns to live in my clothes. The pastel yellow skirt that she's wearing shows off her creamy thighs, the white fitted shirt she's wearing accentuates her curves, and of course, her favorite pink cardigan that I want to peel off her body.

When she comes to a halt between my spread legs, the corner of my mouth tugs into a grin as I snake my arm around her waist and haul her right into my lap.

She's been gone since this morning working at the bakery, which means it's been too fucking long since I touched her, and I need the contact.

"Session went good. I'm a little sore, but I usually am after we hit the cages that hard. And the meeting also went well. We're going to try to get some shoots scheduled before the season kicks off." I brush my thumb along the soft curve of her jaw. "How was *your* day? Any update from the detective?"

"Nothing concrete, but she said they're exhausting all avenues. And we talked at length about Dixon and Brent, and she assured me that she's going to follow up on every lead. It made me feel better talking with her. Knowing that someone is taking it seriously and it's not just a file sitting on top of someone's desk, you know?"

Her pale blue eyes are brighter tonight, and she does look inherently less worried than she has been the last few days, which makes *me* feel better. I hate seeing her worry about anything.

I'm just hoping that these assholes have realized how badly they fucked up now that the police are involved, and they leave her alone. That they don't make the same mistake twice.

I honestly don't think they ever expected Addie to actually go to the cops, but then again, we haven't even been able to prove that it was really *them* behind any of it. Despite the shit that Dixon's pulled in the past and Brent's verbal threats to us, there isn't any real evidence.

But everything's been quiet, so I'm going to take that as a sign that, hopefully, it's fucking over. That they're backing off.

"Good, because I hate when you worry. You get this little line, right here." I ghost my thumb along the spot between her brows that always furrows when she's worried or lost in thought.

Addie's face softens. "Very observant, husband."

"Give me a little more time and I'll have every inch of you memorized." My voice comes out more rough than I intended, and her lips part, those pretty blues widening.

And just like that, I want her again. In the few days following my birthday, we haven't been able to keep our hands off each other. A frantic hunger that we can't ever seem to satiate, no matter how many times I fuck her. Eat her. Kiss her until her lips are bruised and swollen.

Each time, Addie blooms like a fucking flower beneath my hands. She's increasingly less shy, less in her head, more able to embrace her pleasure, and I'm so goddamn thankful I get to witness it.

I'm obsessed with my wife and she's just as ravenous for me as I am for her, and the result has been me taking her on every surface of our apartment.

Like the other night when we were sitting at the kitchen table studying, and she kept glancing up at me, shifting in her seat to the point that she was nearly squirming.

I knew exactly what she wanted, but I wanted to see where she would go with it. So, when she trailed her bare foot up my calf until it brushed directly over my cock, a coy smile on her pretty lips, I hauled her out of the chair and spread her out on the table, then ate her pretty pussy right on top of her textbooks and flash cards.

Needless to say, I think she aced that test. It was a *very* hands-on lesson.

Or the next day, when she walked in during my shower, and I made her take off her panties, sit on the counter with her legs spread, and make herself come while I stroked my cock and watched her.

See? Fucking obsessed with her, and I'm a hundred percent sure that it'll always be that way. That I'll never stop wanting her the way that I do now.

"Oh. I forgot... I made you something today," she says, pulling me from my lust-filled memories. She hops up from my lap and walks over to the takeout box on the coffee table. "The first official batch of beignets since being back in the bakery. And it's a new flavor."

My interest is absolutely fucking piqued. If there's one thing my girl does as well as her art, it's baking.

"I need you to be the taste tester." She slides back into my lap, straddling my hips as she opens the box and pulls out a beignet. My mouth fucking waters when the aroma hits my nose. "It's a strawberry beignet with *homemade* strawberry whipped cream icing."

Strawberries started as *her* favorites, and now they're mine. Probably because her lips taste like them from how much she eats them, and now I fucking crave the taste.

"Say less. Feed it to me, baby."

Her giggle is soft and sweet as she lifts the fried dough to my lips, and I take a bite. Sweetness explodes on my tongue in bright, blinding flavor, and I groan around the mouthful. I'm pretty positive it's the best thing I've ever tasted.

Well, aside from my wife.

"Holy fuck," I mumble. "This is goddamn incredible, Addie."

Her face lights up. "Really? You like it?"

I nod as I swallow the rest. "Fuck yeah, I love it. I want an entire damn box."

"I'm thinking about adding it to the menu and making it a permanent item." Her voice is filled with excitement, and my chest tightens.

I love seeing her face light up like this. Seeing her excited and happy. The bakery being a source of joy again for her.

"Without a doubt, baby. But…" I trail off, dragging the pad of my finger through the creamy icing and then bringing it to her mouth and tracing it along her plump bottom lip. "I think I'm going to need another taste. You know, as the official taste tester."

Her light brow arches, a look of desire flickering her eyes. "Or maybe… *I* need to test it out. To be sure it's the perfect flavor."

My heart rackets in my chest.

She slides out of my lap until she's kneeling on the hardwood between my legs, staring up at me with heavy-lidded eyes. Using her free hand, she glides her hand up my thigh and curves her palm over my already hard cock, causing me to suck in an audible hiss.

Her fingers tighten around my erection, squeezing me through the thin fabric of my gym shorts, and a groan vibrates from my chest. Her fingers slide higher and higher until they're dipping beneath the waistband of my shorts and briefs, brushing over my bare skin.

"Can I… taste you?" she murmurs, holding my gaze steadily.

I can't believe she's *asking* me if she can suck my cock, as if there would ever be a world where I told her no.

Fucking Christ.

I've never seen her so brazen, never so confident in her movements, and I'm so fucking hard that I might actually come in my pants if she keeps touching me.

"Fuck, baby, you never have to ask me that. Literally, ever. Do whatever you want to me."

Her teeth graze her bottom teeth as she nods, a smirk curling her lip up. She looks like a goddamn dream kneeling at my feet, anticipation flickering in her pale irises.

Addie tugs at my shorts while I lift my hips, helping her work them along with my briefs down until my cock bobs free. Her eyes drop to it, and she licks her lips as if she's hungry for it.

Her fingers brush along my cock, spreading the bead of precum seeping from the slit all over the head. A languid exploration that has my entire body taut, my muscles coiling as I attempt to hold on to the small thread of restraint I have left.

It feels too fucking good with her touching me.

My fingers dig into the arm of the couch as she continues her exploration and closes her soft, silky fist around me, pumping once. It's gentle, hesitant almost as she peers up at me through her lashes. "Is this okay…?"

Nodding, I close my fist over hers and squeeze, showing her that she's not going to hurt me. I drop my hand and bring it back to the couch so she can continue. Her gaze drops back to my cock, and I swear to god I almost come with what happens next.

She takes the half-eaten beignet and trails the remainder of strawberry icing down my dick until it's covering it from head to base.

Fuck, fuck, fuck, I'm fighting a losing fucking battle.

After she places the rest onto the floor, she leans forward and trails her tongue along the sugary path, all the way to the head of my cock, then wraps her pouty lips around it, her cheeks hollowing as she sucks.

"Fuck," I grunt roughly, my knuckles turning white with how tightly I'm gripping the arm of the couch, desperate to wrap my fist in her long, silky hair. If I was standing, she'd bring me to my knees right now, in the literal sense.

Jesus fucking Christ.

The sight of my wife on her knees, licking strawberry icing off of my cock like it's a lollipop, will forever be burned into my memory. I'll never be able to eat anything strawberry again without vividly remembering this moment.

I'll dream about it until I fucking die.

I fight to keep my eyes open so I can watch her, the pleasure almost becoming too much, but fuck, I want to *see* her.

I want to watch those plump little lips circling my cock as it slides in between them. I want to watch as her eyes widen when she slides down further, gagging slightly at how deep she takes me down her throat.

Pulling back, she runs her tongue along the sensitive ridge underneath the head, tasting, teasing me until I feel like I'm going to explode, licking my cock completely clean of icing.

"Baby…" I swallow, attempting to breathe as she continues to lap at the head of my cock, teasing the slit with the tip of her tongue. "I'm about to come. Like any fucking second."

I grit the words through clenched teeth, and when I feel the base of my spine beginning to tingle, I reach down and pull her mouth off my cock. As much as I want to paint her throat with my cum, I want to be inside her, making her come with my cock instead.

Another time. Right now, I just *need* to be inside her.

I tug her into my lap, crushing my lips to hers, tasting the salty remnants of me as I sweep my tongue inside of her mouth and suck with a frantic desperation unlike anything I've ever felt.

And she matches me with every breath.

Her thighs bracket my hips, that cute-as-fuck yellow skirt bunching around her waist, the wet heat of her pussy radiating along the bare skin of my cock making my balls ache with the need for release.

"Want your pussy squeezing my cock, baby." I say, gliding my palms up her creamy, exposed thighs, until my fingers graze along the front of her panties. "I can't wait another second to feel you wrapped around me."

We're a frenzy of hands as we tear at each other's clothes frantically. Addie tears my shirt off and tosses it behind her as I drag the fluffy cardigan down her arms and let it drop to the floor. Then, I work on her skirt and panties, yanking the fabric down as she lifts her knees to kick it away, leaving her in nothing but the white fitted tank she's wearing.

I can see the taut, pebbled peaks of her nipples pressing against the front, and I realize she's braless beneath it.

Cupping her tits over the shirt, I press them together and groan. "Fuck. No bra, baby? You can't leave the house like this. I'll have to fight somebody."

I slip my hands beneath the hem of her shirt and tug it off of her in a single breath. My gaze rakes up the flat expanse of her stomach, to her tits. The perfect handfuls with rosy, pink nipples that are hardened into peaks, begging for my mouth.

She's perfection, and she's fucking *mine*.

Leaning forward, I flick my tongue over her nipple before sucking it into my mouth and grazing my teeth along the peak.

My palm curves around her hip and she rocks, dragging her wet heat over me, chasing friction, and I reach between us, thrumming my finger over her clit in rough circles.

With my other hand, I fist the base of my cock, dragging it

through her dripping pussy, coating it in her arousal. One flex of my hips and I could bury myself inside of her.

"Fuck. I don't have a condom, they're in the bedroom."

Her pale blue eyes snap open as her chest heaves, her cheeks blooming red. "I... I'm on birth control. For my periods... If you..." She trails off.

"Are you telling me that I can fuck you bare, baby?" The thought of claiming my wife has desperation tickling down my spine.

She swallows roughly, nodding. "I'm safe. And... I want you to. If *you* do."

My arms wrap around her waist, and I haul her to my chest. "I'm safe too, and there's nothing in the fucking world I want more. Literally, nothing. Are you sure?"

"I want it. I want to feel all of you, with nothing between us."

My balls tighten when she reaches down and wraps her soft fist around me and notches me at her opening while she holds my eyes. Telling me exactly how sure she is.

"You want your husband to fill your pretty little pussy full of cum?"

She slides down a fraction of an inch in response, the head of my cock nudging her entrance, and the feeling is almost enough to have my eyes rolling back.

Warm, wet, heat envelopes my cock as she sinks down on me, inch by inch, until her thighs touch mine and I'm buried inside of her balls deep.

Fuuuuuck.

My vision dances as she clenches around me, adjusting to my cock, and my muscles coil tight. A hoarse grunt falls from my lips, and I reach for her hips, curving my palm over the soft dip.

"Oh..." She moans, her mouth falling open as her hands fall

forward to my chest. She lifts her hips before sliding back down on my cock slowly, in controlled, steady motions.

Way fucking more controlled than I feel. The thread of restraint inside of me is dangerously thin, ready to snap at any second.

After her licking dessert off my cock, I was already on the brink of coming, and now my balls are drawing tight, ready to empty inside of her as my spine tingles, black spots dancing around my vision.

I'm gone for her.

Addie's tits sway with each circle of her hips, and I lean forward, closing my lips around her hardened nipple and sucking. Hard. A needy, desperate whimper sounds from her, and I tighten my grip on her hips, guiding her up and down on my cock harder. Faster. Bottoming out with each flex of my hips.

There's nothing in the world I love more than watching my wife chase her pleasure, those pouty pink lips parted, her eyes squeezed shut on the brink of an orgasm.

"Are you going to come for me, baby? Are you going to let me pump you full of my cum until it leaks out of you? Making you a mess?"

Her pussy clamps down around my cock as she throws her head back and cries out as her orgasm rocks through her. I feel her thighs tremble, and her nails making half-moons on my chest as she rides it out, writhing, grinding her clit against my pelvis.

"Come inside me, Grant, please."

The breathless, raspy tone of her voice combined with the way her pussy's contracting around me is all it takes. My fingers dig into the soft flesh of her hips as I come, doing exactly as I promised, filling her with all of my cum.

My gaze drops to where I'm buried inside of her and I see her pretty pink little pussy stretched around me, our cum dripping out of her and coating my cock.

A surge of possessiveness courses through me at the sight.

Goddamn. I can't believe that she's mine, *really* fucking mine.

When the aftershocks of her orgasm have subsided, she sags against my chest, burying her face in my neck. Sated and boneless from riding my cock is one of my favorite versions of my wife.

Every version of her is my favorite.

"Is it... is sex always like this?" Addie whispers as she drags the tips of her fingers along my chest, making the shapes of stars along my skin.

Bringing my hand to her hair, I brush the damp strands out of her face and shake my head. "Nothing has ever been the way it is with you, Addie. I've never felt the way that I do about you... about anyone. It's different because the way we feel about each other is real. It's different because I love you."

She lifts her head from my chest and peers up at me through her thick, dark lashes. "I love you too. Thank you for loving me... and for being my best friend."

"Always ArtGirl. For better or worse."

chapter twenty-nine

Addie

"I THINK you might be the best husband in the entire world."

Grant's lip twitches from the driver's seat as he glances over at me. "You *think*, baby?"

"Okay, fine. You're definitely the best," I reply sweetly. "Who else would take their wife to get ice cream at almost midnight?"

To be fair, it's *entirely* his fault that I'm up this late. I was nearly asleep when he climbed into bed and wrapped me up in his arms, pressing lingering kisses along the curve of my neck until I was breathless.

Not that I'm complaining, because I got two incredible orgasms out of it, per usual.

I've been craving pecan praline ice cream from my favorite ice cream parlor, and when I told Grant as we lay in bed, he immediately got dressed and said he was taking me, even though it was the middle of the night.

Add it to the very long list of reasons why I'm head over heels in love with this man.

I've never felt like a priority to… *anyone.* Until Grant.

With him, I feel worthy of love. Worthy of being put first. He makes me feel adored and cherished in ways that I never thought I would ever experience.

"If you ask for it, it's yours, Addie," he says as he reaches over the console and curves his large palm along the top of my thigh.

New turn-on unlocked? My husband holding my thigh as he drives. My gaze rakes along his handsome profile as my teeth rake over my bottom lip. The veiny, defined muscles of his arms flex subtly as he grips the wheel, and it's entirely too hot.

"I love you," I say with a smile. "Not *just* because you take me to get ice cream in the middle of the night, but… it definitely helps."

He laughs. "I'm just glad that they're open twenty-four hours, but then again, everything here is."

Lucky me.

Grant's thumb brushes gently along my thigh absentmindedly as he drives, and I sink back into the seat. Although I've lived here my entire life, it still surprises me when I see how alive the city is this late at night. New Orleans is truly a city that never sleeps. A constant stream of people, food, and music. Especially in the French Quarter.

"Did I tell you that Reese invited us to his place for New Y—"

The loud shrill of my phone ringing drowns out Grant, and my brow pinches in confusion as I grab it from the cup holder. My phone never goes off this late. The only people who call me anyway are Amos or Earl, and they're generally asleep by seven since they're up at three for work.

When I see what the notification is on the glowing screen, I suck in a sharp breath, fumbling to swipe my finger along the phone to open it.

"What is it?"

"It's… It's the alarm company, Grant. The alarm's been tripped, and they're dispatching emergency services." My eyes flick to him as a wave of panic makes my chest constrict.

Grant's jaw works before he mumbles, "Fuck."

Oh god… is this happening all over again?

"Addie, baby, it's okay. It could just be a false alarm. We're only a few blocks away—we'll go check it out. Make sure everything's good." He turns down a side road in the direction of Ever After.

He's right—it could be a false alarm, but after the break-in, I can't help but worry as another wave of panic claws at my throat.

I exhale and inhale in a steady rhythm, desperately trying to keep it together, reminding myself that I could be working myself up for nothing.

I hear the wail of sirens echoing off the buildings of the narrow street just as we turn down it. There are fire trucks parked in front of the bakery, their red lights painting everything crimson in their wake as I attempt to register what's happening in front of me.

The bakery… It's on fire. I'm frozen in shock, in pure terror as I watch the place I love more than anything in the world engulfed in a fury of flames.

Grant slams the truck into park as close as he can get, and I don't think, I don't even breathe as I reach for the door handle, wrenching it open and bounding from the truck. I don't make it far before I feel his arms wrapping tightly around my waist, stopping me from running toward the building.

Thick, black smoke billows from the roof as flames lick the sky. The smell of smoke and burning wood fills the air so thickly that I nearly choke. My worst nightmare is happening right in front of me, and I... I'm completely helpless. There's nothing I can do, and the thought makes me want to vomit.

I might, actually—my body is trembling so hard that I feel like I'm going to be sick as a heartbroken sob tears from my mouth, hot tears blurring my vision as I watch my mother's legacy burn.

It's pain unlike anything I've ever felt. I imagine even the burn of those flames wouldn't hurt my body as badly as I feel watching them destroy our beloved bakery right now.

"Breathe, baby. Stay with me," Grant says into my ear, running his hands along my arms soothingly in an attempt to calm me down. I desperately try to suck in a breath.

Up ahead, there are firefighters attempting to tame the fire, their hoses shooting powerful streams of water into the flames. It seems from a distance that... maybe it's just the kitchen that's on fire right now, and the smallest tendril of relief snakes up my spine. I hold on to it desperately because I have to believe that these men are going to save some of Ever After.

I refuse to believe any differently, no matter what it looks like in front of me. I have to hold on to hope because if not, then I'll have nothing.

"W-we have to talk to them, find out what's h-happening." I stumble over my words. "Please."

Grant steps beside me and slips his hand in mine, holding tighter than ever as we walk closer to the bakery. Each step is like a shard of glass puncturing my heart, twisting. The heat radiating from the bakery is palpable the closer we get, making the air shimmer with waves of warmth. Smoke clogs my nose.

They've roped off the exterior of the building with the bright yellow caution tape that you would see at a crime scene and blocked off the driveway.

"Sir," Grant calls, flagging down a man wearing a suit and tie with some type of badge hanging around his neck.

He walks toward us, his jaw set in a hard line. "This area is closed to the public. It's not safe for you to be here."

Grant shakes his head vehemently. "This is my wife's bakery."

The man's gaze flicks to me, and I nod.

"My name is Matty Bishop, and I'm an investigator with the NOFD. I know this is a very difficult time for you, and I'm sorry that we're having to meet under these circumstances," he says with a solemn expression, dark, thick brows pinched together as he speaks.

Thankfully, Grant is able to take over speaking with him because I'm in such shock that I'm frozen. I can't even wrap my head around what's going on, let alone have a coherent conversation. "Do you think they'll be able to stop the fire before it consumes the building?"

Investigator Bishop glances toward the bakery and back to us, "Right now, it's too early to determine the full extent of the damage, but I've been doing this for over a decade, and it looks like they've begun to extinguish it. I don't think it's going to be a total loss. I'll have more once it's safe to enter the building and we conduct a thorough investigation to assess the damage fully."

Oh god. There's... hope. Hope that I'm going to cling to with all that I have.

Grant tightens his arm around me, exhaling a deep, ragged sigh as he nods. "That's reassuring. Thank you and your team for working so hard to get it put out."

"Generally in our investigation, we work to figure out the cause, but upon arrival, we were able to confirm arson since we caught the perpetrator as he attempted to flee the premises.

We're holding him over there for questioning." Investigator Bishop points across the street.

My hand flies to my mouth as I see a familiar face sitting on the curb, handcuffs bracketing his wrists.

Brent.

I'm trembling so hard that my teeth are chattering, and I feel like my legs may give out with a dangerous combination of fear, adrenaline, and anger as I try to let this all sink in.

Brent set my mother's bakery on fire…

"I've called in backup with the NOPD so I can remain on scene, but he's being arrested for arson here tonight." Someone calls his name near the building, and he raises his hand, acknowledging it. "I need to head over there. We're doing everything we can to get this fire out. I'll have some questions later that I'll need answered, so please stay on scene at a safe distance from the fire."

"Thank you," Grant says, reaching out and shaking his hand. "We appreciate it."

Investigator Bishop nods and turns, leaving us alone with my stepfather sitting in handcuffs along the curb.

The fact that Brent is being arrested should bring me a sense of relief, knowing that he'll pay for what he did, but it honestly only makes me angry. That he would do something so vile, so evil.

The shuffle of gravel scraping against the pavement sounds behind me, causing me to jump, and I whip around. Out of my peripheral, I think I see a darkened shadow in the bushes next to the building next door, and I think it looks like a… *person?*

"Grant," I whisper. "I-I think someone's in the… bushes. Over there."

It's so dark that I can't really see if it's my mind playing tricks on me or if there's someone really there. I'm so amped up on adrenaline that I could be imagining it completely, but I would swear that there's someone there. Why would someone be hiding in a bush?

Grant's brow pinches as he squints, trying to see what I do, and then he turns to me. "Stay here, baby, where the investigator can see you."

Abruptly, he takes off toward the other side of the building, disappearing into the darkness, and my heart thrashes wildly as I wait. My eyes continually scan my surroundings, cataloging every sound, every movement. My panicked gaze returns to Brent on the curb near where Investigator Bishop is standing and talking to another person in uniform.

A loud grunt sounds from the darkness, and I gasp, covering my mouth with one hand as I desperately try to see beyond the shadows.

There's another pained grunt, closer this time, followed by the sound of something hard hitting the ground.

I'm going to pass out. Or have a heart attack. In either order.

Tears prick in my eyes, and I squint, trying to blink them away when, suddenly, there's a shadowed body striding toward me, and then I forget how to breathe completely.

I hold the breath inside of me, too afraid to move or make a sound until my lungs begin to burn, and even then, I don't dare to move a single inch.

Then, I see it's Grant walking toward me.

And... he's not alone.

He's practically dragging someone with him, and I wait on a burning, bated breath for the moonlight to illuminate them both. I need to see that he's okay.

I need to make sure he's not hurt.

Oh my god.

Dixon?

Finally, his face comes fully into view as Grant tosses him roughly onto the concrete only feet from where I'm standing. There's a trickle of blood seeping from his nose and split lip where Grant must have hit him. The skin around his eye is red, angry, and beginning to swell, making him squint to see.

I shift my eyes to Grant, running them over his entire body, desperately searching for reassurance that he's okay. I see a bright crimson stain on his gray shirt, and my hand flies to my mouth, covering it.

"It's not mine, baby," he murmurs. "I'm okay."

I nod frantically. "Okay. Okay." I realize I'm repeating it over and over incoherently, but all of this is too much for me to take in. I'm so angry… so hurt, that I feel like I could detonate. A ticking time bomb that's finally reached the end of the fuse.

"Look, man," Dixon grunts, attempting to rise off the ground, lifting on his hands and knees, but Grant plants his foot in the middle of his back and roughly pushes him back to the concrete, where he groans. Rolling to his side, he spits, and blood coats the pavement. "I didn't do shit. It was all that asshole. I said this shit was too far, and I didn't want anything to do with it. I'm not going to fucking jail. Especially not for him."

His beady gaze shifts to my stepfather on the curb, and finally, Brent lifts his head, a deadly look in his dark, black eyes as he scoffs. "You're a fucking pussy, Dixon. You realize that? Shut the fuck up, and don't say another goddamn word."

"Yeah, well, I'd rather be a pussy than someone's bitch in prison. I'm singing like a fucking canary if it keeps me out. All of this bullshit was you, and I'm not going down for you," Dixon mutters as he clutches his side.

I knew it. In my heart, I knew that they were behind the break-in, but hearing him *admit it*?

It's the moment that I feel myself break. Where I'm done

holding back. I'm done letting myself be taken advantage of and hurt.

And for what? What reason could he have for doing this?

I whip around toward Brent, my voice so quiet it's deadly. "Why? Why would you do this? What could you possibly have to gain from doing this?"

Silence meets my question for only a second until Brent laughs without humor. "I hope the motherfucker burns to the ground and there's nothing left but goddamn ashes."

My stomach twists as bile rises in my throat. Grant lunges for him, but I reach out, grasping his arm tightly.

"You're the most evil man I've ever known," I say to Brent as the tears in my eyes fall harder, coating my cheeks. "Tell me why —I deserve that much. I deserve to know how you could do something so evil and cruel. Tell me."

My voice cracks as Brent shakes his head. He peers up at me, hands cuffed tightly behind his back. "Because this piece-of-shit bakery was always supposed to be *mine*. I played the long game. I took your pathetic orphan ass in when you had no one else. This is the payment I fucking *deserved*, and you ruined it. You ruined it all. You stupid, naive little bitch. I was always going to take this place from you. You just made it inherently more difficult." His voice shakes before he pauses. "If I can't take it from you to sell the land—which is worth millions, by the way—then I'll burn the thing to the fucking ground and get the insurance money. If I can't have it, then neither can you."

Anger courses through me in a powerful, all-consuming current. My fingernails cut into my palms as I fist my hands at my sides, making bloody half-moons in my skin.

"It was all about money to you, you greedy, selfish man. All this was was money. Your only motive was to line your pockets.

All of this? Destroying the bakery, the one thing left of your wife, so you could cash in," I nearly spit.

I feel Grant at my side, his arm looping around my waist and pulling my trembling frame against him. If I wasn't so keyed up on my anger, I would probably collapse into him, but right now, all I can focus on is the man at my feet. The one who deserves every ounce of the anger, hurt, and pain I'm feeling right now.

Dixon may be an accomplice, but he's a stupid one. I have no doubt that Brent was the mastermind behind all of this.

Brent's eyes gleam with a chilling light as he chuckles. The sound is completely unnerving. "You have no fucking idea the lengths I would go to make sure the money was mine. I've been setting this up for years. Waiting for the day that I could make it happen. It was pure fucking luck that this dumb fuck and his father fell into my lap. Had he not turned out to be such a pussy and seen this shit through to the end like he was supposed to, I wouldn't be sitting here in fucking handcuffs."

The first police cruiser comes to a skid at the end of the street, signaling this nightmare is almost over, and I use the minutes, maybe seconds, I have left to get the only closure I think I'll ever get from the man who's done nothing but lie, manipulate, and hurt me my entire life.

He planted a seed long ago that had taken root, growing into something nefarious and destroying the things I love most, using the guise of what was best for me to deceive me and water his poisonous plan.

So, I keep my gaze trained on Brent as I lean into my husband, soaking in his quiet strength and fierce protection. He's giving me this moment, even though I know that he probably wants to finish what he started, and I'm thankful that he understands me in a way that no one else does.

"You know, I feel sorry for you," I say over the sound of the sirens and crackling fire. The bitter smoke makes my eyes sting and my nose burn as I suck in an unsteady breath. "I can't imagine how truly miserable your life must have been. How pathetically miserable you must have been to let your entire life be ruined for greed. What about Tad? What about your son? Your own flesh and blood."

"He's a fucking adult, and he doesn't need his daddy to hold his hand," Brent scoffs, eyes bouncing between Grant and me. "Unlike you, he'll graduate college and pass the bar, become an attorney that can actually support himself instead of some silly fucking dream to paint shit for a living."

"Watch your fucking mouth." Grant seethes next to me, his entire body coiled tight, ready to strike. "If it wasn't for her, you'd be out on that fucking pavement."

Bringing my hand to his stomach, I peer up at him and murmur, "It's okay. He's not worth it. He never was."

He gives me a tight, slight nod and draws me tighter against his body.

In the span of seconds, red and blue lights bathe the parking lot, the sound of police sirens blaring so loudly that my ears sting with the proximity.

Dixon makes one last attempt to run for it, but Grant lunges for him, tossing him to the ground with so much force that I wince when his face hits the pavement with a sickening crunch.

"I truly hope that it was worth it," I say, offering Brent one last look, one last moment of attention that he doesn't even deserve. But it's not for him—it's for *me*. "If my mom were here right now, she'd be disgusted by the vile person that you are, but I'm just glad that she never had to see it. Goodbye, Brent."

Everything happens so quickly after the moment that I walk away, tucked into Grant's side, that I can hardly keep up.

I don't look back.

I don't watch as officers haul Brent off the curb or even as they handcuff Dixon and put them both in the back of the cop car. I don't watch as they pull away, the lights fading in the distance.

I simply close my eyes and lean into Grant as he wraps the blanket around us as we sit in the back of the ambulance. The adrenaline of everything that's happened tonight begins to fade, leaving me raw with a hundred tumultuous emotions.

Sagging against Grant's chest, I bury my face into his shirt as the first sob racks my body. I'm emotionally and physically spent, exhaustion seeping into my bones and making my entire body feel heavy.

I feel the soft press of his lips against my hair, his arms tightening around me, holding me through the pent-up release of hurt as it flows out of me.

I lost so much tonight, more than I can even wrap my head around right now. But there's one thing I gained out of all the hurt, pain, and manipulation I've endured.

The love of my life.

In this life and every life.

chapter thirty

Grant

ADDIE FOUGHT exhaustion until the sun had begun to rise, painting the living room in warm morning rays. The shock and adrenaline of the night had worn off, and she passed out, curled into my side, her fingers wound tightly in mine as if she was terrified I'd let her go.

The entire time I washed the smoke and ash from her hair, her body shook with heartbroken sobs that nearly fucking killed me.

It made my chest physically ache. She's my wife, the woman I love more than anything, and I feel so goddamn helpless. I'd do anything in the world to switch places with her and take her pain away. Without hesitation. Without thought.

I've been sitting here ever since she fell asleep, watching the steady rise and fall of her chest, her eyelids fluttering every time she shifts restlessly, a soft sigh floating from her parted lips. I could spend the rest of the day watching her sleep because it's the reassurance I need that she's *here*.

Fuck, I can't stop thinking about what could've happened if Addie had been inside the bakery or if she had run in there and tried to stop the fire.

327

She could've been hurt or worse.

I could've lost her. I could've lost the best thing that's ever happened to me, and just the thought of something happening to her makes me physically fucking ill. Makes my stomach twist into a knot so tight that it's hard to breathe.

I force myself to focus on her sleeping beside me and try not to let my mind wander. The last thing she needs is me losing my shit over what could have happened.

There's a knock at the front door, pulling my attention from Addie. Carefully, I untangle her from my lap, pushing to my feet off the couch, then heading for the door.

When I swing it open, Davis is on the other side, and my brows shoot up in surprise. It's got to be early as shit, although I'm not entirely sure because I haven't checked my phone in a while.

"Dude, I've called you a hundred times. I heard about the bakery on socials. Is Addie okay? Is it salvageable? Shit, I've been freaking the fuck out." His face is lined with worry as he speaks, and I've never heard him so worked up.

"We're both okay. The bakery… we don't know anything yet. We probably won't for a few days. Addie's fucking distraught, dude," I mutter, reaching up to drag my hand down my face. "Come in, we can talk in the kitchen. She finally fell asleep on the couch, and I don't want to wake her."

He nods, following me inside after shutting the door quietly. Once we're in the kitchen, he sits down next to me at the table, and I drop my head in my hands.

I'm fucking exhausted. Not just physically but mentally after everything that's happened tonight.

"What happened?" Davis asks.

"Her stepfather got arrested for arson. He's been working with this dickhead that he tried to set her up with, and I don't know. It was some crazy shit to try and get the insurance money for the bakery."

My hands tighten into fists at the thought, and my knuckles groan in protest. Fuck, I barely even remember hitting him. I was so fucking mad that I just reacted, and given the chance, I'd do it again. He deserved that and more for the shit he put my wife through.

"Shit, man," Davis says with a shake of his head, his unruly auburn hair falling in his face. He brushes it out of his eyes and sits back in the chair. "Are *you* okay?"

For a beat, I'm quiet because I truthfully don't know the answer to that.

"It scared the fuck out of me, Davis." My voice cracks with emotion. "The thought of losing her scares me so much I can't fucking breathe. I just want her to never have to deal with this shit again. It's my job to protect her."

He leans close, placing his palm on my shoulder. "And you are. Shit like this just puts things into a different perspective. You love her, and you both went through some scary shit—of course you'd feel this way. She's your girl, and it's natural that you want to shoulder all the bad things."

I nod as he continues. "If anything, tonight just shows you that life is short, and nothing is ever promised. You just cherish every day that you have together."

I'm taken aback by the Rookie's insight. He's right—it's the same thing that I've thought a hundred times since walking away from that burning building.

"Thank you, for coming here and checking on us. For listening to me," I say.

"Anytime. Anything you need from me, you let me know. I've got class in a few, but text me later when y'all get settled."

We stand from the table, and I reach out to shake his hand, but as his palm slides in mine, he pulls me to him for a hug.

"I know we're not as close as you and your boys, but you're still one of my best friends, Grant. I'm here for you, no matter what."

Seeing this side of Davis surprises me. I mean, I know he's a good kid, but I didn't realize he had it in him to be so introspective. And fuck, I'm thankful for it. I didn't even know how badly I needed this until now.

"I got your back too," I say. "I appreciate you, man. I mean it."

He pulls back, a shit-eating grin on his face. "I always knew you'd love me one day. Been waiting for the day."

I chuckle quietly. "Don't push your luck. I'll text you later."

"Will do." He gives me a quick wave over his shoulder and disappears out of the kitchen, leaving me alone.

I stand from the chair, walking back to the living room to check on Addie, and see her still sleeping on the couch, not having moved an inch.

Before I can even cross the living room to sit next to her and Auggie, who's now cuddled up against her, there's another knock at the front door.

I stride down the hallway and open it quietly. This time, it's Amos and Earl.

Amos looks like he's as ragged as I feel today, and I reach forward, giving him a hug. "Hey. You guys okay?"

When I pull back, he and Earl both nod, even though they both look on the verge of tears. I step back inside the apartment, and once they walk through the door, I shut it behind them.

Amos walks into the living room with Earl beside him, and the moment his gaze lands on Addie, he starts to cry. "Oh, cher.

My darling girl," he says quietly, his hand flying to cover his mouth as a muffled sob echoes around the room.

She doesn't stir as Earl wraps an arm around Amos's shoulder and pulls him into his embrace, running his palms soothingly down his arms.

These two are the only real, stable, loving parental figures that Addie has had since her mother passed away. She's told me bits and pieces of her childhood and how, after her mother was gone, they were the only people that she felt even cared about what happened to her. Amos was the one who taught her how to braid her hair and introduced her to yoga. Earl was the one who taught her to ride a bike and would put Band-Aids on her scraped knees. They helped her with homework and were the ones to give her presents on her birthday.

Not the piece of shit that got every bit of what he deserved last night. Amos and Earl are her parents, and I know it has to be hard for them to know how badly she's hurting. And not just that… but the bakery is a piece of them too.

Amos has been running it since Addie was only a kid. I can only imagine how devastated he is about what happened to Ever After.

"I'm sorry that I wasn't there. I should have been there." He crosses the living room to squat down in front of Addie's sleeping body on the couch. His fingers brush along her forehead, sweeping her hair back from her face. "I'm so sorry."

There was nothing he could have done to stop what Brent and Dixon did. Nothing any of us could have done. The blame is on the assholes who did this, no one else.

"You couldn't have done anything, Amos," I tell him as I sit back down next to Addie. "She'll be glad to know you're okay and that you came. You're the only family she has. You mean everything to her."

He nods, giving me a small smile that doesn't reach his eyes. "And she is the world to us."

I glance up at Earl as he leans against the doorframe with unshed tears pooling in his eyes. Worry morphs his features, and I can't lie, it tugs at my heart. He's this huge, quiet guy with a heart of gold who would do anything for my girl.

"Have you seen it?" I ask Amos, who nods.

"They had the fire extinguished when we got there. It nearly killed me, seeing it like that," he says. "I can't even think about how Addie must have felt."

My gaze lowers to my sleeping wife as I rake my teeth over my bottom lip. It was absolute fucking torture watching her devastation as her mother's dream burned. "She was heartbroken, and it was physically fucking painful to see. But she was so strong, Amos, and I'm so damn proud of her."

Amos is quiet for a moment, his gaze contemplative as he strokes her cheek, then pushes to his feet, taking a seat in the armchair beside me. "You're good for her, Grant. I think I knew that from the first moment I met you. Intuitive and all that." My lip twitches when he says that. He's the guy who pulls a tarot card every day to see what the day has in store. "She's always been the most beautiful, thoughtful, creative girl. Full of wonder and curiosity. But she was quiet and shy, never allowing anyone to get too close. She never gave herself the chance to bloom, to experience life. Until you. I've watched her come into herself more these last few months, and I'll never be able to thank you."

I swallow roughly. "I love her. There's nothing I wouldn't do for her."

His eyes shine, and he nods, reaching for my hand on the arm of the couch. "It's been a privilege to witness the way you love her. Seeing her happy and taken care of is all I have ever wanted for her."

I've never really been the praying type of person, but I've prayed more today than I have in my entire life.

For Addie. For the bakery. For the future that I now realize is never promised.

Last night changed everything, and I know with every fiber of my being that Addie is my forever.

"I've been thinking… and there's something I really need to talk to you both about."

chapter thirty-one

Addie

"BABY... YOUR PHONE IS RINGING," Grant calls from the kitchen. "Want me to answer it?"

"Yes, please. I'm coming," I call back, closing my sketchbook and rising from the comfy chair that's tucked into the corner of our living room. It's become one of my favorite places to sketch, and I've found myself in this very spot more often than not since... that night.

It's been almost a week, and I'm still trying to wrap my mind around what happened.

It *still* doesn't even feel real. Even though the flames are burned into my memory and plague all of my nightmares.

Auggie follows me into the kitchen, undoubtedly so that he can beg his dad for a treat, and when I walk through the doorway, I see Grant leaning against the kitchen counter, nodding while he listens to whoever's on my phone.

His dark blue eyes shift to me when he sees me walk through, and he pulls the phone away from his mouth to whisper, "It's Investigator Bishop."

I nearly trip over Auggie as I rush forward to his side. Grant puts the phone on speaker and hands it to me.

"Hi, Investigator Bishop. Hi," I breathe, my gaze shooting to my husband as I wait anxiously. This is the call we've been waiting on since the night of the fire. Some type of update from the investigation.

The past week has been the worst kind of torture, moving so slowly that I wasn't sure I would make it through.

"Good afternoon, Mrs. Bergeron," he says. "I'm calling to let you know that my team and I have finished our initial investigation and structural assessment of Ever After. While the damage is substantial, the property is not a total loss. Most of the fire was contained to the kitchen and storage areas, so the front part of the building has mostly only sustained smoke damage. I believe it can be restored and renovated to prior standing."

Oh my god. Oh… my… god.

The bakery is salvageable?

A sob escapes past my lips, and I nearly drop the phone as I reach for Grant when the floor feels like it's going to fall out from beneath my feet. His strong hands grasp my forearms, and he drags me into his chest, holding me tight against him as the sound of my soft cries fills the room.

I think… I think I'm in shock.

I was truly expecting the worst, the news that there would be no saving the bakery. That the place I loved was never going to return, and just the thought nearly gutted me.

I didn't want to imagine a world where it doesn't exist. Where every part of my mother was gone. I *couldn't.*

"Your insurance company will work with our agency to conduct a more detailed evaluation to determine the full extent of the damage, but as of now, we do know that restoration is an option," Investigator Bishop says.

I suck in a shaky breath against Grant's chest. "Th-thank you so much. For everything you've done."

"It's my pleasure, Mrs. Bergeron. I'm so glad that this is the news I could be calling with," he replies. "If you need anything in the meantime, please let me know, but we'll be in touch with the insurance company to get the ball rolling once we have the adjuster's information."

I thank him, and we exchange goodbyes, but as my finger hovers over the button to end the call, I stop.

"I'm sorry, Mr. Bishop, I do have one more question," I blurt before he can hang up.

"Of course."

"Am I allowed to go there? I just... I really want to see it for myself," I mumble quietly.

Grant pulls back to look at me, sweeping his thumb along my cheek in quiet reassurance.

After a brief pause, Investigator Bishop says, "You can. It's been cleared structurally, so while I wouldn't advise attempting to go in the dark, it's not unsafe to enter. There is a lot of smoke and soot residue, so please take proper precautions if you do."

As thankful as I am to know that it's not going anywhere, I still want to see it for myself. I'll feel better if I can see the damage. The last time I saw it, it was engulfed in flames, and I'm desperate to replace that image in my head.

"Thank you, again." I set the phone down on the counter next to me once we hang up and glance up at Grant. The hopeful, soft expression on his face is what causes the emotional well to spill over, fresh, hot tears wetting my cheeks and staining his T-shirt.

"I can't believe it," I whisper tearily. "I- I thought that... I would never see the bakery again. I thought the only piece I had left of my mom was gone."

Grant's fingers gently stroke my hair as he holds me against his chest. "I know, baby. But it's not. It's still here, and it's *yours*. No one can ever try to take it away from you again."

With Brent being arrested on felony arson charges, my attorney said he's no longer able to contest the will to try and retain ownership of the property. I couldn't even feel a sliver of relief in hearing that because I wasn't even sure if there was going to *be* a bakery. We had no idea the extent of the damage. Until now.

And now… the hope I've been clinging to is a reality.

"Do you think we could go right now?"

"Of course, baby. Are you sure that you can handle that right now? I just want to make sure you're going to be okay. It's been an emotional few days." The space between his brows is bunched in worry, and my heart swells.

This man always takes care of me. He always considers my feelings and wants to make sure that I'm okay, and it's unlike anything I've ever had.

I nod. "I feel like there's this weight lifted off my shoulders knowing that we can restore it. I know it'll probably take an incredible amount of work, and it won't be easy, but I feel like I need to assure myself that part of it is still there, even if seeing the damage is hard."

Grant looks deeply into my eyes, and apparently, he finds what he was searching for because he kisses me softly and gives me his trademark wink. "Okay, babe, let's go."

I keep reminding myself that no matter what I'm seeing right now, Ever After *can* be saved. That once the debris is gone, the walls have been repainted, and new equipment installed, it will look like the place that I have always known.

Maybe even better.

But seeing it the way it is right now is even harder than I anticipated. My chest feels hollow as I take in the sight of the kitchen in front of me.

The walls are scorched and charred, revealing the framework beneath the drywall. Most of the equipment has been destroyed and melted, leaving behind skeletons of metal. It feels eerily... empty with so much missing. The smell of smoke lingers in the air and clings to every surface, a constant reminder of what's occurred. Soot and ash blanket everything in a charcoal sheen.

I'm fisting my hands so tightly I can feel the skin of my nails as they cut into my palm, and I will myself to release them and try to take a calming breath.

It's fixable. No matter what, we can fix it.

I wish with all of my heart that this hadn't happened. That everything would still remain the same and I could walk into Ever After without it being tainted by what Brent and Dixon had done.

But the reality is that it did happen, and now we have to make the best out of what we've got. I'd take it still standing, in any condition other than being gone.

Grant steps into me and wraps his arms around my waist, pulling me gently back against him. "Are you okay, baby?"

I nod, sinking into his arms. When the world is turbulent around me, his touch always calms me. Like a ship along rough waters and the sail that holds it steady. "Yeah. It's just... hard. Being in the midst of all of these broken pieces. Seeing the place I love like this. I'm trying to see beyond what's in front of me. I'm... I'm thankful that there's even a bakery to come to and that with a little love and renovation, it'll be back to exactly the way it was."

And this time… the people responsible for trying to destroy it are facing felony charges and will pay for what they did.

"You're the strongest person I've ever met," he whispers against my neck. "And I am so fucking proud of you."

My head falls back against his chest. "Thank you. For being here with me and being my strength when I feel like I have none. I'm not sure I could've made it through this without you."

"Yes you could have, baby. I'm just glad that you didn't have to." Grant pauses, glancing around the kitchen. "Do you want to look around? See if we can find anything that's not been damaged?"

I nod. With a chaste kiss against my hair, he lets me go and reaches for my hand. Together, we walk around the empty, wrecked kitchen.

Most of the things in here have been touched by the fire, whether the smoke or flames, but there are a few things that have somehow managed to survive. An old apron on the far side of the room that's only slightly charred. A mixing bowl that's missing a handle.

We stop in front of the stainless steel table where Grant and I stood only months ago and made beignets for the first time. A smile flits to my lips at the memory.

The table is slightly warped from the heat of the flames, and it's come unscrewed from the wall behind it, leaving a huge gap between.

Grant's brow pinches as he peers between the space.

"What is it?" I ask.

"I think I see something behind here. It must have fallen at some point."

He squats, turning to fit one long arm between the space and coming back with a thin black picture frame the size of a sheet of notebook paper.

My brow furrows in confusion. Where did that come from?

Grant hands the frame over to me, and I flip it over to the front. The glass is covered in a thick layer of ash and soot, so I reach out and brush it away, revealing what looks like an old, yellowed newspaper article beneath.

I squint, trying to make out what's beneath the remaining layer of dust and grime, but I can't tell.

Whatever it is, it's old. I wonder how long it's been behind the counter. If the old paper is any indication, I think a while.

"Here, let me see." He takes the frame from my hand and lifts the hem of his T-shirt, cleaning off the glass with it before handing it back to me.

"Oh my god," I whisper when I finally can see what's in the frame. "This is... this is a newspaper article from the local paper from when my mom first opened the bakery."

There's a photo of her standing in front of the bakery, wearing a wide, proud smile as she holds me in her arms. I was only an infant then. Probably no more than three months old or so. Hot, fresh tears prick in my eyes, and I'm hit with a wave of how badly I miss her.

I was so young when she passed away that my memories are hazy, fading over time.

My eyes scan the article as I read it out loud.

"When we asked Cindy what the inspiration for the name of her new beignet bakery was and if it stemmed from her love of fairy tales, she smiled, shaking her head as she said, 'As much as I love a fairy tale, I chose the name for the bakery in honor of my beautiful baby girl, Addie. Because no matter what, I want her to always have her own Happily *Ever After.'*"

The knot in the base of my throat tightens, the emotion stuck there making it impossible to breathe as my heart pounds erratically in my chest.

I… I never knew. I never knew the meaning behind it. That she named the bakery after the dream she had for *me*.

I feel my tears staining my cheeks as I let out a half laugh, half sob, and clutch the frame to my chest. It feels a lot like fate, finding this today. After everything that's happened in the last few months, and after walking into the bakery like this today, finding this of my mother feels like a beacon of… *hope*.

A light in even the darkest time.

I turn, swiping away the tears, and hand the frame to my husband, who takes it, peering down.

"You look like her twin, baby," he says with a smile that lights up his face. "I can't believe I even saw it there. It was wedged between the wall and the back side of the table. Seems like it protected it from the fire."

If there was ever a sign that I would wish to get from her, this feels like the one.

I drag my gaze around the remnants in the room and suck in a shaky breath as I clutch the frame to my chest.

"I never expected to find something like that, especially after all of the damage from the fire, and I know it probably sounds silly, but it almost feels like she wanted me to find it today."

"Doesn't sound silly at all. I think so too, baby. I think that I believe in fate more now than I ever did, and I think it led us right to where we're meant to be," Grant says, his eyes flickering with sincerity.

In a way, I'm thankful for the things that Brent has done. Because had he not tried to force me into marrying someone I didn't know, I never would've gone to that party, and I never would've met Grant.

If he hadn't tried to steal the bakery from me, I never would've fallen in love with my fake husband.

I never would've married the man I now plan to spend the rest of my life with.

All of these things led me to where I am today. With a husband who puts me first and loves me unconditionally.

With a place that I have loved fiercely, devotedly, my entire life and the ability to rebuild the parts he damaged. Making it not only mine but my mom's as well.

It's a bittersweet realization, but all of this taught me to find the beauty in the ruin.

"I think... that my mom led me straight to you, Grant. Even if she couldn't be here, she still made sure that I had my happily ever after by giving me *you*."

He always said he would be my Prince Charming, and it turns out he was right all along.

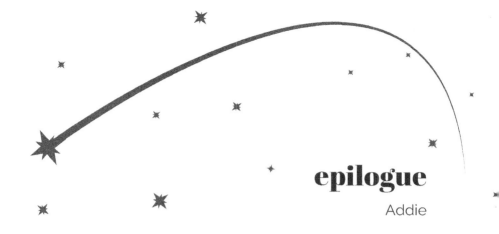

epilogue
Addie

ONE MONTH later

"Where should we start?" Grant's best friend Reese asks as he reaches up and turns the baseball hat around on his head, glancing around the kitchen. "I am at your service, milady."

It's taken a month to get the official approval from NOFD and city inspectors to begin working on debris removal and repairs at the bakery. Time that seemed to drag and fly by all at once. With school and coordinating with the insurance company to get everything needed to start the renovations, it's been a whirlwind. If it wasn't for Grant, I wouldn't have been able to keep up with half of it.

He's been the most attentive, patient, understanding man on the planet, and even though it feels impossible, I love him even more with each passing day. He keeps me grounded and gives me a safe space to land.

How he manages to help with the bakery, spend every night exhausting me until I can't move, play baseball, do a hundred different things for his sponsorship, and still manage to be the most incredible husband and loyal friend is truly beyond me.

In the past month, I've mourned the loss of the place I once

343

knew and worked on accepting that changes had to happen if it meant keeping the place my mother poured all of her love into.

And as I stand in the middle of the kitchen, walls still blackened with smoke damage and charred drywall, another wave of emotion hits me so fiercely that my chest aches.

"I *think* Grant and the guys from the team got most of the charred drywall and some of the broken wood out this morning, so maybe we can start removing the damaged tables and equipment? I think the restoration company will be here later today to set up the ozone generators to help get the smoke odor out." I plant my hands on my hips.

Reese smirks, giving me a dramatic salute that makes me laugh. Grant and I were *not* expecting his friends to show up today, flying in from opposite sides of the country to come and help us with the bakery.

Especially because they're technically Grant's friends, and Ever After is my responsibility.

The thought that Grant's friends flew here at the drop of a hat to be here for us and help when they have their own lives made me emotional in a way that I didn't expect.

"Lane, get your ass over here and help me move these tables. They're heavy as shit, and you're not helping by standing there looking cute," Reese yells to the tall, dark blond guy with unruly hair—Hallie's boyfriend. He's talking with Earl near the back door, and he turns to Reese, giving him the finger, but then strides over to him.

As I watch the guys attempting to move the furniture, Grant's hands bracket my hips before he tugs me back against him. "Hi, ArtGirl."

Just the sound of his *voice* makes me feel more at ease. Renovating a bakery is stressful in itself without everything else, but as always, my husband has the ability to calm me like nothing else in the world. "Hi," I respond with a smile. "I can't believe that everyone flew here just to help us. It was so nice of them."

Grant's lips press along the back of my neck, and I feel him nodding against my skin. "It is. They drive me nuts sometimes, but they're honestly the best people I know. And you already know Reese will use any excuse he can to use the jet."

His laugh vibrates my skin as his head shakes. He's teasing, but I know how much it really means to him to have them here. Not only did his friends drop everything to come when he needed them, but his mom also came to help without even being asked.

And, unsurprisingly, she and Amos hit it off from the moment they met, and it made my heart squeeze to see them together, laughing like they've known each other forever.

"It's just… amazing to see everyone be so supportive and kind. I wasn't expecting it, and I'm already just so emotional about everything that I keep crying. I'm not sad—I'm actually really, *really* happy. Overwhelmingly happy. Thankful. It's ju—" I realize that I'm rambling, so I halt, my mouth snapping shut as I inhale. "I'm grateful. For you and that you have an amazing support system."

"Addie, they're not just here for me. They're here for *you* too. They're our friends and family, and that's what people do when they love each other. They show up."

Once again, fresh tears well in my eyes, and I sniffle, quickly brushing them away before turning to face my husband, wrapping my arms around his neck. "This is the life I always hoped for, and I'm so happy that I get to do it with you."

"Me too, baby. Can I… steal you away for a second?" His lip curves slightly with a grin. "I have something I want to show you."

I nod. I have absolutely no idea what it could even be, but truthfully, I could use a second to just breathe.

He reaches for my hand, sliding his fingers into mine, and then leads me toward the exit at the back of the kitchen. We both laugh when we see Reese and Lane arguing near the stand mixer. Grant just shakes his head and tugs me forward out of the bakery and onto the sidewalk behind it.

I'm completely confused as he guides me to the front of Ever After and comes to a stop in front of the building next door. It's seen much better days. The paint is chipped along the front doors, curling and warping from the heat, the uneven brick front slightly crumbling with old age, and the mailbox next to the door is hanging on by a singular screw. Despite the years of neglect, it's still breathtakingly beautiful. The front windows have always been my favorite part of this place since I was a kid. They're nearly to the ground, covered in a layer of dirt and dust, but I always imagined that they'd let in an abundance of natural light.

"One sec," he murmurs, dropping my hand and reaching into his pocket. When he pulls out a set of keys, my mouth falls open in shock.

Why... Why would *Grant* have keys to this place? It's been empty for years.

Before I can even ask that question, he leads us up to the peeling black front door and unlocks it, pushing it open.

The stale, musty air hits us the moment we walk over the threshold, and I turn to look at him. "Okay, what's going on? Why would you hav—"

My question dies on my tongue when Grant drops to one knee in front of me, holding a dark blue box in his hand as he peers up at me with stormy eyes that nearly match.

Oh my god.

Shaky fingers fly to my mouth, covering it, as a new onslaught of tears well in my eyes, blurring my vision. I blink rapidly, attempting to breathe even as the lump of emotion forms in my throat, making it tight.

I try to speak, but my voice catches, and a breathless laugh escapes from my lips instead.

Grant's mouth tilts into a smile that makes my heart stutter wildly in my chest. "I love you, Addie. I wish that I could've proposed to you this way the first time instead of with a paper ring on my kitchen floor. Because you deserve that. You deserve a wedding surrounded by people who love you and your happily ever after just the way that you imagined it. I want to give it to you. I want to give you everything you've ever wanted, ArtGirl. I want to be your muse, your best friend, and your biggest fan. I want to support you and love you without condition. Our love was always more than an arrangement—it's a testament to souls being tethered by fate. Because I loved you before I ever even saw you.

I'm sobbing as he continues, my entire body shaking with emotion.

"You're the love of my life. In any universe, it will *always* be you. In any lifetime, you will always be the marrow of my bones. A love that transcends time—that's the way I was made to love you, Addie Bergeron. Will you stay my wife? Until the stars call us home?"

I fall to my knees in front of him, throwing myself into his arms so hard that he nearly topples over, burying my face into his neck as my wet tears coat his skin.

"Y-yes, ye-s-s, yes," I chant, over and over, as his arms wrap around my waist and hold me tightly to his body.

He pulls back, tears shining in his own stormy eyes as he

kisses me. His lips press against mine in a series of quick, breath-less movements, and I laugh against his mouth.

"I have something else to show you, baby."

I look up at him, blinking away the wetness from my eyes watching as he lifts the blue box for me to see. When he flips it open, it's not a ring inside of it… it's a key, slotted into the spot where a ring would fit.

My gaze darts from the key to him, and he smirks. "I'm going to get you a new ring, but I want it to be one that you pick out so it's exactly what you want." He pauses, slipping the key out of the box and holding it out for me. "You always said that you wanted to have the bakery *and* display your art for the world to see one day. So, I bought this place for you. And it's in your name only, so no one can ever try and take it away from you. My promise to you that I will never stop trying to make your dreams come true, Addie."

"I love you so much," I sob, crushing my lips to his. I never knew it was possible to love anyone so all-consumingly and wholly.

Nothing in the world has ever felt as right as it does when I'm with him. Like we're two halves of one soul that only feel complete when we're together.

He's the kind of fairy tale that I once thought only existed in books and movies.

Grant Bergeron is my happily ever after, and once upon a time… it all started with ArtGirl and Jockboy.

The Orleans University series is complete!
Click here to see the entire series.

Didn't get enough of the entire Orleans U crew?
Want a peek into the future?

Find out if Grant is drafted into the MLB. What happens with Reese's baseball career? What Lane is up to?

I've got the *perfect* bonus to say goodbye to our favorites.

Click here to subscribe to my newsletter and you'll instantly get your hands on this scene.

Ready for what's next from Maren?
This hero is a little different... he's a bad boy with a **filthy mouth**.
The Bad Boy Rule is available for preorder.
Click here to preorder your copy.

Want a sneak peek of Reese and Viv's book, Catching Feelings?
Turn the page to read the extra spicy Prologue!

then

Reese Landry

I THINK I'm in love.

No, scratch that. I'm *definitely* in love with the girl in the middle of the dance floor wearing hot pink cowgirl boots, cutoff shorts, and a scowl.

Okay, fine. It's not love, but it's *definitely* lust, and when it comes to wanting Vivienne Brentwood, I'm a fucking goner.

I never stood a damn chance.

Those tiny cutoff shorts are molded to her ass, hugging the little dips right beneath her delectable cheeks, and I want to groan out loud in the middle of this honky-tonk bar with how badly I want to touch her. How badly I want to run my tongue along the creamy skin that peeks out the bottom.

Is it because the more I flirt, the more I try to charm her with my good looks, the more she dislikes me?

Absolutely.

I'm a bit of a masochist like that. The harder I try to catch her, the further she runs.

And there's just something about a girl who pretends she wants nothing to do with you but secretly wants to bounce on your cock when no one's around.

And trust me, this girl wants me just as bad as I want her.

She can spew all the venom she wants from those pouty pink lips, but I know the truth, even if she's not ready to admit it to herself.

I've been watching her on the dance floor for the last fifteen minutes, and what little amount of restraint I had left has been dissolved by the five tequila shots I downed earlier.

Viv drops her head back and laughs, swaying her hips to the music, her hands lifted above her head, completely oblivious that every red-blooded guy in this building is watching her the same way that I am.

When the white tank top she's wearing rides up an inch, exposing a sliver of pale skin, I'm fucking *done* watching.

I bring the shot to my lips and toss it back, downing it in a single gulp before slamming it onto the table and making my way across the bar toward her.

The dance floor is crowded with people, but the moment I step onto it, her eyes find mine. Even in the dim, shitty light of the bar, I see the defiance flash in her gaze.

Always a fucking challenge, except tonight, the win will be mine. I'm not leaving here without touching her. We've been dancing around it all night. For weeks, really.

Reaching up, I turn my hat backward as I make my way toward her, never taking my eyes off her.

I can't.

Even if I wanted to look away, I couldn't. I'm in a trance, watching her hips sway to the music. She pulls her plump lip between her teeth and runs her hands down her hips.

Almost like she's dancing for *me.*

When I finally get to her, I reach out, sliding my hands along her waist until my fingers dip into the loops of her cutoffs to pull her toward me. Her soft body collides with mine, and her hands fist into the front of my shirt.

"Um… have you lost your mind?" she says, feigning surprise, but doesn't pull away, and *that* surprises me.

I shrug. "Probably. Don't really give a fuck."

I watch her throat bob as she swallows, and her eyes darken as I move us to the music, pressing us tighter together with my hands resting right above the swell of her ass, testing waters we've never been in.

She doesn't respond, simply stares up at me with those wide blue eyes that I feel like I could drown in.

Leaning down, I dip my head to her ear, whispering, "How about for one night, we pretend you don't hate me, Viv?"

"Why would I do that? Hating you is so much fun," she murmurs coyly.

My hands travel lower, an inch at a time until I'm cupping the soft, bare skin beneath her ass, my thigh parting her legs as we move together to the music. Every time the beat hits, my thumb drags along her soft skin.

Her breath hitches when my thigh brushes against her pussy, and I pull back, staring down at her. "Because I know something that would be much more fun. You can even insult me while we do it."

"And what makes you think that I'd ever want to have *fun* with you, Reese Landry?" The sassy tone of her voice reminds me just how much of a brat she can be.

The song slows, the beat lowering with the lights, and we're pitched into near darkness in the middle of the dance floor. The music fades out, the crowd along with it, and all I can focus on is her pressed against me. How I'm surrounded by her smell. Lavender and something fresh.

She lets go of my shirt and slides her hand lower and lower, so fucking low that I feel her fingers dip beneath the fabric of my T-shirt and brush along the trail of hair on my stomach. The muscles contract under her touch, rippling with each brush of her fingers.

Fuck.

"Kiss me." My raspy command has her pupils dilating, and I pull her tighter against me. In the dim light, I can see her rising onto her tiptoes and feel her warm breath fanning along my lips, and I think this might actually be it.

I'm finally going to kiss this girl, and if I have anything to do with it, I'm going to spend the rest of the night kissing her like I've wanted to since the moment I met her. Even though it's only been a few weeks since then, I've been hooked from that very first insult. Her eyes drop closed, and I slide my hands up her sides slowly, memorizing her curves beneath my palms until I bring them to her face and cradle her jaw as I lean closer.

"Yo." A too familiar voice yells from behind us. You've got to be *fucking* kidding me.

Vivienne's eyes snap open, and I groan inwardly when she steps back like she's been burned, the hazy, heavy-lidded look in her eyes vanishing.

Goddamnit.

I'm going to kill him. The minute I get out of this bar, I'm going to strangle him with my bare hands.

My gaze lands on Grant, who's wearing a shit-eating smirk for interrupting what I already fucking know was going to be a kiss that altered my brain. I narrow my eyes as my jaw works. My teeth grind together when he laughs.

"Sorry to interrupt, but I'm heading out. Meeting up with somebody. You two going to be… good without me?"

"Bye, Grant," I say through clenched teeth. He's my best

friend, but after tonight, he's going to be my best friend from six feet under after he just ruined that moment.

He chuckles, pulling Viv in for a quick hug, then slaps me on the back and disappears through the crowd.

"Viv," I say, reaching for her. She steps back just as my hand lands on her arm.

"*Clearly*, the heat in here is getting to me because I've lost my mind," she mutters before spinning on her heel and sprinting off the dance floor.

Fuck that. I'm not letting her walk away so easily. She was into this just as much as I was.

I follow closely behind on her heels, calling out her name, even as she busts through the exit door of the bar out into the cool night air.

"Viv, wait. Jesus. Just fucking wait," I say, jogging to keep up with her. "Just talk to me."

Finally, she spins around to face me with flushed cheeks. Her long, dark hair whips in the October wind, and I do my best to keep my gaze on her eyes and not how her white tank top is molded to her curves. Only minutes ago, I had my hands on her, and now she's running away from me.

"What? *Please* do not make this a bigger deal than it was, Reese. We accidentally almost kissed. It was a mistake. Now we're going to forget it ever happened. Trust me, I already have."

Chuckling, I step closer until we're toe to toe, and my head's bent as I stare down at her short frame. "Oh? That's what that was back there, huh? A *mistake*?"

"Obviously." She scoffs indifferently. "I was caught up in the moment. I would've kissed *any* guy in there tonight, Reese. Please don't act like you're god's gift to women."

My nostrils flare at the mention of her kissing someone else.

Jealousy unfurls inside of me, and it's not a feeling I'm used to experiencing. Especially over a girl I barely know and haven't even kissed. Yet, it doesn't change the fact that she has me feeling this way.

"Yeah, okay, Viv. And I would've broken his fucking nose, so by all means…" I sweep my hand out toward the bar. "Go back in there and find someone else to kiss. Try me."

Her eyes widen for a moment, like she can't believe that I'm jealous, but guess what… she makes me fucking crazy, so I'm not responsible for the shit coming out of my mouth tonight.

With an eye roll, she pulls her phone out of the back pocket of her shorts and starts tapping at the screen. "Whatever, tough guy. I'm getting an Uber and going home."

"Okay, I'll go with you."

She drags her eyes to mine. "Uh. No, thanks. I don't need a chaperone. I'm a big girl."

"You're not getting into an Uber alone, Viv. You've been drinking, and it's late. It's not the end of the world to share an Uber. I'm a gentleman, and I want to make sure you get home safe."

"*Fine, Father.*" She smarts while she finishes arranging the Uber on her phone.

My lips tilt up at her bratty comment. "I prefer *Daddy*, but whatever works for you, babe."

I pull my phone from my pocket and scroll until the car gets here since she's now ignoring me. I'm not very big on social media, but I try to keep up with a few friends from back home.

After a few minutes of silence, a sleek black Tahoe pulls up to the curb just as I'm shoving my phone back in my pocket.

Viv reaches for the door, but I stop her, opening it. "I've got it."

I'm served another eye roll that makes me want to spank her

ass, and then she climbs into the back seat, and I slide in after her.

The driver pulls from the curb without a word and thankfully cranks the music louder, only slightly drowning out the tension that seems to be buzzing like a live wire between us.

It's hard for me to be quiet or still for any period of time, so I only manage a few minutes before I'm joking, "Did we just have our first fight, babe?"

I expect something smart-ass from her, but instead she actually laughs. "God, you're ridiculous."

I decide I like the sound of it way too much.

I shrug, reaching out to brush her hair off her shoulder, and her gaze flits to me. "Ridiculously *charming*, I know." My smirk widens into a smile, and she rolls her eyes again and huffs, then glances back down at the phone in her lap.

Silence once more fills the cab around us, but I never move my hand, the rough pads of my fingers continually drawing circles on her soft milky skin. I expect her to reach up and stop me, but she doesn't.

The further along we ride, the more she leans into my touch until I feel her pressed against my side as she gazes out the window, watching the cars pass by.

I shouldn't love fighting with her, arguing until I want to either spank her or kiss her, but it seems to be the one thing we seem to do well when we're together.

Bringing my hand down to her bare thigh, I brush my thumb along the exposed skin until she begins to squirm against me.

When it comes to her, I've got the patience of a fucking saint, and this time... I want *her* to be the one to give in.

Inch by inch, I slide my hand higher until I'm playing with the rough hem of her shorts.

My eyes shift to hers, and when she catches my gaze, her

eyes flicker and drop to my lips, lingering for a brief moment before sliding back up to meet mine. When my fingers graze the skin under the hem of her shorts, her breath hitches, and her pupils go wide.

"*Fuck it.*" The words rush from her lips in a whisper as she climbs into my lap, the juncture of her thighs brushing against my already hardening cock, and her lips slam against mine in a kiss that has my balls aching.

It's messy, and frantic, and fucking *hot.*

Her tongue slides into my mouth, and she moans at the contact, sucking my tongue as she explores my mouth with her hands fisted tightly in the locks of my hair. The needy, desperate sound of her whimpers shoots directly to my dick, somehow making me even harder, arousal snaking down my spine.

Finally, we both give in to what we've been dancing around since the day that I met her, that taut line of tension and pent-up need snapping like a rubber band between us. I've wanted her since the moment I laid eyes on her, and finally touching her, *kissing* her, feeling her grinding against my dick feels like I could lift the goddamn world.

Her hips rock, and she nips at my lips while my fingers dig into the flesh at her waist and she pants against my mouth. When she pulls back, searing me with her molten gaze, I'm scared she's going to flee like earlier, but instead, she slides her hand down my chest to the bottom of my T-shirt and tugs it up. Her hand slips into my jeans and palms my aching cock over my boxers, and an involuntary deep, guttural noise sounds from the back of my throat.

This fucking girl.

Her lips tilt into a smirk when she grips me harder. "See how much fun it is to *hate* each other, Reese?"

There's the softest brush of her lips against mine, teasing, taunting, and then I feel her smile against them. If we were any-fucking-where else, I'd put her on her knees and spank the fuck out of her for being such a little brat.

Instead, I slide my hand into the hair at her nape and tug her head back, exposing the column of her throat to press a hot kiss against her flesh. My teeth rake against her pulse point, and then I suck the spot, soothing it as she whimpers against the top of my head.

"Um. Sorry to interrupt, but like, we're almost to your destination. Am I dropping you both off or is there another stop?"

I'm so caught up in the moment, in *her*, that I forgot we're in the back seat of an Uber and the driver's got a front row seat to what we're doing.

Goddamnit.

It physically pains me to tear my lips from her skin, but I do to keep myself from losing the semblance of control I have left.

That's the effect she has on me. Making me lose my head.

Reaching between us, I close my palm over her hand that's still gripping my cock. "What's it going to be, Viv?" I pause, my gaze lingering on her blown pupils. "Are you going to waste more time pretending you don't want this, or are you going to let me fuck the shit out of you?"

Viv pulls me into her dorm and slams the door shut behind us with her foot, all while her hands frantically tear at my T-shirt, lifting and tugging in an attempt to get it off me. Her lips move over mine while she fumbles with the shirt until I finally tear my lips from hers to reach behind my neck and pull it off, letting it fall to the floor. Lifting her off her feet, I walk her backward until her back hits the door, my hips pinning her against it. The motion has my cock jutting against the heat of her pussy, causing us to groan in unison.

"Fuck, I want you," I mumble roughly against her skin. I want her so bad I fucking *ache*.

I had no idea we'd end up here tonight when I almost kissed her at the bar, but I hoped that there'd be more.

That I'd have the chance to do this.

To spend the night, showing her that as much as she hates me, she'll love my tongue on her pussy even more.

When I gave her the chance to walk away in the back seat of the Uber, I thought she might take it. It wouldn't have surprised me if she did. The times we've been around each other, she's spent the entire time insulting me yet... eye-fucking me when no one else was looking. So it was a toss-up of what she'd decide.

She pauses, rolling her lip between her teeth as her eyes hold mine, a war with her body and mind raging behind her eyes.

"*One* night. That's it. Then, we go back to pretending the other doesn't exist. That's all you get, All-Star. Take it or leave it." There's finality in her words, and even though I'm not into it, it doesn't seem like there's a choice.

All I've done so far is kiss this girl, and I already know that one night will never be enough. It won't even scratch the surface of the things I want to do to her. But if it's all I get, I'm taking it.

"Fine, but the entire night, you're *mine*."

If she only wants one night, then I'm going to use every single second of it proving to her that no one will be able to bring her pleasure the way that I can. When it's over, I want to walk out that door confident that she'll never be able to forget tonight. Or forget *me*.

With her still pressed against the door, I slide my hands

beneath her shirt and yank it up, exposing a lacy, pale pink bra that's only a few shades darker than her skin.

A lazy grin curves my lip up as I lean forward and swipe my tongue up the valley between her tits. "I think pink might be my new favorite color."

"Can you *not* talk? Just keep doing what you're doing with your mouth?" With a frustrated whimper, she tugs me back to her chest by my hair, and I chuckle against her skin.

Fuck, I love that mouth.

Giving her exactly what she asked for, I scatter kisses over the swell of skin that spills from the cups.

Her tits are fucking *perfect*. Not too big and not too small. A medium size that look like they'll fill my hands perfectly.

I tug the left cup down, and her pert, rosy nipple strains toward me, a beacon for my tongue.

What I didn't notice in my haste to taste her was the tiny little silver barbell through the middle.

Fuck me.

Her nipples are *pierced*.

"Fuck, Viv, these are so goddamn hot," I tell her as I brush my thumb over the metal. She shivers beneath my touch, her back arching against my fingers. "Are they more sensitive? With the piercing?"

She nods.

Just when I thought she couldn't get any sexier, she almost brings me to my damn knees with the sweetest surprise.

When I wrap my lips around the hardened peak, she moans, tugging at my hair almost to the point of pain, and I relish in the sound. I want to spend the rest of my life listening to her whimpers. Hearing her breathless moans. I flick my tongue over the metal, then suck her nipple into my mouth and roll it between my teeth.

"Stop teasing me, Reese," she pants in a needy, desperate tone. "Get me naked and fuck me already, or we're done with this."

I let go of her nipple and pull back slightly to stare at her, my eyebrow arching. "Do you want to come?"

A beat passes, and then she nods, her blue eyes rolling in frustration.

"Then stop rushing me, Vivienne, or I'll leave you just like this. Wet, needy, desperate for my cock. Without giving you any relief."

Her mouth falls open, and her eyebrows shoot up. "You *wouldn't.*"

I lean forward to suck her nipple into my mouth again and tug—hard—before swirling my tongue around the peak. "Fucking try me."

Pulling away from the door, I turn and carry her toward the unmade bed in the corner, tossing her gently onto the mattress. Those pink sparkly cowgirl boots shimmer in the light as she lies sprawled out before me. I pull them off, then toss them to the side, where they land with a thud. Maybe I should've left them on so I could fuck her in nothing but them. Later.

She sits up on her elbows with her dark hair fanned out around her, her cheeks flushed pink, the skin of her tits blooming red from my lips and my beard scraping against them.

I hope her thighs look the same when I'm done sucking on her cunt.

Her heated gaze burns through me, and my cock throbs when she lifts a foot and drags it slowly down the front of my jeans.

I hiss, the movement almost enough to have my control snapping.

My palm wraps around her ankle, and in one movement, I

yank her across the bed to me as I drop to my knees between her parted thighs.

Deftly, I flick the button of her shorts open and work them down her hips, leaving her in nothing but a scrap of purple lace.

"Tell me what you like," I say, licking my lips as I eye the damp fabric in front of me. There are a lot of guys in this world who aren't into this and would prefer to get their dick sucked, but I love to eat pussy. I want to fucking *devour* this girl.

Whole.

"What do you mean?" Her voice is breathless as she peers down at me.

"What turns you on? I want to know *exactly* how you like it, Vivienne. Talk to me, tell me how you want it. It makes the entire experience better, and I want us both to leave here satisfied."

"Oh, I... I've never been asked that before." She blinks, then tugs her lip between her teeth. The question obviously surprises her, so she's quiet for a minute as she thinks. I want to know it all, her kinks, what gets her off, how to make her come. "I like it rough. I don't like to be handled like glass. And... I sometimes like a finger in my ass when I come."

Most girls have problems with being vocal about their needs, especially during sex, but Viv tilts her chin higher, and her lips curl into a grin.

I knew she would tell me exactly what she wanted. She's nothing if not unfiltered and honest to a fault.

My fingers grip her thighs, holding them open wider for me to settle between them. Her expression turns molten when I drag the pad of my thumb over the damp spot on her panties, brushing over the hood of her clit that peaks against the fabric.

Her back arches, and her hips come off the bed as she sucks in a ragged breath, her fingers flying to my hair.

So fucking responsive, and I've barely even touched her. That tells me that she's just as wound up as I am, and that only makes me harder.

Fisting the lace in my hand, I tug it down her hips and shove it into the pocket of my jeans, then lean forward, dragging my nose up her pussy. She smells so fucking good that my mouth actually waters.

"Did you just *steal* my underwear?" Surprise laces her tone.

Sure as fuck did, and there's not a chance in hell that I'm going to give them back.

"Yep."

The brat laughs. "I knew you were obsessed with me, Reese, but this is too much, even for y—"

Shutting her up, I seal my lips over her clit and suck it into my mouth before circling it roughly with my tongue.

Doesn't she know at this point that her mouthy, bratty little comments only make my dick harder? A special kind of foreplay reserved just for the two of us.

I wet my lips with her, a possessive growl escaping just as she fists both hands in my hair and her hips begin to rock against my mouth.

I'm not sure what I imagined Vivienne tasting like, but whatever it was pales in comparison to the real thing. Sweet and musky and *her*.

Perfection.

Nothing I ever imagined could come close to what it feels like to touch her, to have her hands tugging on my hair when I flatten my tongue and drag it up her soaked pussy.

"Mmm. Is this all for me, baby? I guess hating me gets *you* off as much as it does me. You're drenched."

"Fuck you," she whimpers. Another curse falls from her lips as her head drops back between her shoulders, and the hand that's not holding my face to her pussy travels up to her nipple, pulling at the piercing roughly.

With each rock of her hips, my tongue slides along her pussy, pausing to give extra attention to her clit. I let my teeth graze the sensitive bud when I circle her entrance with my finger, then slide it into her, hooking up to rub her G-spot.

"Right there, right there... *right* there," she chants melodically. Her legs tremble, and I can already feel her cunt tightening and quivering around my finger.

That quick? Fuck yeah.

I smile against her pussy and then flick her clit with the tip of my tongue, teasing and circling until her back is arching off the bed and her arousal is sliding down my hand.

"Look how fast you're coming for me, drenching my tongue. Maybe you *can* be a good girl, Viv."

Goddamnit, this is the hottest thing I've ever experienced. I want her to ride my fucking face so I can *drown* in her.

RIP me, death by pussy. What a fucking way to go.

That's exactly what I want, her smothering me with her pussy. I stop suddenly, pulling my finger out of her and rising to my feet.

Her eyes snap open, blazing, and connect with mine. "Why would you stop when I was about to co—"

I cut her off by flopping onto the bed next to her and scooting up until I hit the headboard, pulling her on top of me in one swift motion.

She looks exquisite with heat in her eyes, her cheeks flushed red, her tits out and on display, and her pussy glistening from my tongue.

"Grab the headboard and ride my face."

Her eyebrows shoot up as if she didn't expect me to want it, but I do, and right the fuck now, or I'll, I dunno... *die.*

My hand hooks around her hip, and I haul her up to my face. After a beat, thank fuck, she springs into action, placing her knees on each side of my head and grabbing the wooden head-board. She's hovering over my mouth with her gaze lingering on mine, so close that I can feel the heat of her pussy, and it makes me impatient. I can't wait another second to swipe my tongue over her swollen folds.

My fingers dig into the soft flesh of her hips as I yank her down onto my face so I can really devour her, sealing my lips around her clit and sucking it into my mouth, alternating pressure. The soft whimper that tumbles from her lips has my cock leaking. I make a vow, right here and now, to spend the rest of the night worshiping her. Getting her out of my system so I don't want her so badly.

I move her hips back and forth, rocking her against my mouth, helping her set the rhythm until she finds her pace and she's writhing on my mouth with her head thrown back in pleasure.

I tease her tight hole with my tongue, groaning when she somehow gets even wetter. I'm having a real-life out-of-body experience right now, and I never wanna come down from it.

"That's it, baby," I praise her. "Fuck my face. Come on my tongue."

I alternate fucking her with my tongue, lapping at her clit, sucking it between my lips and rolling it, then it's only seconds before her entire body goes taut, and she comes with my name on her lips.

"*Reese, Oh... god,*" she moans, dragging her clit over my lips frantically, the friction sending aftershocks through her already sensitive flesh. "Fuck, fuck, fuck."

I can honestly say I have never in my life been so close to

coming in my pants until now, and that's just fucking embar-rassing since I lost my virginity at sixteen.

Once her movements slow and she's able to let go of the headboard, I gently release her hips, and she sits back on my chest, a hazy, unfocused look in her sated eyes.

"Wow. Apparently, there *is* one thing you're good at."

My lips curve into a smirk. "You're only saying that because you haven't had my cock yet, babe."

Even after the orgasm she just had, her eyes darken at my comment, and her expression turns heated, wiping the grin from my lips. I lean up, sliding my hands along her jaw, cradling it in my hands as I dip my head forward to capture her lips.

Part of me regrets ever stepping foot in her dorm tonight. Ever touching her, kissing her, tasting her because I know that she'll be stuck in my head like a sickness I can't get rid of.

I should've known better than to agree to just one night because it won't be enough. I'm not looking for a relationship, but what I want is for more than a few hours with her.

There's no way I can play out every fantasy I've had of this girl in the span of a few hours.

My hands slide beneath the fabric of her tank top where it's still halfway on and yank it up, only breaking our kiss to pull it over her head. My fingers reach for the clasp of her bra and

quickly get it unhooked. She pulls back, letting the lace straps fall down her arms, freeing her breasts completely.

I almost swallow my fucking tongue when my gaze drops to her bare tits. I've never seen anything more perfect in my life.

They're even bigger than what they looked like when spilling from the cups. They're heavy and full. Natural. Sexy as fuck.

Pert, rosy nipples turned up, begging to be sucked. Those tiny little barbells through the center. Which is why I immediately lower my mouth to the peak and suck it into my mouth, then let it go with a pop.

She's straddling my lap now, her bare, still-soaked pussy brushing against my cock through my jeans, and each time she wiggles her hips, I find my control fraying at the edges.

"I need you," I pant, pulling back from her chest.

She nods, reaching for the button of my jeans, flicks it open, and drags the zipper down. Together, we work both jeans and briefs down my hips without her ever moving from my lap.

Once I kick them aside, we're fitted together, skin to skin. I can feel the heat of her pussy along the length of my cock, and when she rocks her hips, a whimper sounding from the back of her throat, I almost fucking lose it.

The thick, weeping head of my cock brushes against her clit each time she moves until we're both groaning, chasing the friction. We're frantically grinding like we're teenagers, and yet it may be the hottest thing I've ever done. Her arms slide around my neck as her fingers tangle into the hair at my nape, and she circles her hips.

"Like this," she breathes. "I want you like this. Just like this, Reese."

I nod with my lips against her already sweat-slicked skin, out of my fucking mind delirious for her. She could ask me for anything right now, and I would make it happen.

Her hand trails down between us, and she closes her fist around my cock, using her thumb to spread the precum seeping from the tip.

I'm pretty sure I'm hallucinating when her gaze lifts to mine and she brings her thumb to her mouth, sucking my cum off the pad.

Fuck. Fuck. Fuck.

"Need to be inside you, Viv. Right the fuck now," I groan.

I can't wait another goddamn second to feel my cock inside her.

"I'm on birth control, and I'm clean," she mumbles against my lips.

I trace my tongue along her bottom lip, grazing it with my teeth and then sucking it into my mouth. "Me too. Testing is a team requirement. You sure?" I say between nipping and sucking her mouth.

She nods vehemently and sinks down a fraction of an inch on my cock, causing us to groan in unison at the feel of her tight heat clamping down on me.

My arms tighten around her when she drops her head back, her mouth falling open, moaning soft and so fucking sweet. Sinking all the way down to the hilt. Until her clit is brushing against my pelvis, until I'm so deep inside of her that the head of my cock meets her cervix, bottoming out.

It feels so damn good that my eyes roll back. Being buried inside of her, feeling her sweet little cunt fluttering around me as she rocks her hips is enough to make my balls draw up.

There's no way I'm lasting being inside of her *bare*.

Not when she's so tight she's practically choking my cock. I already feel the base of my spine tingling with the need to empty inside her.

In one motion, I pull out and flip us over, putting her back on the mattress, and making my way back between her parted thighs, fitting my hips between them. I hitch her leg up on my side with one hand and then reach between us, dragging my cock through her silky wetness, rubbing the blunt head against her clit before sliding home again.

"Right there," she pants when I thrust deep, swiveling my hips and brushing against her G-spot. I slowly pull out of her, only to slam back inside, increasing my pace and fucking her harder and deeper. Trying to plant myself even further inside of her with each surge of my hips.

It isn't enough. I won't ever get enough of her, can't fuck her deep enough. Hard enough.

Her nails drag down my back to the point of pain, and it only makes me more fucking insane with need for her. I want her marks on me.

When her head lolls and her eyes drop shut, I reach down and grasp her face, turning her back to face me. "Watch me fucking you, Vivienne. Watch how good you're taking my cock."

She whimpers, her pussy tightening around me, and when my thumb brushes against her clit, her back arches with pleasure. I can feel how close she is to exploding around me, to flooding my cock with her cum.

At the last second, I pull out of her completely, my heart thrashing wildly. Before she even has a chance to protest, I flip her onto her stomach and grab her hips, hauling her perfect, heart-shaped ass up in the air, leaving her cheek pressed into the mattress. Her pussy and her ass on display, waiting to get fucked. I lean forward and sink my teeth into one pert ass cheek, as wetness from her pussy drips down her thighs.

So fucking wet.

With my hands on her hips, I push back inside of her until my stomach is flush with her ass and I'm buried deep. I grip her cheeks, spreading them open so I can watch my cock disappearing into her pretty little pussy as I fuck her. Watching it stretch to take me, swallowing and coating my dick in her arousal.

I use her hips as leverage as I start to move, pounding into her from behind, her ass shaking with each slap of my hips. My thrusts are brutal and punishing, fucking her up onto the bed while she begs.

"I'm going to come, Reese... Please, I- I..."

I gather her arousal on my thumb, pressing the pad of my finger against her asshole, watching it contract as I slowly press the tip in.

Fuck, yeah.

Taking my time, I dip my finger in, then withdraw it until she's relaxed, and ready for all of my thumb. I press it forward as I fuck her, slowly sinking further into her tight hole until it's finally buried completely in her ass.

She cries out, her pussy clamping down on me while her ass is as full of me.

I guide my finger in slowly, using my other hand to hold her hips as I thrust into her pussy in the same rhythm with my dick, my balls pulling up tight.

I'm so goddamn close.

Slamming my hips forward, I push my thumb deeper in her ass one last time, and she explodes, her back arching, her fingers grasping at the sheets, coming so hard that I can feel her wetness against my fucking stomach.

I groan, dropping my forehead against her back, folding my body over her, emptying myself inside of her, the tight walls of her cunt milking every drop from my balls. So greedy, she wants it all.

I can't even form words as I keep rocking my hips slowly until I'm completely spent, and then we're collapsing onto the bed. I pull out of her gently and drop my gaze to where my cum is seeping out of her pretty little cunt in a thick creamy mess, my eyes flaring at the sight. I have the inexplicable urge to gather it up with my fingers and shove it back inside of her.

"Give me five minutes, and we're doing that again," I say breathlessly.

Viv smirks. "Sure you can get it up again that quickly? It's okay if you're a one and done kinda guy. I won't judge you."

My brow rises. "Yeah? Why don't you climb back on my dick and find out?"

She sits up, her blue eyes flaring with determination as she straddles my lap and then leans down, licking my nipple.

"Okay, let's see who will tap out first, *All-Star.*"

Click here to continue reading Reese and Vivienne's story free in KU!

need moore?

Want instant access to bonus scenes, exclusive giveaways, and content you can't find ANYWHERE else?

Sign up for my newsletter here and get all of the goods!

In your audiobook era? Find all of my audiobooks here!

Want to chat with me about life, get exclusive giveaways and see behind the scenes content? Join my reader group Give Me Moore

also by maren moore

about the author

Maren Moore is an Amazon Top 20 Best-selling sports romance author. Her books are packed full of heat and all the feels that will always come with a happily ever after. She resides in southern Louisiana with her husband, two little boys and their fur babies. When she isn't on a deadline, she's probably reading yet another Dramione fan fic, rewatching cult classic horror movies, or daydreaming about the 90's.

You can connect with her on social media or find information on her books here ➡ here.

Made in the USA
Coppell, TX
14 March 2025

47070248R00249